THE EDEN PROPHECY

a thriller

GRAHAM BROWN

BANTAM BOOKS
NEW YORK

The Eden Prophecy is a work of fiction. Names, characters, places, and incidents either are the product of the author's imagination or are used fictitiously. Any resemblance to actual persons, living or dead, events, or locales is entirely coincidental.

A Bantam Books Mass Market Original
Copyright © 2012 by Graham Brown

Published in the United States by Bantam Books, an imprint of The Random House Publishing Group, a division of Random House, Inc., New York.

BANTAM BOOKS and the rooster colophon are registered trademarks of Random House, Inc.

ISBN 978-0-345-52780-6
eBook ISBN 978-0-345-52781-3

Cover art and design: Carlos Beltran

Printed in the United States of America

www.bantamdell.com

9 8 7 6 5 4 3 2 1

Bantam mass market edition: February 2012

THE
EDEN
PROPHECY

PROLOGUE

Southern Iran, 1979

The desert wind cried like a beast in pain. Ahmad Bashir listened to it as he crouched in the shelter of a hastily erected tent. As the wind howled outside, the tent's thin walls flapped and strained against the poles and stakes that held them in place. The storm was getting worse, not better.

He tried to ignore it, turning his attention to the excavated grave in front of him. There, illuminated by a lantern and the daylight filtering through the canvas of the tent, a partially excavated skeleton rested at the bottom of a five-foot-deep trench.

A stone tablet had been unearthed near the skeleton's feet and a tube of some metal remained clutched in its hand. Bashir examined the metallic tube. It appeared to be made of copper, frayed strands of leather still clinging to it in places. Bashir guessed it had once been wrapped in an animal skin of some kind, a fabric that had been devoured by the desert over the last seven thousand years.

Behind Bashir, a sunburned young man with curly blond hair and long sideburns fiddled with a transistor radio, trying to listen to the BBC news over the noise of the storm. Each time he managed to improve the recep-

tion slightly, the thrashing wind seemed to rise up a notch and drown it out once again.

"Come on," the young man said, twisting the dial in tiny increments.

Bashir glanced at him. "Put it down, Peter." He waved the young man over. "Come look at this instead."

Peter McKenzie was an American anthropologist just out of graduate school. He and several others had come to southern Iran to work on Bashir's excavation. The main effort was taking place twenty miles to the east, where Bashir believed they had found one of the oldest settlements in Iran—older even than the city of Ur, across the border in Iraq. They'd also found directions to a trade route, which had led them to the grave they now stood over.

After discovering it, Bashir and McKenzie had erected the tent to protect the site from the elements, but Bashir had never expected to end up sheltered beneath it himself. A raging sandstorm had seen to that, trapping them for the past two days. With nothing else to do, they'd continued the excavation, at least until events in Tehran had distracted McKenzie.

"It's getting bad," the young man said.

"How can you tell?"

"I can make out some of what's going on," McKenzie insisted. "They've shut down the airport. Flights are being diverted to other countries."

As demonstrations against the shah and American interests grew, most of Bashir's Americans had left, but McKenzie was one of two who had stayed on. A decision he now seemed to be regretting.

"They want the shah returned to stand trial," McKenzie announced. "They're taking hostages."

There had been unrest for months. After decades of persecution, the tables were turning. And while Bashir

thought change was overdue, he had grave concerns about the men who were leading that change.

Some expected them to institute democracy, but most believed they would return Iran to the Middle Ages if they won. Bashir prayed to Allah that it would not be so, but the pendulum had swung so far in one direction under the shah that it was bound to overshoot in the other once he was gone.

"Tehran is a long way from here," he said. "Do you really think they're going to drive through a hundred miles of desert in the middle of a storm just to look for a couple of Americans?"

McKenzie looked around, listening as the wind sandblasted the tent. He seemed to find that logic sensible.

"Anyway," Bashir said. "You're very tan now. I'll put a burqa on you, cover your face, they'll think you're my woman."

"That doesn't make me feel any better," McKenzie said.

Bashir smiled. "How do you think it sounds to me?"

The young American looked no less distraught, but eventually a smile crept over his face. He shook his head, began to laugh, and put the radio down, careful to leave it on.

He crawled over to the trench. "What are you so excited about anyway?"

"Look closely," Bashir said, pointing to the metal tube. Markings could be seen on it. Not drawn or painted, but pounded into the surface as if they had been stamped by some great hammer.

McKenzie's eyes grew wide. "Like the copper scroll from the Dead Sea."

"Exactly," Bashir said. "If our theory is right, this could be as old as the dwellings we found. Seven thousand years. It could tell us priceless things."

Climbing around in the trench, careful not to disturb

anything, Bashir moved to the stone tablet. He swept away the sand with a horsehair brush and studied the symbols. Only then did he realize the tablet was not made of stone but was some type of clay or adobe, fired or dried in the sun. It seemed extremely dense but it would still be a far softer surface than stone.

He moved carefully, blowing air into the crevices and using delicate strokes to reveal the carved markings beneath.

McKenzie aimed a flashlight at the surface.

With the added illumination Bashir could make out the style of writing.

"What do you see?" McKenzie asked.

A wave of elation rose through Bashir, mixed with melancholy disappointment.

"Proto-Elamite," he said, referencing the writing on the stone. Proto-Elamite: one of the most ancient forms of writing known to man. Unfortunately, it was also unreadable. It had never been translated.

Bashir ground his teeth. Whatever secrets were contained on the clay tablet would remain just that. He glanced back at the copper scroll, guessing the information clutched in the skeletal hand would be written in the same style.

"Bad luck," McKenzie said, obviously realizing the same thing. "But it's still an incredible find."

Bashir nodded, but he wasn't really listening. His eyes had been drawn to a mark in the center of the tablet. A circle with four notches on it, like a compass rose. Within the circle was a square and within that square was a vertical rectangle.

The symbol was different from the Proto-Elamite script, in both the way it was drafted and the depth of its carving. Certainly it matched nothing else on the tablet. And yet he'd seen it somewhere before.

The sound of a zipper racing upward and the sudden

blast of wind distracted him. He turned to see Jan Davis, the other American, standing in the entryway, holding the flap open. He looked panic-stricken.

"Close the tent," Bashir said as sand and dust came blasting in.

"We've got to get out of here," Davis said, ignoring Bashir and talking straight at McKenzie.

"Jan!" Bashir shouted.

"They're coming," Davis replied. "They came to the other dig looking for the Americans."

McKenzie looked at Bashir.

"They're coming here next," Davis insisted. "Men with guns, riding in trucks. We have to leave."

"Are you sure?" McKenzie asked.

"They shot Ebi and Fahrid, accused them of being traitors. The rest of us ran."

"Are they okay?" he asked.

Davis looked haunted by what he'd seen. "I don't think so."

Bashir turned back toward the tablet, his mind spinning. He felt instantly sick. Ebi and Fahrid were Iranian like him, from his own university. Two of his best students, now dead at the hands of the revolutionaries.

"Ahmad, we have to leave," McKenzie pleaded.

Bashir knew Peter was correct. Knew he had misjudged the extent to which his country had gone mad.

"Listen," Davis said, turning the radio to full.

Through the static they heard the reporter intermittently.

". . . they've taken the American embassy now, they're parading around in the streets, burning flags, shouting death to America . . ."

"We have to go."

Bashir nodded, slowly coming to terms with it. But as McKenzie stood and gathered a few things, Bashir found

his mind drifting inexplicably back to the tablet. Where had he seen that symbol before?

Jan Davis disappeared from view. McKenzie was halfway out of the tent. "Ahmad, you have to come."

"I'll be all right," he said.

"You won't," he said. "They know you work with Americans. They'll take it out on you when they can't find us."

Bashir couldn't fight the logic, but he did not want to leave. He felt they were close to something important, something that mattered more than revolutions and guns and the ugly transfer of power.

"This symbol," he said, pointing to the tablet. "I've seen it."

The wind howled and the tent shook and Bashir's mind whirled.

"It doesn't matter," McKenzie said.

"It does!"

"Not if you're dead."

McKenzie looked away and then stuck his head back inside. "The truck's leaving."

There was no choice. Bashir knew he had to go. He looked at the symbol one last time, burning it into his brain, and then he went to leave. At the last moment he turned back and grabbed the copper scroll from the skeleton's grasp.

Stepping out of the tent, Bashir was determined not to let the revolutionaries destroy what he'd found. He ripped one stake from the ground and the wind did the rest, filling the tent like a balloon and carrying it across the desert like a kite.

Forty yards away, a big diesel truck waited. McKenzie and Davis were already running toward it.

"Come on!" McKenzie shouted.

Fighting the wind and shielding his eyes, Bashir made his way to the truck. He climbed into the back along

with the two Americans and three others. The cab up front was already full.

In the distance behind them, he could see sunlight reflecting off several vehicles. There was no time to spare.

The truck lurched forward and Bashir lost his balance. He stumbled, put a hand out to brace himself, and dropped the scroll. It hit the back edge of the truck bed and tumbled out onto the sand as the truck accelerated away.

Bashir cringed. He stepped to the edge, ready to jump, but the truck was moving too fast. He grabbed McKenzie. "Tell the driver to stop. Tell him to stop."

Between the roaring of the diesel engine and the howling of the wind, his words were barely audible.

"It's too late!" McKenzie shouted.

"No!" Bashir said.

Desperate beyond reason, he tried to climb out but McKenzie held him back.

"Let me go!"

"No, Ahmad. It's too late."

By now the truck was rolling away at thirty miles per hour. The revolutionaries were approaching from the east. There would be no jumping free, no stopping or turning back.

As this reality seeped into Bashir, he stopped straining. McKenzie relaxed his grasp and then cautiously released him. Bashir squinted through the storm at the scroll, and his heart sank.

It might take hours or even days for the grave to fill with sand, but the scroll would be buried in minutes. And without any marker to lead the way, it would disappear from the world as if it had never existed.

CHAPTER 1

New York City
Present day

Claudia Gonzales flashed her ID badge at the security checkpoint outside the United Nations General Assembly building. There was no real need to do so; the guards knew her well and at this hour of the morning—just after six on the East Coast—she was one of the few diplomats on the scene.

They waved her through posthaste. With a briefcase in one hand and a tall mocha latte in the other, Gonzales made her way to a secure elevator and up to the eleventh floor of the iconic monolith.

Reaching her office before any members of her staff did was a habit she'd kept since graduating from law school. For one thing, it set a good example; it was difficult for her staff to slack off or complain when the boss was working harder than anyone else. It also had a practical purpose. Not only did the early bird catch the worm, but for the busy people of the world, the early morning hours were often the only available moment to actually look for the proverbial morsel.

In an hour the phones would start ringing. Shortly after that, the appointments would begin and then the afternoon teleconferences, followed by press briefings and public hearings. In the blink of an eye it would be

closing time, and the pile of work on her desk would look exactly as it had eight hours before.

To Claudia Gonzales, that was the equivalent of running in place.

She stepped into her office, set down the latte, and turned on her computer. As the machine booted up, she stepped outside, checking the items on her assistant's desk that had come in during the night hours. The world ran 24/7, even if government offices didn't.

There was a report on the continuing blockade of Gaza, another on a human rights situation in East Timor, and an internal-use envelope that lay unopened.

It read "Diplomatic Materials, Private and Confidential." It was listed as coming from the secretary general's office, with Gonzales's name scrawled in the recipient's slot. She grabbed all three items and returned to her office.

Fairly certain there were no earth-shattering details in the two reports, she placed them in her inbox and proceeded to open the big manila package.

Inside was a legal-sized envelope on the secretary general's stationery. Intrigued, she took a sip of her latte, placed it down, and used a letter opener to slice the top of the envelope. There was an odd rubbery feel to the envelope, almost as if it were waterproof. It made her wonder how much the secretary general spent on his office supplies.

She pulled out a folded sheet of paper and began to read.

You will be punished. You will all be punished. We have waited and suffered too long.

Her mood instantly changed. The UN got a hundred threats per week, mostly from crackpots and mentally

unstable individuals who imagined the UN taking over the world with black helicopters. What made these people think the UN was even remotely capable of dominating the world boggled her mind. In the best of times, they had trouble keeping the peace in remote, undeveloped areas.

She read on.

Your efforts have not helped us. You plunge us deeper into despair every day. In the name of progress you enslave us, in the name of charity you starve us, in the name of peace you slaughter us. We can no longer wait for your help, we will change the world ourselves.

Normally Claudia took these threats with a grain of salt, but this letter had come to her internally. Whoever sent it had access to things they should not have had access to. She began to feel sick, her face and hands flushed and sweating.

In our pains we have grown. And you have fed off us. You think you have beaten us, but he who overcomes by force, hath overcome but half his foe.

We cannot reverse what you have done but we mete out your portion of suffering, we bring you down with us. And it is you who will deliver the master stroke for us. That is correct, Ambassador Gonzales, you are the method of our vengeance. If you have read this far, you are carrying the plague already.

Her heart went cold as she read the words. With her hand shaking lightly, she jabbed at the intercom switch on her phone.

"Security," a voice said.

"This is—" She stopped midsentence, noticing some type of reddish liquid left behind on the phone key. She

glanced at her hand, turning her palm up. The tips of her fingers and her thumb were stained reddish brown.

She noticed a strange smell and heard a quiet sizzling sound. Her left hand, still holding the sheet of paper, felt as if it were burning. She flung the letter to the floor with a shout, pushing her chair backward. She jumped up out of the seat, knocking the latte off her desk.

Her palm and fingers were red and bubbling with the crimson liquid. Her heart was pounding.

"Madam Ambassador?" the voice called over the phone. "Are you okay? Madam Ambassador?"

Unable to speak, she stared at the sheet of paper, watching as a red stain soaked through the page from the corners like blood or dye. Despite this strange effect, the words remained clearly readable. The last sentence, in large bold font, read:

Welcome to Hell.

CHAPTER 2

Dubrovnik, Croatia
Twelve hours later

The sprawling warehouse looked to be buttoned down for the weekend. No activity, no traffic on the inadequate, narrow road that ran in front of it, no noise coming from inside. Even a row of parallel loading docks that stuck out behind it sat empty, their garage-style doors down and locked.

A man wearing dark sunglasses and a black leather jacket hopped up on one of the platforms. Despite the apparent lack of operations, he expected that one pallet of goods would be waiting for him.

He approached the door, briefcase in one hand, a .45-caliber pistol in the other. He looked through a small window that rested at eye level.

At first all he saw was his own reflection: close-cropped dark hair, crow's feet streaking from eyes now hidden by sunglasses, two days' worth of stubble coating his face. He noticed the small horizontal scar that ran across one cheek.

He pressed forward, bringing a hand up to block the light. The distorted image vanished, and inside the warehouse he saw four armed men looking bored and impatient. He tapped the window with the barrel of his gun and stepped back.

The men he was meeting would know him as Hawker, a name that had become his persona during ten years spent living on the run. Once he'd been a fast-rising star in the CIA, but an incident he'd pressed too far had spiraled out of control and wound up costing him everything. He'd spent the years since plying his trade as a mercenary, an arms dealer, and a hire of last resort for people who got into situations they had no hope of getting out of.

In a violent world where he could trust precious little to be what it actually seemed, Hawker had learned to hide even from himself. And his real name, like any thoughts of living a normal life, had disappeared like whispers into a swirling wind.

It was a fate he'd come to accept, a self-inflicted wound that had scarred over but would never really heal. And yet, just when he'd thought all hope was lost, a door had opened, a deal had been made with the very government figures who considered him a loose cannon. If he would act on their behalf, he would be taken in and freed from his past.

There was hope now. Hope that one day he'd be able to take up his real name again and that meetings like the one he was about to attend would become the distant, if not forgotten, memory.

Latches clanked as someone released them from the inside. The door began to slide up. As it rose above his head, Hawker took a calming breath and stepped inside.

The four armed men remained where he'd seen them. To his left, a fifth man slammed the door back down and locked it into place.

"This way," the man said.

Hawker followed as they crossed the warehouse floor. Expensive goods filled the place. Crates of electronic equipment by one wall, fur coats hanging in rows, even

a pair of pearl-white, twelve-cylinder, turbocharged Jaguars, still wrapped in protective plastic like they'd just come from the factory.

The guide seemed to notice his stare. "They fell off the back of a truck."

"You mean rolled," Hawker said.

The man smiled. "Yes. That's exactly what I mean."

They continued on, passing the stolen cars and other items and then stopping near the center of the building. Two different sets of long rectangular crates rested there. NATO designations on the crates had been hastily covered with spray paint but were still partially visible. The alphanumeric code FIM-92 was easily readable.

These were the weapons Hawker had come to see, Stinger surface-to-air missiles. An XR designation that hadn't been painted over meant these were extended-range variants. Deadly up to five miles.

The weapons had disappeared from a NATO convoy several years before. The CIA figured they'd been taken for a prearranged buyer or that the thief quickly realized they were too hot to move, for until now they'd never cropped up for sale. But the black market never closed, and eventually rumors began to circulate about a shipment of such weapons.

Hawker glanced at the longer, broader crates to the left.

"Reserved for another buyer," a deep voice said from the shadows.

As Hawker turned, the owner of that voice stepped forward. Bald head polished and shining; jowls, neck, and shoulders forming one great slope. He wasn't overly fat, just incredibly compact, short and stocky beyond what seemed reasonable. He might have been five foot four and two hundred pounds. A tank, a fire hydrant, a bulldog of a man.

His name was La Bruzca, and the ease with which

he'd hidden himself reminded Hawker that the building was essentially a maze and he was a rat in the center of it, with no way of knowing how many men were hidden in the labyrinth. Despite the weapon he carried and his own considerable skills, there would be no fighting his way out of this. He slid the .45 into a shoulder holster.

La Bruzca studied him. "I have heard much about you. They say you are a lost soul, and until you are found, woe unto anyone who gets in your way."

"Don't believe everything you hear," Hawker said.

"If I believed even half of what I've been told, you'd be dead," La Bruzca replied.

Hawker wasn't sure what to make of the taunt, but there was something ominous in La Bruzca's words. He wondered if it was a jab at the number of times Hawker had survived near-certain death. Or if there was some greater meaning.

Could La Bruzca know who Hawker was working for? Hawker doubted it. Then again, this meeting had come about suddenly, through a third party that Hawker didn't know. The middleman was a ghost broker, an unseen player who communicated with both sides for a fee. The possibility of a setup was not beyond reason.

He held his tongue as if the words meant nothing.

"Then again," La Bruzca added, laughing, "I don't believe even one-quarter of what is said."

La Bruzca offered a hand, while the fifth man and another worker began to open one of the crates.

Hawker glanced back at the larger crates. Based on the size and dimensions they had to be larger missiles. But what type? Longer-range SAMs or even surface-to-surface missiles. He'd only been given information and authorization to bid on the Stingers, but if he could find out what they were, that might be of value.

"Additional merchandise," he noted.

La Bruzca nodded. "I carry many things."

"Care to take a bid?"

"No," La Bruzca said firmly.

Hawker cocked his head. "You sure?"

"You are jealous," La Bruzca said, "perhaps because they are bigger than yours."

La Bruzca laughed so hard at his own joke that he began to cough.

"I wouldn't put it quite that way," Hawker said. "But the people I work for might be interested, depending on what type they are."

"They are sold. But if I become interested in taking additional offers, I know how to reach you."

Hawker nodded. No more questions. He tried to memorize the dimensions and color of the crates and then stood his briefcase on a table and popped it open.

"That's a very small case," La Bruzca said. "I hope you brought large denominations."

Hawker pulled out a small set of tools and a pair of electronic devices that looked like testing equipment.

"I brought a down payment," he explained. "And before you get that, I have to inspect the guidance, warheads, and propulsion."

La Bruzca nodded as if it was standard procedure. "Of course you do," he said. "Of course."

Fifteen minutes later, one of the missiles lay on a cradle. A trio of examination ports had been opened. The two ports near the front revealed the guidance system and the battery pack that powered it. The port near the missile's tail gave access to the propellant stage.

Hawker tinkered for a moment, visually inspecting the circuit board and the status of the chargeable battery pack. Then he turned to the tail end of the rocket. Holding a magnifier against the yellow, claylike substance that made up the solid fuel of the missile, he switched on

a UV light. He studied small sections carefully, squinting and looking closely at what the magnifying glass was revealing.

The longer he looked, the closer La Bruzca and the fifth man came.

Finally, Hawker stood back. He shook his head.

"What's wrong?" La Bruzca asked.

"How old are these things?"

"Why?" La Bruzca said defensively.

"Because they're junk," Hawker said bluntly. "And you know it."

"These are top-of-the-line American missiles," La Bruzca said. "Just ask the Iraqis, the Syrians, or the Russians. They're deadly."

Hawker stared at La Bruzca. "Were deadly," he said. "Were."

"What do you mean?"

The question came from the fifth man, the guard who'd walked him in.

"Someone shafted you," Hawker said.

"This is a lie," the fifth man raged, pointing his gun at Hawker.

Hawker glared back at him, wondering how far he could push this without having someone snap. He looked at La Bruzca.

"Did you really get rich by killing all your customers?"

La Bruzca turned to his subordinate. "Put it down," he said, then turned back to Hawker. "You'd better explain your statement, friend."

Hawker turned the UV light back on. "See for yourself."

La Bruzca took the magnifier from Hawker's hand and held it above the propellant as Hawker angled the light.

"This thing sat in a bunker for years before it disap-

peared," Hawker said. "And you and I both know they've been hidden for half a decade since then."

Hawker handed the light to La Bruzca's associate and then pointed to the section of propellant he'd been studying.

"See those hairline cracks? They're your problem, or someone's. The fuel won't burn evenly. Probably detonate on ignition."

La Bruzca leaned in closer. He seemed strangely accepting of Hawker's statement.

"Sorry," Hawker said. "But the only people this thing's gonna kill are the ones who launch it."

As La Bruzca and his man studied the propellant, Hawker turned back to the guidance section. He reached in through the port, using an electrical detector to measure the power supply. He fiddled for a second and then looked at the gauge.

"Guidance looks good. And you seem to have new batteries," he said. "But those are easy to get. A lot easier than military-grade solid rocket fuel."

La Bruzca turned back to him, placing the magnifier down as Hawker snapped the power bus back into place and closed the guidance section.

"And if I don't believe you?"

"Then we disagree," Hawker said, shrugging. "Doesn't mean we can't do business."

"You have other needs?"

He nodded toward the larger crates. La Bruzca shook his head.

"What about Spiders?" Hawker asked, referencing an Israeli missile.

"I can ask around."

"You do that," Hawker said. "The people who hired me will buy anything like that you can get your hands on. British, Israeli, French, even Russian, but nothing Chinese. And the damn things have to work."

La Bruzca did not appear overly fazed. He nodded, appearing to be calculating something, perhaps considering future profits from sales to Hawker's friends. He nodded toward the Stinger.

"This should not get out," he said. A warning to Hawker.

"I'll give them another reason," Hawker promised. "But if I was you," he added, staring hard at La Bruzca, "I'd sell these to someone you don't want to see again."

Hawker snapped the briefcase shut. This was the moment of truth. Would they let him leave?

"Till next time," he said. He was not interested in asking for permission to depart, just in taking it. He turned and began walking across the warehouse floor.

Behind him, La Bruzca and the fifth man discussed something. The words were sharp but whispered, too hard for Hawker to make out.

Hawker kept walking. Trying not to think. Trying not to hope, but silently praying that these men hadn't noticed his sleight of hand. The door was a long way off.

La Bruzca's voice rang out. "Wait a minute, friend!" he shouted. "We are not done here."

Hawker froze. It was not a question. He took a breath and turned.

La Bruzca smiled and rubbed his hands together, then stepped toward Hawker. "Perhaps I can interest you in something else?"

Hawker cocked his head to the side. "Like what?"

La Bruzca smiled generously and for a moment Hawker saw a shopkeeper, a vendor in the market and not an international arms dealer.

"Tell me," he said. "What exactly are you driving these days?"

CHAPTER 3

A half mile from La Bruzca's sprawling warehouse, a craggy hill covered in thick trees and exposed gray rock loomed over the valley. Locals called it the Martyr's Hill, as the dome-shaped rise had been shelled and bombed repeatedly during the Serbo-Croatian War and had been a bloody battleground in the ethnic struggles of this land for a thousand years before that. It stood quietly now, at peace like the rest of this land.

Sitting amid that stillness, huddled under a camouflaged cloak, a man watched from this hill. Pale as bone, with a shaven head, sunken eyes, and the skin on his face stretched and taut, he held up a pair of binoculars, scanning the street in front of the warehouse.

No movement yet, no shooting or shouting. Just as he'd suspected. But no answers, either. And he'd come here in search of answers.

At great expense, this ghost of a man had uncovered the information about La Bruzca and his missiles. He'd leaked it to the right parties and the right parties only. And then he'd come to learn the truth.

With nothing to do but wait, he lowered the binoculars and rubbed at a dark tattoo that marred his neck. It covered a scar where someone had tried to slit his throat eighteen months earlier; a reminder to him that he had enemies on all sides.

Once he'd been a man of power and prestige, carrying a well-known name and a title. Others listened to him, obeyed his orders. But like the man he'd come to watch, the tattooed man had been cast out. Unlike the man below, the world at large would not forgive him his crimes. And that burned the very depths of his soul.

So be it, he thought. To be hated and feared by all was something he could embrace. Far better than a worm begging from the dust. *Far better to reign in hell than to serve in heaven.*

Upon leaving the hospital with his neck sewn together, he'd killed the man who cut him. Shot him and then stabbed him with his own knife and left him in the street in front of his house for others to find. It had been a moment of liberation.

During his life the tattooed man had been responsible for dozens of dead. Men, women, even children had died under his watch. Most had been killed collaterally. A few on direct order. But they were distant actions twice removed. At the time he had felt like a king sacrificing pawns. But to avenge himself in person brought a satisfaction and a wave of giddy power.

Now he would bring revenge to those who had wronged him. If he could not be part of the world, then he would destroy it and all that was good in it.

He chose a new name: *Draco*—Latin for the Serpent. Those who helped him now did not work for him but worshipped him. They were pariahs like he was. Lost souls. He took them in and became their Master, the one who would show them a new way. It complicated things, but it was necessary; a man could not punish the world alone. He needed an army.

When his plan came to fruition the whole world would feel the pain, even those who devoted themselves to him. They would not understand until it was too late; such

was the fate of those who followed. But the others would see and they would know who had bested them.

He wanted one group in particular to bear the brunt of his wrath. And to be sure he had the right targets, he had to know the truth, he had to see the face that had answered La Bruzca's call.

A garage door opened on the side of the warehouse and La Bruzca's thugs pushed a white sedan out onto the drive. It caught the sun, gleaming like polished marble.

Draco raised the binoculars and watched as one man filled the tank from a plastic can while another removed something from the trunk.

La Bruzca came out next, followed by the man in the leather jacket, who opened the sedan's door as if he owned it. He paused with a foot on the sill of the door, one arm resting on the roof, and the other clasping the open door frame.

Focusing the eyepiece, Draco could see their lips moving and watch them laughing, all without sound or context. A smile from the man in the leather jacket breathed arrogance and stirred the bile in Draco's heart. And then he turned and looked directly up the hill, almost right at Draco.

The truth was shown forth. The others called this man Hawker, but Draco knew his real name. And if he had come for La Bruzca's missiles, there could be no denying whom he worked for now.

Draco had his answers. The Serpent would devour the Hawk, but not before destroying everything he might hold dear.

CHAPTER 4

Thirty minutes after leaving the meeting, Hawker pulled up in front of the Excelsior Hotel driving the gleaming Jaguar. He got out, tossed the keys to the excited valet, and walked inside.

He crossed the lobby quickly, making his way to a broad staircase that led to the second floor and a five-star restaurant that overlooked the harbor.

The view was stunning. The hotel sat on the waterfront, jutting up from the seawall and rising several stories as if it were part of the battlements that ringed the harbor. Dorade was the flagship restaurant of the hotel and included a thin balcony that ran the length of the building overlooking the harbor and the Lovrijenac fortress.

The food and service had won awards across Europe. A shame, Hawker thought, as it would honestly be wasted on him. Food was food, you ate it to survive, and if it tasted good that was a bonus, but in general he paid little attention to it.

On the other hand, he needed a place to sit and wait and watch. Departing Croatia immediately would look suspicious, but on the slim chance La Bruzca discovered his deception, Hawker wanted to see the trouble coming, and the table at the end of the balcony would give him a view of the sea and the road leading up to the hotel,

all while allowing him to keep his back to the proverbial stone wall.

He would sit and eat and linger. A bottle of wine on the table would go mostly untouched and then he'd retire to his room, arrange for the Jaguar to be shipped somewhere, and take a cab to the airport, leaving his room paid for but empty during the night.

If he lasted that long it meant La Bruzca had no idea that he'd attached a transmitter to the guidance system of the Stinger missile. It meant that La Bruzca had buttoned up his crates and begun looking for another, less sophisticated buyer.

Hawker was *almost* certain this would be the case. It had gone well at the warehouse. And even if La Bruzca chose to check the missile in question, he or his men would have to know exactly what they were looking for. The transmitter itself was all but identical to the rest of the circuit board. A well-schooled technician might miss it.

In fact, he would have been *completely* certain of the operation's success, had it not been for La Bruzca's odd comment and vague threat regarding what he knew or believed about Hawker.

Reaching the top of the stairs, Hawker turned. He passed the host's stand with a nod to the employees he'd paid handsomely to reserve his table and then strode down the narrow aisle of the balcony.

Evenly spaced tables sat pressed against a waist-high wall on his right. On his left a glass partition kept the remainder of the restaurant out of the ever-changing weather.

He passed a lone patron at the first table and a continental power couple dining at the second. The man wore a thousand-euro suit, while a watch that cost twice that dangled from his wrist. The woman might have walked off the runway somewhere. Dressed in couture, way too

skinny, she looked entirely bored as she sipped champagne.

She flashed her eyes at Hawker as he passed, an act the man with her seemed to notice with disdain. Hawker ignored them both and continued on toward his table at the end of the row.

Halfway there, a red-haired patron turned. The man stretched out a hand and, using a cane, blocked Hawker's path like a toll gate.

Hawker looked down at the cane and then over at the man who held it. Powerfully built, with shoulders like Olympus and steel-gray eyes that seemed out of place beneath tangled hair the color of tomato sauce, David Keegan was a former member of the British SAS and onetime agent for MI-6. Before all that and before an explosion that had torn half his guts out, Keegan had been an alternate for the British national rugby team. What he did now was anyone's guess. Hawker had a few ideas, none of them good.

A porcelain-skinned woman sat across from Keegan, picking at some sashimi, her eyes hidden by mirrored aviators. She dressed the part, but unlike the trophy sitting at table number two, this woman might be as deadly as either of them.

Keegan smiled. "I would have sat at your table, mate, but the view is just crap from there."

"Depends what you're looking for," Hawker said.

The Brit shrugged in agreement. "I suppose it does."

Hawker glanced around. He had no reason to expect trouble from Keegan, he'd even saved the man's life once, but Hawker didn't believe in coincidence, and Keegan's brash manner suggested more than a casual meeting.

La Bruzca's words began running through his mind again. *If I believed even half of what I'm told, you'd be dead.* Could Keegan have known who Hawker worked for now? Could he have given that information away?

With the cane still blocking his way, and damn curious as to what Keegan might be doing there, Hawker grabbed a chair. He pulled it up and sat down in the only spot available: right between the two.

With Keegan on his left, the girl on his right, and his back to the glass wall and the goings-on in the restaurant, Hawker became painfully aware that he was now in exactly the position he didn't want to be.

"What the hell you doing here?" he asked.

Keegan flashed a smile across the table to the girl.

"How's that for a greeting?" he said. "We come all the way from merry old England to find him and he ain't even got a simple hello for us."

"We were at your place in Greece," the girl said flatly.

"Quiet, love," Keegan said. "And order something else, will you. You know I can't stand that stuff."

She smiled at him and took another bite.

"Fish is meant to be cooked," he said. "Now hold this."

As Keegan handed the cane over, Hawker tracked it from the corner of his eye, watching as the girl rested it against the edge of the table.

"So you two are here on your honeymoon?" Hawker said.

The girl sucked at her teeth as if the idea was absurd. Keegan scowled. "Who'm I gonna find to marry me?"

"Only half the women in London," Hawker said.

Keegan looked appalled. "Don't believe a word he says, love; it's more like a third."

"Of course, the other half want to kill you," Hawker added.

"That part might be true," Keegan admitted.

The girl did not seem to care.

"Neither of which explains what you're doing here."

"I'm here to find you, mate."

"I guessed that," Hawker said. "Why? And for that matter, how the hell did you know I was here?"

To do what Hawker did—and survive for any great length of time—took an unusual set of skills: brains, brawn, and quick reflexes. It also required an ability to think two steps ahead of everyone else and doses of absolute confidence and healthy paranoia. Let the ratio get out of whack in either direction and you ended up walking into a bullet or paralyzed by fear.

"Listen, mate," Keegan said. "This is my stomping grounds now. And you've been walking around in it lit up like neon. The whole world knows you're here, because you wanted them to know you were here. Now whether you're buying or selling or—"

Before Keegan could finish, Hawker's left hand shot out, swinging around his old friend's shoulders, grabbing him by the back of the neck, and slamming him forward. At almost the same instant, Hawker's right hand shot inside his jacket, hitting the grip of his pistol, tilting it, and jamming the barrel against Keegan's ribs.

As Keegan grunted in shock, Hawker glanced back. The girl had grabbed the cane. Hawker kicked it with his heel, knocking it out of her hands and sending it flying across the balcony's stone floor.

Buried inside that cane, Hawker knew, were two 9 mm shells that could be fired at the touch of a button and a knife that could be pulled from the handle.

The girl went to move.

"Don't," Hawker growled, flashing enough of the gun for her to see.

The commotion had stirred the other patrons and Hawker realized he was in a precarious situation. But he couldn't let Keegan spit out what he was probably about to say. Most likely, the girl knew everything Keegan knew, but on the odd chance she didn't, Hawker needed to shut him up.

A few tables down, Mr. Thousand Euro Suit had stood

up, tossed his napkin down, and begun coming their way.

"One of yours?" Hawker asked.

Keegan shook his head.

Hawker cut his eyes at the man. "I'd sit down if I was you."

The man stopped in his tracks. Whether he'd seen or guessed that Hawker was holding a gun or just realized this wasn't a person to mess with, he walked back to his table, grabbed his date, and left.

The rest of the balcony began to clear out and Hawker figured he had a minute or so before security showed their faces. He'd dropped enough money on the important people at the hotel that it wouldn't be a problem, but the conversation would be over and the cops might follow.

He leaned close to Keegan's ear. "Tell me who you're working for and what you want, or I'll blow what's left of your guts out and dump your sushi-eating friend over the balcony."

Keegan glanced up at him and then pulled from his grasp. Even now he was strong as an ox.

"Choose your words carefully," Hawker added.

"Same old Hawker," Keegan announced. "Can't tell a friend from a foe."

"Can you?" Hawker said.

Keegan looked across the table at his girl, ignoring Hawker.

"I ever tell you about the time Hawk here found me half blown to bits in the desert. He pushed my intestines back in, wrapped me up, and dragged me a half mile through enemy fire to a waiting air evac unit."

Keegan turned to Hawker, locking eyes with him.

"I don't care what you think, mate, that makes us blood. Understand? I'd go to hell and back for you. So

take that damned gun out of my ribs and listen to me for a minute."

Hawker eased off. The fact that no other thugs had appeared and the girl hadn't shot or stabbed him was somewhat reassuring, but he held the gun on his lap just the same.

"You've got sixty seconds," Hawker said.

"You still into helping friends?"

"You need help?"

"No," Keegan said. "I'm in the information trade now. I run a legitimately illegitimate business these days. Just like you. I'm here for another friend, a less capable friend. A guy I helped you spirit out of Africa five years ago."

A name came to mind: Ranga Milan, a Spanish geneticist he'd met in Africa a decade ago.

"Haven't heard from him in years," Hawker said.

Keegan raised his eyebrows. "What about Sonia?"

For reasons Hawker could never fathom, Ranga's twenty-year-old, American-born daughter, Sonia, had been with him. She was a budding scientist in her own right, but the Republic of the Congo was a dangerous spot, no place for a beautiful young girl. Then again, the whole situation had been a little odd.

Ranga and his daughter were supposed to be working on genetically modified crops, but the paymasters were military men. Whatever the original deal was it seemed to change over time. Veiled threats became outright demands; the generals wanted a bio-weapon.

While Ranga lived in denial, Hawker made escape plans, spending all his time guarding Sonia. Both he and Ranga knew she'd be the target if the generals needed more leverage. They grew closer during that time and she'd convinced herself that she loved him.

Hawker recalled trying to dissuade her from the idea,

though he wasn't sure that he'd tried that hard. Either way, when they'd finally cleared the border and made it to safety she'd begged Hawker to come to Europe with them or to take her wherever he was headed. Hawker had put her on the plane with Keegan and had never seen or heard from her again.

"She was in love with you, mate," Keegan said. "You telling me you haven't spoken?"

"Not since the three of you left Algiers."

"Too bad," Keegan said grinning. "Thought you'd have found her, run off, and had a bushelful of kids by now."

"I think she deserved better."

Keegan nodded. "Probably right about that."

"Did she come to you?" Hawker asked.

"No, mate, Ranga did. He found me in Athens. Don't ask me how. He wanted me to find you. Said he was desperate. Someone was trying to put a bullet in his head."

"Why didn't *you* help him?"

Keegan looked insulted. "I offered," he said. "Even offered to stake him if he needed cash. But he said money wouldn't do it. And he didn't trust me the way he trusted you."

Hawker remembered Ranga being troubled in his own way. He lived in some brooding world in his own mind, alternating between dark spells and manic euphoria as he chased whatever it was that possessed him. How such a brilliant man could seem utterly clueless, Hawker didn't know. But Ranga had pulled it off.

Forcing him to see what was about to happen in the Congo had almost broken him, as if giving up on what he was doing would drive him to madness. After that, mostly silence and then a simple thank-you when he realized what Hawker had saved him and his daughter from.

Apparently Ranga had become no better at choosing his partners.

"What the hell did he get himself into now?" Hawker asked.

"Don't know," Keegan said. "Loose grip on reality, that one. But he looked bad when I saw him. Halfway to dead. Swore there were devils after him. And that he'd done something . . ." Keegan seemed to struggle. "He used the word *unforgivable*."

"He say where I could find him?"

"He said to make your way to Paris. Check in to the Trianon Palace Hotel. He'd find you there." As he finished, Keegan reached into his coat pocket and pulled out a flash drive.

"He gave me this," Keegan said, handing the drive over. "Said you'd understand."

Understand. Right now Hawker didn't understand anything. He had the sickening feeling of a moment spinning out of control.

In many ways, Keegan couldn't have picked a worse time or place to find him, or worse news to tell him. But even with a hundred questions racing around in his head, Hawker knew the bell was about to ring. Time to go.

He stood. "Was she with him?"

"No, mate. I'm thinking she left his crazy little circus the first chance she got."

The situation had always been odd. All families had secrets, but whatever drove Ranga and Sonia both pulled them together and drove them apart

Good for her if she did leave, Hawker thought. And yet, if Ranga was in such deep trouble, she might still be in danger. What better way was there to pressure a father than by threatening his daughter.

"Do you know where she is?"

Keegan shook his head.

"She might be in danger. And she might be in hiding," Hawker said. "Think you can you find her?"

Keegan pursed his lips as if the question was ludicrous. "Sure. And what do I get for it?"

"You get even."

Keegan smiled and then he laughed lightly. "There's no such thing as even, Hawk. You should know that."

"Just find her," Hawker said.

Keegan nodded, which Hawker took as acknowledgment that he would try. "Give me your number."

Keegan handed him a business card.

"You have cards?"

"Don't you?"

Hawker shook his head, typed the number into his phone, and then hit Send. A ringing came from Keegan's pocket.

Hawker hung up.

"Find her and call me," he said. And then he turned to go.

As Hawker strode away Keegan raised his hands, palms outstretched like a man who'd been left with nothing.

"Is that it then!" he shouted, a false look of shock plastered all over his face. "No goodbye kiss or nothing?" He was laughing deliriously by now, probably reveling in the attention of the few people left on the balcony.

As Hawker passed the host's stand and took the stairway down, he could hear Keegan laughing even as he yelled after Hawker.

"And after all we've meant to each other!"

As he left Keegan behind, Hawker regretted threatening him, but sometimes that was the only way to know who was a friend and who wasn't.

He reached the bottom of the stairs, left the hotel, and caught a cab into town. Once there, he cut diagonally across a few city blocks, entered a large office building, and came out the back side. There he grabbed another taxi that took him to the Stradun, Dubrovnik's busiest street.

Feeling certain he'd lost anyone who might have been

following, and mixing with a throng of people who didn't speak much English, he found a quiet corner and dialed a number on his cellphone. The scrambled signal went to a satellite, bounced its way to Washington, and was routed to the person he was looking for.

A female voice came on the line, a soothing voice that he recognized: Danielle Laidlaw, his liaison to the National Research Institute, the organization he now worked for.

The NRI was a strange hybrid of a government agency. It had a large aboveboard department that worked with universities and corporations on cutting-edge research, and it had a smaller, less well known department that functioned like the CIA but in the world of industrial secrets.

Hawker and Danielle worked for the operations department. However, because of his particular background, Hawker had been "loaned out" to the CIA to set up La Bruzca.

"I need extraction," he said.

"You're three days early," she said. "Is something wrong?"

He knew she was referring to the deal with La Bruzca, but his thoughts had left that behind. He couldn't imagine what Ranga had gotten himself into but he knew for the man to reach out, it had to be substantial. He pulled the flash drive out of his pocket, wondering what might be contained inside.

"I'm not sure," Hawker said, eyeing the memory stick. "But I have a feeling something may be very wrong."

CHAPTER 5

Paris, France

Ranga Milan stood at the base of the Eiffel Tower, staring upward. The Iron Lady of France soared above him, a thousand feet of steel bent into a shape that was both structure and art.

Somewhere up on the observation deck, a man waited for him carrying an object with a dual nature of its own: a carved tablet more than seven thousand years old. It was considered a priceless artifact, a remnant of history to most, but Ranga knew better. It contained a secret, hidden since the beginning of recorded time, a secret that could change the future of the world for good or for evil.

Surrounded by the crowd, Ranga felt terribly alone. He'd sent for help but none had come. He'd waited too late, he knew that. But now he was taking a risk that he feared might be too great. He'd come out of hiding and into the open; he was a target.

Dizzy from gazing upward, Ranga lowered his eyes and moved toward the elevator. He edged into a crowd of tourists, fighting every urge to hurry. Rushing would only draw attention. The wrong kind of attention.

From the outside looking in, Ranga had little need to worry. Nearly sixty, of average height and build, he had nondescript features and short dark hair. He was a common-looking everyman. No one ever looked twice.

His background was more impressive. A genetics expert, a former fellow at the prestigious Advanced Genetics Lab of Johns Hopkins University and a onetime Nobel Prize candidate, Ranga had once been a pillar of the community.

Now he was a fugitive.

Listed on Interpol's high-priority register, this nondescript everyman was considered one of the most dangerous people in the world. Not for anything he'd done, for he had committed no crime greater than fraud and theft, but for what they knew he was capable of doing.

In his prior life, Ranga had done research for all the top labs, as well as the U.S. government. His success in manipulating genetic codes and creating new forms of life was legendary, and he had intimate firsthand knowledge regarding the creation of biological weapons.

Beyond that, it was well-known that Ranga Milan needed money. What it was for remained a mystery, but Interpol, the CIA, and other Western security services had long feared he would trade his vast knowledge for the wealth he sought.

So far, Ranga told himself, *I have done no such thing.* It was a partial truth, one he'd risked his life to maintain. But a partial truth was also a partial lie.

He shook the thought away, focusing on the meeting. By holding it here, in the most public space in France, he hoped he would be safe from the people he'd once worked for. He'd believed in them once, believed they had similar desires, but as he discovered the truth he had no choice but to run. Otherwise they would take what he wanted to create and turn it into a weapon like no other that had ever been built.

Ranga shuddered at how close they'd come before he broke away. He cringed in fear that they might find a way to finish what he had already given them. He could

have destroyed the research, should have destroyed it perhaps, but it was his life's work.

And there was still a need.

"Excuse me," he said, brushing past a group of Japanese tourists. *"Merci, merci."*

He squeezed by the group, fitting himself into the front of the crowded elevator. He clutched a computer case to his side and waited as the doors lingered while several more passengers fitted themselves in.

Across the crowded plaza, he saw a gendarme turn his way. Just a casual tilt of the head and then a moment of hesitation, but the hesitation bothered Ranga. The policeman began walking toward the elevator, not hurrying, just strolling, not even really focused on the elevator anymore, but headed his way.

And then the doors closed, the gears whirled, and the elevator began to rise.

As the car raced upward toward the observation deck Ranga exhaled, relaxing for the moment. The computer case slung over one shoulder weighed heavily. Inside lay every ounce of funding he'd been able to put his hands on and it was still ten thousand euros short.

He guessed his contact would do little besides glance at the cash, but the man had his own needs and if an argument ensued Ranga had come prepared for that as well.

A ceramic object in his pocket that looked like a cellphone was actually a handgun. Barely bigger than his palm, it carried four shots. And though Ranga had never fired a gun, under no circumstances would he leave this place empty-handed.

The elevator doors opened and the tourists pushed their way out. Ranga moved with them, wiping a sheen of sweat off his upper lip. He spotted a figure in the southwest corner, at the very edge of the decking. A patch covered one of his eyes and a package rested at his feet.

Ranga walked over. *"Bonjour,"* he said.

The man turned toward Ranga. His weatherbeaten face, tanned skin, and coarse hair suggested a life of hardship. A scar disappearing beneath the eye patch confirmed it.

"The language of the Frenchman is not mine," the seller said coarsely.

"But you make your home here," Ranga said.

"Your money helped me escape," the man said. "But I do not wish to forget."

Ranga had made contact with this man during a stay in Iran. His name was Bashir, a onetime archaeologist and then a curator for a private museum. Bashir had been an opponent of the ayatollahs for many years. He'd kept a low profile until 2009, when he'd stood up and had then been caught and tortured for supporting the Green Revolution after the contested elections.

The hard-liners took his eye and then his family. Bashir had taken revenge by fleeing to France with treasures the world had long thought destroyed. He now sold them to fund the resistance.

"If it is the will of Allah, I will go back one day," he said.

Ranga offered a sad smile. During their time together the two men had debated this concept many times. Apparently neither had changed his position.

"My friend, there is no God," Ranga said. "Neither yours, nor mine, nor any other. There is only man and the stories we tell to explain the unexplainable."

Bashir laughed a little bit. A laugh every bit as sad as Ranga's smile. "They have tainted your mind."

"They have poisoned many things, but this belief is my own."

Ranga said nothing more, not wishing to think of the pain he'd endured at the hands of the radical group he'd allowed himself to join or the despair he felt from their legacy.

"Even as you speak I hear the doubt," Bashir said. "Why else would you want the tablet and the truth it contains?"

Ranga understood how it looked. His interest in Bashir stemmed from the man's knowledge, particularly of the cultures that had grown up in the Middle East thousands of years before the time of Christ. Cultures like the Uruk and the Sumerians and the Elamites, cultures that had left a record of man's earliest quest to understand a being they could neither see nor hear but felt compelled to obey.

Indeed, Ranga was obsessed with the subject, but his reasons were more concrete than spiritual. He could not risk explaining them to Bashir.

"Do you have what you've offered?" Ranga asked. "Or must I wait?"

"I waited thirty years to see it again," Bashir said. "So I understand your need. If I am right, this tablet was carved by the hand of Adam, the first man. Do you understand what that means?"

Ranga tried not to react. He had been fooled by hoaxes before. "How can you be sure?"

"There is no sure," Bashir said. "But the writings that led us to his grave spoke of the Garden, the fall of man, and the exile. They also told us of—"

"Not here," Ranga insisted.

Bashir seemed agitated. "But you must know. It is not what you think. It talks of water, the sword of fire, and of death."

"And of life," Ranga insisted, though he didn't know for sure.

"Yes," Bashir said. "And also of life."

"And what of the scroll?"

"To the auction in Beirut, as I told you," Bashir said sadly.

Ranga felt a spike of emotion, desperation mixed with

panic. He had hoped Bashir would be able to find the scroll he'd spoken of, but in truth it didn't matter now. Not if he was right about the tablet.

"Have you ever chased something that stubbornly remained just beyond your grasp?" Bashir asked.

"All my life," Ranga admitted.

"The scroll has been that way for me. No matter how many times I've gotten close, it has always fled from me," Bashir explained. "I will recover it with what you've given me. I will have it once and for all and I will share with you what it tells me."

Bashir had promised to go to Beirut with the money Ranga was paying him, to bid on the scroll. The effort might avail him, might even prove what Ranga and Bashir both believed about Adam and the Garden, though for vastly different reasons. But now Ranga thought—he hoped—it was no longer necessary. The tablet was all that mattered.

"Let me see it."

Bashir slid the satchel toward him. Ranga opened it. He could see the brownish stone inside and could just make out the carving.

Ranga took a breath and held it. He was so close he could feel it. The end of a quest that had driven him to madness was growing near.

Glancing up, he noticed Bashir's eye shift. Bashir was looking past him, focusing on a spot near the center of the tower. A look of fear grew on his face.

"You've been reckless," Bashir whispered.

Ranga began to turn.

"Don't," Bashir said.

Ranga straightened up, placed the computer case down, and reached into his pocket. Craning his neck around just far enough to see, he spotted four gendarmes spreading out through the crowd. Reflective vests marked them.

Their hands rested on holstered weapons as if they expected a fight.

"The Sûreté," Bashir whispered.

Ranga recognized one of them and felt a wave of fear shoot through him like flash of pain. "Not the police," he said. "It is them. They have come for me."

"Surely they wouldn't—"

"They would do anything," Ranga said.

He pushed the computer bag filled with cash toward Bashir and grabbed for the package. If he could just find a way back into the crowd and down he could—

He took a step but a heavy hand fell on his shoulder like a claw. It spun him around. Ranga placed the satchel down, raised one hand in surrender, and almost simultaneously reached into his pocket and pressed the trigger of his little weapon.

The gunshot echoed through the observation deck. The crowd jumped. The "policeman" fell backward bleeding and clutching his abdomen.

The tourists screamed at the sight and bolted for the elevators and stairwell.

Ranga's hand and side burned from the blast and he stood in foolish shock at what he had done. As the crowd raced around him, he sought a way out. He grabbed the package and tried to move, but more shots rang out. Bullets flew in his direction, forcing him to dive and take cover.

Pulling the zip gun from his pocket, he fired once and ducked behind the ironwork. For a moment he was hidden, but the crowd was thinning quickly and he would soon be hopelessly exposed.

"You can't fight them," Bashir said. "Give them what they want. It means nothing without the scroll."

"You're wrong," Ranga said. "It means everything."

Seeming to disagree, Bashir grabbed the satchel and tried to run, but Ranga tripped him up, the satchel hit

the ground, and the tablet spilled out onto the deck, chipping one corner.

A voice with a Mediterranean lilt rang out across the platform.

"Ranga Milan, you have strayed from the faith. The Master has sent us to bring you home."

He recognized the voice. Marko. The Killer. The Man of Blood.

Grabbing the clay tablet, Ranga scrambled for better cover. He wasn't quick enough. A bullet hit him in the leg, taking his feet out from under him. He fell hard, rolled, and began to crawl, only to have another bullet hit him in the shoulder.

Wincing in agony, Ranga pulled himself into a more covered position. He grasped the tablet and gazed through the iron lattice of the tower.

The "policemen" were moving to new positions, surrounding him from three sides, cutting him off from any hope of reaching the elevator or the stairwell. He could not escape, and with only a few bullets in his small gun, he could not hope to fight his way out.

He looked around in despair.

"Just give it to them," Bashir said. "They will let you go."

"They will never let either of us go," Ranga replied.

From the streets below he could hear alarms blaring. The men surrounding him would not wait long.

He glanced toward the edge of the platform. Out beyond lay the void of open sky.

He could not save himself now. He could not save those he wished to save, but he knew what these men would do with the secret contained in the tablet. He could not allow that to occur.

He ran his hand over the smooth surface and the carved markings. He studied the symbol at the center. A

circle with four notches in it, within which lay a square and a smaller rectangle.

Bashir had called it the Mark of Eden. And he'd been right, but it would do neither of them any good. For if there was no God, as Ranga thought, then his existence was about to end brutally with nothing to show for it but misery. And if there was one, damnation surely awaited for what he had done.

He inched toward the edge.

"Give up, Ranga!" Marko shouted.

"So that you can use me to kill and destroy?"

"Your work will die alongside you," Marko shouted. "Is that what you want?"

Ranga slid a few more inches. "Better than the hell on earth you want to see."

"We do only what is necessary," Marko said. "What you suggested so long ago."

The thought sickened Ranga. It had come full circle, the arrogance he'd always been accused of, the indictment of his profession. Geneticists playing God. And now . . .

What had he done?

Despite a decade of effort, he saw the truth plainly. His work must die. He must die with it.

He inched closer to the edge. He whispered to himself, "I'm sorry, Nadia. I tried."

He turned, fired his last shots blindly, and then lunged for the edge without hesitation.

He made one full step before the crack of a gunshot cut him down.

Ranga's back arched as blistering pain racked his body. He slumped to his knees, one hand on the railing. The tablet fell from his hand, landing on the deck, the Mark of Eden staring back up at him.

He tried to stand but lacked the strength. He reached for the tablet, felt its smooth surface in his hand once more, and then heaved it.

He watched it fall. It spun and tumbled, dropping silently through the air for what seemed like an eternity. Farther and farther down. And then it hit. Shattering into a thousand fragments on the concrete below.

Collapsing facedown, Ranga drifted toward darkness, expecting a bullet to find his skull. But instead of a finishing shot, he felt rough hands yank him up.

"Take him with us," he heard Marko say. "Take them both."

"What about the tablet?"

The second voice sounded nervous, fearful. Ranga understood that, too. The Master would be furious.

Marko was less afraid. "We will find the others, once we have the scroll."

Marko grabbed Ranga by the hair and shook him awake. "And we will force the truth from your lips before you die. I promise you that."

Ranga heard these words through a fog. He saw Marko's unforgiving eyes and felt the hatred in his soul. He knew it was not a lie.

He had failed. He would die in horrendous pain. His dream would be twisted into an endless, living nightmare and hell would come to the earth after all.

CHAPTER 6

Danielle Laidlaw sat in the passenger cabin of a Citation X business jet as it idled on the ramp at an airport forty miles south of Dubrovnik. The main door stood open, the stairs down and locked. Activity was at a standstill.

This jet would be Hawker's method of extraction, a departure in a style appropriate to the people he was supposed to represent. If anyone was watching, all they'd see was Hawker boarding a jet owned by a mysterious corporation chartered out of Malta and known to be involved in international weapons sales.

The only possible link to the United States would be Danielle herself. For that reason she stayed inside, window shades down, restricted to watching the ramp via a closed-circuit camera feed that displayed on a flat-screen monitor at the front of the cabin.

Hawker was late, twenty minutes so far. Not an overly concerning amount, but enough to stir a small degree of worry. She cared a great deal for Hawker. He had a way of bringing out the best and most honorable parts in her own personality. Parts she had lost in her initial climb up the ranks of the National Research Institute.

Her job often required lying, stealing, and deceiving in the name of the greater good. She didn't really have a problem with that. But a time had come when it all went

too far, when the NRI began hiring civilians, putting them at risk and lying about the dangers they would face.

Two and a half years ago, on a mission like that, they'd also retained Hawker. He'd been little more than a hired gun at the time, but as the mission frayed at the edges and then blew itself apart, Hawker had been the one factor that kept the damage from becoming all-encompassing.

The final tally was grave, with more than a dozen deaths and a barely contained scandal that led right back to the agency's then director, Stuart Gibbs. He'd disappeared before Danielle and the team made it home, and the NRI itself had almost collapsed, maintaining its existence by the thinnest of margins.

In the words of one critic, the mission had been "cataclysmic in the scope and magnitude of its failure," but she and several others, mostly civilians, had survived, almost exclusively due to Hawker's efforts.

The experience had been so intense that it took Danielle a while to work out her feelings. Only later had she come to realize the irony of Hawker, the fugitive mercenary and pariah, showing her, the upstanding straight-A government agent, what mattered and what didn't.

It reminded her of deep-seated beliefs about honor and righteousness that she'd somehow buried or rationalized away as a hindrance to getting the job done. It had been the beginning of the way back to herself. And when the dust cleared, she found that she liked new her—the old her—better.

Eventually she'd returned to the NRI with renewed purpose and strength, determined that she could do what was right and still do her job.

Perhaps that was why her feelings for Hawker went deeper than the physical attraction they both felt. She was fairly certain that he'd touched her soul somehow.

Someday, in some way, she hoped, they'd get a chance to see where things might go, but so far Hawker's cover

required him to live exactly as he had for the previous decade. He lived in the shadows as a target for Interpol and American agencies like the FBI that were purposefully kept in the dark as to his change in status, lest it leak out. He never spent more than a few weeks in one place. Not exactly the way to start a relationship.

She'd hoped that after this mission to Croatia they might have some time to be by themselves, but Hawker's message and the information she'd uncovered trying to help him meant there was little chance of that.

As she waited and worried for him, it grieved her that she was here to deliver terrible news.

On the screen she saw an expensive-looking white sedan slide through the gate at the edge of the taxiway. The car rolled across the apron and parked beside the Citation, stopping at the foot of the stairs. Her heart filled with relief when Hawker got out, handed the keys to another man, and then began to climb the stairs.

He stepped through the door and looked directly toward her.

She couldn't help but smile.

He grinned back at her, handsome and rugged.

"I have to ask," she said, playfully, "why are you driving a Jaguar?"

"They didn't have an Aston Martin," he said.

"That's not what I meant."

As the stairs were rolled away, Hawker pulled the door shut, locked it into place, and came back to sit with her.

Pressing an intercom button on her armrest, she spoke to the pilot. "We're ready to go."

The pilot's voice came over the intercom. "We've filed a flight plan to Hamburg. Do you want us to amend?"

"I'll let you know once we're airborne," she said, and then turned her attention back to Hawker. "That's going to be a little hard to explain on the expense report."

"Tell them it's a finder's fee," he said.

La Bruzca had been suspected of trafficking arms for years, but the extent had never been known. Loaning Hawker out to the CIA for a while gave them a chance to get a look at his operation. Danielle had read his report already, including the successful planting of a tracer in the nose cone of one missile. Wherever La Bruzca took his wares they should be able to follow. And if he sold them, the tracer that Hawker planted would lead the CIA right to the end user. She guessed that ought to be worth a car or two.

As the engines spooled up outside the cabin, Hawker's eyes tightened on her. Despite her efforts to turn the conversation in another direction, he asked the exact question she'd hoped he would delay.

"Were you guys able to get a line on Ranga?"

"Yes," she told him. "But it's more complicated than that."

He nodded. "I figured it would be. I don't need you to release the hounds or give me a key to the National Archives. I just want to know if there's anything you can tell me."

She took a breath.

Hawker's fears for an old friend might have fallen on deaf ears, except for a few simple facts. To begin with, Ranga Milan was considered a ticking time bomb, an A. Q. Khan in the making, only in possession of knowledge far more deadly than the simple skills required to build an atomic bomb.

Genetic technology could be almost infinitely dangerous. It was telling that the SALT and START arms limitation treaties and the Geneva Convention all but banned the creation and use of biological weapons, while nations stockpiled tens of thousands of nuclear weapons and pointed them at one another.

The fact was that biological weapons were easily con-

trollable, right up until the moment they were used. After that, all bets were off.

A biological weapon was alive. It could change, mutate, grow, or spread in ways never predicted. Once you sent a plague into your enemy's backyard, no one could promise it wouldn't return home, even with an ocean in between. Nor could anyone guarantee that such an organism would not mutate and overcome defenses and vaccines prepared against it in advance. To use such a weapon was like building a house in a field of dry grass and then setting fire to your neighbor's hut.

Rational minds, even if interested in world domination, knew such weapons were not practical. But in the hands of a fanatic, a suicidal lunatic, or a doomsday cult, such a weapon might be perfect.

And without an announcement by the user, it might be months before something was even noticed, at which point a disease or plague would have spread far beyond its initial starting point and become unstoppable.

Fortunately or unfortunately, someone had recently made such an announcement, in the form of a letter, carrying an unknown virus and delivered to Claudia Gonzales, the assistant U.S. ambassador to the United Nations. Suspicion focused on its being the work of Ranga Milan.

That was fact number two. In the long run it would be the most painful. But under the current circumstances, Danielle guessed fact number three would bring on the most immediate anguish.

"It's more complicated than that because of a pair of incidents that occurred over the last forty-eight hours."

Not wanting to seem evasive, she focused first on Hawker's question.

"Regarding Ranga," she said. "We took the information you gave us. We found him in Paris. I'm sorry, Hawker, but Ranga's dead."

Hawker's jaw clenched and he took a slow breath before responding. "How?"

The file in front of her detailed the life and painful death of Ranga Milan. She could have handed it to him, but that seemed so cold.

"Twenty-eight hours ago, a shooting occurred on the secondary observation deck of the Eiffel Tower. At first blush, it was considered a terrorist incident or even an assassination attempt against an Iranian exile who happened to be there. But we know differently now. Ranga was on that deck."

"You're sure?"

She nodded. "Eyewitnesses and video from the site show two men being captured and hauled off by the Parisian police. Only the police reported no one in custody."

"I don't understand," he said.

"Last night the bodies of four officers were found in an abandoned house on the outskirts of the city. Someone had killed them the day before and taken their place in the tower patrol."

"Someone who needed access to the tower."

She nodded. It was clear the officers had been targeted and taken before the incident. Their uniforms, IDs, and even their cars had been used.

"Any idea who?"

She shook her head. No one had a clue. Certainly no group had claimed responsibility.

"What about Ranga?" Hawker asked.

"They found him this morning," she said. "I'm sorry to tell you this, but he'd been tortured and mutilated in some way."

Understandably she could sense the anger rising in Hawker. "Tortured."

She nodded slowly. "I don't have all the details. I'm hearing it was pretty bad. He was left tied up in another vacant property for the police to find."

After a deep breath, Hawker held out his hand. She passed him the file. It contained everything they knew, including the fact that an Iranian, confirmed to be a member of the Green Revolution and a dealer in stolen antiquities, was still missing, that a large sum of cash was found at the site, and that something had been thrown from the deck. Analysis showed the object to be made of dried clay, but the destruction was so complete it was impossible to determine just what had been destroyed.

She pointed to the file. "There's background information in there," she said, referring to Ranga's profile. "Some of it you may know, some of it maybe not."

Hawker began to read. She could see the tension in his face, could sense him battling the frustration and anger.

"I hate to say this," she added, "but that's not the worst of it."

Hawker looked up.

"The day before Ranga's disappearance, a letter was received at the UN. It carried a rather bizarre rambling threat and also some form of unknown virus."

"I heard about an anthrax scare," he said. "Is that what we're talking about?"

"That's just the cover story," she said. "To keep people calm."

"Anthrax is the cover story?" he repeated. "What the hell is the real story then?"

"It's bad," she said. "It's like nothing anyone has seen before. It may be close to one hundred percent infectious. The threat indicates it is designed to cause a plague."

By the look on his face, Hawker had already guessed where this was going. "And the source?"

"The letter was anonymous, but on an impermeable layer inside the envelope they found fingerprints pretty much everywhere. The prints are Ranga's."

Hawker looked up at the ceiling and exhaled. It wasn't

a look of disbelief but a look of frustration, as if something long feared had just been confirmed.

"He said he'd done something unforgivable. I'm guessing this is it."

"He was your friend," Danielle said, "so I don't expect this to be easy. But I need you to tell me anything about him that we might not already know."

"You know more than I do," he said, holding up the file.

"We don't know what happened in Africa. We have pictures, guesses. You were with him."

He closed the file but held on to it. She sensed a reluctance to talk on his part, but he spoke anyway.

"I met Ranga in '05. I spent fourteen months with him and his daughter, providing protection. First he was looking for funding and then he took a job in the Republic of the Congo in central Africa, studying drought-resistant crops or something like that. I went with them."

He put the file down, pushed it away.

"It didn't take long for them to ask him for something more, something other than what he'd agreed to. Eventually they began to make threats. At one point they tried to take his daughter hostage to force his hand."

Hawker glanced out the window. The Citation had begun to taxi.

"After that he promised them whatever they wanted and things calmed down for a while. I don't know if he believed them or if he just wanted to use them as long as he could, but I almost had to put a gun to his head to get him to leave."

"He's known to be obsessive," she said.

He nodded.

"Usually people like that have an ax to grind. Some perceived slight to avenge. Did you sense that at all?"

Hawker shook his head.

"Did he ever tell you what he was working on? Or at least hint at it?"

Hawker leaned back, a distant look in his eyes, as he tried to recall.

"He talked more about God than genetics," Hawker said. "Wondered how any god could allow what was happening around the world. He seemed to cycle between atheism and fearing that God was punishing him for things he'd said and done. I remember him asking what a man like me thought about divine retribution."

Knowing Hawker's past, she understood why the question might matter. But the issue was Ranga.

"Do you think he's capable of this?" she asked. "Not the construction of the virus—we assume that—but the use of it?"

Hawker took his time. "I know Interpol has him labeled as some public enemy–slash–mad scientist. I'll give you the mad part, but the guy I knew could not be a mass murderer. On our run out of the Congo, he would not carry a weapon because he didn't want to kill anyone."

"People change," she said.

"You asked me what I thought."

"I did," she replied.

"He was trying to get my help for a reason," Hawker said. "Someone was hunting him. My guess is, whoever that was caught him and forced him to send the virus. I mean if you're going to foist a plague on the world and send the letter anonymously, are you really going to be dumb enough to get your fingerprints all over it?"

It was a good point. And the fact that the UN letter had come through internal sources while Ranga Milan was three thousand miles away meant someone else was involved. But who?

Unfortunately, UN security was almost wholly focused on the perimeter. Few cameras or controls were allowed

on the inside, so the diplomats could move and talk freely without fear of being recorded.

Across from her, Hawker leaned forward. Looking into her eyes, his intensity ratcheting up, he spoke.

"I honestly don't know what the hell Ranga was doing. Either then or now. But I know he was basically a good man. I feel it. I saw it. Otherwise he would have just given the bastards in the Congo what they wanted. Or he would have given these people what they wanted instead of ending up dead."

She paused, considering what he'd said and the force with which he'd said it. She knew he was leading up to something. She could guess what it was.

"You want to go after them?"

He nodded. "When this plane lands in Hamburg, I'm off the clock. I'm asking for whatever information you can share. But I can't let this stand."

"I understand how you feel," she said. "I'm not surprised. But there's a bigger issue."

"You're going to fight me on this?"

"No," she said. "I'm going to help you. We—the NRI—we're going to help you. It's an odd coincidence, but Ambassador Gonzales was once an employee of the NRI, ten years ago. And as you're now working with us, the powers that be have determined that we're the appropriate agency to work this case. Back home we're teaming with the CDC to study the virus, out here . . . out here we've been ordered to track down the players involved, if we can. That includes the people who killed your friend."

Hawker sat back again, a look of concern on his face.

"You'd rather do it alone?" she asked.

"No," he said.

"You don't believe we'll be helpful?"

"No," he said. "I don't believe in coincidence, and for the second time in twenty-four hours I'm staring one in the face."

Danielle nodded. She didn't much believe in coincidence, either, but the fact was, Claudia Gonzales had worked for the public division of the NRI, as had several hundred thousand other people over the last decade. Many of them had gone on to important careers in corporate America, politics, and other government agencies. Gonzales had no connection with the operations division, would not even know its real purpose, and certainly, having left ten years ago, knew nothing about Hawker's role with the NRI.

If ever there was a coincidence, this was one.

"Does it change your mind?" she asked.

"No," he said. "Nothing on earth could change my mind right now."

Danielle nodded and pressed her intercom switch, buzzing the pilot.

"We're ready for takeoff," the pilot said.

"Good," she replied. "As soon as we're over international waters, I want you to amend the flight plan."

"Where to?"

"Paris?" she said, looking over at Hawker.

He nodded.

"Direct to Paris," she said, speaking to the pilot.

Hawker leaned back in his seat. He offered a half-hearted smile. "Wish it was under better circumstances," he said. "But it's nice to be working with you again."

CHAPTER 7

La Courneuve, France

His name was Marko. A sullen face, a square jaw, and a large bony brow gave him the look of a giant. He was only six feet tall but thick as a tree, with hands like the paws of a bear. He was first beneath the Master and within the group he was known as the Killer, or as *Cruor*, the Man of Blood, for it was he who put the blades into those the Master marked. It was he who had strangled the life out of the officers from the French police force.

He would do all that the Master requested, because it was his purpose.

Today he waited at the end of the boulevard in a dilapidated shelter that had once been a bus stop and watched as a young man in ratty jeans, boots, and an oversized hoodie walked the trash-littered sidewalk toward him. Rusting cars and graffiti marked the youth's progress— even a van that had burned in the last riots and had yet to be removed.

La Courneuve was a suburb of Paris and one of the toughest slums in Western Europe. Poor French and waves of immigrants settled here, piled in together, jobless, hopeless, soaked in the stench of despair.

The riots of 2005 had begun here after two youths hiding from police were accidentally electrocuted. Media claims pegged the riot on ethnic tensions, but Marko

knew better. There were many ethnicities here, many creeds and colors. All of them shared the anger and frustration of being forgotten, hated, and ignored.

Citizens claimed police brutality on a regular basis, and the police, having been attacked and ambushed so often in La Courneuve, considered it a red zone, where entry was not recommended without heavy support.

Whatever the normal course of action might have been, the police were out in force now. As Marko watched, a small convoy of two cars and an armored SUV cruised slowly down the street. The bodies of the slain policemen had been discovered here and the French police were intent on doling out a reprisal and perhaps even making arrests.

The convoy passed the youth, who did not look up. He knew better than to eye the cops. He continued on, finally joining Marko on the scarred and weathered bench.

"You did as I asked," Marko noted. "I am pleased. The Master is pleased."

"The police have found the bodies."

"Yes," Marko said. "It was planned."

The young man, whose name was Yousef, seemed sick at the notion.

"Why did we want them to be found?"

Marko ignored the question. "Do you feel sorry for them?"

"I hate what they do to us," Yousef said.

"Then they got what they deserved," Marko offered.

Yousef seemed to agree, though Marko could feel some reluctance. "Do I join you now?"

"Are you ready to give up everything?"

"What do I have left?"

"What do you have left?" Marko asked.

Yousef shook his head. "I have no father, no brother. I am French but the French call me 'dirty Arab.' I am not one of them."

"You are a Muslim," Marko noted.

"I no longer pray."

"Why?"

Yousef seemed confused.

"Why do you not pray, Yousef?"

The young man gazed at the ground. "Allah does not answer me," he said.

"You are on the right path," Marko assured him.

A brief pause followed, as if Yousef were contemplating his next words.

"What about the others?" he asked.

Yousef had recruited several friends for the attack. Young men disgruntled like he was. But they did not have the zeal that he had. Marko shook his head. "The others are not worthy as you are. They will be paid and you will leave them behind. Or you will stay."

If Marko judged the young man correctly, this part was harder. It was one thing to give up a country that did not want you, or to reject a god that did not favor you, but to leave friends behind, friends that were the only family a youth from the street had ever known, that was more difficult.

It had been the hardest part for Marko a year before, but like Yousef's friends, Marko's comrades did not really understand where their tyranny originated. They railed against government, the wealthy, and other perceived oppressors. They did not want their lot in life but they wanted others to change it for them.

The Master had opened Marko's eyes to the truth, given him the chance to be free from the lies, and now Marko offered that same chance to Yousef.

"Then I will leave them," Yousef said, staring at the ground. "They will be better off without me."

"No," Marko said coarsely. "It is you who will be better off. But first, there is one more task."

Yousef looked up.

"There is a house on rue des Jardins-St.-Paul. It was the scientist's laboratory. Go there. Bring everything you can find to us. And if anyone interferes, be ready to kill them."

He handed the youth a folded card. On it was the address.

Yousef took it and hid it away.

Marko sensed hesitation. For a moment he wondered if the boy would follow through.

Yousef stood and almost turned to face Marko before catching himself. He checked himself and gazed out along the littered street once again. His body went still.

"You have a question," Marko guessed. "Ask it."

"What will you name me?" Yousef said finally.

"The Master will name you."

"You're the Master," Yousef said, guessing incorrectly.

"No," Marko said. "The Master found me. You will see him one day."

Yousef nodded. "What will he name me?"

Marko smiled. Yousef was ready to give up the past, to let go of his given name and self and take up the destiny that waited before him.

"He will call you Scindo," Marko said. "You are the one who divides."

Even now the young man did not turn to him—he well understood not to look Marko in the eye—but he stood taller and the air filled his lungs. *Scindo* would carry a sense of pride and purpose that no name he'd been given ever had.

"Go now," Marko said, sending the boy forth. "Do as I command."

CHAPTER 8

Hawker and Danielle touched down at Paris–Charles de Gaulle Airport just before noon. Thirty minutes later they were humming along the motorway from the airport into Paris, driving a rented Peugeot.

A conversation via satellite with Arnold Moore, the NRI's director of operations, had confirmed how little anyone knew about the situation. No leads, evidence, or even "chatter" had been discovered to link any known terrorist group to either the situation in Paris or the letter sent to the UN.

They were dealing with either an entirely new group or one that had managed to keep itself hidden from the world. Or the threat was so deadly that even groups that would normally boast about such things were remaining quiet for fear of reprisals.

Understandably, the French had been whipped into a frenzy by the deaths of four police officers, but after rounding up and questioning hundreds of possible suspects they had no new information. At least nothing they wanted to share.

About the only lead they had came from the CIA. Since the Iranian, Ahmad Bashir, was a prominent member of the Green Revolution, the CIA had been keeping track of him, perhaps looking for ways to support him.

With Iran it was always tricky. Open U.S. support for a candidate there could often cost more votes than it earned them, if it didn't get them killed outright. So far they'd done nothing but watch and listen. In the process they'd intercepted a call to him the night before he and Ranga disappeared. It had come from a house in central Paris, and the voice on the phone had since been matched to Ranga Milan.

"This address is a block from the Seine," Danielle said, studying the GPS map on her phone.

"Any idea what we're going to find there?" Hawker asked, navigating a bend in the highway.

Danielle was studying the satellite photo from Google Maps. "Aside from a group of Baroque townhomes and a highly recommended bistro, not a clue."

Hawker had expected a darker neck of the woods, industrial or commercial. Apparently whatever backing Ranga had secured in Paris included enough funding to live well.

"Life on the run, mad scientist style," Hawker joked. "Who needs a spider hole when you can rent out river-front property?"

Danielle laughed lightly, then turned to him. "I've been reading about your friend Ranga," she said. "Do you have any idea how brilliant he was?"

"Can't have been that brilliant," Hawker said. "Or he wouldn't have ended up dead."

Hawker recognized the edge in his own voice. The words had come out oddly, but the truth was, it felt as if his old acquaintance had betrayed him somehow. Never one to be great at understanding his own feelings, Hawker struggled to put his finger on the reasons.

Maybe he felt that way because the situation had brought back just enough of his past to remind him he hadn't always been on the right side of things. Maybe it

was because Ranga had gone and got himself killed some horrible way—so what the hell was the point of saving him in the first place? After all that he and Keegan had been through to drag Ranga and Sonia over the mountains of western Congo, it almost felt like Ranga owed it to them to stay out of trouble.

The thought was ludicrous—Ranga didn't owe him a damn thing. But as Hawker struggled to get a handle on his feelings, he had the sense of firing at a target and hitting all around it but never right on.

He blocked it out and focused on the task ahead. Hopefully they would find something in this town house that would tell them more about whom Ranga was working for and what he'd been doing.

Danielle continued. "Did you know he was one of the first to prove that genetic splicing in the lab is markedly inferior to the way viruses and bacteria have been doing it to their hosts for millennia?"

Her voice was kind. That helped.

"Didn't know that," Hawker said. "Don't even really know what that means."

"What it means is that half the DNA in our genome is now believed to have come from viruses and bacteria, deposited there during infections and now part of what we consider to be *human* DNA."

"So we're part virus?" Hawker asked.

"In a way," she said.

Little could have sounded odder to him than that. "Gives a whole new meaning to the term 'going viral.'"

She laughed. "Your friend also helped decipher the main strands of human DNA and developed three different techniques for gene sequencing that were considered giant leaps in the field."

Hawker hadn't known any of this; it didn't matter to him at the time. But even back then he'd found it

strange that a man like Ranga would be living the way he was.

"So why did he throw away a life of privilege, prestige, and what must have been pretty decent money to hang out in the gutters of the world?"

Danielle shook her head. And Hawker guessed that solving the riddle of who killed Ranga and why might require them to answer that question as well.

He thought about Ranga's message on the flash drive.

I hope this is you, my friend. Do you remember my question? Does Divine retribution exist? I am near to the answer. I fear retribution is coming to me. Not from God but from man. I have done terrible things to keep my hope from dying. But now things have turned. They have everything. They have what they need to deliver a plague, they have everything except the payload. You must help me find it before they do. I'm so close. So close to finishing but they will stop me.

I can pay you if you come to Paris. I can think of no one to trust but you. I need eyes and ears to watch for them. They are everywhere and they are nowhere. They hound me like dogs. They will find me if I stay and they will snare me if I flee. I cannot keep ahead of them much longer. You owe me nothing, but I ask you anyway, for who else can I ask? Who else would come?

The message left much to interpretation. It included an email address for Hawker to respond to. Something that hadn't happened. It never had a chance to. It had taken Keegan two weeks to find Hawker and catch up with him in Croatia. And Ranga had been killed the very next day.

Somehow that made it worse. Hawker guessed that Ranga had died thinking he was alone. Abandoned. Somehow it tore at Hawker's heart that his friend would think he'd been left to the dogs by the one person he'd reached out to.

There was little else in the message. No details as to whom he was running from. No information as to what he was close to finishing.

That was to be expected. If Hawker came, Ranga could have told him, and if he didn't the secrets would remain hidden.

"Next right," Danielle said.

As Hawker followed her directions and maneuvered through the crooked streets of Paris, he considered Ranga's life. At each stage of action, Ranga made choices that led him through doorways and onto different, darker paths. Hawker had been on a similar course once. By luck, or grace, or some miraculous combination of both, he'd been given a reprieve from his own, self-inflicted damnation.

He tried to remind himself of that. He had to focus on finding the people who'd tortured and killed his friend because it was his job, not for some personal act of vengeance. Allowing that to become his motivation might endanger all that he'd found in this new life.

He glanced over at Danielle. She was one of the things he valued most now. Over the past few years they had grown close in fits and starts. Had the information about Ranga surfaced, he might have hoped they'd be driving around the French countryside in his new Jaguar, promising to turn it in to the CIA when they were done and looking for a hotel to disappear into for a week or so.

Some other time, perhaps.

They pulled onto the street containing the address

Moore had given them. Just a normal street in suburban Paris. The town house at the end of the row looked no different than any of the others. And yet as Hawker studied it, he had a sinking feeling about what they might find inside.

CHAPTER 9

Parked across the street from the house at rue des Jardins-St.-Paul, Danielle aimed a cameralike device at the property.

The "camera" was actually an eavesdropping mechanism, able to listen to conversations inside a building by bouncing a laser off the glass and picking up on the minute vibrations caused by voices and sounds. Special types of glass could block or dampen the vibrations, and jamming devices that shook the windows could be attached to glass in an effort to overload the signal, much like jamming a radar by putting out masses of electromagnetic energy, but those things left a specific signature. If they were present Danielle would find them easily.

The readout flatlined. No vibrations, no dampening equipment, no TV left playing to itself. The house was quiet.

She flicked a switch on the scanner, changing it to infrared mode.

Slowly panning back and forth along the walls, she picked up no heat sources.

"No one home," she said.

"Good," Hawker said. "Let's go."

She scanned the street around them. The road was fairly vacant. On a Wednesday at 2 P.M., it seemed most residents were working.

Hawker opened the door.

"Where are you going?" she said.

"Inside."

"Let me go," she said.

He stared at her.

"What do you know about genetics?" she asked.

"Apparently we're all related to viruses."

"Very funny," she said "What about encryption, hacking computers, and bypassing alarms? What about breaking and entering without actually breaking anything?"

It took a moment, but Hawker smiled. "I do like to break things."

"Yes, you do," she said. "Let me go in. I can do it quietly and you can watch my back."

He hesitated and then nodded. "Keep your line open. You go silent I'm coming in."

She nodded, opened the door, and stepped out.

Striding casually across the street, Danielle secured the speaker of her headphone to her right ear. She climbed the steps and made her way to the front door. Holding out a small handheld device, she checked for any alarms. None present, she went to pick the lock. It took a moment, as it was not her most often used skill.

She heard Hawker's voice over the line. "Sure you don't want me to come up and break the door down?"

"I got it," she whispered.

The lock popped. She slipped inside.

Her footsteps echoed on hardwood floors. The large open room in front of her was all but empty. A single overstuffed chair sat in one corner, draped in a dust cover beside a bookshelf devoid of titles.

She went through this room to the kitchen and then a den or bedroom. Little to see, as if someone had recently moved out.

Finally, she entered what might have been a living room. There she found a desk and chair, a large throw rug on the

floor, and stacks of high-tech equipment, including a bank of computers and a wall lined with incubators as well as industrial refrigerators whose clear doors were now covered with frost and condensation. To the left of all that was a Plexiglas-enclosed workstation. It looked to be hermetically sealed, complete with a set of powerful microscopes and the armholes with long rubber gloves attached for manipulating things inside it.

The living room was a makeshift lab.

She stepped over toward the incubators. The first two were warm but appeared to be empty. She could see no sample trays or glass slides inside, only what looked like irrigated soil and wet, muddy clay. A second incubator had a layer of water two inches deep on top of the soil but nothing growing inside. Not even mold.

The refrigerators were next. Condensation on the Plexiglas made it impossible to see inside. She wiped the glass.

Empty.

Each one of them.

A smaller incubator had something moving inside. She looked closer. Rats, some dead, others looking withered and aged, shaking as they tried to move around. The containment habitat was sealed and a thick length of tape covered the seal as if to remind someone not to break it.

"What the hell is all this?" she whispered.

She wondered if Ranga had cleaned the place out or if someone had beaten them to it. Most likely he would have given up the address while being tortured.

She moved to the enclosed workstation and realized the main scope was a scanning electron microscope, an extremely expensive medical device.

She turned it on and looked through. Nothing to see. But the device had an electronic readout and a small keypad. She pressed the power switch and then found a menu to cycle through the most recent images.

Genetic material in the midst of some examination. There was no way for her to tell what it was. She looked around. The computer was her best bet.

She moved to the desk, sat down at the computer, and hit enter.

An encryption screen came up. Not the standard operating software that could easily be breached but a heavy-duty, industrial-grade system. Whatever the computer held, it was well protected.

She pulled a specialized USB drive out of her pocket. It had a program that could auto-launch through most encryption firewalls.

She plugged it in; the green LED lit up and it went to work. If that didn't work, there was the possibility of opening the computer and stealing the hard drive itself. She located the tower under the desk and turned it her way. It didn't move easily. The normal bundle of wires connected to the back of the box was a bad enough tangle, but it seemed to have been augmented by something.

A thin locking cable and a plain red wire held it in place. The cable could be breached easily, but the red wire was suspicious. It terminated in some kind of magnetic switch attached to the back of the computer.

She followed the wire through a hastily drilled hole into one of the desk drawers. There it connected to a brick of what looked like C-4.

Who needs an alarm, she thought, when you can just blow the whole place to hell.

A second length of wire ran from the C-4. It led out behind the desk, under the rug, and across the room. Other wires ran to the incubators and refrigeration units.

She followed one to a credenza against the far wall.

Cautiously she opened the drawer. A stash of binders lay inside. She eased one out. The red wire ran through its binding, but there seemed to be enough slack.

She opened the binder to find handwritten notes. If they

were Ranga's notes—and they did look like a sample of his handwriting that she'd seen—it seemed unlikely they'd be left here unless they were no longer needed. Perhaps whatever samples he had created were enough.

She studied the writing. Tabular entries recording test results. She leafed through the pages, careful not to pull on the wire.

Page after page of numbered experiments, all with failed results. She understood that too.

Despite the incredible things that modern genetic science was capable of, somewhere around 99 percent of experiments were failures. At the big pharmaceutical labs around the world, incredibly gifted men and women often toiled for years with nothing to show for it. One study she recalled stated that a geneticist at a top biotech lab had a fifty-fifty chance of working his or her entire career without ever producing a usable drug.

Part of it was the safety precautions and protocols that purposefully slowed the work to a crawl, but for the most part it was just an incredibly difficult task. Nature had spent five billion years coming up with life in its myriad forms. Five billion years of trial and error. Genetic engineers were desperately trying to take a shortcut in that process.

Outside, half a block down on rue des Jardins-St.-Paul, Hawker sat in the rented Peugeot, watching for trouble. So far the quiet streets of this Paris neighborhood had remained just that, quiet.

A few cars had rolled by. A white Isuzu delivery truck had come down the road and gone around the block and a few pedestrians had strolled by, but none of them had stopped or lingered near the building.

The street was quiet, the neighborhood was quiet, and Danielle had also been quiet for several minutes.

He grabbed the phone and clicked the push-to-talk button. "You finding anything?"

It took a few seconds before the reply came.

"Some kind of lab in here," she said. "Computers, incubators, microscopes. Everything rigged to explosives."

"Wonderful," he said, thinking maybe they should get the French police and the bomb squad involved.

"Any trouble out there?"

"The coast seems clear for now, but . . ."

Hawker's voice trailed off. The Isuzu truck had returned. It pulled up in front of the town house and stopped.

When was he going to learn to keep his mouth shut?

"Hold on a second," he said. "You might have company."

"From where?"

"Front door," Hawker said.

"How many?"

The Isuzu had parked directly in front of the town house, blocking Hawker's view of the entrance. Three men jumped out, dressed like movers. One guy milled around near the back of the van and the other two moved toward the front and the entrance to the town home.

"Two at least," he said. "A third out here."

"I need to know if they're coming in," she said.

Hawker could hear the frustration in Danielle's voice. He knew she would wait until the last second, maybe even push it too far. That was her way. He thought of telling her the men were headed in now, just to get her moving.

"They seem to be bumbling around," he said. "But you might want to look for a back way out."

"I need more time," she said.

"It's not exactly up to me."

Hawker stared at the truck, trying to think of some way to distract the men at the front door, when a shadow caught the corner of his eye. It crossed from behind.

He ducked instinctively just as the side window shattered and the *pop, pop* of a suppressor-equipped handgun sounded.

No time to look back; he scrambled across the car as a third shot was fired. A long finger of padding exploded from one of the seats, marking the bullet's track to his left.

He grabbed the door handle, pushed the passenger's door open, and tumbled out onto the sidewalk. Pulling his gun as he hit the cement, he twisted and fired blindly back into the car and all around it.

Inside the townhome, Danielle heard the shots. She knew the sound of Hawker's .45.

She needed to go, but she felt the answer was close. She flipped through the pages of the notebook, skipping toward the end until she found a page that was only half-full. The last entry was dated one month prior.

She rang her finger down the list.

Series 947—results inconclusive, subject terminated.
Series 948—results inconclusive, subject terminated.
Series 949—results determinable, vitality affected, subject did not survive.

Another gunshot rang out. Danielle glanced that way and then back at the notes.

Series 950—results inconclusive, subject terminated.
Series 951—outcome unequivocal, subject telomeres shortened, activity level unaffected, life span reduced by 51%.

That was the last entry.

Danielle stared at the words as if in a trance. *Telomeres shortened . . . life span reduced.*

Telomeres were molecular chains at the end of the DNA strand. They were known to be connected with

cellular reproduction, cellular life span, and even human life span.

What the hell were these people messing around with?

Another shot boomed outside the door and Danielle knew she'd run out of time.

She ripped the page from the notebook and turned toward the back of the home. Then, realizing the flash drive was still attached to the computer, she ran to it.

A loud crashing noise told her the front door had been breached. She yanked the drive free, turned, and raced to the back of the house.

Hawker lay pressed against the ground, near the rear wheel of the vehicle. The gunman who'd missed him was on the other side of the car, crouched down near the front of the vehicle, no more than ten feet away.

Hawker stared under the car, watching for the man's feet. Then he raised his gun and fired through the car. Two shots, glass shattering everywhere, but the bastard didn't flinch.

The problems as Hawker saw them were threefold. First, he was outnumbered and sooner or later they would come at him from two directions. Second, Danielle was stuck in the building, unless she'd busted out the back as he hoped. Third, the man trying to kill him was up front, protected by the engine block, while Hawker crouched a mere fourteen inches from the half-filled gas tank.

He glanced at the big Isuzu: no one there. He guessed they'd gone inside.

A bullet hit the wall behind him. High and wide.

Time to move. Hawker scrambled backward, scooting on his backside, aiming the gun at the rear of the Peugeot. He fired repeatedly. One shot after another.

Finally there was an explosion. Not the conflagration seen in Hollywood movies, but a bang that blew the

trunk off and shattered the rear window. In an instant the flames were licking around the car.

The gunman on the other side was thrown back. Looking under the car, Hawker saw the man's feet as he stood and ran.

Hawker fired, low and flat, skipping the bullets under the car and off the pavement. With his third shot, the man's ankle exploded and he tumbled down face-first into the street, screaming in agony.

Inside, Danielle had made it through the kitchen to a frosted glass door with a dead bolt. White light poured in through it and freedom beckoned.

She heard footsteps behind her, men shouting to each other. She hastily checked the door for red wires. Finding none, she turned the lock, threw the door open, and raced outside into the rear yard.

Halfway across a man tackled her and pinned her to the ground. She tried to throw him off, but he held a knife beside her face and she went still.

He snatched the papers from her hand, along with the Beretta 9 mm that sat uselessly in a shoulder holster.

"Get up!" the man shouted.

As his weight came off her, she complied. Two other men were with him.

"Take her to the boat," one of them said. The two men dragged her off as the third made his way inside.

Hawker saw the man in the street writhing in pain. He thought of racing past him to the house, but the other thugs had just gone in. And at any rate, if Danielle was smart, she'd gone out the back.

He turned, examining the houses along the street.

Spotting an alleyway between two of the old homes, he ran for it.

Sliding through the narrow chasm, he came out behind the row of houses.

Across the backyards he saw Danielle with two men marching her toward the river. He stepped forward and raised his weapon.

A thundering explosion knocked him sideways.

A flash of heat singed his face. Shrapnel of wood, plaster, and glass blasted him from the side.

He hit the ground hard, rolled over in case he was on fire, and then got to his hands and knees. His head was foggy, his ears ringing. He had no idea what had happened.

As dark smoke billowed around him, he glanced over his shoulder. The townhome had been obliterated from within. Three walls blown out, the roof collapsing, the building was nothing more than a shell now. Flames rose up from inside, chasing the dark smoke as the last wall of brick bulged and collapsed in a sliding pile.

Out in the yard, Danielle and the two men were down. She seemed to have fared better than they had, as if their bodies behind her had acted as a shield.

Hawker climbed to his feet and ran to her, arriving just as she pushed one of the men off. The guy had to be dead, a jagged length of pipe sticking through him.

The other assailant rolled groggily. Hawker dropped down beside him, pulling an old revolver from his hand and tossing it away. The man didn't resist but just stared, glassy-eyed.

"And you think I like to break things," he said, helping Danielle up.

She found her Beretta and put it back in her holster.

"What the hell happened?" Hawker asked.

Danielle looked around, appearing disoriented. "Guess somebody checked out the wrong book."

Ash rained down around them now. Fragments of burning paper falling from the heavens left trails of glowing cinders and smoke as whatever knowledge had been hidden in that building burned itself to dust.

Danielle rubbed her temple, looking down at the dead man.

"Could have been you," Hawker said.

She nodded, and then her mind seemed to clear. She turned toward the river.

"They were taking me to a boat."

Hawker looked that way as Danielle began to walk. The lawn led to a fence with gate, beyond which lay a road and an imposing wall made of stone. A flight of steps cut into the wall had to lead to the Seine.

The sound of a motorboat starting ripped through the air. And Hawker watched as Danielle took off running.

CHAPTER 10

Caught flat-footed, Hawker raced after Danielle as she crashed through an iron gate at the rear of the property, sprinted across the road, and angled toward the wide stairwell. The stairs cut an angled cleft in the wall and sloped down toward the river.

She disappeared down the first few steps as Hawker ran across the street, dodging traffic to try to catch up with her.

The sound of more gunfire rang out, and Hawker tore around the wall's edge and raced down the stairs.

He found Danielle taking cover behind the last pillar of the railing. Someone on the tail end of a speedboat was firing at her as the boat accelerated away, cutting a deep white swath into the calm river.

Hawker stared at the man, wondering if he was looking at Ranga's killer.

He glanced around. There were no other boats tied up by the stairs except an old dinghy with two wooden oars. That wasn't going to help.

Hawker looked back toward the road, had one of those thoughts that he should have tossed out as madness, and raced back up the steps looking for a vehicle.

The Seine flowed through the heart of Paris, for the most part completely and utterly walled in. A thousand years of history will do that to a river in the midst of a

city. And that meant this particular boat on this particular river could be chased by a car.

Hawker pushed out onto the street, looking for a car. A fast car. Nothing, and then . . .

He stepped in front of a moving motorcycle, raising his gun.

The rider skidded to a stop.

"I need your bike," he said.

The rider laid it down without shutting it off and backed away with his hands up.

Hawker shoved the .45 into his shoulder holster and picked up the bike. Throwing a leg over, he jumped on, gunned the throttle, and dropped the red Ducati into gear.

By the time Danielle reached the top of the stairs she had her phone open, trying to get the French police. But the French 911 system seemed to be busy. She looked around, guessing that dozens if not hundreds of calls were being made about the shooting and explosion. It would probably be a minute or two.

She looked around for Hawker and saw a man in a motorcycle helmet without a motorcycle, gesturing madly. Down the road she saw the bike blazing off into the distance.

"Oh hell," she mumbled. The situation was going from bad to worse.

She hung up the phone and focused in on a rubbernecker in a sedan who'd slowed to check out the burning house.

Reluctantly, and knowing there would be hell to pay, she did almost exactly as Hawker had just done.

Raising her gun, she motioned for the man to step out of the vehicle.

He froze as if it was "the end."

She waved the gun. "Move!"

He gripped the wheel, petrified.

She exhaled in frustration. "Oh come on," she said. "Just get out of the car. I'm not really going to shoot you."

Finally, the white-haired gentleman opened the door and stepped out. Danielle took his place, tossed the phone on the front seat, and jammed the car into gear.

A second later she was racing down the street, the Seine to her right, Hawker somewhere up ahead, and the sound of police sirens growing in her ears.

Hawker raced along in the Ducati, weaving in and out of traffic. He had no idea exactly where he was going, but the frontage road along the Seine cut back and forth between buildings and mostly mirrored the water's edge.

A slow-moving truck got in his way and he cut to the inside lane, slicing through the space between two other cars, close enough to reach out and touch both of them had he wanted to.

Shooting out between them, he accelerated further just as the road popped up on a high stretch. From there he scanned the river looking for the boat, catching sight of it about a half mile ahead, hauling ass down the center of the channel. A long white wake stretched out behind it.

Of course, there was one big flaw in his plan. He could follow the boat, but unless the Ducati turned into a Jet Ski, he could not get to it.

He thought of reaching for his phone, trying to shout over the wind that he was the madman who'd just blown up a house and stolen a motorbike at gunpoint, which he was using to chase a speedboat, and politely request backup from the French police. But even in a land where Jerry Lewis was nearly a saint, he guessed that request

might not be taken in the light he'd hoped it would. Besides, his French sucked.

Then he saw a chance. A mile or so up ahead, a line of barges sat on the right side of the river. The boat would have to move closer to the left bank and there Hawker would have his chance.

He twisted the throttle and the bike leapt forward.

As she raced through traffic, Danielle was trying to accomplish a great many things. First, catch Hawker before he did anything stupid; second, avoid killing anyone; and third, stay ahead of the French police.

She saw them in the mirror, blue lights flashing, distinctive singsong wail of their sirens ringing in her ears. She kept her foot down on the accelerator and her eyes forward.

She caught sight of Hawker for a moment, far up ahead, but the sedan was neither as fast nor as maneuverable as the Ducati. He was there for a second and in a blink he was gone, just as another police car swerved onto the road beside her and slammed into the sedan.

She pulled away and regained control and edged in front of the offending vehicle.

"Pull over," she heard from a loudspeaker. "You must pull your vehicle to the curb."

The road bent sharply to the right; she tapped the brakes, squeezed the police car for space, forcing it to drop back, and then mashed on the accelerator once again. It was a bit late to start acting rational.

She made it half a mile farther before two more squad cars pulled onto the road in front of her.

She tried to shoot the gap between them but they closed it. She swerved to the left to cut around but one of them cut left as well, pinning her against the wall.

Another car blocked her way and slammed on its brakes. Danielle tried to stop, but too late.

She slammed into the rear of the police unit. The airbag fired and the next thing she knew she was at a dead stop, dust and residue from the airbag's explosive swirling around her.

Disoriented, she tried to get out. The door opened, then hands reached in and grabbed her, dragging her from the car and holding her to the ground.

Up ahead, Hawker continued racing down the road. Out in the river, the speedboat had slowed a bit, its driver apparently unaware that he was being followed. The boat was pulling closer to the left bank and Hawker knew this was his only chance.

Matching his speed with the boat's, he watched for an opening. He spotted a gap in the stone rail that ran along the river's edge, angled toward it, and accelerated. Cutting across the grass, he lined up with the opening and pinned the throttle open.

At fifty miles an hour, he hit the gap and the bike launched itself toward the speeding boat. The heavy Ducati began to fall away beneath him and Hawker pushed off it, throwing himself to the right.

He heard a tremendous crunch and then he hit the water behind the boat.

Breaking the surface a moment later, he saw the speedboat floundering, the fiberglass cracked and broken where the four-hundred-pound Ducati had slammed into it, like a stone hitting a paper cup.

Shedding his jacket, Hawker swam toward the boat as it began to go down. There were two men aboard. One appeared injured, maybe unconscious, but the other was getting back to his feet. He spotted Hawker, raised a pistol, and fired.

Hawker dove under the water. Bullets cut white lines through the murk here and there as he swam to a new position. He held his breath until the gunfire stopped and then he cautiously popped up.

The man with the pistol was gone, either hiding or gone overboard himself.

Hawker swam up to the swamped vessel. He slipped his own gun out of the holster, put a hand on what remained of the stern, and looked around.

The boat shifted and tilted, debris floating about. Seat cushions, life jackets, and a few empty water bottles bobbed up and down, but Hawker did not see the gunman.

As the boat began to roll, Hawker grabbed the injured man and pulled him into the water.

A moment later the speedboat flipped over. It remained floating, a few feet of the keel sticking out of the water.

Hawker held on to the unconscious man and kicked away from the boat, swimming backward toward the shore, his eyes still on the boat. No movement. He looked around in all directions, but the gunman had disappeared.

CHAPTER 11

Virginia Industrial Complex, Virginia

Arnold Moore, director of operations at the National Research Institute, sat at a metallic desk with a glass top. Papers arranged in neat stacks lined both sides of a computer monitor that would fold flat into the desktop for more workspace if he needed it. To the left and right, printers and scanners and screens for satellite video-conferencing sat dormant, only their "standby" LEDs blinking softly in the semidarkness.

Across the desk from him stood one of the NRI's best young minds, Walter Yang, a geneticist out of Stanford. If he wasn't working in the lab, Walter was living online as a devotee of massive multiplayer computer gaming and anything that might lead to a hive mind. He seemed impressed with Arnold's digs.

"This office rocks pretty hard, Mr. Moore."

Rocks. Moore did not think it *rocked,* unless that meant it did not suit him.

Moore's new suite at the Virginia Industrial Complex was a study in order and ultramodern design. It impressed others, especially its designers, and it bothered the hell out of Arnold Moore.

It was too sterile for him, too precise and lacking in individuality.

Even the walls bothered him. They were special Kevlar-

coated glass, which could be turned instantly opaque at the press of a button. Someone's idea of hip, high-tech décor, apparently designed to go with the NRI's mission. When told about it, Moore had assumed someone was joking: the head of a secret agency working in a glass cube? He'd darkened the walls on day one and had yet to allow the light back in.

"Yes," he said politely. "You would think that, Walter. Part of the joy of being young. Things can *rock*. Now talk to me about this UN virus."

Walter cleared his throat and looked down at his notes. And Moore realized his own level of crankiness had reached an intraday high. The UN had been quarantined for three days and the natives were growing restless. The only saving grace was that Claudia Gonzales had arrived at work so early, she'd opened the offending letter before most of the staff had even arrived.

"Sorry," Yang said.

"Don't be," Moore said. "Just tell me some good news."

"We do have good news," Yang insisted. "The CDC has exhausted its review of the sample and determined that it matches nothing in the database."

"So we're dealing with an entirely new virus?"

Yang nodded.

"How exactly is that good news?" Moore asked.

"It relates to the pathogen's virulence," Yang said.

Moore stared at him.

"We define virulence as the ability of a pathogen to cause disease," Yang said. "It depends primarily on three things: the ability of the pathogen to infect cells; the ability of the pathogen to spread and what routes it takes to spread—what we call *vectors*; and finally, the damage it does to the infected cells."

"Okay," Moore said. "So tell me where we're winning."

"Well," Yang said. "The epidemiology of this virus is

quite impressive. It shows incredible speed and effectiveness at invading a host cell. It seems to attack all cells in the body. And so far our tests indicate it would spread through a large number of vectors."

"In English, Walter," Moore asked.

"Sorry, Mr. Moore," he said. "I'll try to be clear. In general, certain viruses attack only certain types of cells. Respiratory viruses attack cells in the lungs. Herpesvirus attacks skin cells. But this UN virus is highly and rapidly infectious across a wide range of, if not all, types of cells in the human body. That is extremely unusual."

"We see this in Ms. Gonzales?" Moore asked.

Yang nodded. "A CDC check shows that she is dealing with the infection in many different areas. Bronchial cells, muscle cells, liver, kidney, and lymphatic cells. Basically every system in her body shows traces of the infection."

Moore exhaled wearily. "Unless you're the beneficiary of her insurance policy, this doesn't qualify as good news, either."

"No," Yang said. "I mean, of course we'd prefer to see a smaller cellular range, and to be honest we'd certainly prefer a contagion that had fewer open vectors to be transmitted through, but—"

"How contagious?" Moore asked.

"Our tests confirm that it has the ability to spread in an aerosol, through sneezing and coughing like the common cold, through insect vectors like mosquitoes and ticks, etc. Just like malaria or West Nile virus, and through birds, like H1N1 or SARS."

Neither did this news seem to qualify as positive, but Moore guessed Yang would get around to that. "How did it get into the ambassador's system?"

"The envelope was lined with plastic," Yang said. "In effect, it was hermetically sealed. The interior of the envelope was a vacuum until she tore it open. The note inside was written on special paper that reacted with oxygen

and the heat of her fingertips. As it turned red it generated heat, which caused the virus and a thin layer of gel it had been deposited on to aerosolize. As she read the letter, the ambassador breathed it in."

"And the red coloring?" Moore asked. "The blood on the letter?"

"A cheap parlor trick," Yang said. "A side effect of the heat. Like invisible ink reappearing."

"Someone has a flair for the dramatic," Moore said. And yet, he reminded himself, no one had claimed responsibility. Something didn't add up.

"Because of that and the other things it's able to do, the CDC is calling it the Magician virus."

"Great," Moore said. "Now that we have it named, I'm ready for the good news."

"Oh yeah," Yang said. "Here's the cool part, the really interesting part. So this virus is highly contagious outside the body and extremely infectious in the body. But aside from a fever and a monster headache, Ms. Gonzales is doing well. In fact this virus, which seems to be attacking every cell in her body, doesn't seem to do much once it wins the high ground."

Moore shifted in his seat. It seemed an odd bit of luck, too odd to actually be luck. "What are you telling me?"

"Most viruses take over a cell, inject their DNA, and force it to produce millions of copies of itself. Then they explode out of the cell, killing it or leaving it to die and moving on. The cell death all over the body causes the sickness. This UN virus enters a cell, forces the cell to reproduce its copies, and then—bizarrely—leaves the cell intact, with a small remnant of its DNA now encoded into the DNA of the affected cell."

"Remnant?" Moore asked suspiciously. "What kind of remnant? Does it do anything?"

"We're studying it now," Yang said. "But it seems to be completely inert."

Moore looked around his office, thinking and wondering. He considered the design of the room, how it seemed useless and excessive to him but had a purpose in the mind of the designers.

The Magician virus sounded like the brilliant creation of some disturbed mind. Most likely the mind of Ranga Milan. He guessed that this useless bit of DNA left behind had some purpose to its designer as well.

"I'll take that as a stroke of good luck and something we shouldn't count on continuing," he said. "But I want you to study it. Let the CDC work on the main virus, and by all means keep up with them, but I want you to look at that inert DNA coding and figure out if it means anything, anything at all."

Walter Yang stood. "What about the quarantine?"

Arnold was already reviewing his notes, head down. "What do you mean?" he said without looking up.

"CDC wants to send the ambassador home."

Moore stopped and looked up. "No," he said. "Hell no. Anybody tries to bust that quarantine you stop them. Shoot them if you have to. Understand?"

"I'm not issued a weapon, Mr. Moore."

"Then get one," Moore said.

Yang seemed unsure, so Moore decided to be clear. "Listen to me," he said. "We're involved in this for a number of reasons, most of which I can't explain to you or the CDC. But one thing that you should know is Claudia Gonzales once worked for the NRI. Ten years ago she was one of us. That may be an odd coincidence or it might mean something. The bottom line is, we've been put in charge through a presidential order and until I say so, until we know for sure that this bug isn't a Greek bearing some mysterious gift, nobody leaves quarantine. Nobody. Got me?"

Yang nodded firmly, seeming far more subdued than

when he'd come in. Getting growled at by the boss when you figured you'd done well could do that to a person.

"Good work," Moore said. "I'm sorry the crusty old bastard you work for didn't say it earlier."

Yang hesitated.

"Yeah," Moore said. "I'm talking about me. Now get out there and dig. A lot may depend on what you find."

Yang nodded, then left the office with some juice in his step. Moore's intercom buzzed. The voice of Stephanie Williams, the NRI's director of communications, came through loud and clear.

"Arnold, you got a second?"

"All yours," he said. "What do you have for me?"

Because of Hawker's unique cover, Williams had set up special channels of communication with Hawker that no one else in the organization aside from Danielle and Arnold Moore knew about.

She also kept track of the two agents when they were on assignment.

"I have information on Hawker and Danielle," she said.

"What's the word?" he asked.

"I'm afraid you're going to be busy."

That did not sound good. "I'm already busy, Ms. Williams."

"We're getting radio chatter from France on the police bands. Something about a house exploding, a shoot-out, and a high-speed chase in central Paris. Suspects are Americans. One male and one female."

Moore cringed. "Good God," he said. It never rained but it poured.

CHAPTER 12

Danielle sat in handcuffs, waiting in the private office of the commandant of the Police Nationale in central Paris. Hawker sat next to her, cuffed as she was, and seemed to be favoring his right shoulder.

For the moment they were alone.

"You all right?" she asked.

"Landed on my shoulder when the house blew up," he said. "Hitting the water didn't help it much."

To be honest, she was surprised he'd even survived. "Why'd you go after them on that bike anyway?"

He looked at her. "Why did you run to the river?"

"I thought they were getting away."

"There you go."

She exhaled in exasperation. "Yes, but all I wanted to do was spot the boat and contact the police, not risk life and limb five times over on some insane stunt. That may have been the dumbest thing you've ever done."

"Don't be so sure," he said. "There's a lot of competition for that title."

He made it a point to be funny, but the situation was not all that humorous. They'd been here for three hours, allowed no outside contact, not even with the embassy. Their papers had been confiscated and they hadn't even been questioned yet. The situation could go either way:

They could be released, or if a pissing match developed, they might not see the outside world for months.

To be honest, she wondered why they were being held in this office and not some dark cell. It made even less sense that they were being held together. Perhaps the commandant did not want the world to know they were there. Perhaps he was watching or listening, hoping they would give something away.

At that moment the door swung open. In walked Commandant Lavril, chief of the Paris police. He eyed them with some disdain and closed the door gently before walking to the chair behind his desk.

It was a massive, incredibly impressive desk, the kind that told anyone sitting across from it where the power resided in this particular room, the kind that might protect one from a bomb blast or a tornado or a meteor strike if one hid underneath it.

Danielle wondered how the hell they'd even fit the giant desk into this small room. Maybe the walls had been built around the monstrosity.

"Your papers check out," the commandant said, flipping through the pages of their passports. "Your consulate confirms that you are here as part of your embassy's security detail."

He dropped the passports and glared at them.

She and Hawker had been given covers. No one at the embassy would recognize them on sight, but they'd been told what to say if something happened—as it quickly had.

"So that gives you the right to carry guns in my country," Lavril said. "But not the right to use them on French citizens or to blow up our buildings."

"You seem awfully concerned with the people who tried to kill us," she said.

He shrugged. "They are French, you are not."

"I promise you if a Frenchman was mugged on the

streets of Washington, we wouldn't be asking him what he did to provoke the attack."

"You might," Lavril said, "if he blew up half a block in Georgetown."

The brawl was coming; she could feel it. She would go for the high ground and the commandant would stand and defend it. But begging was not her way.

"I don't know how long you intend to hold us," she said, "but you and I both know what's going to happen. Sooner rather than later, a call is going to come in. From the right person in my government to the right person in yours. And after long conversations, which you will never know about, someone else is going to call down here and you're going to be forced to release us whether you like it or not."

Lavril simmered and she wondered if she'd hit close to the mark. Maybe that call had already come in.

"So are we free to go?" she asked.

Hawker smiled and held up his hands as if Lavril might just unlock them right then and there.

"No," Lavril said drily, "you are anything but free."

Hawker's false smile faded and he dropped his hands with a noticeable wince from the shoulder pain.

Lavril continued. "At best, I will allow you to contact someone. But not until I find out what you were doing here. And what exactly is going on."

"What's going on," she began, "is that two American citizens were almost killed at the hands of the terrorists on French soil. It can't look good for the Sûreté that we had to save ourselves."

Lavril laughed confidently. "We are no longer called the Sûreté, madam."

Strike one.

"But since we are freely offering opinions, I will share one of mine: I have had two terrorist incidents in three

days. Both involving Americans. It would take much to make me believe they are unrelated."

"What you believe is irrelevant to me," Danielle said.

"What I believe will prove to be incredibly relevant to you," Lavril corrected. "I assure you of that."

He looked at her oddly and then at Hawker.

"What about you?" he asked. "Do you speak?"

Hawker glared at Lavril. "Better to hold one's tongue and be thought a fool," he said finally, "than to speak out and confirm it."

"So you are a fool," Lavril said.

"I must be," Hawker said. "How else would I end up in here?"

"Hmm," the commandant mumbled. "I don't think either of you are fools. And the fact that you quote the proverbs is more telling than you know. My nurse tells me you are a man covered in scars. Bullet wounds, knife wounds, even a few broken bones that seemed to have healed a little bit off."

Because several pieces of shrapnel from the building had cut into Hawker and his shoulder had been injured, the first thing the police had done was remove his shirt, pull out the shrapnel, and stitch him up.

Two stitches here, three stitches there. Some gauze and tape on a third smaller cut.

They had of course relayed Hawker's physical description to Lavril, partially because it would have seemed noteworthy and also because scars could help identify people. As far as Danielle knew, Hawker wasn't in anyone's database, but she couldn't be sure.

"*By their fruits you shall know them,*" Lavril said, quoting scripture himself. "You are a killer: an assassin. Sent here to clean up a problem your government has been aware of for years."

Danielle rolled her eyes. "Oh come on."

"Monsieur Milan was on Interpol's list," Lavril re-

minded everyone. "No doubt he was on your list as well. One of your most wanted. Admit it, you came here for him."

The words soaked in as Lavril glared down at them.

"And if you killed him," Lavril added, "then you are responsible for the deaths of my officers, my men. In which case I will not release you, even if God himself calls on your behalf."

He leaned back in his chair, tapping his pen on the desk like a drummer, waiting.

Now Danielle understood. In a way, she couldn't blame Lavril. She'd lost people under her charge before. There was no deeper well of determination than finding a way to right such an act.

"We didn't kill Ranga Milan and we didn't kill your officers," she said. "You know that. We came through customs two days after it happened. Besides, if we'd killed Ranga or your men, do you think we'd still be here?"

"Then you must have a different target," he said.

Danielle remained still.

Lavril got up and came around to the front of the desk. He folded his arms, leaning back, resting against it.

She guessed it was a deliberate, practiced move. Sitting on the low-slung couch, with Lavril towering over them, they were at a distinct disadvantage.

"Perhaps your target was these terrorists—as you call them," he said. "Though I must admit they seem a little out of their depth."

He picked up a rap sheet of sorts.

"Roland Lange," he said, apparently naming one of the men. "Two counts of purse snatching last year. Three counts of disorderly conduct, and minor assault. He's gone from swearing at the police from the crowd, to a slab in the morgue, with a hunk of metal where his liver should be."

Danielle squirmed a bit.

Lavril continued to read. "Dibea Monsigne was once an accomplice in a bungled car theft. Has been charged with two counts of assault for fights he seemed to have lost . . . public drunkenness . . . disorderly conduct."

Lavril put the paper down. "The others are similar. Criminal masterminds one and all. And now they're dead."

"Dead?" she asked.

"All of them."

That didn't make sense. The men in the house, yes. The poor bastard who'd taken the stick of rebar into his ribs, too, but the others . . .

"What about the one on the boat?"

"In a medically induced coma, due to a major head injury."

"What about the other man in the yard?"

"A bullet to the head, small caliber. Perhaps point two five."

Danielle's mind reeled. That man had been alive if not well when they'd left him. Certainly she hadn't shot him, and Hawker had trailed her by only seconds. Even in his anger she couldn't believe he would do such a thing.

As she went silent, Hawker finally stirred, which seemed to please Lavril. "And the man in the street?"

"Do you even have to ask?" Lavril said.

"I shot him in the leg,"

"And in the head."

"I shot him once," Hawker said. "I had no reason to see him die."

"And if you had such reason?"

"Then I'd have killed him with the first bullet," Hawker replied sharply, no doubt confirming the commandant's belief that they were some kind of hit squad.

A smile curled across Lavril's face as he weighed Hawker's statement. Whether he believed what he'd been told or not, Danielle couldn't tell, nor did she really care. Her

thoughts were now occupied with the dead men who'd been alive when they left.

Someone else had to have shot him, either the French police—which seemed unlikely, since that wasn't their reputation to begin with and the building had been surrounded by onlookers long before the police arrived—or . . .

Another member of the group. One who had remained unseen, one who had escaped. A trailer. A control.

"You have our weapons," she said. "Neither were twenty-five caliber."

"You drove five miles," Lavril said. "He went into the water. Easy to lose a weapon doing such things."

"You don't believe that," she said, "so why don't you just drop all this, tell us what you want, and we can get this game over with."

"You are very direct," Lavril said. "I admire that." He looked down at her. "You know, much has been made of the rift between your country and mine. We agree as often as an old married couple. It is easy to understand. European soil has been soaked with blood for five hundred years as men from Paris, Berlin, and London tried to control the world. We have finally let it go. But you . . . Your country is younger, only now feeling the pain that comes from reaching beyond your grasp."

Lavril smiled, then went on. "You see our reluctance as weakness and you resent it. We see your confidence as arrogance. But in truth, it is only time that divides our perspective.

"In time you will see things as we do now," he continued. "Perhaps that will be unfortunate. There are times for caution and discretion, and there are times for anger and for . . . revenge."

Slowly Lavril's focus shifted from her to Hawker. And Danielle sensed a moment that she had begun to fear. Hawker's own anger had remained beneath the surface

so far, but she had no doubt that the fires of vengeance were smoldering inside him.

Lavril reached into his desk drawer, grabbed a file, and then fished out a photograph. Leaning forward he pushed it across the desk. She and Hawker stretched to see it.

It was Ranga, naked and bloodied, on his knees with his arms held up, tied in ropes. His head drooped and his body sagged, held only by the rigging that bound his arms. Bruises, welts, and blood covered his face. Slashing cuts covered his chest and torso, and burn marks left his skin peeling and blackened.

"We believe the burns were done with a blowtorch," Lavril said. "In places, they were down to the bone."

Danielle felt as if she was about to be sick. She saw Hawker from the corner of her eye, staring unblinking at the image as if looking away might indicate some weakness.

Mercifully, Lavril took the photo back.

"Whoever killed him could have easily dumped his body somewhere, but instead they left him like this. It is for a reason."

"A message," Hawker said.

Lavril nodded.

"To who?" Danielle asked.

"To the whole world," Lavril said.

He glanced at the photo. "There was a strange mark burned into his chest. Very hard to make out."

He pushed another photo toward them, this time a close-up of Ranga's chest. It looked like he had been branded.

"Numbers and letters," Lavril said. "G, E, N, two, one, seven."

"And what's that supposed to mean?" Hawker asked.

"Earlier you quoted Proverbs to me. Surely you recognize it? Genesis, chapter two, verse seventeen."

Hawker looked back to the photo, silent as to whether he knew the meaning of those verses, but thanks to a strict Catholic upbringing the text popped into Danielle's mind almost immediately.

"And ye shall not eat from the tree of knowledge of good and evil," she said. "For when you eat of it you shall certainly die."

As she spoke the words, Danielle's mind reeled. Ranga was a geneticist obsessed with the building blocks of life, the very ability to control it, change it, even create it. Knowledge previously reserved for God alone.

If the brand was a message, was it a warning? Or a punishment from some radical group that did not want him doing such things?

"We believe a cult is responsible," Lavril insisted. "We believe they murdered both your citizens and mine."

He looked at Hawker. "You are angry. For reasons you will not say, this is personal to you. And if that's the case, then I would like to make you a deal."

CHAPTER 13

As she sat there Danielle realized how plainly Hawker had telegraphed his feelings. Add to that his reckless chase of the man on the boat and it was easy to see that he was already more vested in this incident than he should be.

Clearly Lavril had sensed this as well. "Tell me what this is all about and I'll tell you what I know. As it turns out we may want the same thing."

"You first," Hawker said.

Lavril smiled. Of course he wouldn't go first, Danielle knew that, but now Lavril knew he had Hawker on the hook. He would play it as a trump card, using Hawker's desire for revenge to reel him in. Possibly driving a wedge between Hawker and her in the process.

She didn't want him to answer, silently prayed that he wouldn't answer, but she knew that he would. And the only way she could think to counter the pain it would bring was to take the hit for Hawker. Before he took it himself.

"You want to talk," she said. "Let's talk. Ranga Milan was murdered for something he was working on. And we were sent to find the people who did it."

Lavril looked eminently pleased with himself. "What did you find in the house on rue des Jardins?"

"A lab filled with equipment," she said. "Rigged to

explosives. Since the men who attacked us blew themselves up trying to get whatever was inside, I can only assume it was Ranga's."

She kept going. "It looked like Ranga was working on something viral and connected with cellular decay. Shortening cellular life spans. I don't know why or for what."

"A weapon," Lavril asked.

"Probably. Or a drug, or something that could be turned into either."

Lavril stood still, calculating. "Is Paris at risk?"

Danielle shook her head. "As far as I could tell, whatever stock had been present was already gone, moved or destroyed. And that explosion was extremely hot."

"Over a thousand degrees," Lavril said. "Thermite mixed with C-4 according to our bomb squad. Three other buildings burned and the fire melted the steel railings across the street."

Danielle nodded. "I'd guess he rigged it that way on purpose," she said. "To destroy any evidence or any pathogens, or both, should something like this occur."

"So a plague is not imminent?"

"I wouldn't think so," Danielle said, realizing he was focused particularly on that subject. "Do you have reason to think Paris is a target?"

Lavril had been caught in his own trap, asking one too many questions. "We received a letter," he said. "The writers claim responsibility for the incident at the tower. And they promise to wreak a plague far worse than any that has gone before upon the rest of us."

Danielle's eyes widened. "Is it authentic?"

"It relayed the details of each man's kidnapping and murder as proof of its authenticity. And then it followed with a list of threats.

"It promises a plague that will wash away 'all false evidence of a false god.' It then says: 'All shall fall, Canterbury, Notre Dame, the Dome of the Rock, and the Wall at

its feet. Mecca, Jerusalem, and the Holy See: All will be powerless to the truth revealed.'"

Danielle listened intently. Canterbury Cathedral was home of the Church of England. The Dome of the Rock was the second most holy site in Islam, Mecca being the first. The Wailing Wall was the last remnant of the Jewish Temple. And the Holy See was of course the home of the Vatican. Could some madman really be declaring war on every major Western religion at once?

Lavril continued reading. "This is just the beginning," he said. "It goes on to promise the power of life and death will lie in the cult's grasp. 'You will lay all of them down and worship us,' it says.

"The letter is signed 'Draco—the serpent.'"

It sounded like madness, like the deranged ramblings of a hundred other groups, but if this group had what Ranga had been working on, and if the notes she'd seen in his lab were accurate, they might just wield some great power over life and death.

"Do you know who they are?" Hawker asked.

"Murderers," Lavril said. "Beyond that . . ." He shook his head.

It certainly sounded like some type of cult. Perhaps that explained the torture and burning Ranga had endured; perhaps it had been some ceremonial punishment. Perhaps that explained the brand seared into his chest. The French policemen were not killed in the same way.

As Lavril spoke, she saw Hawker's eyes narrow, saw his jaw clench, and she wished she could speak to him alone, warn him of what she feared.

"What do you know?" she asked Lavril.

The commandant pursed his lips as if thinking hard about what he was about to say.

She would say nothing further, not without something from him. "Quid pro quo," she said. Something for something.

"Your scientist had been tortured; you know this," Lavril said. "But he also had old wounds. Healed wounds. Perhaps it was not the first time."

Danielle took that in.

"And he had stingers in his skin," Lavril added.

"Stingers?" Hawker asked.

"From a jellyfish," Lavril said. "On his hands and arms and neck. Does it mean anything to you?"

"No," she said. "What else?"

"Asbestos and heavy oil under his fingernails."

It sounded like a random list of things. Almost as if Lavril had made it up on the fly, yet Danielle sensed honesty from the commandant and guessed that these facts would help in some way at some time. For now she racked her brain and came up empty.

Lavril looked on expectantly. "Does it mean anything to you?"

She looked at Hawker, who shook his head. "I wish it did."

Lavril looked down at the floor, as if disappointed. He scratched at a spot beneath his ear in an almost subconscious way, then looked back up.

It seemed he'd decided something.

He went back behind the desk, sat down, and began scribbling on several sheets of paper.

"Your job is to seek these men, yes?"

Danielle nodded. Hawker did the same.

"Then you will be released," he said, glancing briefly at Danielle and then focusing on Hawker once again.

"They killed one friend of yours," he said. "They've murdered four of mine. This is not America. Rarely is anyone shot here. And the police . . . we have not lost an officer in almost twelve years." He shook his head. "Those men had families. To us this is a tragedy. It will haunt us for an age. But no matter how angry I am, I cannot chase

these men out of Paris; I cannot hunt them to the ends of
the earth. But you can."

Hawker nodded.

"What will you do when you find them?" Lavril asked.

"After what you've shown me," Hawker said. He
shook his head.

Lavril nodded knowingly. He slid two sheets of paper
across the desk toward them: signed release forms, with
the key to the cuffs sitting on top.

"If you find them . . . ," he began, then stopped. "When
you find them, please give them our regards along with
your own."

Danielle hesitated. With all the talk of Adam and Eve
she felt as if they were making a deal with the devil
themselves. She stared at the key as if touching it would
bring dark consequences. Beside her Hawker stretched
forward and snatched it. Apparently he had no such
qualms.

He unlocked his cuffs, dropped them onto the desk,
and then handed the key to her.

"Where do you suggest we start?" he asked.

"The man who was with Ranga on the tower has been
identified as an exiled Iranian named Ahmad Bashir. He
had a ticket to Beirut on Air France 917 for tonight. A
similar ticket was issued to another passenger using the
address at rue des Jardins."

"For what?" Hawker asked.

"I don't know," Lavril said. "But it must matter."

Danielle unlocked her own cuffs, stunned at the turn of
events and the deal that had just been made. She feared
the ground they now stood upon, but after all they'd been
through, she wouldn't let Hawker stand alone.

She tossed her cuffs to Lavril a little quicker than
might have been necessary.

"There is a car waiting for you," Lavril said.

She turned and made her way toward the door without responding.

Hawker lingered.

"Your friend does not approve," she heard Lavril say.

"I don't need her for this," Hawker said calmly.

The words stung, but Danielle kept walking as if she hadn't heard.

For Lavril, Hawker's connection to Ranga made him the perfect choice to go after the killers, but it also made him the worst possible choice of all.

Danielle tried to think of a way to reach Hawker, to convince him that he was going down the wrong path, but she feared confrontation might just push him so far away that she would never be able to bring him back.

CHAPTER 14

Yousef sat against the wall in the back room of an abandoned house. He had done what he was ordered to do. But he had failed, failed to get the scientist's samples or documents, failed to do anything but escape and survive.

He shivered in the darkness and the filth. His clothes had dried hours ago after his swim in the Seine, but now he'd drifted into shock.

He'd lost everything. His friends were dead. The police would find him soon. And he had lost any hope of ascending within the brotherhood.

He pulled a lighter from his pocket and flicked it.

Rats scurried away from the light, disappearing into a gnawed-out section of the wall.

In the dim orange glow, Yousef studied his surroundings: trash and decay scented with urine. Back where he'd started.

He felt the weight of the pistol in his hand. The weapon seemed heavier now, more substantial than when Marko had given it to him. It had drawn no blood, at least not yet.

He put it down and pulled out a cellphone, dialing from memory.

As it was answered, Yousef began to speak.

"I have failed you," he said.

Marko's voice came through the speaker, heavy and calm. "Where are you, Yousef?"

"I'm back in La Courneuve," he said. "The police are looking for me."

"Yes, they are," Marko said, then paused. "But they will not reach you before I do."

The words struck fear into Yousef.

"Are you coming to kill me?"

Marko laughed, and in the empty darkness of the house, the sound echoed. It haunted Yousef to the point where he thought of hanging up, of running. But where could he go? He looked at the gun on the cold floor. He thought of using it on himself, ending the misery before Marko and the others punished him.

"You have done better than you imagine," Marko said finally. "The Master is pleased with you, Scindo. We will not leave you behind."

For a moment the chills stopped. Yousef was alone and ready to die just to end the pain, but Scindo was not alone.

"Stay where you are," Marko said. "I am coming for you."

CHAPTER 15

Barton Cassel IV walked into his office on the thirty-eighth floor of the Cassel Pharmaceuticals office tower in downtown Nice. An American who preferred to be considered a citizen of the world, Cassel had taken over the family business from his father at the ripe old age of twenty-nine; thirty years later he'd transformed it from a sleepy little drug distribution company to an international producer of four blockbuster medications. CPC (Cassel Pharmaceutical Corporation) revenues had reached almost $3 billion per year. Profits would hit $200 million for the trailing twelve months, depending on the exchange rate.

Such wealth had transformed Cassel into an international playboy of sorts. He owned yachts anchored in Miami and Monaco; he had purchased a run-down castle and transformed it into a thirty-thousand-square-foot home where he threw lavish parties that attracted supermodels, movie stars, and Formula One drivers. Recently he'd toyed with the idea of buying some type of title so he could be officially addressed as Duke, Prince, or Count.

But for all his wealth, Barton Cassel IV was not a man without problems. To begin with, his four blockbuster drugs generated 95 percent of the company's revenues, but three of them would go generic within the next year; the fourth would follow shortly, crippling CPC. Reve-

nues would drop by half, and without huge layoffs and other cutbacks, especially in the horrendously expensive research and development budget, profits would disappear and the red ink would flow as if a dam had burst.

Despite a massive effort Cassel had nothing in the pipeline to replace them. And cutting the R and D budget meant there would be little likelihood of coming up with anything anytime soon.

That was one problem. As he switched on the light in his sprawling office, a second, derivative problem stared him in the face.

"Hello, Barton," a voice said.

Cassel looked up. On a couch near the small kitchen and wet bar that were part of his office, he saw a man with a shaven head and a dark, rectangular tattoo wrapping halfway around his neck like a collar.

Cassel knew the voice, the tattoo, the ugly gaze.

"What the hell are you doing here?"

"I came to bring you news," the tattooed man said.

Cassel looked toward the door, a bit too obviously.

"Don't bother," the tattooed man warned. Then as if it weren't a threat: "You're going to want to hear what I have to say."

Cassel fumed. He had the best security service in the country, multiple layers of protection from the street on up; he had cameras and scanners and even a key-coded lock on his own door that he'd just opened. All designed to keep him from dealing with "stuff."

The man across from him definitely qualified as stuff.

"How the hell did you get in here?"

The tattooed man laughed. "Did you really think your store-bought security would keep me out? I spent half my life figuring out how to get through systems like yours. Most of them a hell of a lot better than your pathetic little show."

Cassel shifted in his seat. He knew all this, of course; it

was the danger of dealing with a man from such a background.

"I paid a heavy price for relying on my own security once," the tattooed man said. "A heavy price. I suggest you avoid making the same mistake. You're not out of reach. No one is."

The man across from him had once been respected and powerful, Cassel knew that. It was the only reason Cassel had listened to him when he'd first come in, the only reason he'd agreed to work with him. Not the only reason perhaps—desperation played a part—but what Cassel hadn't realized was that far more than the man's appearance had changed.

The man called himself "Draco" now and he seemed to think of himself in bizarre, vainglorious tones. Apparently suits and ties being replaced by tattoos and Goth-like clothing were more than a cosmetic change. Madness had come and settled in. Draco had gone from being merely ruthless to vicious, sadistic, and erratic in his behavior.

Perhaps a fall from such high places did that to a man. Cassel had no desire to find out personally.

"What kind of news do you have?" he asked.

"I need more money," Draco said.

"That's not news."

"Put another million dollars into the account," Draco said, as if Cassel worked for him.

"Another million? And what do I have to show for the millions I've already spent? Do you have my sample? Do you have the proteins you promised, or the coding?"

"I have a sample, but it's not the sample you want."

Cassel squinted. Draco held up a small vial the size of a thimble, sealed but unlabeled.

"What the hell are you talking about? Our deal was for the drug Milan was working on. What's this?"

"Partial delivery," the man said. "Some of Milan's latest work is contained in that vial. Enough for you to see where it's going."

"I'm not paying you millions of dollars to *see where things are going*," Cassel said, anger overriding fear and concern. "I want the fucking drug you promised, the one you said would change everything."

Draco tilted his head, the tattoo-covered scar around his neck stretching oddly. "Give me my money and let me continue the search."

Cassel's mind spun. *Continue the search*. The man spoke the words like he was looking for a lost dog. If Cassel counted right, he'd killed nearly a dozen people on this search already, including Ranga Milan, the man who was supposed to give them what they were after.

"I'm done with you," Cassel said.

Across from him Draco sat taller. "Are you now?"

"Think you're going to kill me and walk out of here?" Cassel asked. "No way."

Draco stood and stepped forward. Cassel reached his hand toward a red button on the desk.

"I touch this button and they lock this place down, and I don't care how store-bought they are, you'll never get past them if I'm not with you."

Draco walked ominously toward Cassel, putting the vial down on the desk in front of Cassel.

"Inside is the virus sent to the UN a week ago," Draco said. "Ranga's prototype. They're still trying to figure out what it is. I would hate for them to know it was designed with equipment you gave us."

"They'll never trace it."

"I'll prove it to them if you make me."

Cassel drew his hand back.

"While you've been dutifully hiding, burning and destroying any evidence of our partnership, I've been tap-

ing, recording, and tracking every one of our transactions. I have enough to prove where my money came from and what we agreed to do. It makes no difference to me. I'm a wanted man anyway. But you . . ."

Cassel stared at him. "I have people who will hunt you down," he insisted.

"Yes, I'm sure you do," Draco replied. "And you're willing to take risks. That's why I came to you. But now you have exposure and, as someone once told me, *It's a terrible thing to live with exposure.*" He pushed the vial across the table. "Put two million in the account."

"You said one."

"For my troubles."

"And then what?"

Draco smiled a sinister grin. "I know someone who can finish the synthesis for you. I just have to reel her in."

"Who?" Cassel asked, curious despite all that had gone on.

"The one who led us to Ranga in the first place."

"His daughter."

Draco nodded.

Despite his revulsion for Draco, Cassel warmed instantly to this thought. Ranga had almost completed work on something magnificent. If CPC could get it and tweak it, move it away from what Ranga wanted and toward something more commercial, Cassel could turn it into the single greatest drug of all time. He would measure sales in the billions per month. And that was just the beginning.

The problem lay with the complexity of what Ranga had done. Even with a sample, it would take years for his people to deconstruct the changes and coding. His daughter, Sonia, was known to have worked with Ranga for years before the two had a falling-out. If anyone could finish the serum he'd been working on quickly, it was probably her.

Perhaps Draco's skills in the criminal arts remained useful. If he could get into Cassel's office unannounced, what was to stop him from finding and abducting Ranga's daughter?

"You can bring her in?" Cassel asked.

"We won't have to bring her in," Draco insisted. "With the right offer, she'll beg us to let her on board."

CHAPTER 16

Hawker crossed the tarmac of Paris–Charles de Gaulle Airport beneath a dark and threatening sky. Danielle walked ahead of him as they approached the NRI Citation that had brought them in forty-eight hours before.

The plan was to get to Beirut, find out what Ranga and Bashir were looking for down there, and see if they could develop a lead as to who'd kidnapped them and why. It was thin as hell but it was all they had.

As she looked up, a figure stood by the aircraft waiting for them, a sturdy gray-haired man in a green overcoat: Arnold Moore.

Great, Hawker thought. He looked like an angry parent come to collect his wayward children.

"Done remodeling Paris, you two?"

"For now," he heard Danielle say. "Come to chaperone us?"

"As if it would help," Moore replied.

A short time later, the three of them were airborne and headed to the southeast, toward Beirut.

Danielle explained their misadventures to Moore. Hawker noticed that she left out any mention of the deal with Lavril. It was a kindness he hadn't expected and didn't really deserve. It made him realize how some of the things he'd said must have sounded to her; hurtful and selfish, and yet she protected him. It reminded him

of the argument with Keegan and the fact that he seemed to have better friends than maybe he warranted at times.

As Danielle finished, Moore spoke his own piece. His voice was grave.

"The French shared the letter with us," he said. "We ran everything we have on these people through the database. Using the letter of responsibility, the manner of Ranga's death, and the religious branding, we've come up with a profile."

He handed them a pair of matching dossiers.

Hawker scanned the front sheet: a Mossad report on a group that called itself the Cult of Men.

"They're an extremely obscure group. Responsible for several killings over the last year or so, but nothing before that."

"Whose side are they on?" Hawker asked.

"Their own, it would seem."

Danielle was reading further. "They've claimed responsibility for the deaths of Israeli settlers, Hamas militants, and even Christian pilgrims trying to bring about the onset of revelation. The first attack claimed and attributed to them was the bombing of a building in Belfast.

"Consistent with the letter," Danielle said. "A lunatic fringe, even to the lunatics."

"The thing is," Moore added, "Mossad doesn't believe they were responsible for any of those things."

"Then why claim them?" Danielle asked.

"Cobra's hood," Moore said. "It makes them look bigger than they really are."

"So why do we think they're involved in this, then?" Hawker asked.

"One of their few known members was photographed with Ranga six months ago."

Hawker suddenly wished he hadn't asked.

"Mossad has them pegged as antireligionists. Blaming God for the state of the world."

"Whose God?"

"Any God."

"Any God?"

"Yes," Moore said. "Their position is that God or the concept of God is the enemy of man. Religion causes war, death, subjugation, et cetera, et cetera."

"Great," Hawker said. "Everyone's killing in the name of God. Now we have a group killing in the name of no god at all."

"How does this connect with the attack on the UN?" Danielle asked. "They're not a religious organization."

"We haven't figured that out yet," Moore said. "But no one says these people have to be rational or consistent."

She nodded.

"Truth is, this group has been extremely secretive," Moore added. "We're trying to back-trace them but it's almost like they came into existence out of the blue. We know where Al Qaeda trains and where they're based and who they recruit. We know the same information for the IRA and the KKK and Hamas, but no one seems to have any idea who these people are, how they're funded, or even how many members they might have. It's like they have no history."

"Even that tells us something," Hawker said.

"What's their goal?" Danielle asked.

"It's a little murky," Moore said, "but the theme is simple: Religion is bad. In their propaganda it's always religion that has corrupted men, not saved us. One threat announcement concluded with the words: *You have listened to the lies and gone forth and multiplied—and you are now a plague upon the face of the earth. Too many, too fast—you starve your brother or kill him for food. Greedily you engorge without restraint, and know not that you are eating death.*"

Hawker listened to Moore. The words sounded familiar to him. As if he'd heard them before.

"Is that a quote? Tennyson or something?"

"It's a corruption of Milton," Moore said. "From *Paradise Lost*."

"Referring to Eve eating the apple," Danielle said.

Moore nodded. "It's not the only reference they've made. In the first letter they borrowed another phrase of his. *He who overcomes by force, hath overcome but half his foe.*"

"Sounds like they're trying to tell us something," Hawker suggested.

"They seem to be choosing the role of Satan," Moore said. "Defeated by God, now trying to destroy his creation: mankind. And yet from the letter to the UN and this reference they seem to imply we'll do it to ourselves."

Hawker considered what was being said. There was something else to it. The bitterness in the words, the choice of verses. The choice of referencing Milton in the first place. It seemed almost . . . He couldn't put his finger on it, but he was certain there was more to what was being said than met the eye.

"Great," Danielle said. "So what do these people want? Are they against God or are they against man?"

"Religious influence on man," Moore said. "That's the best we can distill it down to. All classic religions seem to want their people to reproduce as rapidly as possible, perhaps because failure to do so makes you weaker in numbers than your enemy. But synthesizing the UN letter and these other letters together it seems they blame the world's problems on this and on the overpopulation resulting from it and Western introduction of medicines and other technologies that have reduced infant mortality and the death rate, while not reducing the birthrate equally."

"So the plague is for culling the herd," Danielle said.

"The logical response in livestock."

"Humans are not livestock," she said.

"Perhaps to this cult we are," Moore said.

Hawker remained silent. He'd seen too much of man treating his fellow man worse than livestock to doubt it.

"Ranga's notes suggested he was working on something that would drastically reduce life span," Danielle said. "It appeared as if he was getting close. Could that be culling the herd?"

"Perhaps," Moore said.

As Hawker listened, it became clear they were facing a group with dangerously warped minds. His deal with Lavril likely didn't matter. These were not the kind of people who came in from the cold or allowed themselves to be arrested. He was all but certain they'd have to kill these men to defeat them. So be it.

"Ranga got caught up with these people somehow," Hawker said. "If we could retrace that avenue, maybe we find out where they hide. Hit them before they hit us. Act instead of react."

Moore looked at him thoughtfully. "I think we know what avenue Ranga connected with them on," he said. Without elaborating he cued something up on the screen on the bulkhead of the aircraft.

Hawker turned to watch. At first he couldn't tell what he was looking at. The video was poor and the room shown was badly lit. It turned out to be an auditorium of some kind. And then, as the camera zoomed in on a group of people sitting onstage, he recognized Ranga. He was younger, slimmer, wearing a white shirt and a thin black tie.

The moderator was talking, saying something about the challenge of feeding growing populations through the use of genetically modified crops.

The question was posed to Ranga as to what progress could be expected in the next twenty years.

"Drought resistance is important," Ranga insisted, "for lost crops mean no harvest at all, which is the worst-case scenario. But you must understand that all things in nature are compromises. Drought resistance comes with a price: It can result in smaller yields under normal circumstances. Just the same, designing crops that yield more food per acre brings a risk: They require more water and more fertilizer and are often at the highest risks of failure under stressed conditions."

A question from the audience prompted him.

"So what's the answer, Dr. Milan?" someone asked. "Is there hope?"

Ranga cleared his throat. "In some sense we are searching for the impossible," he said. "The best answer would be a crop that resists stressed growing conditions, produces more food per acre, and does not drain the soil or water table excessively. We are looking for ways to do this," he said proudly, then continued less energetically. "But it's a bit like trying to make an elephant fly without asking him to lose any weight."

Laughter spread through the crowd.

"It's problematic," Ranga continued. "We do what we can. But if you must know, we are really attacking the issue from the wrong direction. It is often said that the world produces too little food. But rarely is it stated that we consume too much."

Hawker sensed the pause. Ranga had always paused before stating his most important point.

"There will soon be seven billion people on this earth. In twenty years that number will near ten billion. And despite slowing growth rates, some projections go as high as twelve to fifteen billion by 2075. The earth cannot sustain such numbers. Especially if we all wish to live like Americans."

A grumble went through the crowd.

"Make no mistake," Ranga continued. "In every corner of the world people dream of living like an American. But that means each person consumes six times as much food, water, and fuel as the worldwide average. That would be the equivalent of a planet with fifty billion people on it."

A collective gasp escaped from the audience.

"Like any population growing out of control, be it animals, insects, or bacteria, such growth ends in a crash. Our species will eventually crash as we destroy the host and starve."

"The host?" It was one of the other panelists.

"The earth is our host," Ranga replied, then turned back to the crowd. "The real solution lies not in growing more food but in reducing the population. The sooner we take action the less radical it will need to be, but based on religions that demand we all go forth and multiply and on both cultural and secular morality of reproductive rights, we will likely only act when it is far too late. At that point the action will have to be drastic. Beyond voluntary birth control, beyond individual decisions, beyond the Chinese one-child rule."

An uneasy question came from somewhere off camera. "What exactly are you suggesting?"

Ranga cleared his throat again. "Just as it is possible for us to engineer crops, it is within our grasp to engineer humankind. A virus could be created that would spread randomly from person to person. It would bring with it genetic coding that would either sterilize some percentage of those it attached to, or reduce fertility or drastically shorten life spans. If the average life span were forty to fifty years—as it was once in this world—population growth would be severely curtailed if not reversed."

"What!" someone shouted.

"Are you out of your mind?" a second voice said.

"Please," Ranga said, speaking over a murmuring, restless crowd. "This may be the only real solution. There are either too many of us making too many babies, or we live far too long. One variable must change. It is up to us which one."

It was an academic argument, delivered to the wrong crowd. They broke into jeers and shouts.

"You're a freak," someone shouted.

"Nazi!"

"Calm down," the moderator requested.

Other shouts came forth, but Ranga did not back down.

"You live here in a big country, with plenty of space. But go to other places. See the crowds in the slums. See the children naked and begging. That is overpopulation. Not a crowded freeway or a line at a restaurant. It's hundreds of thousands begging. People crawling on each other like ants."

A shoe came flying onto the stage, barely missing Ranga's head. He ducked and then looked out into the crowd. The discord was so loud it became hard to hear him, even with the microphone.

"You have to understand!" he shouted, trying to get his point across. "If we don't do this ourselves, nature will eventually do it for us. Nature will always cull the herd."

More shouts and accusations came from the crowd. The moderator took the microphone and started pleading for calm. People began to walk out, others pressing up onto the stage pointing and shouting. The room became chaotic; something crashed into the table, and then the tape ended.

Hawker stared at the static on the screen, blindingly aware that Ranga had used the very term written in the cult's letter. If the jury was still out on Ranga, they had to be leaning toward conviction now.

"I'm sorry," Danielle said.

He appreciated her words, appreciated that there was no "I told you so" tone to her voice.

"Not your fault," he said.

His thoughts turned back to the tape, and the friend who now sounded like some version of the Nazi regime's Dr. Mengele. Ranga looked awfully young, thinner, smoother face, fuller head of hair.

"When was that tape made?"

"In '98," Moore said. "At a conference on food production, two years before he went on the run."

Hawker looked up at the ceiling and exhaled. "Well, my old friend certainly *sounds* like a lunatic," he admitted.

He looked at Danielle and tried to telegraph his regret without saying it. She turned to Moore.

"So what are we dealing with here?"

"Walter Yang and the CDC are analyzing the data you pulled off the computer. I'll let you know what we can find."

"And this group?" Hawker asked. "Can they really be capable of what they're threatening?"

"They wouldn't be the first to try," Moore said. "Jim Jones poisoned more than nine hundred of his own people with cyanide in Guyana. He and his thugs shot everyone who tried to interfere, including a U.S. congressman. The Aum Shinrikyo cult dumped Sarin nerve gas into the subways of Tokyo. Twelve people were killed, thousands more injured, but the scary part came when police raided the cult's headquarters. They found anthrax and Ebola cultures, explosives, hallucinogenic drugs, and storehouses of chemical precursors. Based on what they had on-site, they could have manufactured enough Sarin to kill four million people."

"I remember that," Hawker said. "I didn't know they had anthrax and Ebola. Why didn't they use them?"

"They weren't ready," Moore said. "Rumor had it the police were about to raid them, so they went suicidal. Same with Jim Jones. He was getting a lot of heat about keeping people trapped there; that's what Congressman Ryan went to check out. When things start to look bad, the leaders of these groups snap. Suicide pacts, murder suicide, mass killings. The endgame is always the same."

"Whoever's leading this cult, he sounds a lot like Shoko Asahara," Moore added. "The guy who led the Japanese cult. His obsession was bringing about some type of apocalypse that combined the writings of Revelation with Buddhism and the predictions of Nostradamus."

"Another lunatic," Hawker noted.

"Like I said, they don't have to make sense," Moore noted. "They just have to get others to follow them. In Asahara's case those who didn't were jailed in cells at their headquarters or killed. In Guyana the same thing. Waco was the same."

"We've seen that they're capable of murder," Danielle said. "And torture as well, in a very direct one-on-one style. Releasing a bioweapon might be easy by comparison."

Moore nodded. "And if Ranga's work went the way it seemed to, they might be close to possessing one: a weapon with the power to either sterilize a good portion of the human race or cut their life spans in half."

For the first time in a long while Hawker felt a wave of uncertainty. He couldn't imagine his old friend being part of such a group, but he'd obviously been just that. At least he'd tried to break away. "We have to stop these psychopaths, whatever it costs."

He looked at Danielle, who nodded.

"So what do we do in Beirut?" she asked.

"Bashir was a known dealer in stolen art," Moore said. "Beirut is one center of that trade. Gateway to Europe, as it's often been called. We know somebody there

who might be able to help. Might be able to get you into the party."

"For what?" Hawker asked, thinking it sounded like an absurd waste of time.

"To follow the lead," Moore replied sternly.

Danielle took the middle ground. "You think they were using stolen art to fund Ranga's experiments, or even the cult itself?"

Moore shook his head. "We thought of that. And we haven't been able to link anything else to them, so maybe. But the word is Ranga was a buyer, not a seller. Why? We have no idea. One of you is going there to find out."

"One of us?" Danielle said.

"Our other lead is in Dubai," Moore explained. "A venture capital fund-raiser for a start-up drug company called Paradox. They once claimed Ranga as one of their founders."

To Hawker that sounded even thinner than the Beirut lead.

"A land with bombed-out buildings and dangerous black-market activities or a high-tech ball in one of the most luxurious cities on earth," he said. "Guess I know where I'm going."

Moore nodded. "You're going to Dubai."

Hawker tilted his head. He wasn't sure he'd heard that right.

"We got a call this morning on your line," Moore explained. "Sorry it didn't go through. But once you two got plucked we had to shut things down, divert all data to Central Communications. A man named David Keegan called you. Former MI-5 striker, if I'm not mistaken."

Hawker nodded. "He gave me the information on Ranga."

"Yes, well, he found the person you asked him to look for," Moore said.

Moore reached over and clicked an icon on the laptop in front of him.

Keegan's voice came from the speakers. *"Listen, mate, I've found your girl. Told you, you should have married her, she's some big shot at a pharma company now. You'd done like I said and you'd be sipping champagne and buying polo horses instead of dodging bullets and hanging out with the likes of me. Anyway, she's in Dubai for a shindig with her company, Paradox. I'll text you the info. You take it from there. Let me know if you need anything else."*

The playback ended. Hawker looked on as Moore clicked the *x* and closed the program. Whatever doubts they'd had about his objectivity could have only been confirmed by the words Keegan had chosen to use. Perhaps that was even why Moore played it. A preemptive shot, like Danielle's the day before. Hawker understood.

"Were you really going to marry her?" Danielle asked, sounding half-shocked, half-amused.

"It's just Keegan. He thinks he's funny," Hawker said.

"Mmm-hmm," she said, smiling. "Does sound kind of funny."

"Sonia is now a geneticist in her own right," Moore said. "She's also part of Paradox. She'll be in Dubai giving a speech to potential investors. You're going to meet her, Hawker. And you're going to find out what she knows."

CHAPTER 17

Yousef stood in near-perfect darkness, with only a pin-point of light aimed down at him from above. He wore sweatpants. His hands stretched out to either side—cuffed to rails on the right and the left.

Metal walls sweated around him while machinery hummed and a strange vibration grew and faded and then returned again in a slowly repeating pattern.

Shadows moved just beyond his view and then passed him. Shapes dressed in black, hoods partially covering their faces. As each went past, a blade cut his arm. Just deep enough to make him bleed.

He winced at the pain, saw the knives retracted in the dark, felt the blood trickling down his arm and heard it dripping drop by drop onto a metal tray.

It flowed to a space in front of him, where they tossed their relics: crucifixes, golden pendants in the shape of the crescent moon and the Star of David, other symbols that he did not recognize.

As the last cut was made, Yousef was already shaking.

In front of him the group stood, but in the darkness he could see little.

He felt a presence behind him but he knew not to turn.

"What is the lie that we have been told?" the figure behind him said.

Now Yousef recognized the voice as that of Marko. It was deeper and echoing in the metallic chamber but he was almost certain.

"That we are fallen," the group replied in unison. "That we are incomplete."

"Do you lay down the lie?" the voice said.

"We lay down the lie," they said together. "We take up our truth."

"And what is the truth?"

In his dizzy state, Yousef listened. He tried to remember what was being said; he would have to remember these words.

"That together we are whole."

"From where comes the truth?" the voice behind him asked.

Yousef felt as if he'd been drugged. It was the air and the loss of blood, he thought. His head was spinning.

"Cruor speaks the truth," they said, speaking as one. "Blood speaks the truth."

"And who speaks to Cruor?"

"The Master."

Marko's hand, the hand of Cruor—the Man of Blood— pressed onto the back of Yousef's neck.

"Do you lay down the lie?" he asked.

Yousef knew what to say.

"I lay it down," Yousef said. "There is no God. Only man. There is no punishment. Only life. There is no death for us. Only for others."

He looked down at the metal tray. A thin layer of his blood had spread across it, soaking all the religious icons, drowning them in blood of man.

He smelled fire, and he looked over to see a glowing rod being carried through the darkness. There were letters and numbers on it. It was the brand of the brother-

hood. It signified the moment when the first man had rejected God.

All the brotherhood wore it. None could be part without it.

"Do you accept the brand?" Cruor said.

Yousef stared at it. The heated metal glowed red in the dark, as if it wanted to taste his skin.

"Do you accept it?" he was asked again.

What had God done for him? he thought. If it was the will of God that he live in the gutter, tormented by the police and the drug dealers, sometimes lacking even the basics of life, then what use was God for him?

He would be part of something. He would have power. Like they did.

"Do you accept it?" he was asked a third time.

"I accept the brand," he said, steeling himself for the pain.

"Then you shall be Scindo," Cruor said.

And the glowing metal was pressed into his flesh.

Yousef howled in pain, trying to pull loose from the cuffs. Steam and smoke rose from his chest and the stench of burned skin filled his nostrils. He leaned forward and retched even as cold water was thrown upon him from all sides.

He fell to his knees, his arms held up by the cuffs. His body heaved and he vomited again as a layer of burned skin peeled off and fell to the floor beneath him. He looked to it, a twisted version of the mark in his own flesh. On his chest it would become a scar, a brand that marked him for what he was.

Soaking wet, blood dripping, dry-heaving on his knees, he heard a voice. And then other voices.

"Scindo," they whispered. "Rise, Scindo. Rise."

He pulled on the bars to which he was cuffed, grasping them and straining with what strength he had left.

The voices grew louder until they were shaking the room. He felt their power. With one last effort, he heaved himself up until he stood before them. Yousef was banished; he existed no more. He had become something greater. He was now Scindo: the one who divides.

CHAPTER 18

Hawker stood near the exit door of a sleek monorail as it cut across Dubai and angled toward the Persian Gulf. In the distance the sun had begun to drop, lending long shadows to the afternoon and drawing out the hues of red and yellow that normally lay subdued under the blistering white light of the day.

The monorail was part of Dubai's never-ending push toward the modern and spectacular. It ran all over the city. This particular line took them toward the coast.

Up ahead he could see their destination: the magnificent Burj Al Arab hotel, rising 1,052 feet from the man-made island on which it had been built.

The incredible wedge-shaped building soared into the sky like a sail on the horizon. Its western edge stood sharp and vertical like a mast, its eastern side curving gracefully back toward the ground like the billowing canvas of a spinnaker. A winglike structure protruded forward like the bridge of a great ship, and in its sheltered rear section a helipad jutted out some eight hundred feet above the waterline.

There were few things in the world that Hawker considered impressive simply in and of themselves, but setting eyes on this building, he added one to the list.

Far behind him, in the central part of the city, the tallest building in the world towered like a spike, but the Burj

Khalifa did not hold the eye or move the spirit like the structure in front of him.

For a moment Hawker was speechless.

Unfortunately the man beside him was not.

"It was hella hot when we got off that plane," the man said, pulling at his silk tie. "Damn hot. Worse than I expected."

"It's a desert," Hawker said. "And it's July."

The man looked up at him. "That's a good point. You are damn observant. No wonder you went into the security business."

The man laughed at his own joke and Hawker struggled to decide if he wanted to laugh with him or slap him. "Yes, sir," he said, somewhat painfully.

Had Danielle been sent to the fund-raising event, she would have gone as an NRI representative or even a proxy for some company on the NRI's list of civilian partners, but Hawker's knowledge of genetics would have lasted ten seconds in such an environment. That made such a proposition more difficult.

Thoughts of flying *his* turbocharged Jaguar in from Croatia, tooling down the coast, and driving up to the Burj in an Armani suit and posing as an investor were likewise dashed, since that required a specific invite to what was essentially a closed party.

Besides, Hawker knew little more about venture capital or international business than he did about genetics. And even if he could pass off the role, he guessed that Sonia would recognize him fairly quickly. She might have changed from a twenty-year-old to a young woman, but he didn't look that much different; a little gray in the stubble of his beard when he didn't shave, a few more lines on his face and around his eyes. But that was it. Not enough change to fool someone who had spent the better part of a year pining for him.

So if he couldn't pretend to be someone else, then he had only one other choice: pretend to be himself.

Moore had pulled some strings and one of the venture capitalists had suddenly lost his security team. With a diplomatic problem holding his own men up, Mr. James B. Callahan of Fresno, California, found himself needing to hire someone. And the U.S. embassy found itself recommending someone they'd never heard of before.

But orders were orders, and Hawker had signed on for forty-eight hours of close protection. He wondered if he could survive forty-eight hours of listening to Callahan.

Callahan turned to their host, an Emirate man wearing a *kandura,* the traditional long white cloak worn in the region.

"How much does real estate go for around here?" Callahan asked. " 'Cause you can't buy a pot to piss in near Silicon Valley without a million bucks."

The Emirate man smiled politely and glanced at Hawker as if looking for help. Hawker just shrugged and rolled his eyes. Unfortunately, shooting Callahan and throwing him off the train would blow his cover.

"If you like, I can put you in touch with a broker," the Emirate man said politely.

"I like," Callahan said. "Oh yeah, absolutely. I like. Heard about that island you got, the one that looks like a palm tree. Might want to buy me something there."

The Emirate nodded and Callahan turned to Hawker. "I got a good feeling about this," he said.

Funny, Hawker thought, because he felt just the opposite. As if he were heading toward some type of doom long avoided but always creeping closer. He'd always known that Ranga and Sonia were keeping some great secret during their time in Africa. Whatever it was, it drove them on, binding them together yet also forcing them apart. Even then, Sonia spent nearly as much time in the lab as her father, receiving an education at his hands.

It was only when the generals started pushing him harder that Ranga began working in the lab alone. Did he want to protect Sonia or to keep her from knowing what he was doing?

Hawker didn't know and at the time hadn't asked. Questions and explanations weren't part of the deal. But after viewing the tape and listening to Ranga speak, Hawker wondered if he'd been protecting a lunatic.

He wondered if things might not have been better had he let Ranga and Sonia die or languish as captives all those years ago. If he had, the world might not be staring down the barrel of a heavily loaded gun.

As the thoughts swirled, he felt a little guilty about lumping Sonia in with her father. Truth was, he didn't know what her part was in all of this, either then or now. Had she gotten away from Ranga's circus as soon as she had the chance, like Keegan suggested? Certainly, it seemed like she'd built her own life. Then again, Paradox, the company she worked for, listed Ranga as an original principal. Was it simply a natural place for her to land, a place where the Milan family knew a few people?

Hawker felt now much as he'd felt when seeing Keegan: There are no coincidences. Ranga, Sonia, Paradox, this plague—in his heart of hearts he was certain there would be some connection. And that thought bothered him more than anything else.

Ten minutes later, as they stepped out into the lobby of the hotel, the Emirate man joyfully bid them adieu. In a private room at the base of the hotel, Callahan was introduced to several staff members of the drug company. He signed papers of confidentiality and was scanned from head to toe for recording devices or other electronic equipment. An aide held out a plastic bag, into which Callahan placed his BlackBerry and his iPhone.

Then he and Hawker, who underwent the same treatment, were led to an elevator. It started upward, moving

smoothly and rapidly until it stopped and the doors opened to the top-floor ballroom.

Amber-colored marble stretched out ahead of them. Blue light shone through the tinted floor-to-ceiling windows that looked out over the Persian Gulf. Out on the floor millionaires mingled, whispered, and snacked on Beluga caviar.

Callahan stepped out with Hawker at his side. A quick check told Hawker the place was secure.

"You're in good hands here," he told Callahan. "I'm going to walk the perimeter, make sure there are no threats or weaknesses the hotel security has overlooked."

Callahan laughed. "That's why I like you," he said.

"Because I do my job?"

"No, because you take it so seriously," Callahan said. "We're cool here. Nothing's gonna happen. Hell, the only reason I brought you was for looks."

Not that he really cared, but he had to know. "What do you mean, 'looks'?"

"A guy ain't squat at one of these things if he don't have his own security," Callahan said. "It's like a platinum card—except everybody has those now—no, it's more like your own jet. You don't want to be the guy who rents."

Hawker actually smiled. He wondered how someone so idiotic could be worth so much money. Either it was all an act on Callahan's part or there really was no justice in the world.

"Go find yourself a few drinks," Callahan said. "And if you can find yourself a girl, have at it. I'll pay you a bonus."

Hawker nodded and walked off, feeling as if he'd just been paroled or something.

He checked a few doors, studied the hallways in and out, and found himself lingering near the wall of glass on the eastern side of the building. Below he could see the coast of Dubai, in the distance the city lights, and up

above, the base of the circular helipad that jutted out from the roof.

A waiter stopped by and Hawker took a glass of champagne.

A second waiter followed, holding a tray toward him.

Hawker studied the tray: thin crackers, caviar, and foie gras, if he wasn't mistaken.

"I'm guessing you don't have a cheeseburger hiding back there somewhere," he said.

The man stared at him.

"Never mind," Hawker said. He held out a hand, passing on the food.

The waiter moved off and Hawker began to scan the room.

Filling out the incredible space was an international group of investors and medical professionals. Whatever Paradox was selling, a pretty distinguished group of guests seemed interested in buying.

Wealth from twenty countries walked the floor. Americans like Callahan, Middle Eastern men in traditional garb, Chinese, Japanese, and Russian attendees could be seen and overheard. Aside from the waiters, Hawker was undoubtedly the poorest man in the room. It left him feeling oddly out of place.

And then he spotted Sonia, standing near a podium, in a form-fitting white cocktail dress. Leaning close to a thin, gray-haired man, she seemed to speak in hushed tones. A whisper here, a nod there, a smile and a handshake for someone who stopped by.

She was all grown up now, no doubt about that. The awkward beauty of a twenty-year-old had morphed into a gorgeous thirty-year-old with curves and confidence. From what he saw, she was in her element, shining as the center of attention while everything else swirled around her.

She said a few more words to the man next to her, a

partner or executive by the look of things, shook another set of hands, and then exhaled at a break in the
pressing crowd.

As she took a breath her eyes came up; her gaze
stretched out across the ballroom as if to relax for just a
moment, and in the process landed directly on Hawker.

He saw her pause. Her expression changed, signaling
a moment of confusion and indecision. He guessed she
wasn't sure what she was seeing or didn't believe what
her mind was telling her. And then she drew in a breath,
her lips parted in surprise, and Hawker knew that she'd
recognized him.

The gray-haired man tapped her on the shoulder. She
turned toward him abruptly, but in a second she was back
on form. And Hawker realized that Sonia wasn't just part
of the show—she was the main attraction.

Moments later the lights began to dim. Sonia and the
gray-haired man stepped off the platform and Hawker
lost them in the crowd. At each end of the room, huge
plasma-screen monitors began to descend from the ceiling while some type of spalike music rose up.

The show was about to begin. Whatever Sonia had
been up to for the last few years, whatever Paradox was
selling, Hawker and the rest of the crowd were about to
find out.

CHAPTER 19

Upon their arrival in Beirut, Danielle and Moore had been whisked away to the American embassy. Waiting in a secured communications room, Danielle took the opportunity to talk with Moore about Hawker.

"I'm not sure Hawker is the best person to be on this mission," she said.

Moore remained stoic. "I was wondering when you'd mention that. What are your thoughts?"

"He has a stake in it," she said. "He wants his friend to be cleared, wants to believe in him."

As Moore considered her words, Danielle felt sick inside. She felt as if she were stabbing Hawker in the back somehow. She believed what she was saying and, more important, she believed she was speaking in Hawker's best interest, whether he knew it or not.

Moore seemed less concerned. "Who wouldn't want their friend to be proven innocent?" he said. "He seems objective to me."

Danielle struggled. Perhaps objective versus subjective was the point, or at least it might become the point.

"There's no one else I know more interested in doing what's 'right,'" she said. "But if what's right from his point of view conflicts with what's right for the rest of the world . . . we know where Hawker comes down on that. He believes in the tribe around him. That's what matters.

It's the reason we love him, and the reason he frustrates us so badly. Even in Mexico he threatened to let the world burn if it came down to choosing between those he loved and everything else."

"And did he?"

"No," she said, remembering how Hawker had ultimately chosen. "But it's still a blind spot."

Moore stopped scribbling the notes on his pad and turned toward her. "We all have blind spots," he said. "Sometimes they're what make us who we are."

"I know, but—"

"Hawker joined up for a reason."

"Because he wants a clean slate," she said.

"That's not why he joined," Moore insisted.

Danielle sat back, fixing her gaze on Moore in an inquisitive way. She was pretty certain she understood the deal they'd crafted for Hawker and what he was getting out of it.

"We're his tribe now," Moore explained. "You in particular. He joined up so he wouldn't be alone."

"And the fact that he's now making contact with a woman from his past, someone he obviously had feelings for?" she asked.

"You tell me," Moore said. "Would he choose her over what's right?"

She hesitated. How could she know?

"The feelings between you two are no great secret," he said. "Can *you* be objective about it?"

"It's not his body I'm trying to save," she said defensively.

Moore made a face as if he were weighing the possibilities. "Then you watch him, you make the call."

As she considered Moore's directive, a great irony struck her. She had always been good at seeing the forest for the trees, focusing on the bigger picture. But now her mind was on Hawker. She was the one seeing it on a

personal level, trying to spare her friend from the dark road he seemed to be heading down.

She didn't want Hawker getting pushed into a corner and forced to choose. He'd suffered enough of that already.

A moment later the feed from NRI headquarters in Virginia kicked in and Danielle recognized Walter Yang from the NRI's medical science department. Dressed in a white lab coat with rimless glasses, Walter looked every bit the PhD in molecular biology and genetics that he was. For reasons she could not fathom, he was also wearing a holster with a pistol secured in it.

Moore cleared his throat. "Why are you armed, Walter?"

"You told me to shoot anyone who tried to break the quarantine," Yang said.

Moore looked distraught and glanced over at Danielle. "Remind me not to use metaphors when speaking to the sciences department," he said, and then he turned back to the screen.

"Have you shot anybody yet?"

"No," Yang said proudly. "No one has tried to escape."

"Good," Moore said. "Let's keep it that way. Turn the gun back in to security, forget what I said about shooting people, and tell me what you've discovered on the data Ms. Laidlaw provided."

Yang looked disappointed for a second, then brightened. "First off," he said, "the data are incomplete."

"I was in kind of a hurry," Danielle said, realizing that Yang would know nothing about where the data came from or how it was collected.

"Sure," he said. "Well, the good thing is we have enough here to reconstruct the gist of this clinical trial: several years of work on a long list of deliberately mutated viruses. Things don't go straight-line, of course, but in general each new series seemed to improve on the last."

"Can you see a connection with the UN virus?" Moore asked.

"I can't speak to their genetic similarities, because the data contains only trial results, not the actual genetic coding, but based on the range of infected cells claimed in the trials, the UN virus and trial 951 are likely highly related but not the same. Given some modifications, both could probably be used in genetic therapy."

"Ah," Danielle said. Onscreen, Yang grinned and nodded.

"Someone want to enlighten the old man?" Moore asked.

Danielle took a shot. "Genetic therapy has been talked about for years. The first moves from the lab to the medical profession are just starting to take place, from what I understand. Basically, patients with genetic disorders, mutations, or certain cancers can't be treated with normal drugs because the issue isn't sickness, it's defective coding. No matter what drug you use to treat the symptoms, each time the defective cell divides and the DNA replicates, it copies the mistake into the new cell."

"Like cheating off a kid who doesn't know the answers," Yang added.

Moore turned to the screen, his eyebrows up.

"Not that I ever did that," Yang said.

"The only way to break the cycle," Danielle said, "is to patch the DNA so the newly replicated cells carry the correct code and not the defective gene. Best way to do this is to design a virus that can be released into the body carrying a DNA 'patch' that corrects the genetic code. From then on, when the cell divides, it makes a nondefective copy of itself."

"Like cheating off a kid who actually knows his stuff," Moore said, reusing the analogy.

Danielle smiled and looked at the screen. "If we take Dr. Yang's computer analogy, it's like downloading soft-

ware to your hard drive. If that software contains a bad virus, you're in trouble; if it contains a patch to fix a flaw in the original programming, your computer now runs like it was supposed to."

Yang took over. "The problem is the average human body contains a billion cells. Can't exactly reset the codes one by one. So one way to reach the defective cells is with what we call a carrier virus. We modify the virus to carry the updated human DNA and then inject it into the defective area of the patient. The virus then does what it's designed to do, spreading across the cells, implanting its new DNA into the cells, and reproducing by the billions. Those copies do the same thing, and so on and so on, like that shampoo commercial from the seventies.

"The end result is a regeneration of sorts in the specific organ or system that was defective. It's not a hundred percent, but you end up with far more healthy cells than unhealthy ones, and over time the healthy cells crowd out the weak and the dying."

From an academic perspective, Danielle understood Yang's excitement. But knowing Ranga's radical position on population and his work on telomeres, she grew more worried. Used malevolently, Ranga's trial 951 might age every cell in the human body, radically reducing life spans just as he suggested the world might need to do.

"Can it be weaponized?" Moore asked.

Yang nodded. "Both the UN virus and 951 can survive outside the host, both can be carried by air or other vectors such as birds or insects. Aerosolized dispersal from crop dusters or via airburst from missiles or artillery shells would create a very effective biological spread."

"So how did they go from the inert UN virus to this trial 951?" Moore asked.

"It might be as simple as changing payloads," Yang said.

"Payloads?"

"Those blank spaces I told you about," Yang said. "As it stands right now, the UN virus is an empty carrier, but it has been designed with a space holder for whatever the user might want to put inside. That's the payload. Designing the virus itself is the hard part, like designing a ballistic missile. In comparison, putting a DNA patch in the leftover spaces would be relatively easy. Like loading the warhead onto the missile. You can go conventional, you can go nuclear. In this case, they could put a corrective gene in those blank spaces or they could put something devastating. That might be what they did with 951."

Danielle thought about what would happen if the code from trial 951 were placed inside the UN virus. Pretty soon the whole human race might look like the aged and dying rats she'd seen in Ranga's lab.

Danielle was thirty-seven, in the prime of her life. In the world Ranga envisioned, the world he might have been trying to bring about, she would be in her last days, an old woman feeling infirmity and facing death. In fact, her life might already have been over.

"Anything else?" Moore asked.

"Not yet," Yang said.

"All right," Moore said. "Turn in your gun. I'll touch base with you in twelve hours."

Yang signed off. Moore turned to Danielle. "So the UN virus does nothing," he noted. "Then why send it?"

"Could be a message, like Ranga's well-staged death," she said. "If the goal is extortion, making your point without killing anyone at first is a pretty good start."

"No one's called with any demands," Moore said.

"Maybe they're not done making the point," she said.

Moore looked as if he agreed. "We're pessimists," he noted. "Anything you can think of that might make the future seem a little bit brighter?"

"Only the obvious," she said.

"Which is?"

"They don't have anything to put inside. They don't have a payload yet."

"Ranga gave them a blank virus," Moore said, following her line of thought.

She nodded. "Why else would they need him back? Why else would they go to his lab?"

Moore's face brightened. It was all speculation but it made sense. "Ranga breaks away without giving them the crucial payload, they hunt him down and catch him, but instead of killing him outright they grab him and torture him."

"And he gives up the address on rue des Jardins," she said.

"And he's willing to give it up, because he's got the place wired to blow," Moore finished. "Score one for Hawker's friend if that's the case. So what would they do next?"

Danielle tried to put herself in their place. It didn't take much. "They'd find someone to finish the job."

"Ranga's daughter."

It didn't have to be her; there could be others. The evidence showed Ranga and Sonia hadn't worked together in years, but that hadn't stopped the NRI from sending Hawker to Dubai. Which was exactly where Danielle felt she should be.

"What the hell am I doing here chasing after stolen art?"

"Whatever's about to be sold here, it was important to Ranga and Bashir," Moore reminded her.

"But how?" she asked. "How could *this* possibly have anything to do with *that*?"

"That's what you're here to find out," Moore said. "You have an invite to a private auction tonight courtesy of a friend of mine, Mr. Faisal Najir. He'll expect you to come dressed for the occasion."

Danielle looked at Moore suspiciously. "Where?"

"Center city," Moore said.

Danielle recalled Beirut's city center as a bombed-out wasteland. "That's no-man's-land."

"Up on the surface it is," Moore said. "But don't worry, you'll be underground."

CHAPTER 20

As Hawker watched, a pair of huge plasma screens descended slowly from the ceiling at each end of the ballroom. All eyes turned toward one or the other, causing the crowd to part in the middle like the Red Sea. He could see one screen from where he was, so he held his ground and kept his back to the wall.

"*Welcome to the city of the future,*" a voice said, mixing with the music. "*Here you will see your future, a future without sickness, a future without infirmity, a future without dying.*"

He leaned forward to get a better view of the screen. It showed a man stepping off a yacht with a beautiful young woman on his arm. He was silver-haired and obviously in his midsixties; the woman—of course—might have been twenty-five. But as they walked toward the camera, the image changed. The gray in his hair disappeared, the lines on his face faded and vanished, his shoulders straightened, his chest filled, his gut shrank to nothing.

"*With Paradox you will see yourselves at age one hundred, living more vitally than you do today at forty, fifty, or sixty,*" the voice promised.

By the time the yachtsman passed the camera, he looked to be thirty-five or so, a paragon of health and virility. The woman on his arm no longer looked out of place.

"*Aging is nothing more than the dying of cells. But*

reversing this process at the cellular level will reverse the effects that you feel."

On the screen a CGI animation showed cells dividing; it zoomed in on the DNA strand as the double helix split and reconnected. Tiny links at the end of the chain fell off, drifting from the screen. Those were the telomeres, as Danielle had explained it to him. Like the tips on your shoelaces. When the telomeres were gone the rest of the lace began to fray.

"This is not a resurfacing project designed to hide the damage of age. Nor is it an attempt to make you look younger, or even feel younger—this is a revolution. When you join us you will be remade, younger, stronger, more virile. Youth will no longer be wasted on the young."

A cheer went up from the audience and Hawker stood amazed. Not because a raft of the wealthy were interested in turning back the hands of time, but because the graphics on the screen showed cellular activity, with labels and subtitles.

These were the very subjects of Ranga's notes, according to Danielle. More shocking to Hawker was a graphic in the lower corner. It indicated a trial number: Series 951. It might have meant nothing to the others, but Danielle had recalled the lists of experiments ending with Series 951.

The same number Danielle had recounted as the last entry in the notes. Sonia's presentation was promising to extend life, using the very same data and a virus with the very same trial number that Ranga's notes had indicated would destroy life.

A seed of anger returned to Hawker's heart.

The best-case scenario had Sonia as just another snake-oil salesman, promising the rich what they wanted to hear, but Hawker didn't believe in the best-case scenario.

And the worst: that Sonia's company and all of this were part of Ranga's plan, part of the cult's plan. What

better or more ironic way could there be to spread a disease than to get rich people to pay millions for the privilege of being infected. Come here for the serum of life, only don't expect to live much after you take it.

And if that was the case, it meant something far more sinister was going on.

CHAPTER 21

As the video presentation wound down, Hawker found himself needing space to think. He moved from the window and began examining the service passages of the hotel. He could still hear the spa music in the ballroom, although the voice-over had been replaced by a dozen individual speakers and models who were milling around in the crowd, talking in person to the wealthy men and women.

He paid attention to it only sporadically. Instead he studied the back halls of the hotel and the unmarked doors that led to prep rooms, kitchens, and fire escapes. If trouble came, it would be one of these areas that proved to be the weak link in the chain. At the same time, these back-of-the-house areas would allow the greatest chance to escape and evade it; but first, one had to know one's way around.

He came out of a staging room filled with audiovisual equipment and moved down the hall to an unmarked stairwell. It led up to the heliport that lay above them and down as a type of fire escape.

Down the hall a door to the right was locked; to the left he found a dead end. He turned back and saw two people walking toward him: Sonia and the gray-haired man.

They exchanged glances.

"I've got this," he heard Sonia say.

"Are you sure?" the man asked.

"Yes."

He kissed her on the cheek and took the stairwell up to the heliport.

"Can I help you find something?" she said to Hawker, sounding very official.

That was a hell of a question. She came closer, moving forward with confidence.

"What makes you think I'm looking for something?" he asked.

She slowed, glancing up the stairs. The sound of footsteps climbing was still audible.

"You were always looking for something when I knew you."

She didn't sound so official anymore.

Up close she was even more beautiful than she had been from a distance. Her soulful hazel eyes, her smooth, tan skin glowing against the white hue of the cocktail dress.

"Maybe we all were," he said.

"Searching for answers together?"

"Better than searching alone," he added.

As she spoke he noticed a different look in her eyes, a weary sadness she'd hidden behind the smiles and the salesman's confidence. Truthfully he wondered how she maintained it at all, considering what was going on.

"Did my father send you?" she asked.

The question struck Hawker oddly. Obviously Ranga had tried to contact him, but the way Sonia asked the question, she sounded more upset or aggravated than concerned. The reason hit him suddenly: No wonder she was able to star at this reception, no wonder she was able to hold it together—she didn't know that her father was gone.

"When did you last speak with him?" he asked.

"Six months ago," she said. "We had a tenth falling-out. Or maybe an eleventh. This one appears to have stuck."

If they'd fallen out months ago, he wondered, then how could her data trial match the number of his most recent work? He kept that to himself. She was lying. There could be many reasons for that, the easiest of which was she didn't know what Hawker was doing here, but if he cornered her now, she would just cover up the lie with another lie.

"Why?" Hawker asked. "What's been going on?"

She looked away as if deciding where to start. "My father is still a refugee," she began. "He refuses to—"

Hawker raised a hand, stopping her. He wanted to hear every word, but something was wrong. He glanced up the stairwell. He should have felt a draft when Gray Hair opened the door to the roof. But he hadn't felt it yet.

He took Sonia by the elbow and moved down the hall.

As a flood of different emotions washed over him, Hawker tried to remain cool. He had to remind himself that the woman in front of him was not the young girl he'd protected years ago. That somehow she was mixed up in what was going on.

"How much do you know about the people your father was working with?"

"Not much. He was always secretive."

"What caused your falling-out?"

"Life," she said. "Changes. I couldn't live his way anymore."

"I mean specifically."

"I'm on the board at Paradox," she said defensively. "Obviously he's no longer any part of this company, just a name on the founders list."

"So he was jealous?"

"No," she said. "He was worried."

"About what?"

"About what we're doing," she said, growing aggravated. "Why are you asking me these things?"

"Something bad has happened," Hawker said.

Her expression changed, worry replacing the aggravation. She shrank back, beginning to shake. "Please tell me he's okay," she said. "Please, Hawker. Please tell me he sent you to find me and talk me into coming back."

Tears were welling up in her eyes.

"I . . ."

A group of people turned down the hall, two men and one woman, carrying drinks. They spoke loudly and asked about the restroom.

Sonia got it together and pointed to the doorway just before the stairwell. The guests moved off.

"Where is he?" she asked. "Tell me where he is."

"I'm sorry," Hawker said. "I couldn't reach him in time."

Her knees buckled at the sound of his words and Hawker had to grab her by the arms to keep her from falling.

She looked up, the tears overflowing her eyes.

"Why?" she asked. "How?"

"Somebody he was working for killed him," Hawker said. "He got a message to me asking for help."

"Why didn't you?" she asked, pleading as if it could be changed now. "Why didn't you save him?"

"I tried."

She wouldn't look at him. She began to pull away. He held on to her.

"I need to know who he was working with," he said. "It's important."

She pulled out of his grasp, holding her hands up as if she could ward him off. "Get away from me."

The moment was hellish to Hawker, every trigger of guilt and anger and vengeance, all being hammered repeatedly and at the same time.

"Sonia," he said sharply, trying to get her attention, "you could be in danger. I need to know what you know."

He wanted to whisk her up in his arms and carry her away from there. To take her somewhere safe, where men like those who'd killed her father could not hope to stray. But there was something larger at stake and Hawker knew he had to hold back.

She didn't run. She just stared, a hand on the wall to steady herself.

As he waited for her, a commotion down the hallway caught his ear. Glaring down the hallway looking for the source of the noise, Hawker caught sight of a body tumbling down the stairwell from the upper level.

Gray Hair.

He hit the bottom landing, clutching his throat and bleeding profusely.

Before she could see it, Hawker pushed Sonia back into an alcove.

One of the bathroom seekers ran to assist Gray Hair, not realizing what had happened.

"What the hell . . ."

The words barely escaped his mouth before a cascade of gunfire rained down from the stairs above.

Too late.

Hawker grabbed Sonia and pulled her into the storeroom with his hand over her mouth. He led her to a table, and they crouched down.

"What's going on?"

"Quiet."

"But—"

He silenced her with a glance and they waited. Nothing happened for a moment, and then the lights on the eighty-first floor went out and the sound of machine-gun fire thundered down the darkened hallway.

CHAPTER 22

Danielle's trip through Beirut was a surreal journey, a passage through a city that had long been at war with itself. Most people knew of Beirut's sad recent history, a place being torn apart for thirty years by civil war, invasions, and strife. What most people didn't know was that Beirut had once been a shining beacon of prosperity and multicultural cooperation.

After World War II, the population had been divided roughly fifty-fifty between Muslims and Christians and the power had been similarly shared. For twenty-plus years it had remained that way, with a strong commercial sector, a rapidly growing economy, and a thriving tourist industry.

During those years Beirut had been a nexus for much of the Arab and Western worlds. Europeans came to its beaches and casinos almost as frequently as they went to Monaco and the south of France. Beirut was the gateway to Europe in one direction and the gateway to the Middle East in the other.

But then the sorrows came. The Muslim population grew faster than the Christian, and demands for more power by Muslim leaders were met with suspicion and resistance from Christian ones. Soon the city and the country around it were in a state of civil war, a war that

would eventually draw in Syria, Israel, and the United States.

A decade of that madness left the city divided, with a Christian side, a Muslim side, and a vacant central core acting as a sort of unofficial demilitarized zone.

On each side rebuilding efforts went on; on each side those who wanted peace fought with those who wanted aggression, while the two sides faced off against each other across the vacant no-man's-land.

But the will of the Lebanese people to thrive seemed greater than the ability of fate to keep them down. At various times in past millennia they had rebuilt after massive earthquakes, invasion, occupation, fires that had burned the city to the ground.

As Danielle rode through the city in a silver SUV, she noticed cranes sprouting from every block. Bulldozers and construction equipment clogged the streets and horns honked in frustration, marking an odd kind of progress. Beirut was filling in the wound that had cleaved it in two, and while many complaints were made about the pace, style, and final design of all the work, no one really wanted it to stop.

On the Muslim side, Danielle passed modern-looking hotels, office buildings, and other structures most in America would be shocked to find in Beirut. She made it to the shore, drove past Pigeon's Rock, and arrived at the St.-George Yacht Club.

It was a busy place as well. Hundred-foot yachts anchored at various spots in the harbor. Farther out, eighty-foot sailboats bobbed on swells as smaller craft moved here and there.

She parked, made her way down the pier, and arrived in front of a sleek-looking motor yacht named *Phoenician Builder.* A guard checked her credentials and waved her on board. A second crewman led her to a shaded deck where Faisal Najir sat enjoying a late lunch.

Najir sat alone, wearing slacks and a white linen shirt open to the third button, just far enough to display a dark, hairy chest and several medallions hanging from his neck. His olive skin glowed with the sun and his wild mane of curly hair seemed to enjoy the breeze that swept over the boat. A pair of bodyguards stood a few steps behind him.

As Danielle approached, he stood and extended a hand.

"You are Danielle Laidlaw," he said confidently.

"And you are Faisal Najir, master builder," she replied. "A friend of Arnold Moore's."

"And lucky to be both," he insisted.

He waved a hand at the empty seat. "Please."

Danielle sat. A waiter appeared, filling her glass with water, as if they were at a restaurant. She glanced at him and then at the bodyguards.

"Can we talk privately?"

Najir nodded to the guards and they moved away, beyond hearing range.

"Did Arnold tell you why I'm here?"

"You wish to attend an auction of . . . how to say it: unsavory items. No, no, 'items with unsavory backgrounds' sounds better."

Danielle was unsure which would turn out to be more unsavory, the items for bid or the crowd bidding on them, but that was the gist of it.

"Do you know of such an auction?" she asked.

"I do," he replied. "You wish to bid on something or just observe?"

She nodded. "Both. Specifically anything a man named Bashir or another man named Ranga Milan might have been interested in."

A look of discomfort registered on Najir's face. He glanced away for a moment.

"Do you know them?" she asked.

"Not the second name. But Bashir is well-known here.

He is well liked. I am friends with Arnold Moore but I will not assist in incriminating or otherwise harming Bashir."

"It's not something you need to worry about," she said.

"It is something I choose to worry about," he replied.

Danielle realized he'd taken her statement the wrong way. "Bashir is missing," she said. "The other man I named is dead. We don't know why, but tonight's auction held great interest for both of them. It may have something to do with what happened to them."

The words lingered, laid out there as bare truth for Najir to ponder. Danielle preferred to be straightforward when she could. With little time, she thought it best not to beat around the bush.

"So the Iranians finally finished him," Najir said.

"We don't think it was them," she replied. "But whoever it was, they may be more dangerous than any existing regime."

"What are we talking about?"

"A cult that wants to destroy God."

He laughed lightly. "What does God have to fear from man?"

"Not God, specifically," she said. "God's children. People."

"Which people?"

"All of us," she said. "At least all the children of Abraham."

Now Faisal nodded. Abraham was in a sense the patriarch of the three great Western religions: Judaism, Christianity, Islam.

"We have reason to believe they may be able to do great harm."

Bashir put his hand on the glass in front of him as if he were about to have a drink, but he did not lift it. He seemed too deep in thought.

"Do you know why I have these bodyguards?" Najir said.

She could guess but didn't.

"Because I told the Syrians to get the hell out of my country, demanded the Israelis stop bombing us, and warned the Iranians to never come here again."

It was a proud statement. She sensed it was true.

"Left alone, we Lebanese will find a way to live together. But there is a price to pay for bravery."

"I know," she said. "I've seen it firsthand."

"And been part of it, I'd guess," he said. "Otherwise Arnold would not speak so highly of you."

Never one to take compliments well, she wasn't sure how to respond.

"I don't need you to go with me," she said. "Just get me inside. Tell me what to look for and who'll be there. I can do the rest."

Najir took a drink of water and then broke a corner off his bread. He dipped it in olive oil and turned back to her, his smile as warm as the Mediterranean sun. "That will look suspicious," he said.

"Because I'm a woman?"

"No," he said smiling. "Because they will be surprised *not* to see me."

She smiled back at him. "Of course."

"We all have temptations we find hard to resist."

"That we do," she said. "When's the auction?"

"After the evening prayers, we will meet some of our brothers from the other side of the city. And then you will see what Bashir wanted to see."

CHAPTER 23

Hawker and Sonia took cover in the audiovisual control room while a wave of panic swept through the outside. Sporadic gunfire was interspersed with screaming, and then they heard nothing but silence.

"What's going on?" Sonia asked.

He was pretty damn sure that she knew what was going on.

"My guess?" he said. "These are the people your father was working for."

Another burst of gunfire echoed.

"They're killing those people," she said.

That was a distinct possibility, Hawker thought, but he didn't want Sonia to feel that.

"I doubt it," he said. "They're looking for you."

"Me?"

"After they took your father, they went after a lab he'd been working out of. There can be only one reason for that: he didn't give them everything they wanted."

"And they think I'll have it?" she asked. Fear filled her eyes. The type of fear he'd seen once before, years ago, when it seemed they might all die before they got the chance to leave the Republic of the Congo.

He didn't completely trust Sonia—there were too many red flags for that—but he was certain of one thing: No

way on earth would he let this cult get their hands on her and do what they'd done to Ranga.

A small boom echoed from the main room. It sounded like an explosion.

"We have to do something," Sonia said. "We can't just hide here."

Hawker intended to do just that. Sooner or later it would turn into a standoff. Hotel security would rush in and Dubai's antiterrorist forces would appear. If he guessed right the attackers did not want that. They had to find Sonia quick and get her out of there, probably by using the helicopter they'd flown in on.

The problem was, it wouldn't take them long to go through the attendees, and then they'd start checking the rooms off the main hall, like the one he and Sonia were in now.

He glanced around, looking for a weapon. As he did he noticed light coming from a long flat panel near the wall. It looked like a mixing room of a recording studio. The controls for the audiovisual displays were still lit from within: The power was still on.

Right off the bat he'd assumed the attackers had cut the line, but that was easier said than done in a big hotel like the Burj. Somehow they'd taken out the lights, but that was it. For all he knew they'd just turned off the damn switch.

"I'm not going to let those people die for me," she said.

"A lot more people will die if they get their hands on you. Trust me."

She looked at him as if the statement confused her, but for reasons he couldn't quite put a finger on, it seemed like a performance. He hoped he was wrong, but once again he heard Keegan's words in his head. The man was right. He couldn't tell a friend from a foe.

He crawled to the panel, conscious of more shouting outside in the hall. After a second of looking it over—and realizing he knew nothing about how to work it—he began throwing switches, pressing buttons that seemed to represent Play and pushing levers that he guessed would control speakers or lighting effects.

The sound of the spa music rose up again. He could hear it from the main room. He pushed the lever to full, and then pressed Play on what looked like a giant DVD player.

The music grew louder and the voice of the spokesman cut in, but at a hundred decibels or more.

"You are here in the city of the future," it boomed.

He threw a bunch of other levers and then grabbed Sonia.

"Come on."

Out in the ballroom the guests lay flat on the floor. Three of them were dead, blood pooling around beneath them on the marble floor. Several others had suffered beatings.

A group of thugs in black fatigues and ski masks had fanned out around the perimeter. They'd gotten control quickly and now pointed automatic weapons at the men and women corralled between them.

At the center of that group, two others stood. One held his weapon at the ready; the other, without a mask and displaying a long blond ponytail, walked among the prone hostages like a wolf on the prowl.

He stopped.

"You."

He pointed toward one of the Paradox personnel.

"Get up."

As the man stood, Ponytail grabbed him by the throat.

"You're a spokesman?"

The man from Paradox nodded fearfully.

"Then speak. Tell me where she is."

"Who?"

"Sonia Milan."

The spokesman choked at a lump in his throat. "She went down the east hall," he said finally. "With Hendricks."

"Hendricks? The old man?"

The spokesman nodded.

Ponytail shook his head. "We killed Hendricks. She wasn't with him."

"I swear they went together, right before you got here," the poor guy said.

Ponytail brought a pistol up, placed the barrel against the man's forehead, and cocked the hammer.

"I swear it! It's the last I saw of her! I don't know anything else!"

"Then I don't need you anymore," Ponytail said.

He pulled the trigger. The man's head exploded and he fell backward, dead. Screams rose and were quickly stifled.

"Anyone else have any better information?" Ponytail shouted. "You know, the kind that might keep you alive?"

Before anyone spoke, the huge plasma screens lit up and began dropping slowly on their hydraulic slides. The music came up seconds later, blaring at a painfully loud volume, making it hard to hear. And then the voice-over began. A calm, soothing voice, played so loud it blocked out the music and distorted the speakers.

"Welcome to the city of the future."

In the center of this madness the men with guns looked suddenly nervous. The ones on the perimeter stepped back a few paces, their hands tightening on their weapons.

"You have come here to see your future."

The flickering of the screens was disorienting in the darkness.

"What the hell is this?" one of the thugs asked.

Their leader remained calm.

He grabbed one of the hotel staff and shoved the pistol in the man's face. "Where's the control room?"

The man pointed to the east hall.

The east hall again.

Ponytail shoved him back to the floor, waved two of his people over, and stormed off the dance floor, heading for the darkened recess of the east hall.

Hawker held Sonia's hand as the two of them slipped out the back door of the control room and entered the west hallway. The setup was simple: a big horseshoe with the ballroom in the middle, the east hallway coming out of one edge and the west hallway on the other side.

With the sound system raging and the plasma screens bathing the main room in an ever-changing flicker of light, it would be hard to notice two people sneaking around. Though that cut both ways.

Hawker stared down the hall. "All we need is a little fog and we could make a rock video," he mumbled.

As the light brightened he caught sight of something more useful: a janitors' closet. He pulled Sonia toward it and opened the door. Buckets and mops, tarps, and all kinds of supplies filled the small space. Perfect.

"Get in the back," he said, pushing her inside. "Lie on the floor behind all that crap and make it look like this room is empty in case they look for you. Whatever happens, wait here. Don't make a sound, no matter what. Just like in Africa. Understand?"

She nodded tearfully.

"Relax," he said, smiling. "I'll be right back."

He shut the door, wondering if he would indeed be back. First he needed a weapon.

* * *

As Ponytail and his two men moved down the east hall, the cacophony of sound and voice diminished slightly but the flickering screens lit them up like a strobe. It gave him a sense of danger he'd not expected to feel.

"Go slow, boys," he said, ghosting the left wall with his gun raised.

The others did likewise, but no one challenged them and they reached the AV room unhindered. One of them pushed on the door.

"Locked."

Ponytail fired away at the handle until the doorjamb and the handle were blasted to splinters. One of his men kicked it in and the door swung open to darkness.

Stepping inside they saw nothing.

A rear door beckoned. He waved his men on.

"Find her!"

As the men went out the door, Ponytail looked around the room, checking the nooks and crannies.

"Sonia!" he called.

No response and he found no one hiding. He stepped to the audiovisual controls, raised his rifle, and unloaded on it, shredding the entire panel.

"You're going to piss me off, young lady," he mumbled to himself.

When the echo of his shots died, the eighty-first floor went silent once again. Ponytail checked his watch. They were running out of time.

Hawker inched his way down the hall, hands up in case anyone saw him. The chaos seemed to be keeping everyone interested, at least until the sound of rifle fire overrode it and the speakers and plasma screens went dead.

So much for plan A.

He stared through the suddenly complete darkness for something, anything.

He found what he was looking for under a glowing sign: the fire alarm.

He elbowed the glass and yanked the handle down.

A piercing wail went out across the floor. A long blast, followed by four short blasts and accompanied by flashing strobes and emergency lights.

As the alarm shrieked, a figure appeared down the end of the hall. Hawker dove just as the man opened fire.

Booming gunfire and the sharp sound of ricochets mixed with the piercing tone of the alarm and the flashing lights.

Seconds later another man fired. But this time from the rear of the hall. In the madness and the dark, the gunmen were shooting at one another.

The man near the ballroom went down.

Hawker glanced back and then took off running. He launched himself toward the injured thug, hammering him with a forearm as he landed. More gunfire snapped; bullets tore holes in the walls and skipped off the marble floor. Hawker wrested the thug's gun loose and fired back down the hall, lighting up the guy at the far end.

With confusion now reigning and gunfire all over the building, some of the hostages had panicked. Without waiting, they made a break for the stairwells; others remained where they were. One of the terrorists opened fire on the crowd and Hawker saw a couple of people fall.

He aimed and pulled the trigger, dropping the man. But another one found Hawker and fired back.

Hawker dove away, hearing the bullets whiz by. All hell had broken loose and the remaining terrorists were fleeing, running toward the east hall and firing back into the crowd as they did.

Hawker knew they were heading for the stairwell and back to the helicopter on which they'd come. He let them

go and raced back around the corner into the west hall, fighting his way through a crowd.

He reached the janitors' closet where he'd hidden Sonia and pulled the door open.

"Sonia, it's me," he said.

Silence.

"Sonia?"

He stepped inside, but she was gone.

CHAPTER 24

An hour after dusk, Danielle stepped out of the silver Mercedes SUV and into the geographic center of Beirut. Ahead of her was a building that had been bombed, shot to pieces, flooded, and then had become a home of refugees and wildlife during the decades of sorrow. It was now reclaimed and fully restored. The National Museum.

Next to the museum a nascent hospital sprouted on one side, while the other side was home to the new government library, also freshly reconstructed. Its façade was a mix of old stone walls and modern tinted glass. All three buildings looked spectacular lit up for the night and fitted out for a ball.

Security was heavy. Cameras, bomb-sniffing dogs, and Lebanese soldiers with rifles seemed to be everywhere.

The valet drove the SUV away and Danielle stepped forward. Lights, music, and a red carpet beckoned. She climbed the stairs in a charcoal-colored gown of smooth, shimmering material. It flowed smoothly as she moved and accentuated her tan skin.

Najir and his bodyguards flanked her, each of them in a tuxedo.

It almost made her laugh. During her early years with the NRI, she and Moore had attended many functions, conferences, and charity balls. You went where the contacts were, and in the high-tech world of industrial es-

pionage, that meant following the money, the investors, the inventors.

For years her closet had been filled with gowns like the one she now wore. And then a funny thing had happened. Beginning with the Brazil project, Danielle had traded in her cocktail dresses and makeup for boots and mosquito repellent.

The mission to Brazil took them deep into the heart of the Amazon. Later it was Mexico, from the Gulf Coast through the jungle to the mountains. The fanciest outfit she'd worn was a simple cotton dress, and that had been borrowed. Most of the time it was cargo pants, T-shirts, and backpacks. Despite the stares from the men around her, Danielle felt a little awkward dressed to kill once again. A square peg in a round hole somehow.

It made her wonder how Hawker was faring. If she felt out of place, she wondered how he could possibly hope to pull off an upscale event like the one in Dubai.

She hadn't been told what his cover was. *Perhaps he'd sneak in as part of the waitstaff, with caterers or the cleaning crew.*

Listen to me, she thought. In truth, she guessed he'd clean up pretty good and felt a slight pang of jealousy at not being there to see it, especially while an old flame of his would apparently get the full treatment.

She put the thought aside and focused on the moment.

"You're rebuilding quite well," she said.

"We're always rebuilding," Najir said. "We must find a way to stop tearing down."

She smiled and noticed the Phoenician Builder logo in half a dozen places where the reconstruction was ongoing. "It's a good business to be in around here."

"We make no money off this one," Najir insisted. "We are rebuilding the hospital and the wealthy families here are paying thousands to have their names attached to it. This party is a celebration. While it goes on above, we

will be met and taken to a separate area, where some of the patrons will be given a chance to bid on the artwork."

"And that part's not for charity," she guessed.

"Not unless you consider Swiss bank accounts charity."

"Do you know what we're bidding on?"

"I have talked to some people," he said. "Bashir has several items here for sale, early Mesopotamian art."

"I'm not interested in what he was selling," she said.

Najir nodded. "Except it's believed he is selling them to raise funds for the one he wants to buy."

"Which is?"

"The main item in the second lot. It's labeled 'Copper Scroll—Proto Elamite.' Originally it was offered with a carving of Gilgamesh, the famous king of that period. But now they are separate."

The names meant nothing to Danielle, and by the look on Najir's face, they meant nothing to him. She suddenly wished she had an expert with her. Still, she was glad the one person who came to mind was somewhere else, safe and sound.

"And if I need to buy?"

He glanced over at her. "Ranga Milan is dead, you say?"

She nodded, wondering what that had to do with anything. "You said you didn't know him."

"An oversight," Najir said.

Danielle couldn't tell if he was lying or speaking the truth.

"I did not remember him," her host insisted. "I met him twice. Bashir introduced him to me a year ago and I introduced him to these people. As I told you, they know me. You cannot just arrive at an auction like this and bid. You have to be vetted first and prove your ability to pay. Mr. Milan needed an account they could access. I set one up for him."

Something told her Najir had his hands in all kinds of business dealings.

"You're some kind of middleman in this?"

"I am trusted," he said, "by all sides. It has its rewards."

"You take a cut," she guessed.

"If you bring in a bidder, you take a percentage of what that person pays."

"Incentive to find others and bring them to the table," she said.

"Exactly," he said. "For tonight, I have set up an account and indicated that you are here to bid on Ranga's behalf."

Anger flashed through her. It made sense, but she resented such a move being made on her behalf.

"That makes me a target," she said.

"Aren't you already?"

"Of course I am." That's why she carried a Kahr P380 pistol in her purse and a small carbon-fiber knife in the heel of her shoe.

"And you are also dangerous," Najir added, smiling and playing to her ego.

"More than you know," she promised.

"Then you will be fine."

She nodded. She intended to be. "Ask next time," she said.

"Of course," he said, nodding in a slight bow. "You have my word."

She and Najir spent a little over an hour at the reception before a tall, thin man tapped him on the shoulder. He whispered something and moved off. Najir offered his arm to Danielle.

"We are to follow," he said.

They crossed the room, avoiding any obvious places to hold an auction and taking a rear stairwell that led to an old gated freight elevator.

Danielle eyed the mechanical cage suspiciously.

"In there?"

"The auction is down below," Najir assured her.

Moore had said she'd be going underground, and Najir had indicated they would be bidding on items from somewhere beneath the ballroom, but considering the way they were dressed, Danielle had assumed it would be a lower level of the museum or library.

Half her instincts nagged at her to turn away, to beg off and ask if there was another way down, or decline completely. But the rest of her thoughts focused on what was still at stake, the fact that she had her own weapon, and the fact that she was very dangerous if she needed to be.

She pulled free from Najir's arm and waved a hand toward the cage.

"After you."

He stepped onto the elevator, Danielle followed, and the thin man climbed in last and pulled the gate shut. He pressed the button and the bulky mechanics of the elevator clanked to life.

The car released with a jolt and began dropping into the darkness.

CHAPTER 25

With shouts and commotion and the wailing of the fire alarm echoing around him, Hawker stared into the recesses of the janitorial closet. He could not believe his eyes. As each flash of the fire alarm lit up the tiny space, he expected to see Sonia there. But she was gone.

He turned. "Sonia!" he shouted, adding his voice to the madness.

The *whoop, whoop* of the alarm drowned out any reply.

Either she'd found a better place to hide or . . .

He began to move, slowly at first, because he didn't want to believe what he was thinking. And then he ran.

He sprinted down the hall with the rifle in his hand, well aware that any security team that reached the floor would shoot him on sight.

He made it to the stairwell, where crowds were trying to force their way down.

A burly man got in his way. "Move!" Hawker shouted, shoving the man to the side.

Hawker needed to get to the stairs, but to go up, not down. He pushed through the crowd. Climbed over the railing and dashed upward.

When he broke out into the open night air he could see across a catwalk to the helipad. A French-made Dauphin

helicopter was winding up. Two armed men were dragging Sonia toward it.

Resisting the urge to shout to her, Hawker dropped to one knee, steadied himself, and fired. His first shot took out the man on her right, hitting him in the upper center of his back.

Sonia and the man on her left fell forward, sprawling on the catwalk. The thug reacted quickly. Turning and aiming, he fired back down the catwalk blindly, but there were only so many places an attacker could be.

As Hawker crouched, the thug moved backward, instinctively using Sonia as a partial shield.

It didn't matter. Hawker needed only one second of separation.

The thug shoved her in the helicopter and Hawker pulled the trigger, killing him with a head shot and sending him tumbling off the catwalk.

Before he could do more, shots fired from within the helicopter forced him to take cover. He tried to pop up, but at each hint of a move more shells pinged off the catwalk around him.

"Sonia!" he shouted.

There was no way she could hear him now. The roar of the helicopter had become deafening. As he felt the rush of the downwash, he knew the pilot had added pitch. The copter was taking off.

He fired blindly and then ran.

The copter was rising up, its landing gear stretching as the weight came off. Sparks and tiny pieces of shrapnel told him more gunfire was coming in that he couldn't hear. He dove, aimed, and fired again.

Half a dozen white-ringed holes appeared in the Plexiglas bubble at the front of the copter and the roar of the rotors instantly changed. The pilot slumped forward. The Dauphin rose up unsteadily, began tilting over, and then smashed back down on its side.

The rotors shattered, flinging shards of carbon composite material in every direction.

Hawker lay flat. A cut on his arm and one on his shoulder testified to how close the flying knives had come.

Glad to be alive and glad the helicopter hadn't gotten away, he looked up. A new wave of horror rushed through him.

The Dauphin had landed on its side, with half its tail over the edge and part of its landing gear caught up in the three-cable guardrail that surrounded the helipad.

The cables were stretching and their poles were bending and twisting as the copter tilted slowly, threatening to tumble off the edge.

Hawker ran forward and scrambled onto the shifting craft. He looked inside, aiming his rifle. The doors on both sides of the helicopter were open. Sonia was looking up toward him, her arms wrapped around a seat belt in a death grip. The strain on her face showed as she tried to hold on, and with good reason. A blond man with a ponytail had a bear hug around her waist.

He looked up at Hawker with a snarl. Beneath them, a thousand feet below, Hawker could see the street filled with cars and emergency vehicles.

Hawker reached in and grabbed her, but his added weight caused the helicopter to shift further. It creaked ominously.

"My arm!" Sonia cried.

"Hang on!" Hawker shouted.

A sound like that of a ricochet echoed through the night. The helicopter dropped a foot or more, as one of the three cables had snapped.

The jolt caused Sonia to slip. She screamed as her arm stretched unnaturally.

Hawker tried to get some leverage and pull her out, but there was no way he could dead-lift the combined

weight of the two of them. Holding Sonia with one hand, he felt behind him, found the rifle, and swung it around, aiming into the passenger space.

"No!" the ponytailed man shouted.

Sonia screamed with him, but the crack of the rifle drowned both voices out.

Ponytail fell, dropping into the darkness.

Hawker let the rifle go and grabbed Sonia with both hands.

"Pull!"

"I can't!" she cried. "It hurts!"

"Pull anyway!" he shouted, leaning back and trying to yank her out.

She came up sixteen inches or so, enough to get her foot inside the fuselage.

The copter shifted again and another ping and rip sounded as the second of the three cables snapped. The final cable wouldn't hold the weight for long.

"Come on!" he shouted, pulling with all he had.

Sonia screamed in pain, but she pulled hard and pushed off with her foot. Hawker leaned back, wrenching her toward him and pushing off with his legs as the last cable snapped.

He and Sonia fell backward as the helicopter dropped away.

Lying on the helipad, clutching her to him, he heard nothing but the wind for several long seconds. And then the sickening crunch of the impact below, followed by the echoing boom of an explosion.

In seconds the smell of burning kerosene reached them, and waves of black smoke began to drift upward and across the helipad. It didn't matter: She was in his arms and she was safe. They were both safe. Now all they had to do was get the hell out of there.

Hawker eased Sonia off him and then helped her stand.

Her face was white. No tears, no words. It looked like shock.

"Come on," he said.

He took her by the hand and led her back toward the shelter of the hotel.

A crowd of people had gathered there, watching the spectacle. One opened the door for him, some of them clapped. A figure stepped forward. It was James B. Callahan. The loudmouth was gone; he looked shaken but relieved.

"You're not security, are you?" he said.

"I am, I'm just not yours," Hawker said as he pushed on past.

Back inside the hotel, things on the eighty-first floor were less chaotic than Hawker would have expected. Twenty or thirty people had been injured in the shoot-out and a dozen killed, including the terrorists. But in the aftermath a sense of action had overtaken the crowd.

Where Hawker expected panic, there was little. With security now swarming through the room, a sense of calm was being restored. And because the fund-raiser was connected to the medical profession, many of the attendees were or had once been prominent doctors. Some of them seemed to revert almost instantly to their training.

In an impromptu scene of multicultural cooperation, jackets were discarded, sleeves were rolled up, and men and women sprang into action. In an instant there were people helping the wounded, attending to the distressed, saying prayers for those who were beyond help.

Holding her injured arm, Sonia stared at the scene as if in a trance. "Savi," she whispered.

"What?" Hawker asked.

Sonia looked up, more alert suddenly. "These people

came for me," she said. "That means Savi and Nadia are in danger."

"Savi and Nadia?" These were names Hawker didn't know.

"We have to get to them," she said, color returning to her face. "Please. We have to go."

By the time they reached the lobby, fire and police units had completely surrounded the building. A group of paramedics rushed past, piling into the elevator car.

The hotel's manager saw Sonia and the bloodstained dress.

"Praise be to God that you're alive," he said. "Are you badly injured?"

"No," she replied. "But I need a car."

He shook his head. "A car will never get through."

The gridlock outside was unimaginable. The causeway was thin enough to begin with, but the mangled wreck of the helicopter had taken out half the road. It now lay burning in the shallow water.

"Please," she begged. "I need to leave."

He studied her and Hawker for a moment.

"We have a boat," he said. "For tourists."

"Thank you," she said.

Moments later, Sonia and Hawker were on a small boat that the hotel used for tours up and down the Dubai coast. It took them across to the shore, where a car waited. Thirty minutes later they were in downtown Dubai as Sonia raced into an opulent apartment complex.

Three stories up, she pounded on a door.

"Savi," she shouted. "Savi!"

The door opened and a white-haired woman of sixty stood there. A shawl draped her shoulders and she looked shaken. She and Sonia embraced.

"We heard about the attack," the woman said. "We were so worried."

The woman stared at the blood on Sonia's dress.

"It's not mine," Sonia said.

Hawker guessed it had come from the men he'd shot around her.

"And who is this?" the woman asked suspiciously.

"A friend," Sonia said. "Someone I haven't seen in years. His name is Hawker."

The woman stepped back. The look of suspicion faded, turning into a look of surprise and then warmth.

"So you're the one," she said.

Hawker's brow wrinkled. "The one what?"

"The one who brought them out of the Congo," she said. "Ranga said you would help us. He wasn't sure he could find you in time."

"He didn't," Hawker said, sadly. "At least not in time for him."

The old woman looked away but she held firm, far less shaken by the news than Sonia had been. At least outwardly.

"That's not a surprise," she said.

"We need to talk," Hawker said. "But after what happened tonight, I doubt any of you are safe here."

He glanced around the apartment. There was utter order to the place, as if it had never been lived in. The sign of people who knew they might have to move quickly. "Looks like you're ready to go."

"We can be out the door in two minutes," Savi said, opening a closet that held suitcases, already packed. "Get your things," she said to Sonia. "And wake your sister. She's asleep."

More news to Hawker. He'd never known Sonia to have a sister.

"It's okay," a meek voice said from the darkened hall. "I'm already up."

Hawker turned.

A young child stood there, perhaps three feet tall. She came forward and hugged Sonia around the waist.

Hawker stared. The child wore exceptionally thick glasses. Her face was wrinkled, her hair white and thin, and her skin marked and discolored with spots.

At first, he thought it was a trick of the light or an illusion of some kind, but then she turned toward him, straightened her glasses, and smiled. Now he could see her plainly. And he found himself staring into the face of an eighty-year-old woman.

Sonia crouched down and wrapped her arms protectively around the child. "This is my sister," she said. "Her name is Nadia. She's eleven years old."

CHAPTER 26

Danielle Laidlaw held on as the antique elevator shook and shimmied and descended two levels. When it stopped it opened onto a corridor of sandstone walls. A sporadically lit hall beckoned with work lights and bare bulbs along one wall. Construction equipment rested on one side; other sections were roped off.

"What is this place?" she asked.

"As we rebuild the city we find more and more of our history," Najir said. He pointed to what looked like an excavation. "This section was once a Roman bath."

Three men waited there, two holding guns.

"This way," the thin man said, leading them on and following the hall to the right.

The corridor led them to a stairwell with a curved archway at the top. Old city architecture, cut from the sandstone.

"Where the hell are we going?" she asked.

The thin man stopped and turned. He glanced first at Najir but then responded to Danielle.

"The auction is down below. Forty steps. If madam cannot make it or is uncomfortable, I can inform the host that she has canceled. However, the deposit will not be returned."

Danielle exchanged glances with Najir and then stepped through the door.

"Madam will be fine," she said. "She just likes to know what she's getting into."

Their host stepped aside and held the door. Danielle went through first, with Najir following. They descended the stairs in semidarkness. Literally and figuratively they were getting in deeper, and Danielle felt less and less properly dressed for the occasion.

"We are passing through six thousand years of history," Najir said. "Down below are the first extensive catacombs ever discovered in Beirut. Phoenicians buried their dead there, as did the Romans centuries later. Some crypts are believed to contain the bodies of Crusaders from Europe."

"Just as long as we don't end up buried down here ourselves," Danielle said.

Finally the stairwell bottomed, and a few steps ahead they reached an iron gate that might have been built during the Crusades. Two men stood guard, weapons at the ready. They let Najir and Danielle pass through the gate.

"You sure about this?" she asked.

"We're safe here," Najir said.

During her time with the NRI she'd been through dozens of encounters and emergency situations. Her training had included survival school and other tests, the result of which was a supreme confidence in her ability to deal with any situation. But her instructors had a favorite saying, one they all seemed to repeat: *The good operatives can get themselves out of any situation; the great ones avoid the situations in the first place.*

As she looked at the gate and the walls and the narrow stairwell, Danielle felt herself walking into a trap, despite Najir's confidence.

Najir nodded his agreement and the two moved out into the hall, which ran in both directions. The floor and walls were wet, and water pooled in places.

The name Beirut meant "the Wells" in ancient Phoenician, and for good reason. The city had a high water table

and wells did not have to be drilled too deep to reach good, potable water. Here in the catacombs of the old city, they might have been close to that water table.

Not another soul was in view, but twenty yards farther a door beckoned. Muffled sounds were coming from beyond it. Najir knocked.

A bolt was heard sliding and then the door opened to reveal a large, brightly lit room filled with a dozen people, all dressed for the party upstairs.

The room was sandstone, like the rest of the catacombs, but swept clean. Modern track lighting illuminated the space, computer terminals were set up here and there, and a small wet bar stood in one corner. Alcoves ran off the main room in spots and another gate barred the far end. Walking in felt like entering a very private lounge.

A moment later the tall, thin man appeared, a new look in his eye. No longer the humble servant, he walked with an owner's pride in his step. Apparently he'd entered the room some other way.

"Now that we are gathered," he said, calling the group to attention, "please take your time and examine the items for purchase."

With an ancient key he opened the gate at the far end and the group filed through to examine the prizes.

Danielle moved slowly, trying to make some sense of things. The first two items appeared to be Greek or Minoan masks. The small clay Gilgamesh statue was the third item in the lot and the copper scroll was fourth. A clay tablet with Sumerian writing on it and the stone head of a statue from the first Persian Empire came next.

Standing next to these items was a four-foot staff with an iron tip on one end and silver barb on the other. The spear was known as a dory; this was the weapon of a hoplite soldier from Sparta, allegedly from the Greek golden age.

The final items were writings on papyrus. They would

need cleaning and restoring to be read, but if the information sheet was accurate they were written in Aramaic, like the Dead Sea Scrolls.

In a twist that Danielle found strange, some of the items were authenticated by newspaper reports and even insurance claims detailing their thefts from various museums and collections. All except the copper scroll.

"You see anything you like?" Najir asked.

"Not sure I like any of it," she said. "But Bashir was interested in that scroll."

"He called it the find of a lifetime," Najir said.

"Why is there no authentication?" she asked.

"Either it came directly from an excavation, not uncommon, or from a private collection," Najir said.

That sounded like a prime setup for a hoax. She studied the scroll's description. Forty inches long and marked with raised writing, it lay curled up like a poster or a giant metallic Swiss roll. A set of photos purporting to show the script unrolled looked like they'd been taken by an amateur in bad light. The abstract data listed no place of origin and nowhere could she find any type of translation suggesting what information the scroll held.

"If no one has looked at it—no one from the archaeological world—how do we know it didn't get hammered out in someone's garage?"

Najir shrugged. "Caveat emptor."

"Buyer beware."

He nodded. "You do what you must, but as I told you, Bashir is normally a seller. He does it to raise funds for the opposition in Iran. If he was planning on spending money, it would have to be for something very important."

Important to him, Danielle thought. But why it would matter to a geneticist or a doomsday cult trying to infect the world with a plague she couldn't possibly fathom.

"I could use a drink," she said.

"I'll get it," he said. "Make sure not to stare; it will only increase the cost. There's bound to be a shill or two down here somewhere."

Danielle smiled to herself, glancing around at the other patrons. She counted eight groups in all. Three couples and two men by themselves, all looking like the Mediterranean version of old money. In addition there were three other groups, including two Arab men—power brokers or their minions by the look of things—and a younger European man who sported a large ring and expensive suit but who didn't quite look the part of a dilettante.

As the man picked up a glass of wine, Danielle studied his hands. They were rough, with thick callous pads edging the top of his palm. This was a workingman, a proxy, not someone spending his own money. Maybe that's the way it worked down here.

Najir returned with two glasses of champagne. He looked disappointed.

"What's wrong?"

"I know some of these men," he said. "I'm afraid this is going to be an expensive evening."

Danielle laughed and took a sip of the champagne. She hated to admit it but she was starting to have fun.

A moment later, the thin man ushered them into one of the alcoves. Expensive chairs and a small table were placed there; matching setups graced each alcove, one for each of the bidding groups.

He placed an iPad in her hand. "This will tell you the bid on each item," the thin man said. "You can see each additional bid as it comes through."

"But not who makes the bid," she guessed.

"No, madam. Our buyers prefer to retain their anonymity."

"As do I."

The man scooted off, heading to the next alcove, and Najir sat down. He leaned over the table.

"You're not going to bid on everything, are you?"

"I might," she said. "But I promise not to *buy* everything."

Najir took another sip of champagne, seeming only slightly mollified.

A high-toned bell rang. "The bidding will now commence on item one," the thin man said.

Danielle studied the iPad. Within seconds, four bids appeared. As each new bid topped the old, a green bar tracked upward toward a reserve mark. The current bid was $120,000 for the Sumerian tablet.

"This is a pretty sophisticated setup," Danielle said. "How much do you know about it?"

"The thin man runs it," Najir said. "The art comes from all over, but mostly from Iraq. Sites there are still being looted, even as other items are discovered and returned. Some have been stolen, recovered, and returned several times already."

Danielle looked back at the iPad. The bid had reached $200,000, the reserve mark. It quickly went above that.

She noticed that the bids were numbered, just like the paddles at a regular auction. A good trick: it maintained anonymity while allowing the bidders to know whether they were bidding against one person in particular or the whole group, facts that tended to trigger different types of pride responses and drive the bidding higher.

The first item closed at $280,000.

Out in the center of the room, two guards secured the prize in a felt-lined, polished wooden box, and the thin man's voice came through the hall.

"Bidding begins on the head of Persian goddess."

This time Danielle pressed in a bid, $100,000: half the reserve.

"Be careful," Najir said.

As they spoke, the price doubled and then doubled again. To Najir's relief, Danielle laid off as a heated competition developed between two parties. It went back and forth several times until one of them withdrew.

"Four hundred and seventy thousand for a head," Danielle mused. "Wonder how much you get for the whole body?"

"More than we have to spend," Najir insisted.

In the center, the guards boxed up the statue's head, placed a wax seal against the edge of the case, and marked it.

"A seal," Danielle said. "For authentication."

"A formality," Najir said. "You don't steal from this kind of people, not if you want to stay alive."

The bell rang a third time and the bidding commenced on the Gilgamesh statue. It went quickly, and then they were on to the fourth item: the copper scroll.

The initial bid came in at $100,000.

A bid of $150,000 came in from number four.

Danielle bid $200,000.

Number eight bid $250,000. Number four raised that to $300,000 and Danielle topped them both.

Najir glanced at the number but said nothing.

The bid hit $500,000, from number four again.

Then $550,000 from Danielle, $600,000 from bidder number two, and $650,000 from number four.

"Be careful," Najir said. "They're baiting you."

Danielle didn't think so. In fact, she felt more like she was baiting them. If Bashir wanted this item so badly, forcing someone to bid into the extreme might make them a suspect in what had happened to him and Ranga.

A $700,000 bid came in from number eight, instantly topped by number four to the tune of $850,000. It seemed a huge raise, almost unnecessary; a nervous bidder trying to knock others out of the game, throwing money away.

She felt Najir wince as she entered $875,000 on the

touchscreen and then $925,000 after number four answered.

"I'd like to know who that son of a bitch is," Danielle whispered, but none of the alcoves faced any of the others. No bidder could be seen from where they sat, and even if they could be, the small taps of a finger would be hard to make out.

When $975,000 came in Danielle tried to top it, but a red bar on the iPad flashed. She tried again, but the same red bar popped up.

The thin man appeared. He whispered discreetly.

"Does madam have additional equity she wishes to pledge?"

She looked at him and then at Najir. "*Does* madam have additional equity that she could pledge?"

Najir clenched his jaw. And then slowly, appearing as if it pained him, he nodded.

"What limit?"

"Full credit," he said. "Three million dollars."

The thin man looked pleased. It seemed a killing was about to be made.

"Though we don't intend to use it all," Najir added, glaring at Danielle.

The thin man tapped his own iPad a few times and the bar on Danielle's screen turned green. She'd noticed that bidder number four had topped her by smaller amounts each time. She hoped that meant he was running low on funds.

She took a deep breath and typed in a new figure. One that would turn Najir green.

She pressed Enter and the screen cycled. The new bid was $1.5 million.

A collective gasp wafted through the room, emerging simultaneously from the other alcoves. Najir hung his head at the sound. He seemed to guess.

Danielle turned to show him but he held out his hand. "I don't even want to know."

She turned back to the screen, waiting for number four to top her bid. Waiting, and wondering what she might do if he did. And then . . .

The screen went gray and a window popped up indicating that she had been awarded the scroll. It requested a code for verification—in effect, an electronic signature.

With a little trepidation she handed the iPad to Najir.

"At least you're getting five percent," she said.

"Making five percent on my own money is a good way to go out of business," he said. Despite looking stricken, he typed in his code.

The deal was done. Danielle now owned the copper scroll Bashir had been interested in. Whether she had just wasted a million-five or gotten something worthwhile, she had no clue.

Before she could even think about it, there was some commotion down the hall.

It sounded like anger—no doubt from bidder number four. Sharp words were being exchanged, albeit in a hushed tone.

A glass smashed and Danielle heard the sound of someone stomping off. The heavy door opened, and then closed with a reverberating thud.

The thin man came to the center of the room, where he could be seen from all the alcoves.

"Bidder number four has decided to withdraw," he said. "But the auction will continue."

Danielle wished she knew who bidder number four had been; perhaps she could pry it out of the thin man. She had a hunch it was the false dilettante. She tried to lock his features in her brain: six feet tall, broad shoulders, dark curly hair, and wide-set brown eyes; his teeth were uneven and at least two were chipped. When she got the

chance she'd describe these details to Moore and have someone back at the NRI run the profile.

Bidding began on the next item, and Najir offered the iPad back to Danielle.

"Want to finish me off?"

Danielle smiled. Despite Najir's dour expression, she had no doubt that a U.S. government check would be forthcoming to replenish his bank account.

"That's all right," she said. "I've got what we came for."

She turned to where the guards were boxing up the scroll. They placed it in the case and moved to seal it, but as one of the guards poured the wax, a minor vibration shook the room.

It was very slight, almost unfelt, but enough to make the filaments in the track lighting dim for an instant and a few glasses clink almost inaudibly together.

Danielle glanced around the room. The burning candles moved sideways for a second, as if air had been sucked from the room.

No one else seemed to notice. Bidding on the hoplite's staff was still going strong; the sounds of whispers and quiet murmurs from the other alcoves continued. But the hair on Danielle's neck stood up.

"Something's wrong," she said.

Najir nodded.

"Let's get out of here."

She put the champagne glass down and stepped forward just as a heavier boom sounded.

Still distant, this one shook things more visibly. Dust snowed down from the rafters; bottles clinked together on the wet bar. A glass fell to the floor.

This time everyone noticed.

Danielle and Najir moved first, pushing toward the exit, but another explosion rocked the building, blowing the door open and sending a wave of dust barreling toward them.

CHAPTER 27

Danielle crouched down and covered her nose in an attempt to keep from choking on the dust.

Najir gave her a handkerchief, which helped a little.

"Do you think we should go?" he asked.

She wasn't sure. The explosion had sounded like a stun grenade used somewhere down the hall. She thought of the armed men they'd passed there.

Listening through the open door, she heard shouting, and then one of the guards stumbled into the main room, bleeding.

The thin man rushed up to him, and the two of them tried to close and bar the door; but just then it was smashed inward. Both the thin man and the Arab were flung away from it.

One of the auction guards fired a weapon and bullets began flying through the chamber. Danielle dove back into the alcove.

Lebanese words were shouted through the chamber.

"We are under arrest," Najir said, putting his hands up.

"Arrest?" she asked.

"It seems this is a raid."

"You guys own the police," she said. "It doesn't make any sense."

"Someone here must owe a bigger chit," he said.

The thin man backed into the alcove with them, hands

above his head. The uniformed troopers moved in, point-ing guns in each alcove, taking positions near the center of the room. Fifteen feet away, too far to lunge for. An-other figure walked by slowly, inspecting the situation. He seemed to be their commander. He looked briefly at Najir and Danielle and then moved on, examining the remaining artifacts.

Danielle's mind flashed back to what had happened in Paris. The men who killed Ranga posing as police. She thought about his statement, *They are everywhere and they are nowhere.* That could only be if they constantly seemed like others until revealing their plans.

"Something's wrong here," Danielle said.

"Yes, but it will be remedied," the thin man said.

"No, it won't," she whispered, quietly enough so the trooper facing them could not hear. "This isn't a raid—it's a theft."

"What are you talking about?"

"We have to do something or they're going to kill us all," she explained.

The thin man turned. "Are you insane?" he said. "Why should I listen to you?"

"Because I know who you are. You're the number two here. That Arab guy who just took the door in the face, he's your boss. He's an Iraqi. Just low enough on the totem pole not to get his own playing card, but I'm guess-ing you're one, too, and now you're his lieutenant."

"We are equal partners," he said.

"Great, didn't mean to insult you," she said. "But ei-ther one of you should be able to tell what you're seeing," she said, then elaborated. "Look at their shoes. Do those look like soldiers' shoes to you?"

The thin man glanced at the guards' footwear: They were hiking boots, not polished soldiers' boots like those of the men upstairs.

The leader walked by again, counting. He seemed to

be looking for something. His shoes were more professional, but they were a businessman's shoes, not combat boots.

"Imposters," the thin man whispered. "But what can we do?"

The leader of the faux troops stopped to speak with the two guards at the center of the room. Whispering in their own right, probably discussing execution orders.

"How did you get down here?" she asked.

"These are the catacombs. There are many ways."

Before she could make an additional statement, the leader stepped toward their alcove. Without a word he grabbed Danielle by the hand and dragged her from the spot. She did not resist much. But that was to the man's detriment, for he kept his grip halfheartedly.

As he glanced away toward the front door, Danielle flipped her hand, reversing the grip by grabbing the man's arm under his elbow and twisting it. Her other arm came down like a hammer and shattered his elbow.

At almost the same moment Najir shoved the thin man toward one guard and lunged forward, tackling a third.

Danielle whipped around, grabbing the hoplite's dory. She came up swinging, jamming the silver butt into the first guard's neck and swinging the spear end around, smashing it across the temple of the other guard.

Four of the men who'd broken in were down or occupied, but the others had begun firing.

Danielle and Najir ducked into separate alcoves as gunfire erupted. From the rear of the chamber the auctioneer's remaining security members returned fire.

The thin man scrambled to her side, crowding her.

"Get behind me," she said, shoving him farther into the alcove. She needed room to swing the spear.

"Faisal!" she shouted.

"I'm all right," a call came back. "Get out if you can!"

She turned to the thin man. "Where's the exit? The one you came in through?"

The thin man pointed toward the back of the room, but there was no way to make it without getting shredded from one or both sides. Shells cut close to the wall, blasting bits of the stone out.

She glanced forward. The men were dragging their injured comrades toward the front door, but they had something else with them. And from the size and shape of the box, Danielle guessed what it was.

"They have the scroll!" she shouted.

"Then I'd better get my money back!" Najir yelled.

The last of the men stepped near to the door, and then Danielle smelled something far worse than smoke. Gasoline.

As she looked around the edge, a book of lit matches was tossed through the closing door. It landed on a pool of liquid that could only be petroleum. In an instant the front of the room was ablaze.

The gunfire ceased but the smoke and heat grew quickly in the unventilated room.

"We have to go now!" she shouted.

Najir emerged from his alcove, limping and bleeding. Danielle grabbed him and supported him.

"I'm okay," he said. "I'm okay."

She looked at the thin man. "You'd better show us the way out now."

"This way," he said.

With the thin man leading the way and Danielle still carrying the dory in her hand, the group moved to the back, checking for survivors and dragging the wounded with them.

A stairwell opened beneath a trapdoor and the group took it down, arriving at a new level even with the water table of the city. A thin walkway ran beside a wide aqueduct filled with water.

The thin man pointed to a second stairwell he'd come down earlier.

It sounded like walking right back into trouble to Danielle. "They'll probably be watching it," she said. "What's this way?"

"I don't know," the thin man said.

Danielle looked at the Iraqi.

He shook his head.

"Let's find out," she said.

Along the thin edge of the aqueduct, they traveled into absolute darkness. At one point the ledge disappeared completely and they were forced to wade in the storm drain for a half mile before spotting a shaft of light prying its way through the pitch dark. Another stairwell, poorly lit, but it seemed bright and cheery after the darkness of the tunnel.

They pushed through it and made their way to street level. Danielle and the thin man pushed the heavy grate up and over and the survivors of the incident began to drag their way out and disappear into the night.

The thin man and his boss remained behind, huddling with them in an alley lit only by blue moonlight.

"I must thank you," the thin man said. "I should have known it wasn't a raid. We bribe all the right people."

"You can repay us with information," Danielle said. "Starting with the names of the people who were at this party."

"I cannot," the man said. "Not if I wish to live."

"What about addresses, where these people have their things delivered?" she asked. "Clearly no one walked out of here with a statue or a fifty-pound clay tablet or five-foot spear."

"Banks in London, Cairo. Office buildings in Abu Dhabi," he said. "They won't do you much good."

The man was afraid of blowback. "One name then," she said. "Your bidder number four."

"I told you, I cannot—"

"In case you missed it, he wasn't around when the soldiers came in."

The thin man hesitated, as if he was attempting to remember. He conferred in Arabic with the other Iraqi.

"He was angry about your last-minute infusion of cash," the thin man said.

"And he took the scroll," she said. "I didn't see them carrying anything else out. Ten to one this was the backup plan," Danielle said.

"I know him only as Marko," the thin man said. "His account is here, his vetting was Greek, his delivery address is in Kuwait—Kuwait City."

"And what about the copper scroll," she said. "Where did it come from?"

"A private owner," he said. "A man who buys and sells; he is not even a big player. I understand the scroll was found in the desert by Bedouins some years back. No one knows exactly where."

"Why would anyone want something that bad?"

The thin man shook his head.

"Come on," she demanded. "Half a dozen people have already been killed over it. It can't just be art."

"I have no idea what makes it so special to anyone. Until tonight, I expected few bids aside from Bashir. That is why it was originally paired with the statue."

She glanced at Najir. He looked increasingly bad; blood continued to flow from his wound. They couldn't wait much longer.

She looked back toward the thin man. "You have pictures of that scroll," she said, looking back toward the thin man. "Better pictures than what I saw?"

The thin man nodded.

"I need them," she said. "You get them to me, we're square."

The thin man spoke with the Iraqi for a second and then he nodded.

"Where do I send them?"

She pointed to her wounded host. "I'm getting Najir to the hospital. You get the pictures to him. He'll know how to find me."

CHAPTER 28

Carlsbad, California

On a day when the marine layer had burned off and the sun shone warmly over Southern California, Professor Michael McCarter sat on the rear porch of his son's house, babysitting his five-year-old grandchild. The boy was attempting to hit an oversized plastic golf ball with an oversized plastic club. So far the little guy had hit almost everything else around him, including both of McCarter's shins. But he hadn't given up.

The sound of the phone ringing got McCarter's attention. "You keep swinging," he said. "Grandpa has to get the phone."

The boy smiled with the type of gleam only a five-year-old could possess, and then whammed the head off one of the prize roses.

McCarter stepped inside, shaking his head and mumbling, "It's a Cinderella story . . ."

He closed the screen door behind him and picked up the phone.

"Hello."

"Professor," a female voice said.

McCarter did not struggle to place it—they were too close for that—but his emotions were mixed. On the one hand, he cared greatly for the person on the other end of

that line. On the other hand, he now wished it had been a telemarketer.

"Please tell me you're retired," he said, "and you need a reference or a place to crash."

"Afraid not," she said. "Looking for some help. Knowledge really. Got a minute?"

McCarter felt his throat closing up. He'd worked with the NRI for the better part of two years, first as a consultant and then as an operative of some kind—he still wasn't quite sure what his title had been. They'd turned out to be the two most thrilling, important, and mind-altering years of his life. They'd also been incredibly painful and dangerous. Having barely survived, he'd been damn glad when they were over.

Danielle and Hawker had been part of his world then, but he'd bid them farewell six months ago and hadn't heard from them since. Not that he'd expected to, at least not until one or both came to their senses and gave up risking their necks around the world.

"I'm finally walking without a limp," he said, thinking about the bullet wound that had almost cost him his leg.

"Don't worry," she said. "I'm not asking you to rejoin the team, just need your take on something."

McCarter felt somewhat relieved by that statement. "Are you with Hawker?"

"He's elsewhere right now. And I'm guessing he's got his hands full, although probably in a much more interesting way than I do."

McCarter wondered what she meant. He chose not to ask.

"So what have you gotten yourselves into now?" he said.

"I can't tell you," she said. "But I have photographs of an ancient scroll that need to be looked at. Not a normal scroll, either. It's made from pounded sheets of copper."

"Like the copper scroll from the Dead Sea," he said.

"So I'm told, although it's been said that this one is much older."

"Where did it come from?"

"Somewhere in Iraq," she said. "Or maybe Iran. Some of the writing on it is supposed to be Sumerian. Although it could be Klingon for all I know."

McCarter laughed. "I can work on the Sumerian for you. And I know a few Trekkies who can do the Klingon, if you need it."

"Good," she said. "I'm sending an encrypted email."

"What's the password?"

"The date our last adventure ended," she said. "Do you remember?"

It had been the culmination of years of research, a moment that had changed his perspective on what man was truly capable of.

"How could I forget?"

"Good," she said. "The file's on its way. Moore knows how to reach me when you have something."

McCarter knew how to reach Arnold Moore, and though he would have preferred just to deal with Danielle, he guessed she would be on the move constantly.

He looked around at the nice suburban setting he now called home. He was wearing flip-flops, a faded Hawaiian shirt, and some old comfortable jeans. He felt safe and secure and blissful in his son's house.

And yet the call from Danielle sparked worries in his mind. Worries for her and Hawker, worries for what they might be involved in trying to stop. Worries for his children and most of all for his grandchild.

"Should I be afraid?" he asked.

"You won't be in danger for doing this," she insisted.

"That's not what I mean."

Danielle hesitated; an ominous sign.

"It may be nothing," she said.

"But . . ."

"We're trying to stop something from happening," she said. "Something that none of us wants to see occur."

Of course they were. What else would they be doing?

"The scroll may have nothing to do with it," she added. "Or it might. It's just a lead we have to run down, but the quicker the better."

For a moment McCarter thought of digging deeper; if he pried she would tell him. She owed him that. But then he decided he didn't want to know. If the answers were too terrible, it would distract him.

"How bad is it?" he asked.

"Bad enough that I need all the help you can give us," she said.

McCarter took a deep breath. "I'll get to the file as soon as it comes in," he said. "I'll be as quick as I can."

CHAPTER 29

Hawker stood near the aft end of a forty-foot cabin cruiser as Savi piloted the boat away from one of Dubai's marinas. Behind them the lights of the city blazed into the night, obscured in places by the smoke rising from the base of the Burj Al Arab. The glare made it impossible to see anything else. No stars, no features on the water beyond fifty feet or so. Looking ahead it seemed as if they were sailing into a void.

In some ways, that matched the feelings Hawker fought to silence. The situation reminded him of the past, the dash across the Republic of the Congo and into Algeria he'd guided Ranga and Sonia on in a desperate attempt to escape dangerous men. But the facts were plain then, or at least he'd thought they were. He didn't know the facts here, not enough of them anyway.

He needed to press Sonia about her father, the people he'd been mixed up with and the work he'd been doing. That was all that really mattered, but the sudden turn of events—the revelation that Sonia had a sister and the young girl's odd condition—had stunned him, blinding him in a sense to what was up ahead.

Sonia had taken her sister into the forward cabin, bringing with her some medications and hoping to put her back to bed. She did not seem to be in pain, nor did she seem

undeveloped mentally. To keep her calm as they drove to the boat in the middle of the night, Sonia had practiced spelling and math with her. Then the little girl had picked up a book and begun reading on her own.

At first he'd guessed that maybe her aged appearance was just cosmetic, and then she struggled climbing into the boat, because of a knee that Sonia said was arthritic. And the thick glasses suggested vision problems like many older people had.

He suddenly remembered Ranga's questions about retribution and divine punishment and his speech about humanity living too long, a speech given before Hawker had even met Ranga, before he had even become a renegade. If Hawker had the dates right, it was the year before Nadia was born. Since then she must have been hidden with Savi: Ranga's sister, Sonia's aunt. Certainly the little child hadn't been with them in Africa.

Crazy thoughts ran through Hawker's mind. Thoughts he wanted to banish but couldn't. Could Ranga have done something to Nadia? Could he have administered some drug or experimented with some type of genetic therapy on his own child? Could Ranga have created a prototype of his life-shortening drug and given it first to his own child? Aging her, like the rats Danielle had seen in his lab?

He prayed it was something less evil, but he couldn't say it was impossible.

For one thing, that might explain why Ranga wondered about divine retribution even as he claimed not to believe in any God. The scientist messing with the code of life, an act previously reserved for the Almighty alone. It reminded him of Pharaoh determining the last of God's plagues by threatening to kill the son of Moses, destroying his own child and all the firstborn of Egypt in the process.

The door to the front cabin opened and Sonia came up from below. She reached out to Hawker, took his hands, and squeezed them in a gesture of thanks. He gazed at her face. The exhaustion showed through.

"I need to ask," he said. "What do you know about the men your father was mixed up with?"

Sonia looked away, let go of his hands.

"I don't know much about them," she said. "After we left Africa, Father and I went different ways. We had contact at times but . . ."

She looked back at him. "I told you, ten fallings-out, and at least nine reconciliations."

"Why?"

"Because I wanted a different life."

"So why go back to working with him then? I know you've had more contact than you're admitting," he said.

She looked away again.

"Why?" Hawker asked.

"For Nadia," she said plainly.

Somehow the child's condition played in this, but what mattered most was the cult, the danger.

"Why would your father work with a cult?" he asked.

"He had nowhere legitimate to turn, so he always ended up with these kinds of people."

"How long had he been working with them?"

"A year or so?" she said, her gaze falling away. "Did they hurt him?"

It was an odd question. "They killed him, Sonia."

"I know," she said. "Dying is one thing, but I just . . . I always feared that someone would hurt him. Make him suffer. There are worse fates than dying. In Africa they threatened such horrible things."

Hawker understood that thought. He didn't know how to answer.

"Please tell me he didn't suffer," she said.

He didn't want to lie to her, but she didn't need the details. "People like these don't let someone go easily."

She looked out into the blackness of the night, her body tensing as if fighting back tears. Hawker decided to change subjects.

"What's wrong with Nadia?" he asked. "What happened to her?"

Sonia sat down on the padded bench and studied Hawker.

"You mean, what's *happening* to her."

"Happening?" Hawker said. "As in *still happening*?"

Sonia nodded. "Yes. And unfortunately what's happening to her is happening to all of us."

"I'm sorry," Hawker said. "I don't understand."

Sonia brushed a strand of hair back over her ear and motioned to the seat across from her.

Hawker sat, guessing it would be a long story.

"She's aging," Sonia said. "Only far more rapidly than the rest of us are."

"You mean it's not just her appearance?"

"Nadia is only eleven," she said. "Nineteen years younger than me. Yet she has advanced osteoporosis. Her eyes are filling with cataracts; her skin is so brittle that if you grab her, she'll bruise or bleed. And soon, hopefully not too soon, she'll need dialysis because her kidneys are failing."

Hawker looked away, finding it hard to believe such a thing was even possible. If Ranga had done this . . .

"How did it happen?"

"It's a genetic disease," Sonia said. "They call it progeria, or Werner syndrome. It's caused by a defect in the way her DNA repairs itself."

"It's naturally occurring?" he asked.

"If you call that natural," she said.

Hawker took a deep breath. He was damn glad to hear that Ranga hadn't caused it, at least not directly. "What I mean is, no one did this to her?"

She looked away. "Only God, if you believe in that sort of thing."

Hawker believed in God. He'd seen enough horror in the world to make him angry at God and wonder where He was, but he'd also seen what he considered miracles.

"Is there any way to stop it?"

Sonia smiled a half smile as tears welled up in her eyes again. She seemed lost like him, looking for answers that were not there.

"We're trying," was all she could say, wiping away the tears.

"We," Hawker noted. "You and your father?"

She nodded.

"Is this what you were working on in Africa? Is that what this has all been about?"

She took a deep breath. Hawker guessed he was right, but he wanted to hear it from Sonia, he wanted to understand finally what had been hidden all this time.

"My mother died giving birth to Nadia and a year later we detected the disease in her. Father tried to convince the company he was working for to fund some research, or to allow him to use their equipment to do his own research on his own time. But no one wanted to help."

"He worked on it anyway," Hawker said.

"He did it without their knowledge. Maybe that was foolish, but what else could he do? When they found out, they were furious. He took the data, the samples, and what money he could and he ran. I had just finished my sophomore year at Princeton. I wanted to help. I forced him to take me with him."

She looked to the woman piloting the boat. "Nadia went with Savi. I went with Father, first to Costa Rica

and then Africa. We thought that in the right place, a place with no restrictions, we might find the answer in a year or two."

She laughed sadly. "Didn't exactly turn out that way."

"That's why he stalled in the Congo," Hawker guessed. "He thought you were close."

"Father always thought we were close."

Hawker was beginning to understand Ranga's fanaticism. He'd always wondered how a man could seem kind and good and yet knowingly endanger his daughter the way he'd endangered Sonia. But he was trying to save the more helpless of his children.

He glanced toward the forward cabin where the young girl was sleeping. "So what causes it?"

"There are different types," she said. "In Nadia's case, structures in her DNA that we call telomeres are rapidly shortening. We all have them. Every time our cells divide, the telomeres shorten. It happens in all of us, but in her case, they shorten far too much with each regeneration.

"Some progeria patients are affected in a different way—they don't get cataracts or all the signs of aging—but Nadia has a form in which virtually all her cells are affected. Her telomeres are all but used up."

"Used up?"

"Without a breakthrough, she'll die of old age before she turns twelve," Sonia said.

The words hit Hawker like a ton of bricks. They reminded him of another child he'd met who never had the chance to live.

"So all this," he said. "The money, the research, the lies to people who wanted other things from him: All of that was for her?"

Sonia nodded. "Would you do any less?"

Hawker grew silent, hoping he would do as much.

With a better understanding of Ranga's obsession and even his odd dealings with those who'd acted as bene-

factors, Hawker considered the current situation. Ranga had been working on something in secret. His lab in Paris proved it. But if the data Danielle found was correct and the information in Ranga's notes was true, it sure didn't seem like he was headed in the right direction.

Sonia's company, Paradox, seemed to be closer, although glossy ads and a slick sales presentation didn't mean they'd discovered the fountain of youth. And then there was the matter of trial 951.

"What about Paradox?" Hawker asked. "Your father is listed as one of the founders. Is that why he started it?"

A look of disdain came across Sonia's face. "Father started Paradox to move money about," she said. "I was the one who realized we could do more."

Sonia's aunt joined the conversation. "And he never agreed with it," Savi said. "He told you it was too public. He said something like this would happen."

"To him," Sonia clarified. "There were people looking for him, not me."

He'd obviously stumbled on some long-simmering argument. Something he didn't have time for. "Does your company have a solution for Nadia?"

She hesitated. "Not yet," Sonia said. "But we're working on it."

"So the big shindig at the top of the hotel . . ."

"We need funding," she said. "No one wants to cure progeria. At least not businesspeople."

"I would have thought—"

"Progeria is extremely rare. It would cost ten thousand times more to develop a treatment than you could ever make selling it. Even if you sold it for a million dollars per dose."

"Can't you get grants?" Hawker asked.

"Not with my family name," she said. "Besides, dribs and drabs of money won't save Nadia."

Hawker understood. As in many other things, economics drove the bus. "So you sell the idea of eternal youth to those who might spend ten million."

Sonia nodded back toward Dubai. "There are people in this world with money to burn. People with millions and billions that are just sitting in the bank doing nothing—even in these times. If Father taught me anything, he taught me that."

She shrugged. It was just a fact.

"With that kind of wealth the only downside to life is that it ends."

"This was your idea."

"Father kept looking for someone to take pity on him," she said. "I chose to find people who would *beg us* to take their money. With Paradox we'd have unlimited funding and we wouldn't have to run or hide or lie about what we're working on like Father always did."

There was a new sense of pride in Sonia's voice as she spoke. Paradox was her creation, not just another step following in her father's footsteps. Hawker had to admit it was a brilliant move. And by basing Paradox in a nation without stringent standards or an entrenched bureaucracy like the American FDA, she and her fellow researchers could do almost anything they wanted.

"Long life equals big money," Savi noted with some disdain. "But if it's just for the rich, how does it make this world a better place?"

"I don't care about the world," Sonia said. "I care about Nadia. And Father. Paradox was their way out. It would have worked, for both of them. But now . . ."

Her voice trailed off as if she realized that that particular dream was shattered beyond repair.

Savi shook her head. "Your father wanted to keep the research secret. That's why he did the things he did. Why he went through all he went through."

"I went through it with him," Sonia reminded her.

Savi nodded. "I'm sorry, Sonia," she said. "He didn't want people to live forever."

"I heard a speech he gave once," Hawker said. "He talked about forced sterilization, culling the herd. Was he really that radical?"

Sonia looked embarrassed at this revelation. "Father didn't really believe in those things. He was just trying to make a point. What he wanted was birth control and responsibility and family planning."

Savi spoke up. "When Ranga and I were children, Mr. Hawker, we traveled with our mother. She was a nurse. She went on missions to the poorest parts of the world. Slums like Dharavi, outside Mumbai, or Kibera near Nairobi. The poor live there among filth you couldn't imagine, crawling all over one another like ants. They survive just long enough to have more children and increase the population and suffering. Medicines and food are delivered by those who wish to help. People like our mother. And so fewer die in childbirth, fewer die in childhood, and ever more are confined to utter misery."

Hawker remained quiet.

Savi turned toward him. "Have you ever been to a place where parents burn their children with scalding water, Mr. Hawker? Or poke their eyes out with a stick so they will be more pitiful when they go and beg? Or kill them because they cannot afford to have one more mouth to feed?"

"You'd be surprised where I've been," he said, coldly.

"Then you understand why my brother spoke as he did," she replied.

As Hawker listened he got the feeling that Savi and Sonia had practiced defending Ranga for a long time. And in a way, Hawker did understand. In the poorest, most overpopulated parts of the world, Western help in the form of medicines and food had wreaked havoc. In lands where large numbers of children were the norm because

so few survived to adulthood, Western efforts had changed the equation drastically.

Where once a family had ten children and counted on two or three to become adults, now nine or ten did. Five generations used to take the population from four to twenty; now it took them to a hundred or more. There was simply not enough food or jobs or water or land for such growth.

But to pretend that only evil and misery came from such places was a conceit of the rich and a lie. He'd seen great love and affection and joy in some of the poorest places he'd ever been to.

"I'm not judging him," Hawker said. "I'm only trying to understand. And to figure out who took his life and stop them from harming anyone else, including the three of you."

For a second Savi looked embarrassed. "I'm sorry, it's just . . ."

"It's okay," he said, then turned to Sonia. "I'm sorry I couldn't get to your father in time. But he mentioned a breakthrough. Said he was near the answer. I think the people who killed him were after that. Do you know what it was?"

Sonia's face brightened. Her eyes found Hawker and appeared both tremendously innocent and somehow prideful and strong and wise all at the same time.

"After years of pure research, Father decided to take a different route," she said. "He studied animals blessed with long life spans, tortoises and parrots and things like that. And then he worked with stem cells, and compounds that could affect those stem cells."

She glanced toward the forward cabin.

"Some of mine have been given to Nadia. They're a part of her now. It seems to be helping."

"And the breakthrough?"

"Father became convinced that if a genetic defect that

destroyed telomeres existed in nature, then the opposite must already exist somewhere as well. He began to research stories of long life and even legends of immortality. It seemed so very odd, but he felt there would be some truth to whatever stories existed.

"He became friends with a man named Bashir, an Iranian archaeologist. They were quite a pair. Two bitter old madmen, it seemed. Father looking for immortality and Bashir chasing a dream he said he'd once lost in the desert sands."

"What dream are we talking about here?" Hawker asked, recognizing Bashir's name.

"Bashir's great obsession," she said. "Every equal of my father's. He claimed he'd once found the grave of Adam. And clutched in Adam's hand was a scroll of copper, which Bashir had become certain would lead him to the Garden of Eden."

Hawker felt as if he were treading water, reaching for the bottom with his feet only to find each time that there was no ground beneath him.

"The Garden of Eden?"

"I know how it sounds," Sonia said. "But Bashir believed they could find it, and Father believed he could save Nadia with what he would discover there."

Hawker fought to contain his skepticism. "And what would that be?"

"A miracle from God, to some. A miracle of science, to my father," she said. "The hope of immortality."

He looked at her. "Immortality?"

She nodded. "In the book of Genesis, it was called the Tree of Life."

CHAPTER 30

Scindo stood with Cruor in the same darkened room in which he had been named. He was here for a different reason now. Another man stood in front of them, an older man with gray hair and reddish brown skin. Cruor called him Bashir.

"We have something for you," Cruor said.

"I want nothing of yours," Bashir said.

Cruor laughed, a deep, sickly laugh.

"What I give you was never mine, but once it was yours. Or so you say."

From Bashir's features and accent, Scindo knew he was Middle Eastern, Persian as opposed to his own Arabian heritage. Why he was present, Scindo didn't know; that he'd been beaten was obvious. There were bruises around his face, and he hobbled when he walked.

He was also missing an eye, but that scar was old.

"You were friends with Ranga," Cruor said to the prisoner. "He told us what you believed."

"You tortured it out of him."

"This was before we caught both of you, before Ranga had betrayed us."

"You murdered him for leaving you," Bashir said.

"No," Cruor said. "We punished him for betrayal."

"What right do you have to punish anyone?" Bashir asked, straining, angry.

"We claim the right, as gods have done for millennia," Cruor said. "Ranga understood this. He was part of it. He knew the punishment. We all know it."

Cruor carried with him a long cardboard tube, which he placed down. Scindo did not know what lay inside.

"I won't help you," Bashir said. "I have been tortured before. What can you do to me that they have not already done?"

Cruor reached out and grabbed Bashir by the face, pulling him closer and examining the old scar.

"We can do worse," he insisted. "I promise you."

Cruor released Bashir and shoved him backward into a chair. He picked up the long cardboard tube and opened it.

Scindo had expected to see a weapon, a spear or a sword or some kind of blade. Instead what he saw looked like a thin, curved piece of metal.

Cruor placed it down on the table and began to unroll it.

Bashir stood. He moved forward slowly, as if drawn to the table.

As Scindo watched, Cruor unbent the copper sheet, rolling it out with great effort and precision. Eventually, when the sheet had been made somewhat flat, he and another man clamped the edges to the table.

Scindo stared. He saw that symbols had been pounded into the copper.

"You have been looking for this half your life," Cruor said. "We give you a chance to read it."

Bashir looked up.

"Be careful you do not lie to us. We will have others to check what you say."

"Why would you care?" Bashir asked. "It's ancient."

"It exposes the lie," Cruor said.

"What lie?"

"The lie of God," Cruor said.

Bashir looked confused.

"For one small act of disobedience, God cast humanity from paradise. For one mistake He confined us to a harsh life and to certain death. Some go to heaven and some to hell, or so we are told. But if a man can live forever, he has no need for heaven or hell or the claims of a false god."

Bashir struggled to respond, but he looked as if he did not know what to say.

"It is the first lie!" Cruor shouted. "All the other lies have come from it. Go to any corner of the world. There you will find men begging a god they cannot see for forgiveness, for life. We will not beg for what we can take . . . and give if we choose."

Bashir backed away. Cruor grabbed him.

"Look at it," he said.

"You're insane," Bashir said, panicking. "All of you, more insane than those who kill for greed or lust."

"The truth is written there!" Cruor shouted. "You said it yourself."

"No," Bashir said. "I will not show you."

Cruor shoved Bashir's head toward the scroll, slamming his face into it. "You will show us the way."

"Go to hell," Bashir managed.

Cruor pulled him back and struck him across the face, sending him flying into the wall.

Remaining on the floor, Bashir cowered as far from the Man of Blood as he could get.

Cruor motioned to another member of the brotherhood, who grabbed Bashir and dragged him forward. With a knife, Cruor cut Bashir's hands free. Then, one by one, he chained them to the rails where Scindo's hands had been cuffed days before.

"Scindo!" Cruor shouted, pointing to Bashir's feet.

Scindo dropped to the ground and shackled Bashir's

feet. Despite the man's struggles, he quickly pulled the straps tight so Bashir could no longer move.

"What are you doing?" Bashir shouted.

No answers.

Cruor moved toward a door. The other member of the brotherhood removed an acetylene torch from a rack and turned the handle for the gas.

With a spark, the flame lit. A jet of white and blue.

"I'll read it," Bashir said. "I'll tell you what it says."

Scindo knew it had to be done, but he felt sick inside. He looked to Cruor, who paused in the doorway as the man with the blowtorch moved up beside Bashir.

"Wait," Cruor said.

Scindo's heart pounded in his chest; a sense of relief swept over him. The Persian had come to his senses. Perhaps Cruor would spare him.

Cruor smiled at the man with the torch.

"Have Scindo do it," he said with finality. "He must earn his stripes." And then he stepped out and slammed the metal door shut.

CHAPTER 31

Hawker stared dumbfounded at Sonia. He remembered the branding on her father's chest, the verse from Genesis. He knew that Ranga had been interested in ancient artifacts, and that Bashir had been a noted seller of such things—that's why Danielle had gone to Beirut—but what Sonia had just told him sounded patently absurd.

"The Tree of Life?" he said. "As in Adam and Eve, don't eat from this tree or you'll die, Tree of Life?"

"Actually," she said, "Adam and Eve were allowed to eat from the Tree of Life. And in doing so they remained young and healthy and immortal. It was the Tree of Knowledge that they were warned against eating from."

"Right," Hawker said, trying to remember his Sunday school teaching from so long ago. "And your father thought this was real?"

A question came from Savi. "Don't you believe in the Garden of Eden, Mr. Hawker?"

"On a physical level?" he said. "No."

"Interesting," she said. "So the Fall of Man, the doctrine of Original Sin, God's punishment for us: Are these not things you accept?"

The last thing Hawker had expected this evening was a discussion of religious doctrine. Still, he felt the need to answer, as if Savi was testing him somehow.

"The fall of man—I see it every day," he said. "But we're capable of great good and righteous sacrifice ourselves." This was something he'd almost lost belief in until recently. "As far as Original Sin goes, I have enough of my own to worry about."

"And God's punishment?" she repeated.

There was definitely a test in her words somewhere. As if she was probing for an answer.

In truth, much of what religious groups called God's punishment made little sense to Hawker. The soldier guarding the Ark of the Covenant getting hit by lightning for touching it as he tried to stop it from falling to the ground. Moses doing everything God asked but being forced to wander the desert for forty years and then barred from entering the Promised Land because he had one moment of arrogance. It all sounded a little harsh to him. A little too human, like the men who wanted to instill a doctrine of absolute obedience regardless of right and wrong. Something he had always railed against.

"I've done plenty of things God would be right to punish me for," he said. "But Adam and Eve? They took the apple—or whatever it was—after being tricked by the serpent. If I remember rightly, the Bible even mentions that the serpent was filled with guile the likes of which Adam and Eve had never seen."

"The serpent was the devil," Savi noted.

"I know that," Hawker said. "But my point is this: If God is all-knowing, then He had to know what would happen when the devil found Adam and Eve in the Garden. And if He's all-powerful, then He could have stopped the serpent from getting in there in the first place by snapping His fingers. So Adam and Eve made a bad choice. But to some extent—if you believe it all really happened that way—then somehow God was partially responsible. And punishing humanity for that makes no sense to me.

Would you punish your child for being tricked by a predator that you allowed into their world in the first place?"

Savi smiled. "You seem very intense on this point."

"Men twist God's words," he said. "And it's usually those who claim divine authority."

"But you believe?"

"In God, yes. In man's descriptions of Him, some of them very much. Others don't seem like they're talking about the same guy."

Savi looked at Sonia and then back at Hawker. "So you are a man of faith, but you reject some teachings and accept others," she said suspiciously.

"To accept everything you're told or to reject everything you hear are the two signs of fanaticism," he said. "And I reject that above all else."

She nodded. "I see. And so if God didn't know what would happen in the Garden, then He's fallible. And if He did know, then He's culpable. Is that what you're saying?"

Hawker was done playing games. "I'm saying the least He could have done was hire a gardener to kill the snake."

Sonia laughed and Savi's smile continued. "And if He didn't?" Savi pressed.

Hawker wondered what she was getting at. "Then it's because the whole thing is a metaphor. We're all innocent till we fall. We all make our own choices. You, me, everyone. We're all Adam, we're all Eve."

Sonia looked over to Savi, who suddenly seemed less excited. Perhaps it wasn't the answer she was looking for.

"He sounds like Father," Sonia said.

With that, it came to Hawker that he'd had a similar conversation with Ranga a decade earlier. Right before Ranga had left Africa. Had he already been thinking along such lines back then?

"Yes he does," Savi agreed, the slightly sour look re-

maining on her face. "He also sounds like Pelagius, who suggested a similar thought in the fourth century."

"I don't know who that is, but he sounds like a smart man," Hawker said.

"He was a British monk who became very influential," she said, "until Saint Augustine and the Council of Carthage declared him a heretic in 418."

Hawker nodded ruefully; he'd walked into that one. "Too bad I wasn't there, I could have backed him up," Hawker said, willing to offer assistance based on his general distrust of authority and a high esteem for anyone who questioned it.

"I'm thinking your help will be of much higher value here," Sonia said. "And at any rate, it's not the theological argument that matters to me. Or that mattered to Father. It's the physical reality we're interested in."

"Right," Hawker said, remembering where they'd started. "You're telling me the Garden of Eden was a real place. Where God put Adam and Eve until they sinned. And your father and Bashir had figured out how to find it."

Sonia took over. "Not exactly," she said. "God may have had nothing to do with it."

Hawker stared at her.

"Let me explain it this way, so that you won't think were crazy," she said. "How much do you know about genetics?"

It was the second time in three days someone had asked him that question. Since he'd answered Danielle, some guy named Yang had given Hawker a two-hour crash course before sending him to Dubai. It hadn't helped much.

"More than I want to at this point," he said. "And that we're all related to viruses."

"Genetics teaches us things," she said. "It lets us track

the migration of *Homo sapiens* by following mutant genes. A mutant gene that misses a population tells us that population has branched off before the gene appeared in human code."

"Okay," he said. "And . . ."

"And it tells us there are different ways to attack different problems. For instance, with aging, some animals have slower rates of aging and thus longer lives. There's a trade-off in what they are able to accomplish in those lives, but the fact of the matter is they live longer.

"Other animals have extremely short lives but reproduce rapidly, ensuring the survival of the DNA. Plants live tremendously long lives in some cases. There are trees on some ancient mountains that were alive when Christ walked the earth."

"So trees live long lives," Hawker said. "That doesn't mean they're the Tree of Life."

"No," Sonia said. "Only that they've found one of the secrets. Another form of life that's found a different type of the secret is *Turritopsis nutricula*, a kind of jellyfish that grows into adult stage, reproduces itself, and then, instead of dying, reverts back into a juvenile phase. Instead of a linear life span, this creature lives a circular one. Old then young, and then old and then young again. Ad infinitum, at least until something eats it."

Hawker remembered Lavril, the French commandant, mentioning that Ranga was covered in jellyfish stings. Could this have been the reason?

"Did your father work with these everlasting jellyfish?"

"He did," Sonia said. "But they act on a different principle than what Nadia needs. *Turritopsis nutricula* reaches maturity and then reactivates its stem cells. Starting over. In essence, it's not that it doesn't age, it just ages in both directions. Nadia, and all of us, we're far more complex

organisms. While reactivating our stem cells might help, the problem in Nadia's case is that the new cells they create will still have the same genetic code and thus the same genetic defects as the old ones."

"She needs something more," Hawker said.

"We can't just turn her aging switch off, or start her cells over. We have to rewrite her genetic code so that the new generation of cells she produces are free of the progeria defect. Over time she will grow young again, even as she grows to maturity."

"And how do you do that?"

"You find a gene that resets the telomere chains in Nadia's cells and then implant it into every cell in her body."

Hawker considered the data Danielle had discovered in Ranga's Paris lab and the information Moore had given him on the UN virus. The gist of it was viruses being used to infect people. A 90 percent cellular infection rate or something. He guessed this was what they were getting at.

"You use a virus to do the implanting."

Sonia nodded. "With the right kind of virus, a virus that attaches to human cells but does not destroy them, we can implant whatever we want into human DNA."

Hawker thought again of the data Danielle had found, including a trial that indicated 90 percent success rate in infectiousness but was rejected because the mortality rate was unacceptable.

He, Danielle, and Moore had assumed that meant human mortality. And that it had been rejected as unacceptable because the mortality rate was not high enough to achieve this perfect weapon. Now he was thinking just the opposite. Perhaps this trial had been deemed unacceptable based on the cellular mortality rate. And not because it was too low, but because it was too high.

"You have the first part done," he said, guessing but pretty certain.

Sonia nodded. "Father did. He sent me the data a month ago," she said. "I swear I haven't seen him for ages, but he contacted me out of the blue."

A desperate act, like reaching out to Hawker. Most likely Ranga knew or feared what was coming and didn't want it to end.

"Trial 951," he said.

She looked surprised.

"I saw it on your presentation."

Her face relaxed. "Yes. Exactly. We have the delivery vehicle, the carrier. Now we just need the DNA patch to put inside it."

"Trial 951 shortened life spans in your father's tests," he said.

"It doesn't have to," she said. "We can engineer it to do the opposite. We just need to find the right payload."

"In the Garden?" he guessed.

"All viruses have a host," she said. "A reservoir where the virus rests not destroying or harming them. Ebola, Marburg, all of them, they exist somewhere, dormant or semidormant until they come into contact with people. Why do you think they called it the swine flu or the bird flu? Because those animals are the reservoirs."

"And in this case?"

"Somewhere in the ancient world there was a tree," she said. "And from that tree came a fruit, and within that fruit rested a virus. A virus that changed the DNA of those who ate it, lengthening their telomeres and giving them incredibly long, maybe infinite lives.

"The ancients didn't know why," she added. "All they knew was that those who ate from this tree seemed to live forever. They prescribed it as a miracle sent down from God. They called the place where the tree grew the Garden of Eden and tree itself was named Life."

Hawker understood now where they were going. Sonia spoke once more to clarify.

"It's not mysticism," she said. "It's not religion, it's not spirituality. It's science. And if we can find it, we can save Nadia."

CHAPTER 32

Barton Cassel stepped out of an elevator into the basement garage beneath the CPC building. The tension in his body had been undeniable all day long. He hadn't eaten, he hadn't slept, several stiff drinks had done little to calm him down.

After making a good show of work for three hours it was time to go, before anyone noticed what he was desperately trying to keep from telegraphing to the world: fear.

His bulletproof Lincoln Town Car coasted to a stop beside him. One of Cassel's bodyguards climbed inside. Cassel followed.

The car made its way through the parking garage and out onto the main street. Cassel reached for the decanter in the center console nook, hoping the fifth dose of Glenfiddich 40 might do what the other four had failed to.

He'd gone against the wishes of his psychopathic and now unwanted associate—the man who called himself Draco. He'd tried to grab Ms. Sonia Milan during the one moment she popped up to the surface, her fundraiser in Dubai. And he'd failed.

It had all gone terribly wrong. And while no one had put the details together, the CNN broadcast looped endlessly, replaying the sight of a burning helicopter at the

base of the tower, security forces racing around with machine guns and walkie-talkies, and then the dead bodies, including one that had fallen from the tower with a bullet hole in its skull.

Cassel poured the whiskey. The $2,600 bottle was supposed to be sipped, allowed to evolve and breathe like a wine. Cassel gulped it down and tried to remind himself of the layers of insulation between him and the men who'd raided the tower.

His contact worked with a middleman, and that person had hired the leader of the group; the leader had in turn hired the rest of the men.

If the group's leader was among the dead, that might break the trail right from the start. But if the man had survived and rolled over on the middleman . . . He wondered how long trouble would take to work its way up the line.

The fact that his contact was no longer reachable scared the hell out of him. What other reason could he have for not answering?

Glancing out the window, Cassel hoped the leader of the commandos was dead. That would do it. That bastard dying would do just fine.

Another sip of the Glenfiddich and a few deep breaths calmed him. It would be all right, he told himself. Someone down below would be sacrificed and the rising tide would never reach him.

The rising tide.

He could see the ocean out the window. This wasn't the route to his home; it was the coast road that wound its way east along the cliffs.

"Driver!" he shouted. "Where the hell are we going?"

The driver turned and Cassel heard a spitting sound.

Thew! Thew!

The bodyguard slumped forward. Blood spattered on Cassel. He dropped the glass.

"What the hell?"

The car leapt forward, snapping Cassel's neck back and throwing him off balance.

Fear coursed through Cassel's body. He grabbed for the door handle, planning to jump, but they were doing sixty miles per hour, with a thin guardrail that might cut him in half if he hit it and an eighty-foot drop to stony beaches if he didn't.

"Go ahead," the driver growled. "Jump."

The Lincoln whipped through a turn that threw Cassel to the other side of the car. He ended up on top of his bodyguard, who was still alive but gurgling blood.

He pushed off. As the car reached a straightaway he regained his balance.

"Jump!" the driver shouted again. "Jump, damn you!"

This time Cassel recognized the sinister voice.

He looked forward and saw the tattoo peeking out of the driver's collar. "Draco!" he shouted. "Are you insane?"

"Your words," Draco said. He pressed a switch and the sound system came on. Cassel recognized his own voice over the speakers.

". . . *I'm not listening to this psychopath anymore. Find some guys, grab Ranga's little girl, and bring her to us.*"

Another voice replied, distorted by some type of voice-changing technology. "*It won't be that easy. She stays underground almost like her father.*"

"*She's going to be in Dubai,*" Cassel heard his own voice say.

"*That's high stakes.*"

"*Just do it! I don't care what it costs.*"

"*What about Draco?*" the distorted voice asked.

"*I want that freak watched 24/7,*" Cassel's voice said. "*He gets near this building again, kill him.*"

Draco whipped the car into another curve. And then

he threw something into the backseat with Cassel. The object landed next to him and Cassel looked at it out of reflex.

Partially wrapped in bloody white cloth were human fingers.

"He laid a hand on me," Draco said. "It was a big mistake."

Feeling like he might throw up, Cassel pushed the cloth onto the floor out of sight as the Lincoln accelerated more.

"What do you want?"

"I want you to jump," Draco said.

"Go to hell!"

Draco slammed on the brakes. Cassel wasn't ready. He slammed into the divider between the back and front seats. A tooth flew, his lip exploded in a spray of blood, and then the accelerator slammed down again and Cassel was whiplashed into the back.

"Remember your seat belt next time," Draco said, laughing maniacally and pinning the accelerator to the floor.

Dazed, exhausted, and scared to death, Cassel resorted to the only thing he had left. "I'll pay you. Two million, just like you asked."

"Too late."

"Five million, ten million!" he shouted. "Whatever you want!"

Draco slammed on the brakes again and threw the wheel over. The Lincoln skidded a hundred feet before coming to a stop by a cliffside view.

Cassel went for the door but Draco turned and fired.

Pain shot through Cassel and he grabbed his gut. Blood trickled from a small wound, oozing between his fingers.

Draco stared over the barrel of his pistol, made all the more menacing by the long suppressor attached to the front.

"Call," he said. "Make the transfer."

Cassel reached into his jacket pocket, pulling out his phone. He dialed, his hands shaking. He spoke a code.

"How much?"

"Ten million ought to cover it."

Cassel spoke another code. "Transfer ten million," he added. "Yes," he said. "Ten million. Immediately." A third code confirmed his authenticity.

Draco looked at his own phone and grinned as the funds appeared in his account.

He opened the door, keeping his eyes on Cassel.

"Never make a deal when you're not the driver," he said. "I learned that lesson the hard way. Now I pass it on."

He took a step farther away and Cassel began dialing 911. As he did, Draco tossed something into the car. Cassel focused on it, hoping it wasn't another body part. It was gray can with some type of appendage on the top.

An incendiary grenade.

Cassel grabbed the door handle, flung it open, and jumped out just as the explosion flashed through the car.

The blast launched him forward, over the edge of the cliff. He fell, covered in flames and trailing smoke. The stony ground rushed up at him. He hit with a sickening crunch, rolled once, and was engulfed by the flames.

CHAPTER 33

At his son's home in Carlsbad, Professor McCarter had spent seventeen hours poring over the photos Danielle sent him. He'd referenced, cross-referenced, and double-checked his work. And he still felt a surge of nervous energy pouring through him that made it difficult to sit still.

Needing to communicate with Danielle securely, he'd driven downtown in the dark of night, piloting a faded red Mustang along the I-5 freeway, through a corner of Balboa Park and a good chunk of San Diego proper before turning onto the Coronado Bridge, which took him up and out over sparkling moonlit water of the bay.

Arriving at the naval base, McCarter offered his driver's license. A quick check by the guard showed his name on a list and the gate began to go up.

McCarter saluted the guard, who didn't respond but leaned close to McCarter's open window. "You're a civilian, sir," the guard said. "Don't salute."

"Right," McCarter said. "Gotcha. Ten-four."

Ten minutes later, McCarter sat in a secure room with a scanner, a computer, and a flat-screen monitor for teleconferencing. As he waited for Danielle to dial in from wherever she was, he thought about what he'd found.

The copper scroll was an elegant solution to an ancient problem: recording things in a secure, portable manner.

Bark paper and papyrus were fragile, stone tablets were heavy—for some reason the Flintstones came to mind—but copper was soft and malleable. It was relatively light, especially when pressed into thin curved sheets. It had been mined for ten thousand years. It would not weigh a traveler down or break if dropped, or fade or burn or be eaten by moths.

There were some in the archaeological community who expected to find copper scrolls everywhere, recording great events or even transactions of travelers, but that hadn't happened. A few copper sheets had been found in various places (tin had also been used) and of course there was the copper scroll from the Dead Sea, but little else.

It was telling that the Dead Sea Scrolls, including the copper one, came from a group of outcasts. And that the information on the copper scroll was not the biblical information found on the parchment and papyrus scrolls, but directions to treasure hoards supposedly owned by those who'd written the scrolls. This was something they wanted to keep secret and avoid losing once they'd recorded it. Something they might have needed to bring with them if they moved, but could not allow to be destroyed either by fire or moth or time.

In a way, McCarter found a similar dynamic on the scroll in Danielle's photos. It contained something the writer had not wanted to lose, directions to something secret and of incalculable value even to those who lived seven thousand years ago. And based on the story it told, it seemed the writer needed that information to be portable, since he was on the run.

Figuring out what that information was hadn't been easy.

The first section of the scroll was written in a script known as Proto-Elamite. It appeared in a slightly different form than any examples he could find, but that

really didn't matter much, because whatever form it was in, Proto-Elamite was a dead language. No one knew what its strange symbols represented.

Fearing they were done before they started, McCarter examined the rest of the scroll. To his great delight he discovered writings in two languages that were known.

The first of these was a type of cuneiform writing. Cuneiform meant "wedge" and this type of writing used different wedge-shaped symbols. The particular style turned out to be Sumerian, a text that had evolved in southern Iraq sometime around 3000 BC.

Sumerian had been widely translated and was one of the most well-known scripts of the ancient world. Finding it, McCarter felt their luck improving.

On the last section of the scroll he found stampings in a style known as Akkadian or Eastern Semitic. This language was also known. It had been used mainly around 2500 BC across central and northern Iraq and into what was modern-day Syria. For the most part, Akkadian looked like different types of weirdly shaped arrows pointing in various directions.

Seeing this setup had sparked euphoria in McCarter's heart that had yet to subside.

The copper scroll was a trilingual inscription, and there could be only one reason for that: translation. It would be the equivalent of the Susa find or the better-known translational discovery: the Rosetta Stone.

Most knew the Rosetta Stone's connection with modern decipherment. Discovered in Alexandria in 1799 by one of Napoleon's soldiers, and then taken by the British in 1801, the Rosetta Stone contained a decree of an Egyptian king, handed down in 196 BC.

The orders had been carved onto its granite surface in three separate languages: ancient Egyptian hieroglyphics, Demotic or written Egyptian, and ancient Greek. By comparing the three writings, scholars had been able to

make the first real reading of Egyptian hieroglyphics and begin unlocking the secrets of the pharaohs.

With notable exceptions, most dead or lost languages could only be revived or learned this way.

Linear Elamite had been partially deciphered this way after a bilingual text had been discovered in 1905 in Susa. But Proto-Elamite remained completely unknown. It was so much older and more primitive that most scholars doubted it would ever be translated.

Staring McCarter in the face was the chance to prove those scholars wrong, the chance to unlock knowledge and history that until now were just interesting symbols on clay and stone. That fact alone was incredible enough. But the story McCarter found in the pressed copper was enough to make it seem almost irrelevant.

The information on the copper scroll was not just a random decree or royal accounting or even anything as momentous as a treaty between far-flung peoples. It was a message in a bottle, sent by someone trying desperately to ensure that their story would survive. As McCarter read it, he began to realize that a version of it had indeed survived, spreading around the world in languages that did not even exist when it had first been written down.

A soft pinging tone came from the monitor and the screen lit up. Moments later McCarter saw the classically striking face of Danielle Laidlaw.

After brief hellos, McCarter began to explain what he'd found.

". . . the story being told is a version of Genesis," he said. "It focuses on the Garden of Eden and the Fall of Man, though with many differences from the biblical account."

"That makes sense in some ways," Danielle said. "Does it mention weapons or plagues or anything like that?"

"No," he said, wondering why she would ask. "But it

does make the rather incredible claim that there was more than one Garden of Eden."

She looked stunned. "More than one Garden of Eden?"

McCarter cleared his throat. "Yes," he said. "Well, sort of. Not exactly. Kind of . . ."

"Professor," she said, stopping him in his tracks. "We've done this dance before. Can you just get to the main point?"

"Sorry," he replied. He cleared his throat. "The authors of this scroll talk about many gardens containing trees bearing miraculous life-giving fruit," he began. "They speak of one in Egypt, tended by the pharaoh's most trusted priests, and one in India, near the river Ganges, another in what is now Ethiopia, and even one in Macedonia or Greece."

"Okay," she said, "so there was more than one Garden of Eden."

"No," he said, correcting her again. "More than one . . . miraculous garden. *Eden* is the name of a place, an area, believed to be derived from the word *Edin* in Sumerian, which means 'open plain.' If we go with that concept, we find an *Edin*—an open plain—stretching across central Iraq where the Sumerian civilization thrived. It's mostly desert now, but seven thousand years ago it looked like the American Midwest in the time of the settlers. Horses, plentiful game, flowing grass. Somewhere in this area was one of these miraculous gardens. This would be the Garden of—or the Garden in—Edin."

"The Garden in the Open Plain," she said. "Doesn't exactly have the same ring to it. What else do you have?"

He could sense she was in a hurry, as always, but even though she seemed interested in the information only as pure information, McCarter felt certain that as he explained, Danielle would come to feel a sense of wonder.

"In the days before this scroll was stamped, the other miraculous gardens had withered and died."

He glanced at his notes. "One by one the others turned barren," he said, reading aloud and using his finger to mark his progress on the page. "They did not bear seed to plant new trees. They did not bear the seedless fruit that gave life to the aged. After a time of years, the first Garden was the last. The Garden in Edin still bore fruit."

"Go on," she said.

"The great drying came," he said, looking up. "I think this refers to something we call the 5.9K event. About six thousand years ago, northern Africa, the Middle East, and parts of Asia went from a relatively humid climate to the deserts we see today. The cause is unknown, but based on the type of seeds discovered and fossils in the record we know it happened rather rapidly."

She nodded, appearing to understand. "Go on."

"If this is what they mean by the 'great drying,' then we can peg the time of this scroll being written or stamped to somewhere between 3900 and 3400 BC."

"Okay," she said. "What else?"

"It goes on to say that word went forth as to barrenness of the Garden in Edin, but that was a lie, the trees continued to bear fruit."

"So the Garden in Edin was the last place these trees grew," she said. "Could that be the source of the Bible story?"

"Very possible," McCarter said.

He watched as Danielle scribbled down more notes. She seemed closer to frustrated than impressed.

"What else?" she asked, still not looking up.

"According to the scroll, an island known as something like 'the Table of Sand' existed in the center of a great river. Only the king of the people and the strongest and most honorable of his soldiers knew of its whereabouts. They kept it secret, guarded it day and night, and in return they received gold and onyx."

"Items also mentioned in the Bible," she noted.

He nodded and continued. "The kingdom became wealthy because they gave to the leaders of other lands the fruit of this garden, and those who ate of it lived for ages longer than those who did not."

At this point, Danielle exhaled and looked up. "That's all very interesting, Professor, but I'm afraid it doesn't help me much."

"Perhaps I could be more helpful if I knew what you were dealing with," he said.

She hesitated. "Maybe you're right," she said. "A radical group stole this scroll. They claim they can prove that God doesn't exist and that they've taken the power of life and death for themselves. Normally we'd write them off as lunatics full of talk, except they may be close to building a powerful biological weapon."

McCarter's heart all but froze.

"For some reason they're interested in this," Danielle continued. "Because of that, we are as well. Except it doesn't seem to have any connection to the threat, even if it means something symbolic to this cult."

McCarter thought about what she was saying, and tried to see the connection himself.

"Does it tell you anything of value? Anything beyond a different version of the Genesis story?"

"It tells you how to get there," McCarter said.

"To get where?"

"To the Garden in Edin," he said.

She paused, looking at him as if she'd heard him wrong.

"I thought the Bible already told us where Eden was," she said.

"It does," McCarter said. "Except the geographic description doesn't really make any sense. That's why people have been looking for it unsuccessfully for thousands of years."

He glanced at his notes. "The Old Testament or the Torah describes Eden as being in the east. That doesn't exactly narrow it down. It also describes rivers that either led into or out of Eden, but even here we find confusion. In addition to the Tigris and Euphrates, which we all know about, one river the Bible references is named the Pishon, which is said to flow around the entire land of Havilah, where gold and onyx are found. All this points us to Iraq, possibly Iran, but very definitely the Middle East. *Havilah* means 'stretch of sand,' by the way, which connects nicely with the 'table of sand' from the scroll."

"That sounds helpful," Danielle said.

"The problem is," he said, "it then goes on to describe another river called the Gihon, which flowed around the entire land of Kush. Unfortunately, Kush is strongly thought to reference a well-known kingdom in Ethiopia along the Nile. This is not just the work of modern scholars. The Bible constantly refers to Kush in connection to the Nile."

"I see what you mean," she said. "These are not very good directions."

"Not good for finding one place," he said, "But if there's more than one Miraculous Garden of Life . . ."

"Of course," she said, sounding impressed, "you never cease to amaze me."

"Thank you," he said, feeling very proud of himself.

"Can you tell me how to find one of them? Any one of them?"

"This scroll tells us of a specific journey *from* the Garden in Edin. And it gives it a marker that we could use to find it today."

"I still don't see why that would matter to them. How does finding Eden disprove the existence of God? It's like saying the discovery of Camelot would prove that King Arthur wasn't real. It's backwards."

"Unless," McCarter said, "something in Camelot proves that someone else was king."

"Maybe," she said. "But that's for theologians to argue. We're trying to prevent these freaks from obtaining whatever they need to finish this weapon. Unless you've found something like that in there, I'm afraid this is a dead end."

"Sorry," McCarter said. "Or maybe I'm not. Maybe I'm happy about that. But there's nothing in here about weapons or the power to kill or destroy."

She went silent for a moment, scribbling more notes, and he thought it might be the opportunity to ask a question.

"Are you going there?"

For the first time, she smiled. "You're not coming along if we do," she insisted.

"Of course," he said. "Not now, but I'll make you a deal. I'll tell you where it is, and once you and Hawker have gone in—done your thing and killed all the baddies—I get first crack at the excavation."

He paused. "That is, assuming you don't get yourselves blown up by terrorists, jailed by government authorities, or smote down by angels with flaming swords. Like those who are prophesied to be guarding the place."

"Angels with swords of fire," she said. "Maybe we should hope they are guarding the place. Might save us a lot of trouble and the world some agony."

"Maybe," he agreed.

"You know where it is," she guessed.

"Not yet," he insisted. "But there are enough landmarks in this description to give you a general area. From there you can begin the search. It might actually be easy to find."

As he spoke the words, McCarter remembered scoffing at a similar statement Danielle had made during their trip to the Amazon two and a half years ago.

"You realize the irony of what you're suggesting," she said.

He laughed. "Yes, but the Miraculous Garden in Open Plain of Edin has a marker, and with a little help from your friends with the satellites, we should be able to pin it down rather quickly."

She looked conflicted: part eager, part suspicious. He could only imagine the weight she carried on her shoulders. He guessed she hadn't told him the worst of it.

"Figure it out," she said finally. "I'll let you know."

CHAPTER 34

Hawker stood on a second-floor terrace. It overlooked a courtyard, complete with gurgling fountains, manicured palm and olive trees, and a twelve-foot wall topped with vicious-looking iron spikes, security cameras, and razor wire.

The up-lit palms soared past him, taking on new shades as the daylight faded and the dusk approached.

Traveling by boat through the night and half the next day, he, Sonia, Savi, and Nadia had made their way through the Persian Gulf to Kuwait. A slip at a private marina waited for their unnamed boat and thirty minutes by car had brought them here: Savi's home.

As he looked around, it seemed like Ranga's sister possessed a substantial amount of wealth, but according to Sonia it was all spent. The large house, the sloop they'd traveled in, all of it was mortgaged to the hilt and utterly dependent on Paradox getting funding.

With that in mind, Sonia had returned to business mode, spending the last hours of the day calling investors, talking with various members of the UAE security apparatus, and trying desperately to put a different spin on what had happened, one that might allow Paradox to rise from the proverbial ashes.

Yes, of course they would come back to answer ques-

tions. They'd only fled out of fear for their lives. No, they didn't know who had attacked them or why.

Hawker wondered about that. The thugs who'd hit them in Dubai were far more professional than the group in Paris. They were Caucasian men, not locals. And they were armed to the teeth and using a stolen helicopter. It was such a different mode of operation that Hawker wondered whether these were core members of the cult or another player. Like everything else in this mess, he could only ask the question. There were no answers.

And Danielle was faring no better. He'd received a text saying she'd lost out on the scroll but had their old friend Professor McCarter examining photos of it. She doubted it mattered much and Hawker felt the same.

Moments later a second message had come in from her. It read: *Have you figured it out yet?*

Hell no, he hadn't figured it out. It seemed like a bunch of puzzle pieces lying at his feet, but instead of a coherent whole it was like the pieces all came from different boxes with different pictures on the top. Not only did nothing fit, but even if you smashed them together and forced them to fit the result was a disjointed mess.

And so it went. As he waited for Sonia to finish, Hawker shared a cup of tea with Savi and Nadia, which the little girl proudly prepared and served. With teatime over, he wandered about, watching for trouble. Shortly after nightfall, he found himself in Savi's library.

He studied the selection.

A huge tome titled *History of the Middle East* rested side by side with various medical journals. Next to them were several works on the archaeology of the region, and then textbooks on genetic sequencing, two of which Ranga had written himself.

Hawker found little order to the arrangement. Not alphabetic or by type of book. Not even by subject.

A book on the Sumerian horse culture stood one space from a thick hardback called *Atrocities of the Crusades*.

"Haven't you guys heard of the Dewey Decimal System?" he wondered aloud.

The next book held a familiar title: *Paradise Lost*, the very book the cult had quoted from in their threat. He pulled the tattered copy from the shelf. Several pages were dog-eared. He turned to one of them. Underlined in red ink was a verse from the epic poem.

The first sort by their own suggestions fell,
Self-tempted, self-depraved.

He knew the verse was a reference to Satan's fall. By his own choice Satan had challenged God and been cast out. Hawker wondered if this was how Ranga felt. For a man who claimed not to believe in God, Ranga had talked about Him an awful lot. Had Ranga's own search, his own belief that he could change the code of life, caused him to fall?

Hawker flipped the pages and found another underlined verse. As he read a voice spoke it from behind him at almost the same time.

"*The more I see pleasures about me, so much more I feel torment within me.*"

Hawker turned to see Sonia.

They stared in quiet stillness for a moment.

"Are you a fan of Milton?" she asked.

The more appropriate question, he thought, was whether she and her father were fans of Milton.

"I tried to read it once," he said, closing the book. "Too close to home. So I put it away."

"It's brilliant," she said. "It explains many things about the state of man."

"The verse you quoted," he asked. "Did you underline it?"

Sonia shook her head. "Those were Father's marks, but that one's my favorite."

"What does it mean?"

"I take it as the pain of reality," she said. "Knowing what you cannot have is infinitely worse than not being able to have it in the first place. The pleasure of wanting causing the pain of lacking that very thing."

He nodded. That's what he remembered. Too close to home.

"You know, the cult that your father got mixed up in seem to be fans of Milton as well."

"I know," she said.

Of course she did. "You know more than you're telling me," Hawker said bluntly.

Tears filled her eyes; she turned away.

"Sonia."

She looked back at him, dabbing at the drops of liquid running down her face. "How far did you get in *Paradise Lost*?" she asked.

"Not far enough to take a test," he said.

"Do you know who Urial was?"

He shook his head.

"Urial was the brightest of all God's angels. The Angel of the Sun and the very eyes of God. But in his reverence for what God had created, Urial stared too long at the Garden of Eden. He meant no harm by it, but through this fault, he accidentally revealed the location of the Garden to Satan. And thus the story begins."

"You led your father to these men," he guessed.

"The other way around," she said. "I led *them* to *him*."

The thought shocked Hawker. "How?" she asked.

"Before I realized what we could do with Paradox, we'd reached a point of desperation. Everything was tapped out. There was nowhere left to turn. A man came to me interested in genetics. He was odd but he said he

had money. He wanted someone to work on a genetic problem the rest of the world was ignoring. It sounded perfect. I told him about my father. If anyone could help him, it was my father. I was proud. I was desperate. Father needed another hand, and by the time I'd realized the danger, Father was tangled up in it as deep as ever."

"They wanted a weapon," he said. "Like the generals in the Congo."

She nodded. "And just like in Africa I couldn't get Father to break away. This time until it was too late."

He sensed her drowning in guilt. He'd lived that way himself after certain failures.

"I understand what you're feeling," he said. "I can only imagine how much it hurts. But there is a bigger issue here."

"Yes, there is," she said. "My sister will die if we don't do something soon. That's bigger to me. I need to find the Garden, Hawker. I need to finish this."

"You don't understand, Sonia. These people want to finish something, too. They have your carrier virus; they sent it to the UN to scare the hell out of the world, but it doesn't do much, not without your payload. Your father rigged his lab to explode to keep them from getting 951. He suffered at their hands but he didn't give it up, because he knew what would happen if they got ahold of it. He gave his life. He destroyed his life's work to prevent something far worse from happening."

"Worse to some," she said.

He stared at her and wondered if she could really mean what she was saying.

"To see my sister die after knowing my father threw his life and half of mine away trying to save her is as bad as any plague."

"You don't mean that. You don't want to see a billion children suffering like she is."

She hesitated, choking up and fighting it off again.

"No," she said finally, "but I wish I did. I want to feel that way, to care more about Nadia than anything else, or what good am I?"

He could sense Sonia on the point of breaking. She felt as if the answer was out there, just around the corner. Exactly as Ranga had felt through ten years of searching.

The more I see pleasures about me, so much more I feel torment within me.

She looked up at him. "Besides," she said, "he didn't destroy 951. He sent it to me."

"The truth at last," he said. "And the cult knows that, or at least they suspect."

She remained quiet. Maybe she was beginning to understand.

"They came after you for a reason," he said. "I have to take you where they can't get to you. Stick you in the president's bunker or Fort Knox or somewhere like that, where they'd need an army to even get close to you."

"They got into the UN," she noted.

She was right about that. Despite intense efforts, no one knew how the cult had pulled that one off. It suggested someone with infiltration skills, someone well acquainted with government systems and a background in the type of spycraft that it would take to break into such a place. That seemed a little beyond a cult of the lunatic fringe but it had happened. Another puzzle piece from a different box.

"You're right," he said. "But I promise this will be different."

"Why?" she whispered. "Why save me?"

From a personal perspective, because the idea of her being harmed by these thugs was too agonizing to think about, but as he kept saying, there were bigger reasons.

"With your father gone and his lab destroyed, you're the only link to 951. Without you they can do nothing.

But with you, if they get 951 from you, they can murder half the world."

She gulped at a lump in her throat. "Then why not just kill me?"

"Because I'm going to kill them instead."

Silence hung over the room.

Sonia sat and buried her face in her hands as if she might burst into tears. He could only imagine the strain. He was asking her to hide until he could make the world safe for her. It might take months or years or it might never happen, and in the meantime, Nadia would wither and die. And her father's life and half of hers would be in vain.

"You don't understand," she whispered. "They don't need 951. They don't even really want 951. They want the seeds from the Garden. The fruit of the Tree of Life."

This didn't make any sense to him. "Why?" he asked. "You can't kill with the Tree of Life."

She looked at him sadly. "They're devils, Hawker. They don't want to *just* kill, they want to destroy. Even in the Garden, Satan didn't kill Adam and Eve, he just tricked them into bringing death onto themselves."

"Meaning what? What are you getting at?"

She sighed and a weight seemed to come off her shoulders, as if she'd finally decided to put down the burden of holding in what she feared most.

"A virus that kills millions or even billions won't destroy the world," she said. "It would be a horrendous tragedy and we might not recover for centuries, but in the long run it might even help the world. And in any event, we could fight it, just like we fight every other disease and condition. Theoretically we could even create a counter-virus or use gene therapy to patch the DNA their plague destroyed. This is not what they want."

"So what do they want?"

"They want to take the virus from the Tree of Life," she said. "They want to mate it with the carrier virus that they already have and then spread it around the planet."

Hawker could hardly follow. He had to be missing something.

"The virus from the Tree of Life?" he asked. "The same one you want? You're telling me their big threat is to infect us with a plague that makes us live forever?" Hawker's tone had become incredulous, but it sounded like being threatened with cake and money and good looks all at the same time. "I'm sorry, but that doesn't sound so bad."

"Not to you," she said. "Not at first. But as time goes by and the virus spreads, and virtually all human life spans are doubled, tripled, or quintupled, what do you think will happen? When the old don't die and the young don't grow old and child-bearing age lasts a century, instead of a decade or two, the population will utterly explode. And in very short order, this planet will die under the weight of humanity."

Suddenly Hawker began to understand.

"Seven billion now," she said. "Fifteen billion in twenty years. Thirty billion people on this rock by the middle of the century. There will be nothing but war and misery and starvation. It will no longer matter if there's a heaven, because earth will become hell itself and the immortal humans will be consigned to it for all eternity."

As the words rang in his ears, Hawker felt as if he'd been blindsided. Rarely could he remember being so stunned and shocked or feeling so simple and ignorant and blind. At this moment he was the fool he'd claimed to be in Lavril's office. In fact, he was worse.

"They could come up with an antidote," he stammered. "Fight it like you said."

"And who's going to take it?" she asked. "If everyone else will, that would be awfully nice, but are you? Am I?

Most people are going to refuse to take a suicide pill just for the greater good of the world."

"It wouldn't be a suicide pill," he said, realizing he was wrong even as he spoke the words.

"Of course it would. It would be exactly that. A pill that makes you live a far shorter life. What else would you call it?"

Hawker went quiet. It was the same argument Ranga had made as a young man. There were too many people in the world. And it was the same response: fine, but someone else can decrease the population, not me.

"If the carrier virus can spread the plague, another version can spread the antidote," he said. "Something to cause the telomeres to shorten. We can use 951 to off-set it."

"Yes," she said. "Sounds like a great idea. In fact it's exactly what you thought my father's murderers were about to do. Now you're suggesting it as if it sounds rational."

"It's different," he said.

She shook her head. "Only your perspective has changed."

He knew she was right.

"A worldwide genocide. Is that what we need? A final solution? My father was derided for suggesting something similar years ago. He was called a fascist and a fanatic. But it doesn't sound so fanatical to you anymore, does it?"

It still sounded fanatical and fascist and evil to him. He was just grasping at straws. But what else could the world do? Forced sterilization? You might have to sterilize 90 percent of humanity just to keep the population stable.

And who decided which 10 percent got to reproduce? A lottery? An even division among all races, creeds, and colors? A scientific board choosing which traits would

survive and which would die? Once again they were right back to the master race.

More than likely, the rich and powerful would get eternal life and the chance to pass on their genes, while the poor would be sterilized without their consent.

And if they did nothing, the whole world would be covered in humanity with no space to breathe or good food or clean water. Exactly what Ranga had always fought against and now he might be the cause of it.

Unforgivable. Hawker now understood what he'd meant.

"Once this genie is out of the bottle, it can never be put back in. It cannot be treated. It cannot be cured any more than 'life' can be cured."

"I'm sorry," he said. "I'm a fool who should have kept his mouth shut. I now understand what you're afraid of. Why you fear it so deeply."

"I don't want to be the cause of that, any more than my father did," she said. "But I don't want to give up on the only chance I have to save Nadia. I want to give her and others like her a life."

"And they want to destroy," he said. "They think if they succeed in spreading this virus there will be no hope. No reason for hope. From their point of view, they will have destroyed God's creation. Paradise will be lost forever."

Hawker thought about the situation. The world was staring down the barrel of a gun, but a gun has no power without a bullet inside it.

"We have to find the Garden," he said. "If it exists, we have to find it before they do."

She nodded.

It seemed an absurd quest. But Sonia and her father were trained scientists, not spiritualists or religious fanatics. If they believed the Garden existed and believed it could be found, then he had to give them the benefit of

the doubt. And that meant great danger still hung over the world.

"I have to make a call," he said. He stood, walked out of the library, and found his way back to the balcony, the phone to his ear.

Danielle answered.

"I haven't figured it all out," he said.

"I wouldn't have thought you had," she replied, sounding oddly surprised by his statement.

"But I know what we have to do next," he said. "I know where we have to go."

"If you say the Garden of Eden I'm going to throw up."

"That's their next target."

"Hawker, it's a dead end," she said, sounding exasperated. "These people are fanatics. We need to focus on the virus, not chasing them all over the world."

"I know what it means," he said, thinking of the original threat. "*We mete out your portion of suffering, we bring you down with us.* They want the whole world to suffer, like the poor already suffer. Ranga said they would turn this place into hell on earth and he's right, that's exactly what they're going to do, by granting everyone eternal life or something close to it."

He explained what he knew and the conversation he'd just had with Sonia. Slowly, like him, Danielle came to realize the consequences.

"Well, believe it or not," she said, "I think I know where to look."

"Iraq," he guessed, thinking that most scholars he'd heard of placed the Garden of Eden somewhere near the Euphrates and Tigris rivers.

"That would be too easy," she said. "McCarter has it located in western Iran."

"Can you get us in?"

"No one will authorize us to go across the border," she said.

"That never stopped us before."

"And it won't stop us now," she said. "But we're on our own. Can you meet me in Al Qurnah, north of Basra?"

"I need a place to stash a few people in Kuwait," he said.

"Have you been picking up strays again?"

"Good people," he said. "Sonia's sister and aunt. I can't leave them out in the open."

"I'll talk to Moore, find you a safe house," she said. "See you in Al Qurnah."

CHAPTER 35

Given the choice, Hawker would have connected up with Danielle, hired a few gunslingers, and made the run into Iran without Sonia along for the ride. But despite his insistence, Sonia would not give up the information she held. Whatever the final secret of the Tree of Life was, she kept it to herself. He was forced to take her along.

After stashing Savi and Nadia in an NRI safe house of sorts, Hawker and Sonia made the journey into Iraq by car. After a quick stop at the border they traveled northward, headed for the city of Al Qurnah.

Stepping out of the car at the prearranged location, Hawker spotted a familiar face, David Keegan, wearing desert camouflage and looking like the Royal Marine he'd once been. Turned out Keegan was the only gunslinger Hawker could find on such short notice.

After a brief reunion, the three of them drove on.

"Just like old times," Keegan said. "A road trip with nothing but trouble up ahead."

"Yeah," Hawker said. "It's like we're getting the band back together."

Five miles down the road, Hawker pulled in beside a flatbed truck with a tarp over some large object in back.

"And who's that?" Keegan asked, looking at the woman standing beside the front wheel.

"A friend of mine," Hawker said. "Keep your hands off."

Keegan chuckled. "It's not my hands you should be worried about, mate."

Hawker stepped out and introductions were made.

"I'm Danielle Laidlaw," she said to Sonia. "I work for the National Research Institute."

Sonia seemed a little confused. "You're with the government?" She looked at Hawker as if she'd been betrayed.

"Nothing I could do," he said. "The French grabbed me in Paris. The only way I could get out and help you is if I brought them along."

"What do you want?" Sonia asked.

"The same thing as you," Danielle explained. "To find these seeds and determine if anything can be done with them."

"So you'll take them from me," Sonia said defensively. "After all this."

"No," Danielle said. "We'll work with you. We'll even fund your experiments. You'll be allowed to do what you need for your sister and other patients like her, but only once we've altered the delivery virus and ended its ability to cause an epidemic."

Sonia brightened but appeared uncertain. She looked at Hawker, touching his arm as she spoke. "Is this legitimate? Can I trust them?"

"As far as I know," Hawker said, looking at Danielle. "So far they've honored what they promised me."

Sonia turned back to study Danielle. "Okay," she said. "If Hawker trusts you, I trust you."

She squeezed Hawker's arm again as if excited about the possibilities. And Hawker noticed what appeared to be very mixed emotions on Danielle's face. He understood, but they had a job to do.

The deal made, Danielle shook hands with Keegan.

He smiled broadly. "Hawk here says you're single and that you might be available."

Danielle cut her eyes at Hawker.

He shook his head.

"I'm single for a reason," she said. "Most people annoy me."

"Funny," Keegan said. "I know just what you mean. By the way, how do you feel about sushi?"

"Can't stand the stuff," Danielle replied, then turned and headed for the rear of the truck, ending all further conversation.

Keegan grinned. "That one's a keeper."

"Get in the truck," Hawker said, holding the door for his friend.

As Sonia and Keegan settled into the cab of the vehicle, Hawker caught up with Danielle at the rear of the flatbed.

"Friendly little thing you've got there," she said.

"Which one?"

She tilted her head like a puppy and opened her eyes, wide and innocent. *"Oh Hawker, is this okay?"* she said. *"If you think it's okay, it sounds okay to me.* I thought I was going to gag."

"It's a good thing she likes me," he said. "Since the cover you chose is so diabolically tricky. Nothing like telling people exactly who you are."

He climbed onto the flatbed and looked under the tarp.

"No need for a cover," she replied. "Truth works better here."

"A little heads-up next time," he said. "I don't think that well on my feet."

"Yeah," she said. "Especially when you've been off them so recently."

Hawker looked under the tarp. An airboat that might have been at home in the Everglades sat chained to the bed of the truck. "This looks good. We have weapons?"

She nodded, opening a locker. Four AR-15s sat in a rack, grenade launchers slung under two of them. A well-stocked box of clips sat to the left of the rifles.

"We can put the other two on that tripod if we need it." She pointed to a mount on the front of the boat.

"What else?"

"Body armor. Radar-absorbent coating on the boat. And we can make smoke if we need to."

It wouldn't be much if they ran into the Iranian military but it would help if they encountered anyone else.

"How far in are we going?" Hawker asked.

"Nineteen miles across the swamp, the last eight on the Iranian side. From there it's five miles over land."

"You sure it's deserted?"

"The last satellite pass was three hours ago. Nothing for miles."

Hawker looked up; it was almost dusk. They would move under cover of darkness.

"This seem too easy to you?"

"Of course," she said. "Should be a piece of cake. That's why I doubled my insurance policy before I came out."

Thirty minutes later Hawker was backing the flatbed into the water at the edge of the Hawizeh Marsh, a wetland that extended on both sides of the Iran-Iraq border.

Danielle climbed aboard and made sure all systems were go, then waved Hawker, Keegan, and Sonia aboard. With the retaining straps disconnected, the airboat floated off the back of the truck once Hawker had backed it far enough in.

"Ready?" she asked.

They nodded and Danielle engaged the secondary motor.

For stealth, the black-clad skiff moved under the power of a quiet electric impeller. The impeller sucked water in through a wide opening in the front, accelerated it, and pushed it out a narrower vent in the rear. It was an almost silent way to travel, but it was slow. They could move no more than seven knots with this motor. That meant a three-hour transit time to the other side.

If they needed to take some evasive action or to race back to the Iraqi side of the border, the big air fan could push the boat at fifty knots, while the large air rudder would make it possible to turn on a dime.

For now they glided silently in the darkness, cruising across an area that was once a battleground.

Because the swamp straddled the border, Iranian troops had once been ordered to cross it in en masse. For the most part they were unarmed draftees, acting as human cannon fodder for those who carried weapons behind them.

In response, Saddam Hussein had electrified parts of the swamp, killing the Iranians by the thousands. There was no evidence of that now, but Danielle felt great sorrow around them as they moved through it.

"So tell me what the professor thinks," Hawker asked. "And how glad he is not to be here with us right now."

Danielle had to laugh. She explained McCarter's theory that according to the copper scroll, there were many gardens, and that the river flowing around the land of Havilah, much like that flowing around the land of Kush, was an explanation of how the Garden was arranged, with four canals and a circular moat surrounding an island.

Once the 5.9K event hit and the Middle East began to dry up, the Garden in Eden, fed by canals that diverted water from the Tigris and Euphrates rivers, survived. As long as the same mixture of waters could be brought to

the Garden, the ancients believed they could keep the Tree of Life producing.

"It makes sense," Sonia said. "My father found that in each of the cultures he studied, there were trees or plants that had life-extending properties, all of which died from some type of drought or rot."

"How does this help us?" Hawker asked. "If this place has been abandoned for seven thousand years or so, then how do we expect to find anything?"

Danielle saw him studying the satellite picture. She knew the answer but Sonia spoke first.

"Seeds can survive given the right conditions," she said. "They can survive fire, they can survive drought. Winters, summers, volcanic eruptions. They can live like dormant programs in a computer, waiting until the right moment wakes them up."

"What kind of moment?"

"Application of temperature and moisture," Sonia said. "Given the right mix, a seed senses somehow that it's time to come to life."

"After seventy centuries?"

"Possibly," she said. "Given the right conditions. But we don't need the seeds to come to life on their own. We only need to find one. The virus should still be on it."

"How can you be sure?" Danielle asked.

"Viruses are extremely hardy in some ways," she said. "Because they're really just packs of chemicals that do nothing until they come into contact with a cell, they can remain dormant for extremely long periods of time— given the right conditions."

"Don't they have to eat or anything?" Hawker asked.

"No," she said. "They don't ingest food, or break it down or create heat or have any cellular processes."

"How do they live?"

"Some scientists believe they're not alive. They're just

random coding, floating around out in the world. Until they come into contact with a cell of some kind they are as inert as any stone."

"So given the right conditions," Danielle said, "the virus you're talking about could still exist, even if the tree or the fruit doesn't. As long as it has a place to hide."

Sonia nodded. "Once we find it, we can extract the DNA and clone it. Viruses are very simple. I can do it in twenty-four hours. And then we can create our own Tree of Life, without the tree I guess, and from that develop the serum I told you about."

Despite a level of jealousy that surprised her, Danielle found herself admiring the young woman. She appreciated those who tried to do what others said was impossible. Danielle had grown up living that way herself. It had pushed her onward to becoming an operative for the NRI.

"DNA has been extracted from fossilized plants and animals for years. A seed preserved in the right kind of mud might be almost intact," Danielle said.

Sonia smiled and Danielle guessed the support felt good to her.

"Is that what we're looking for?" Hawker asked. "Seeds in the mud?"

Sonia gave a wry smile. "In a way, that's exactly what we're looking for."

Before she could elaborate, the military-grade scanner Danielle carried squawked and the sounds of a conversation in Farsi came over the speaker.

She tensed a little bit listening. Their biggest fear was that Iranian defense forces would spot them and attack or capture them. The main danger was helicopters. Though a helicopter or aircraft could be spotted a long way off, it would still be able to close on the airboat quickly. The scanner would help, detecting communica-

tions between the air units long before they were in range.

As Danielle listened, she could make out one voice mention altitude and range, but she wasn't sure what else was said and she didn't hear the distinctive background vibration that would tell her it was a helicopter.

"It's okay," Hawker said, pointing up and to the left. "It's just airline traffic and a routing center somewhere."

Danielle followed his gaze. A few miles off and twenty thousand feet above, the blinking red dot of an airliner's beacon could be seen heading southeast, crossing the sky in silence.

She glanced at the second device just to be sure. The display on the radar warning receiver, or RWR, remained green. They hadn't been painted. She guessed Hawker was right. So far no one knew they were there.

Sonia looked at Danielle. "This is why I like to keep him around. He makes me feel safe."

Oh God, Danielle thought. The respectful feelings vanished. "Somebody shoot me," she mumbled.

Fortunately no one responded and a moment later they came upon a strange sight. From a distance, it looked as if a Quonset hut had been dropped into the water and now sat there, an island in the marsh. But as they closed in on the structure it became clear that the "hut" was not some prefabricated building: It was a lodge of sorts, constructed of reeds.

Danielle's briefing had included mention of these huts but also that she was unlikely to see any. They were the creation of groups known as the Marsh Arabs, a Bedouin-like people who lived out on the swamps instead of in the deserts. They were almost extinct.

"It's *mudhif,*" she said, "a communal meeting place for the people who used to live here."

"What happened to them?" Hawker asked.

"They fought against Saddam and after he crushed

them they fled back here to the swamps. So Saddam drained most of the wetlands. Diverting the water. The swamps turned to desert and the people had nowhere to hide."

Danielle looked back at the *mudhif* they were now passing.

A magnificent labor, built on a man-made island of mud and grass, the *mudhif* was the size of a school bus, constructed entirely out of woven reeds. But the structure was dilapidated now, falling apart. It seemed that those who had built it were gone and there was no one left to repair or use it.

"A century ago, there were a hundred thousand people living out here," she added. "Now . . . probably a thousand or so, spread over the whole of the marshland."

"Poor sods," Keegan said.

"War destroys everything," Sonia said.

Danielle agreed. "McCarter told me these people were linked to the Sumerians, the civilization that built the cities of Ur and Uruk around 3000 BC. Their word for this whole area is *Edin*—it means the open plains."

Danielle did not consider herself a sucker for circumstantial evidence, but as she'd listened to McCarter's theory, she'd thought "why not." They'd discovered other, perhaps stranger things, working together.

And it wasn't only the Old Testament that spoke of eternal life from a tree in a garden. McCarter had explained that other cultures had their own stories about immortality. Carved tablets describing the Sumerians as the keepers of the Immortal Garden had been found in Iraq; Egyptian records counted several pharaohs living into their nineties when the average human life span was twenty-seven. Fruit from a tree in the oasis of Ra was said to be responsible. That tree had been a gift from the king of Sumer.

He quoted texts she'd never heard of: Apocryphal Bible

texts, like the book of Enoch, which claimed the Tree of Life was a type of tamarind tree. Syrian texts on Alexander the Great, which held that his reason for conquering much of the world was to find the Garden of Eden; he failed and died in his thirties. The Epic of Gilgamesh, an ancient Sumerian story of a god-king who quested for the secret to eternal life after his friend Enkidu was killed. Gilgamesh eventually arrived in a garden filled with jewellike trees. Later Gilgamesh found a plant that granted eternal life at the bottom of a shallow lake. He retrieved the plant, only to have it stolen by a serpent.

Another miracle, another serpent. She hoped their quest would turn out differently.

Three hours later they'd crossed the swamp and beached the airboat at the edge of the mudflat. Hawker unloaded a pair of ATVs while Danielle collected the equipment they would need: two GPS receivers already programmed with the information McCarter had given them. Two sets of night-vision goggles. Flak jackets, helmets, gloves, guns. She had four pistols, one for each of them, and both she and Hawker would carry rifles.

She handed a Beretta to Sonia. "I'm okay. I have my own," Sonia said.

Danielle paused. She guessed that someone who'd been in danger for years would be a fool not to have their own gun. She put the Beretta back in the locker and turned to Hawker's friend Keegan. He stood on the airboat.

"Not coming?"

"Lot of hiking where you're going," he said.

"Probably."

"I'll stay here," he said. "Make sure no one steals our tires."

It made sense. From the satellite pictures it was obvious that the site had some difficult terrain. Keegan would struggle out there.

"Here," she said, handing the second pair of night-

vision goggles to Hawker. "Sorry I don't have a pair for your girlfriend."

Hawker chuckled and Danielle wasn't sure if he was laughing with her or at her.

"I assume she's going to share your ride," Danielle said.

"Unless you want her arms wrapped around you?"

She slammed the flak jackets into his chest, purposefully putting extra effort behind the handoff. "Keep dreaming."

They climbed onto the ATVs. Turning the keys brought up low-level illumination on the instrument panels but produced no sound. The four-wheelers were completely electric.

"Keep your headlight off," she said. "With the goggles and the starlight we should be fine."

Danielle took a moment for her eyes to adjust to the glowing green view of the world. Her bearings established, she twisted the throttle and accelerated silently into the night.

Moments later she was racing through the desert in near-total darkness and silence. It was an odd feeling. The acceleration of the vehicle was instant, the speed and agility right there with a top-of-the-line motorized ATV, but apart from the almost inaudible electric whirring, the only sound came from the tires and the wind. It gave her the sensation of literally flying through the night.

Keeping a sharp eye ahead, Danielle glanced at the GPS, adjusted course slightly, and accelerated again. Fifteen minutes later they zoomed out of the mudflats and began racing across dunes of sand that rose and fell like waves on the ocean. Travel here was smoother, if a bit slower.

Beyond the dunes they came to a broad wadi, a dried-up riverbed that was once part of the canal system. She

drove beside it for a mile and then down into it. Three miles to go.

With the scanner and radar warning receiver strapped to the bars of her ATV showing no sign of activity, Danielle felt certain that no parties were aware of their presence. She hoped their luck held and she accelerated a bit more, anxious to get whatever they could find and get the hell out of Dodge.

She curved to the left, weaving around a dead tree. The walls of the wadi were built-up sand for the most part, but in places rubble of stone blocks showed through, remnants of the time when this had been a canal.

She followed the path, came around a turn, and all of a sudden she was there.

CHAPTER 36

Hawker followed Danielle's lead, chasing her across the mudflats, desert, and scrubland, slightly annoyed at the pace she kept. His aggravation came not because it was nearly impossible to keep up with her—which it was—or because he and Sonia had spent twenty minutes eating sand—which they had—but because separated as they were he had no way to communicate with her. They couldn't use a radio without facing the same risk of detection as the airliners that had flown overhead during their ride across the swamp. And if anything went wrong Danielle would never know until she stopped and wondered where he and Sonia had gone.

He did his best to keep up, having better luck once they were in the wadi. Five minutes on he saw her race around a half-buried dead tree. He followed, with Sonia holding tight. On the other side he found Danielle stopped—parked at the edge of a deep pit.

He slammed on the brakes and the ATV skidded. The wheels dug into the sand, Sonia's weight pressed against him, adding to his own, and they almost went over.

The ATV stopped with Hawker hanging over the handlebars and peering down into a five-story drop. A massive void lay before them. It was like standing at the edge of an open-pit mine. The far wall might have been half a mile away.

At the bottom, sand piled up in sloping heaps against three of the four walls. He guessed that showed the direction of the wind. In the center, raised up almost to their level, lay a flattish table perhaps the size of a dozen football fields.

Stone ruins covering one section appeared to be mostly crude structures. On the far edge lay a much larger structure, one that seemed to protrude into the ground.

The ATV slipped a bit. Realizing he was still hanging over the edge, Hawker pushed off the handlebars, straightening up. With his hand on the clutch he walked the ATV back a few steps, flipping up the night-vision goggles as he went.

"A little warning next time," he suggested.

"Like you gave me in Paris?"

There was not much he could say to that.

Danielle smiled. "Would you like a drink?" she said. "You must be thirsty after eating so much dust." She was obviously enjoying the moment.

"Didn't know you were such a comedian."

"There's a lot you don't know about me."

That much was true. *Maybe someday.*

Behind him, Sonia stepped off the ATV.

"Is this it?" she asked.

Danielle nodded. She pointed to the walls of the pit, the moat that surrounded the structure in the middle like a castle.

"If this whole theory is right, we're looking at the land of Havilah, 'the table or stretch of sand,' closely related to the name used in the Bible and 'completely surrounded' by the river Pishon."

Sonia pulled off her helmet and shook out her hair.

"And in the middle?" Hawker asked.

"The first and the last of the Miraculous Gardens of Life," Danielle said. "The Garden of—or in—Eden."

It seemed both correct and wrong. The place was barren, quiet, and deserted. It seemed the opposite of life in its current state and yet the stars above were so brilliant in their intensity, it almost felt as if God were watching.

"How is it no one ever found this place?" Hawker asked. "Especially if this Bashir guy has been looking for it all his life?"

"Because," Danielle said, "until a few years ago, when Saddam drained the swamps, this whole area was underwater. Since then it's been kind of a war zone."

That made sense. Too bad for Bashir, maybe for the rest of the world, too.

Sonia reached into her pocket and pulled out a folded-up piece of paper. Scratched into the paper was a drawing of a large, lush area surrounded by water and walls.

"This was drawn up from a Sumerian description of the place where life flowed."

She held it out at an angle. It didn't really match, but with imagination Hawker could kind of see the resemblance.

"So now what?"

"Down inside," Sonia said. "If they still exist, what we're looking for will be in the main building."

They tied a rope to one of the ATVs, climbed down into the moat, and crossed the open area. Making their way up to the platform was far more difficult but eventually they reached the first tier.

Strange rows of rocks stood piled and aligned in places, but most of it was a jumble. Since the water had drained away, the area had become bone dry. The only erosion had come from the wind. Like the sites at Ur or the pyramids of Giza, what hadn't been disturbed by man lay pretty much as it once had.

They crossed the lower, outer platform and scaled a crumbling ten-foot wall onto the main level of the platform.

Sonia moved toward the main building, appearing for all the world like she knew what she was looking for.

"The people who lived here predated the Sumerians," she said. "Some scholars call them the Elamites."

"Elamites—Edenites," Hawker said. "Got to be the same."

"We call them the Elamites," she said. "We have no idea what they called themselves."

Danielle laughed and leaned in to Hawker. "She's too smart for you. She should date McCarter instead."

Hawker had to laugh. He was enjoying the moment. No one was shooting at them or trying to blow them up, Sonia seemed to be glowing as she neared the end of her quest, and every jealous bone in Danielle's body had begun to act up.

"Never thought you'd be the jealous type," he replied.

"Just trying to save you some heartache."

They followed Sonia through the broken remnants of the large structure. Here and there she looked at parts of the ruins, eventually coming to an opening that led underground.

"Can I use the light?" she asked.

So far they'd been maneuvering by moonlight, but to go where she was going required artificial illumination.

Hawker nodded. "Just keep it covered until you're inside."

Sonia pulled her flashlight out and stepped to the edge. She made it down a foot or so and then turned on the beam, covering it with her hand.

Danielle and Hawker moved up to the edge.

Hawker followed Sonia's light and Danielle came in behind him. They moved into an empty room that looked like it might have been hollowed out of the rock itself to make a storehouse. Most of it was filled with sand, but like the moat outside, some sections seemed to have been sheltered. Or cleared.

Hawker bent close to Sonia as she ran her hand across one of the stones.

"What are you looking for?"

"Growing stones," she said.

"What's a growing stone?"

She explained. "According to the Sumerian part of the legend, the life-giving tree bore two kinds of fruit: the seedless kind that was consumed, and on rare occasion a seeded bud. They were so valuable and few, that upon their reaching fullness, they were plucked, surrounded in wax, sealed into a ball of gold, and then placed inside bricks of mud and clay. The clay was then baked at a very low temperature until it hardened into tablets. Tablets upon which the story of their existence was carved."

"So the seeds aren't in the mud," Hawker noted.

"They are," she said. "It's just the mud is now a brick."

"Look at this," Danielle said.

They turned her way. With the edge of her knife she was scraping off soot and creosote from the stone walls. Shining the flashlights around what was left of the structure showed the same soot everywhere, baked into the stone.

"There was a fire here," Danielle said. "Big enough, hot enough to heat these rocks and scar them."

She scraped off a bunch more of the soot, filling a small plastic bag.

"What, are you with CSI now?"

"McCarter wanted samples so he could try to carbon-date the place."

"What does he think about all this?"

"He read the scroll," she said. "It says two people were kept here to tend the Garden. They were given everything by the king but were never allowed to leave. They partook of the seedless fruit from the Tree of Life and thus lived for ages."

"Sounds familiar," he said.

"It parallels very nicely," she said. "Apparently the keepers of the Garden weren't permitted to know of the outside world. They were born here, told that this was the entire world, and made to live all their lives here. They were given food and wine and other treasures. Everything a person could want, but they were never allowed to leave."

"Because if they left, they could tell someone where the Garden was," Hawker guessed, assuming that was one thing the king couldn't have.

"Exactly."

"Bashir told my father the scroll was found in the grave of the first one," Sonia said. "Adam."

She looked around. "A long way from here, though."

"The scroll says they were tricked into leaving by one of the king's guards," Danielle explained. "According to McCarter, it doesn't mention anything about knowledge of good and evil but it does mention knowledge of a wider world."

"And once they left and gained this knowledge?" Hawker asked.

"Can't go home again," Danielle said. "Once they'd left, the king needed to find and kill them, lest they tell anyone about his garden."

" 'So now you will suffer death,' " he said, quoting Genesis.

She nodded. "They had eternal life and everything a person could want and now the king, the one who had provided them with everything, sent orders that they be killed. Life in the Garden, death outside."

"So the king becomes God in the text," Hawker said.

"A different kind of God," Sonia said.

"Different than the Abrahamic God?" Danielle asked.

"Not by name," she said. "But by actions. If you read

Genesis carefully, you'll see a different character from the all-knowing, all-powerful God we meet in the rest of the Bible. He often seems surprised by things, like the serpent tricking Adam and Eve. Sometimes he seems confused or even afraid. When he comes to see Adam and Eve after they've eaten the apple, they hide and he doesn't know where they are. He demands that they *show themselves*. He doesn't know who told them they were naked. He asks them *if they've eaten from the tree he told them not to*. And when they say yes, he asks them why, *what made them do that*?"

"Religious people will tell you that's not what He meant," she added. "Usually right after they tell you to read the Bible literally, but that's what it says."

It felt odd to Hawker. Even though he considered the Garden of Eden a metaphor, there was some natural resistance to anyone offering a different view of the Bible. He felt it himself this moment, even though he had his own different views.

"Is this why Savi was upset when I called it a metaphor?" he asked.

"She was hoping you would see it our way," Sonia said.

In hindsight he could see it that way. He didn't necessarily agree with it, but his mind was open. In fact one thing he'd always wondered jumped out at him—if Adam and Eve were the people from whom all others came, how come they ran into other humans shortly after they left the Garden? If anything, that seemed to suggest a more earthly and different reality, more like what was being told in the copper scroll. People who had no knowledge of the outside world might think they—and the king who came around—were the only ones who existed. At least, that is, until they stepped into that outside world and ran into more people.

"Ever wonder what would have happened if Adam had refused to eat the fruit after Eve had taken a bite?" Hawker asked, thinking it sounded like Eve might have left, snuck off this castle/island, and then returned to tell Adam of the outside world. And then perhaps Adam went, too.

"Or if Eve had killed herself like Judas, before luring Adam in," Sonia said.

There was an odd tone in Sonia's voice, made odder by the way it echoed around beneath the stone outcropping.

"Either way, Adam would have been awfully lonely at night," Danielle said.

Hawker had to agree. "Better to die with love than live without it."

"The thing is," Danielle said, "according to the scroll, the keepers of the Garden, this first one and his wife— whether it was Adam and Eve or not—they did try to come back here, only to find the Garden in flames. War had broken out between the king and the traitor who tricked the keepers of the Garden and as their swords clashed, the last of the miraculous gardens burned."

As Danielle scraped another smudge of black carbon off the stone walls, Hawker wondered if the image of this garden in flames while men fought over it was the source of the Bible verse that told of God preventing humans from returning to Eden by stationing mighty angels with flaming swords at its entrance.

Fire, swords, no return; maybe,. or maybe he was just trying to fit those puzzle pieces together again. To see a picture where there wasn't one.

Danielle tucked her sample away and scanned around the ruins. "McCarter asked for samples of wooden beams and things like that, but I don't see any."

Hawker followed her gaze. The whole structure was stone, cut and laid precisely. He remembered McCarter

telling them about stone blocks and how, without mortar, they'd hold themselves in place far longer than cemented structures.

The weight of the stones did the work. And with no mortar or cement to dissolve, the structure would last as long as the stone itself. That's why the great pyramids around the world still looked relatively close to their original shape.

He'd said if humans disappeared from the earth today, a visitor five thousand years later might find no sign of the modern world, and yet the pyramids of Giza would still stand.

Hawker glanced at Sonia. She was studying the layer of soot as Danielle had, but she'd moved from the walls to what looked like a threshing stone on the floor. She examined it for a moment and then moved on.

One by one she studied each and every block and mud brick as if she was looking for clues. Finally, after pulling one heavy stone out of the ground, she stopped. Her eyes fixated on something underneath it.

Hawker looked. It appeared to be another rectangular brick about the size and shape of a cereal box. In the glare of Sonia's light, he saw markings.

Sonia began to scrape away the dirt and then stopped, looking disappointed.

"This isn't what we're looking for," she said.

"How do you know?" Hawker asked. "Can you read it?"

"No, but I'm looking for the sign."

"What sign?"

Danielle answered from another section of the ruin. "This one."

Hawker and Sonia turned. Danielle was pointing to another of the flat, rectangular bricks. Like the one Sonia had looked at, it lay one level down, beneath another stone.

A carving appeared in its center. The mark looked like a rectangle, surrounded by a larger square, surrounded by a circle with hash marks pointing out in four directions, like a compass rose.

Sonia moved toward her. "That's the one."

"You guys want to let me in on your little secret?" Hawker asked.

They exchanged glances and smiled. Suddenly it was a girls' club, like best of friends, with him on the outside.

Sonia dropped to the ground and began digging around the edges of the tablet. Danielle turned to Hawker.

"When McCarter translated the writing on the copper scroll, he found a symbol at the bottom of each column. It was the only symbol written the same in all three languages," she said.

"That symbol," Hawker guessed.

"Exactly," she said. "It is a combination of the Sumerian symbol of life and"—she looked around—"a representation of this place."

Hawker thought about that. The platform in the middle, the larger, sunken platform surrounding it, the curving sides of the pit surrounding the square shape of the platform: It certainly made sense.

"What are the lines branching out from the circle?"

"The four rivers of Eden," Danielle said. "Or in reality, the four canals. They controlled the water to the pit, keeping it level, keeping it a certain depth and temperature. Because if McCarter and Gilgamesh are right, the Tree of Life didn't grow on the land, it grew in the water, on the lower terrace."

"It's as if the story took on different forms," Danielle continued. "The Garden of Hesperides to the Macedonian Greeks. The plant under the water in the Epic of Gilgamesh. The story of Adam and Eve in Genesis."

"And what's this place?" Hawker asked. "This build-

ing. I don't recall Adam and Eve doing any construction work."

"Like anything, we're talking about a legend that traveled the known world seven thousand years ago. It might have been written down in a few places like these tablets or the copper scroll, but those types of things were far too valuable to move around."

"Not to mention heavy," Sonia said, still digging at the edges of the tablet, trying to pull it loose from the ground.

"Besides," Danielle added, "at the time, ninety-nine percent of the people wouldn't have been able to read them anyway."

"So the story changes," Hawker said.

"McCarter told me that myths form like that," she added. "Stories begin as basic truth, but over time concrete things are replaced by the idealistic. Buildings and clothing no longer figure in the narrative because the Garden is no longer a working garden but has become a paradise. The work of men and women to till the land and shape the ground and divert the water is replaced by the power of God."

"He should really be here," Hawker said.

Danielle smiled. "He probably should."

Hawker looked around. Despite being submerged for the last few centuries, the place was empty. It resembled many ruins in the modern world: picked over and barren. For all he knew the smoke and soot were not from the previous age but from Bedouins who might have camped here six months ago. Or before the swamp covered it.

If there had ever been gold or onyx or aromatic spices here, they were long gone. About the only thing that remained were the stones and the carved bricks, like the one Sonia was still struggling with.

He dropped down beside her, grabbed a stone as a

makeshift tool, and began scraping along the sides of the tablet, trying to help dig it out.

"You sure this is the one?" he asked.

"It has the symbol on it," she replied. "The symbol of the Garden. The symbol of life. The seeds from the tree are inside."

Hawker put his hand on the surface of the tablet. It wasn't made of stone; it was a brick of mud and clay. It had been formed by human hands. Just like the scroll said.

Sonia smiled in the dark. Hawker turned and glanced at Danielle, who was also smiling. It felt at long last like a moment of victory.

And then a burst of static came from the scanner on Danielle's belt.

Hawker's eyes fell to the scanner. The green LED was fluctuating: Some kind of signal was being picked up, probably blocked by the stone of the building.

Danielle must have realized this, too. She pulled the scanner from her belt and held it to her ear as she moved toward the entrance.

A second wave of static came over the speaker and then words too faint for Hawker to hear.

Danielle heard them, though. She turned back toward him. "We've run out of time."

CHAPTER 37

Better get that thing out of the ground," Danielle said.
As Hawker attacked the hard-packed dirt around
the edge of the tablet with his jagged stone, Danielle
climbed back to the surface. A glow hugged the horizon
to the south, but it wasn't the moon—that wouldn't
come up for hours.

She climbed to a higher point, up on one of the piles
of stone.

Dust, illuminated by the lights of several vehicles, rose
in a cloud. She could only guess at the distance, maybe
a couple of miles.

She heard another radio transmission and realized the
voices were speaking English.

"How did they find us?" Sonia asked. "How could
they know where we are?"

"They have the scroll," Danielle said. "And they must
still have Bashir."

The poor man had never resurfaced, either dead or
alive. She guessed they'd kept him around for a reason.

Still, she'd rather deal with their enemies than the Iranian military. And they'd already found what they were
looking for. If they could just get it out of the ground
and get moving the cult might never know they'd been
there.

Hawker reached under the tablet and pried it loose. After pulling it out of the ground he heaved it up on his shoulder, like a boom box of some kind.

"How much time do we have?" he asked.

"Five minutes at best," Danielle said. "But I don't think they know we're here. Otherwise they wouldn't be charging this way with their lights on."

"Good," Hawker said. "Score one for us."

Danielle moved off, making her way toward the edge of the main platform. Hawker and Sonia followed.

Danielle slid down to the lower level, the level that would have been underwater when this place had been a garden. Hawker came to the edge and slid down beside her, moving awkwardly with the heavy stone. Pausing, he looked over at the pit they would have to cross in a moment and then climb out of.

"This ain't going to work," he said.

She had to agree. Getting the forty-pound tablet down into the chasm was one thing, bringing it back up was another.

"Break it," she said, pointing to one of the large blackened stones on the ground. "Crack it in half."

As Hawker studied the sharp edge of the blackened stone, Danielle turned to Sonia. "Will it be okay?"

"It should," Sonia said. "We'll have to break it sometime anyway. All we really need is what's inside."

Danielle aimed her flashlight toward the stone. Sonia did the same.

Hawker raised the tablet up off his shoulder and slammed it down onto the sharp edge. The brick tablet cracked, not only in half, but into three major pieces and a handful of smaller chunks and shards.

Danielle studied the ground, moving the beam of her flashlight around. She had expected golden pods to drop out, like ball bearings or Christmas ornaments or seeds from a pumpkin. But there was nothing of the sort.

She crouched to examine the pieces. Sonia and Hawker did the same. But there was no sign of anything like what they hoped to see. Sonia put her hands on one of the pieces, picking it up and examining it.

From the south they could hear the sound of engines approaching.

"Just grab everything," Hawker said. "We'll figure it out later."

Danielle clipped the flashlight back on her belt and grabbed a piece. She jammed it into the pack with McCarter's samples and zipped the top shut. Sonia did the same with the piece she'd been studying, and Hawker grabbed the last section.

By the time Danielle looked up, Hawker was already on the move. She followed with Sonia trailing behind. They went down the slope and across the bottom of the pit, chasing after Hawker.

She could hear the approaching vehicles clearly now. There was an odd timbre to the noise, one she couldn't place. She moved across the dry moat, quickly reaching the edge. Hawker was halfway up the rope already.

She held the end for Sonia. "Go," she said.

The young woman grabbed the rope without saying a word and started to climb. Whether it was the weight in the pack or thoughts of failure swirling in her mind, Sonia did not move quickly.

Hawker had reached the top and lay flat, looking back down. "Come on," he whispered sharply.

Sonia began to move a little quicker, finally cresting the edge. Danielle began climbing immediately. Her arms were burning by the time she reached the top. She stepped toward her ATV only to have Hawker pull her to the ground.

He pointed out across the sand. The strange-sounding vehicles had reached the far edge of the moat and were prowling the perimeter.

As they turned off their headlights, Danielle understood why the engines had sounded so odd. The vehicles
were sand rails, dune buggies with unmuffled motors.
She counted four of them and a foreign-looking offroad
vehicle something like a Humvee.

At least eight men had dismounted.

Carrying guns and flashlights of their own, they
picked their way toward the edge of the pit. She saw one
man step out of the Humvee-like vehicle, but he never
strayed from its side.

This man began directing the others, but they moved
in a ragged fashion, speaking in loud voices without dis-
cipline. It sounded like Farsi at one point and then broken English.

"Locals, just like in Paris," she said. "These guys hire
locals to do their dirty work and then kill them to ice the
trail. Those poor bastards think they're about to get
paid."

"That's not what they did in Dubai," Hawker said.

Perhaps not, but it was clear in this case. Danielle
guessed that the guy with the radio and whoever else
was in that Humvee were members of the cult, directing
the show.

Danielle almost felt sorry for the men—except for the
fact that they would kill her, Sonia, and Hawker if they
got the chance.

"Not our problem," she said.

She took another look at the sand rails. They looked
like fast machines. She remembered racing something
similar as a child along a beach in North Carolina. She
doubted the ATVs would be able to outrun them.

She glanced toward her four-wheeler.

Hawker nodded. "Quietly."

She turned to Sonia. "This time you're with me."

Sonia looked confused but didn't question it. To Danielle, the thinking was clear. She was fifty pounds lighter

than Hawker to begin with and he was carrying the heaviest piece of the stone. She and Sonia on one rig would be much faster than Hawker and Sonia had been on the way in.

Hawker smiled.

"Don't get any ideas," she said.

Still smiling, Hawker pulled his rifle from the scabbard on the side of his ATV. With another glance at the men in the moat, he climbed on.

Danielle did likewise, pulling the straps on her backpack tight.

Without engaging the motor, she walked the ATV back from the edge, turning it through 90 degrees in the process. A necessary act, since they'd foolishly left them pointing toward the precipice upon arrival.

Sonia remained on the ground, staring at the men. Frozen once again.

"Come on, Sonia," Hawker said. "We need to move."

"Those are the men who killed my father," Sonia said, as if mesmerized.

"They might be," Danielle said. "All the more reason to put them behind us."

Sonia nodded, then slowly stood, moving toward the back of Danielle's ride.

As she did her footing gave way, not enough to make her fall, but enough to send a tiny avalanche of rocks and sand tumbling down the edge of the moat.

Click, clack. Crunch.

The tumbling rocks might as well have been gunshots in the silence of the night.

Flashlights swung their way.

"Not good," Danielle said.

Shouts followed. They'd been spotted.

Sonia climbed on board and Danielle gunned the throttle, racing past Hawker and out into the night.

As she accelerated down the dry riverbed, she heard gunfire from behind.

The shooting was too close to be the Iranians. Hawker had to be blasting away at them, trying to keep them pinned down.

It would work for a minute, but once the men on the rim started firing back Hawker would have to flee or risk getting caught or killed himself.

Danielle raced on, trusting his judgment.

With Sonia clinging tight, she rounded a curve in the bend of the river and glanced at the GPS. In a half mile she would turn west and cut through the dunes toward the marshland and the waiting airboat.

She hoped Hawker would catch them by then and that they'd be able to lose any pursuit before they reached that point.

As Danielle and Sonia raced away, Hawker cracked off a half-dozen shots from the ArmaLite. He saw one man fall and get up again. The others took cover.

He aimed toward the sand rails and opened up with a hail of shells. Sparks flew from where the vehicles were parked, but before he could land any fatal blows, explosions of dirt began to kick up around him and bullets began to whistle by.

He shuffled backward to the ATV, shoved the rifle back into the scabbard, climbed back on, and gunned the throttle.

In seconds he'd left the shooters well behind him.

He flew along the dry riverbed, traveling at breakneck speed and suddenly realizing a problem. His helmet, and the night-vision goggles attached to it, sat strapped uselessly to the peg behind him.

He had no time to stop and put them on. He squinted

into the wind, trying to navigate by the starlight that
spread itself over the desert sand.

Danielle had reached the turnoff. She slowed, looking
for the best place to climb up the slope of the bank.
Finding a promising spot, she shouted to Sonia.

"Hold on."

She gunned the throttle again and they raced up and
out onto the open desert. A minute later they entered the
sand dunes.

Like someone skiing huge moguls or avoiding massive
swells at sea, Danielle did the best she could to race
around the dunes, sticking to the low points. To speed
across the top kicking up a rooster tail was just asking
to be seen and then shot.

Lower was safer, even if it meant constant course
changes and turns and rechecking the GPS. Trying to do
all that and keep the ATV moving at full speed took all
Danielle's attention. She couldn't risk a glance back to
look for Hawker, but Sonia could.

"Do you see Hawker?" she shouted.

Danielle felt Sonia's weight shift as she turned. She reduced the speed for a moment, to give her a better look.

"No!" Sonia shouted.

A second later something caught Danielle's eye to the
left. She glanced toward it and hoped it was Hawker.

"Damn."

The sound of an unmuffled engine roared in her ears
as lights blazed toward them from the dune above. The
sand rails had found them.

CHAPTER 38

Hang on!" Danielle shouted.

One buggy raced down toward them from the top of the dune. A second followed on a slightly wider track.

Danielle curved away from them, snaking between a group of smaller mounds in the dark. The ATV bounced and skidded. Left, then right, then left again. Suddenly the world filled with light as one of the dune buggies dropped in behind.

The light was so intense that Danielle couldn't see through the goggles. She flipped them up just in time to see an outcropping of rock.

She cut right, leaning hard to keep the ATV from flipping.

They missed it. But the sound of a heavy crunch and a sudden return of the darkness told her their pursuers had nailed it head-on. Whether they would be permanently out of the action or only held up for the moment she didn't know. But she'd take what she could get.

Flying along at top speed in an attempt to catch up with Danielle, Hawker had encountered another problem: He'd become utterly lost.

The riverbed looked different: more dead trees, more rocks, less smooth ground to rumble over. He hadn't

seen this on the way in and that could mean only one thing: He'd stayed in the wadi too long and gone too far north.

He looked for a way out, found a slope that seemed climbable, and raced up it, pressing his weight forward to keep the ATV's nose down.

Cresting the top of the climb, he saw lights racing westward across the dunes, three pairs in the lead and two in a trailing group.

Hounds after the fox, chasing Danielle and Sonia.

He accelerated forward, got the ATV up to full speed, and pulled the rifle out once again. Because the throttle was on the right, he switched the rifle into his left hand, holding it against the handlebar and accelerating further.

He couldn't remember firing a rifle left-handed, but there was a first time for everything.

Danielle continued around the dunes, trying desperately to keep moving in the general direction of the airboat. It was only a mile off now and Hawker's friend Keegan was waiting there with more firepower. Maybe enough to help even the odds.

She whipped into a right turn and the ATV almost flipped. Sonia had moved the wrong way.

A moment later it happened again.

"Move with me," Danielle shouted.

"I'm looking for Hawker!" she shouted.

"Forget about him. You need to move with me or we're going down."

For emphasis Danielle took another turn they didn't have to take, but Sonia got the message and leaned into it hard, if late.

Lights flooded the desert in front of her as one of the

sand rails barreled toward them, attempting to cut her off. Danielle cut toward it like a fighter pilot breaking toward a missile. Her turn was too sharp for the buggy to copy, and it overshot her and vanished in the dark.

Another narrow escape.

Danielle wondered how long their luck would last. To be honest she was surprised they'd gotten this far. She feared for Hawker, wondered where he was, and prayed that nothing had happened to him.

Still traveling full speed, Danielle raced up the next dune and then down. From the top she could see the lights of the others trailing them; they'd spread out in a wide V. An attempt to keep her from breaking containment and disappearing into the night, she thought, or . . .

She looked ahead—they were nearing the marsh now. Climbing over the top of the last dune, she caught sight of the reeds at the water's edge. Her worst fears were realized.

The men in the sand rails were chasing her and Sonia all right, but they were also herding her toward a second group. A half-dozen men and another Humvee waited by the shore.

Danielle hit the brakes and turned, but this time Sonia's lean came way too late and the ATV flipped, flinging both of them off and into the sand.

Tumbling and then sliding to a stop, Danielle quickly looked up. The ATV was upside down, its wheels spinning. She scrambled back to the overturned rig, and pulled the rifle loose. She turned and opened fire, just as the three sand rails came flying over the crest of the dune and down at them.

She hit one of the dune buggies. It went off course, flipping and tumbling down the hill, one wheel flying through the air like a Frisbee. The other two turned wide, made a long stretch outward, and then turned back. They began

circling her and Sonia, penning them in halfway down the last dune, five hundred yards from the marsh.

Fifty feet away Sonia had gotten to her hands and knees.

"Over here!" Danielle shouted.

Appearing groggy from the fall, Sonia crawled to where Danielle was.

"Where's your gun?" Danielle shouted.

Sonia reached into her pack and pulled out a small pistol. She gripped it awkwardly.

"Fire only if they start to close in."

Danielle could see the men from the water's edge heading up toward her. The Hummer followed, moving at a crawl, pointing its blazing high beams right into her eyes.

Danielle ripped off a group of shots and the Humvee's lights went dark. Then she hunkered down behind the overturned ATV.

The men weren't firing yet, but it was hard to watch them all and sort of dizzying and confusing trying to keep track of the two dune buggies racing around in opposite directions as they circled.

Beside her Sonia fired wildly and well behind one of the racing buggies.

"Wait till they're closer!" Danielle said.

"I don't want them to get closer!" Sonia shouted back.

Danielle had to agree with that thought, but they didn't have all that much ammunition.

She glanced toward the edge of the swamp and realized something new. Keegan and the boat were gone.

Hawker's plan for a mad charge had come with one deficiency: The vehicles he was chasing were faster than he was. They ran away from him without ever knowing they'd been challenged.

He continued on, following their lights and aware that they were heading in the general direction of the marsh. When their progress stopped and the lights began dancing in strange circles Hawker feared the worst. It reminded him of a wolf pack having finally downed its prey.

He pressed forward, down through the dunes and up over the last one. He saw Danielle and Sonia on the ground, crouching in the cover of the overturned ATV. He saw the sand rails circling them like hyenas and a group of men marching toward them.

Now was the time for the charge.

He gunned the throttle again, aimed for the point where he'd intersect one of the sand rails on its wide circle, and raced down the last dune, opening fire as he went.

Within a few seconds he'd riddled the first vehicle with shells. Its gas tank exploded and it rolled away, burning.

From there he raced around wide, opening fire into the pack of men.

Danielle and Sonia must have joined in because as his weapon ran dry he could still hear gunfire and see the men scattering.

He glanced over toward Danielle. The last of the sand rails was racing toward her and Sonia. Hawker saw three men hanging on to the back, like firemen on a ladder truck.

As the vehicle raced past, the men jumped off. They lunged forward with nets in their hands, as if they would capture the two women like lions.

Hawker turned that way, accelerating. The nets were thrown, engulfing Danielle and Sonia. Gunfire flashed from Danielle's position and one of the men staggered back clutching his chest. But the second man tackled her and she went down, tangled in the net, while the third fought with Sonia.

Hawker raced in at full speed, swinging the empty rifle like a club.

It whammed against the side of one of the men, ripping out of Hawker's hand and pulling him off balance. He flew off the ATV and rolled. As he got up, he saw Danielle retraining her rifle and aiming through the netting. She blasted the third assailant off Sonia. The guy Hawker had hit lay flat and unmoving.

What had started as a rout was fast approaching even odds. But they still needed to get to the water.

With his ATV zooming out of reach, Hawker ran toward the women. He pulled the net off Danielle as Sonia untangled herself.

"I need a weapon," he said.

Sonia handed him her pistol.

"Where's your friend?" Danielle shouted, firing a carefully aimed shot in one direction and then the next, trying to keep the rest of the men at bay.

Hawker looked toward the swamp and realized what Danielle was saying.

"They must have chased him off!" he shouted. "Don't worry, he'll be back."

"He better make it quick. I have two more shells."

Hawker reached into his vest, pulled out an extra clip, and handed it to her. "I won't be needing this."

Danielle snapped off her last two shots, popped the empty out, and jammed the clip Hawker gave her into the rifle.

As she racked the slide, Hawker looked over the field. The men attacking them had been scattered. Some were cowering behind overturned vehicles, others taking what cover they could out on the open ground. There was no one between them and the marsh.

"How many of them are left?"

"No idea," Danielle said. "Seven or eight. Maybe a dozen."

"I can't believe they haven't shot us yet," he noted.

"They're not going to shoot," Sonia said.

He turned.

"They want me," she explained. "Just like you said. They killed my father because he wouldn't help them and now they want me—alive."

That was one of the reasons he'd wanted her in the safe house.

He looked around, pissed at himself for not forcing her to go with Savi and her sister.

"Sooner or later they're going to try another run," he said. They'd go for him and Danielle and then they'd swarm Sonia and take her. No way in hell he was going to let that happen. But how to stop it?

Hawker looked around. His own ATV was gone. A runaway that had zoomed off into the darkness, it probably wouldn't stop till it hit the Persian Gulf.

"Does this thing still run?" he asked.

"I think it will," Danielle said.

Hawker grabbed the handhold and pulled with all his might. The ATV came up slowly and then went over and landed back onto its wheels.

"You two get on this thing and head for the marsh," he said. "Keegan's out there somewhere."

"What if he's not?"

"He is," Hawker insisted. "If you don't see him, just drive right into the damn water and swim for it. He'll find you."

He took Danielle's rifle.

"What about you?" Sonia asked, fear in her eyes.

"I'm going to make these people wish they'd messed with someone else tonight."

Danielle's face was white, but she tried to play along. "He'll be all right," she said. "This is what he does."

Sonia didn't look convinced, but she nodded her head.

Danielle flipped the switch and the ATV's panel lit up. "We have power."

Danielle climbed on and Sonia settled in behind her.

"Go!" Hawker shouted.

The ATV's wheels spun, showering Hawker with sand as it raced away toward the water's edge.

Almost immediately several of the men and the last of the sand rails moved to cut the women off.

Hawker targeted the buggy and lit it up with three quick bursts. Desperately trying to keep the alley open he fired a burst at the men on the right and then at the group on the left. Alternating his shots like this he tried to keep them pinned down as Danielle and Sonia raced for the water.

It looked as if it might just work. The men who'd come to get them were cowering. They'd bit off more than they'd expected and had begun regressing into survival mode, staying down even when they didn't have to. Danielle was still accelerating, head down, throttle wide open.

And then, right in front of his eyes, something happened that Hawker could not believe.

CHAPTER 39

Danielle held the ATV's throttle at full and the four-wheeler flew down the sand gathering speed. Seeing no sign of Keegan or the airboat, she planned to race into the water as far as possible and then dive off with Sonia in tow.

They could swim out into the dark and hide in the reeds and the murk of the swamp. Their pursuers were still unlikely to shoot at them for fear of hitting Sonia, and eventually they'd have to leave or risk trouble with the Iranian military. But that did not help Hawker, and unless Keegan showed up and began throwing some fire support their way, Hawker wouldn't last long.

As they roared down the hill and onto the mud flat, Danielle listened for Hawker's shots. She knew he was deadly accurate, enough that she didn't look to either side, only ahead. If someone popped up it would be the last thing they did.

No one rose to challenge them, no one cut them off. Fifteen seconds and they'd be in the water.

And then suddenly, something was wrong.

She felt Sonia's hands slip from her waist, felt her fall away, and felt the ATV surge forward with the sudden reduction in weight.

She slowed slightly and turned a bit, enough to see.

Sonia had fallen in a heap, tumbling like a ball.

"What the hell?"

Danielle began a turn to pick her up, but shots flew her way. Tracers that she hadn't seen before in this fight. It was like they knew Sonia had fallen and could now open fire. She cut away from the incoming, but a shell or two hit the front right wheel.

The tire exploded. The ATV went down hard like a racehorse with a broken leg. Danielle flew off again, hit the mud at the swamp's edge, and slid forward like she'd landed on ice. Covered in mud, she hit the waterline and lay sprawled in muck.

A group of men were moving toward her, a second group racing toward Sonia. Unbelievably, the young woman stood and began to move toward them.

Staying low, Danielle unholstered her Beretta. From behind her a great noise came zooming forward. The airboat roared out of the darkness with Keegan at the helm. Rapid fire from the twin guns on the tripod scattered the men who'd come for her, but it was too late for Sonia. The men had her and were dragging her off.

Danielle raised her gun to fire but couldn't without hitting Sonia. She heard a shot from Hawker's ArmaLite. But then nothing.

The tables had been turned. They hauled Sonia into the waiting Humvee, threw her in the back, and slammed the door. Seconds later they were racing off. The other men piled on the sides of the second Humvee and the surviving sand rail, and the ragtag convoy raced off with its prize.

In a moment they were gone, disappearing into the dunes.

Danielle looked around. The light from the burning vehicles flickered across the desert, illuminating the wreckage of the battle: dead men, ruined machines, smoke, flame. Up on the slope, alone in the center of the carnage, it lit upon Hawker, stunned and immobile and staring after the departing vehicles.

*   *   *

Hawker could not believe what he'd just seen. Their enemy had taken Sonia. What's more, it seemed as if she'd given herself up willingly at the very edge of freedom.

Why?

His mind raced, but he found no answers. Had she fallen? Had she been injured by some gunfire he didn't see? Had she been trying to save them by sacrificing herself?

He had no idea. And in truth, the reasons didn't matter. They had her and they had the stone and things were infinitely worse than they'd been twenty-four hours ago.

On the sand beside him, the man Hawker had clubbed with the rifle was coming to.

Hawker looked down. The young man looked familiar. Hawker had seen him in Paris. This was the man who'd managed to jump off the boat and disappear into the Seine.

The man looked up with glazed-over eyes, and the fury that rose in Hawker became hard to contain. Twice this man had tried to murder friends of his; twice he'd been the cause of anguish and grief.

"You're a dead man," Hawker growled.

A wave of fear washed across the man's face.

He turned from Hawker.

"Look at me, you son of a bitch!" Hawker shouted.

The man did not respond. He was moving his arm toward his face. He had something in his hand, something small.

Danielle was coming up the side of the dune.

The man's hand moved.

Hawker snapped the gun toward him.

"No!" Danielle shouted.

Hawker's rifle cracked and the echo of its report rolled across the night.

CHAPTER 40

Danielle stared at the man on the ground. Hawker had blown a hole in the man's hand and he now clutched it, writhing in agony. A black pistol lay on the ground beside him.

"I thought you were going to kill him," Danielle said, sounding relieved.

Hawker turned to her and the look on his face froze her heart.

"I am going to kill him," Hawker said. "But not before he tells me where they're taking her."

The scanner on Danielle's belt began to squawk again. She could hear the words, enough to make out that they were saying something about Americans near the swamp.

"You're going to have to do it somewhere else," she said.

Hawker seemed to know that. He'd already slung Danielle's rifle over his shoulder and was bending down to pick up the injured man.

Danielle helped, using a strip of cloth to bandage the man's hand and then tying his wrists with another strip.

Hawker threw the man over his shoulder and carried him down the slope. Danielle ran ahead, climbing aboard the airboat with Keegan and breaking out extra ammunition.

She saw Hawker wade into the water and toss the man on board like a sack of flour before climbing on himself.

"Let's go," she said.

Keegan gunned the throttle and spun the wheel. The airboat turned and raced out across the swamp.

CHAPTER 41

Hawker stood in the kitchen of a small house, in a vacant section of Al Qurnah, washing the grime from his hands and face. Burying his face in a towel, he tried to think and clear his head even as it pounded with post-battle adrenaline.

His eyes burned from the sand and the wind while his mind burned with rage. Try as he might, Hawker could not come to grips with the sight of Sonia falling from Danielle's ATV and then running toward their assailants.

As Danielle put in a call for Moore to contact them, Keegan came up and put a hand on Hawker's shoulder.

"I'll guard the bugger," he said, referring to their prisoner, who sat tied and gagged in another room. "You want me to cave his head in?"

Hawker intended to interrogate the bastard but he needed to get his wits about him. Although anger could be useful it had to be wielded with control.

"I'll do it myself if it comes to that," he said.

Keegan nodded and walked out of the kitchen, just as Danielle came in, looking keen to wash her own face.

"I'm sorry," she said. "We'll find her. Somehow we'll find her."

Hawker appreciated the kindness. He wasn't used to it, and so he appreciated it all the more.

He moved over as Danielle took off her jacket and shoulder holster. His own holster lay on the counter, and as he glanced at it Hawker's eye fell onto the gun in the holster. It was a smaller pistol, not the 9 mm Beretta that Danielle normally carried.

"You handed this to me," he said. "Where'd you get it?"

"It was Sonia's," she said. "Somehow we traded."

"You give it to her in the first place?"

"No, she had it with her."

Hawker studied the weapon. It was a .25-caliber automatic. The sight of it left a sickening feeling in his stomach, a possibility he didn't want to consider.

He handed the towel to Danielle, stepped away to grab his phone, and sent a text message to a number in France.

A moment later Moore was on the satellite line and the three of them were having a teleconference.

". . . the CDC confirmed all the numbers on infection rate and virulence. And the threat is now receiving the highest-priority response," Moore said.

"Meaning what?" Hawker asked.

"Stockpiles of antivirals are being increased. Interpol is redoubling its efforts and the president is going to brief leaders of NATO countries in the morning."

"That's all political bull," Hawker said. "We need to do something and we need to do it now."

"I'm open to suggestions," Moore said.

"We should be going after these bastards," he said. "We should have full recons of southern Iran going by now. We should have strike teams in there, we should have helicopter patrols scanning the coast, and we should be violating Iranian waters looking for a getaway boat because these anti-God lunatics are probably not planning on staying in the Islamic republic."

He noticed Danielle studying him, her eyes kind. Moore was blunt.

"Hawker, I understand that Sonia is your friend but a mini-invasion of Iran is—"

"It's not about her being a friend," Hawker said. "She's the key now. They came after her in Dubai to disrupt the fund-raiser—which put her back in Ranga's shoes: desperately looking for funding—and because they wanted to grab her in person. If they had gotten what they needed out of Ranga there would be no need for them to take her. But Ranga pulled some kind of trick on them."

"Like what?"

Hawker shrugged. "Maybe he told them that everything they needed was at the lab, hoping they'd blow themselves up going to get it. Or maybe they killed him too quickly by mistake. Either way, they didn't give a damn about her until he was dead. There can only be one reason for that."

"Because they want her to finish what he started," Moore said.

"Exactly."

"Suppose that's correct," Moore said. "Any idea how long it will take to synthesize the serum?"

"She said she could do it in a day."

Moore took a breath and nodded. "Yang insists that's the simplest part."

"How long do think she'll hold out?" Danielle asked.

"Not long," Hawker said. "A day, maybe two; depends what they do to her. Depends on if she even wants to hold out."

Neither of them asked him to elaborate, which he was thankful for. In his anger he'd begun to say things he wasn't sure he meant.

"I'm afraid they might not have to do anything to her," Moore said.

Hawker looked up. "What do you mean?"

"Two things have happened," he said. "First, someone hit Paradox last night and made off with computer records and various stock from their lab. No one's sure, because the company is in a shambles, but we're guessing they have the viral stock for 951."

It kept getting worse.

"In addition," Moore said, "the NRI office that you dropped Sonia's aunt and sister at in Kuwait went dark at almost the same time. Someone hit it hard. Both of them are gone."

A new wave of bitterness swept forth as he pictured the little girl with her arthritis and failing vision being manhandled by the cult's thugs.

"How did anyone know they were there?" Danielle asked.

"Don't know," Moore said. "They might have been watching the house."

"This isn't my first dance," Hawker said. "I promise you no one followed us."

"Could have been a tracer, or from an aircraft or a neighbor's tip," Moore said.

Hawker tensed, trying to contain himself. This latest news was throwing him off balance. How the hell was this group always one step ahead of them? It was as if the cult knew their playbook. As if they were listening in. Which would be impossible unless . . .

The only one who knew they were going to Iran besides him, Danielle, and Moore was Sonia. And the only person who knew where the safe house was besides him, Danielle, and Moore was Sonia.

Hawker prayed he was wrong, and just as paranoid as everyone accused him of being, but the image of Sonia falling off the back of that ATV almost deliberately continued to run through his mind. He'd begun to think that Sonia was involved with the cult somehow.

Ranga had warned him to trust no one. He hadn't listed an exception for his daughter. Could their falling-out have been more than just another argument?

The thought made Hawker sick, but it didn't affect what they had to do now. The next move had to be the same.

"If they have her sister, then Sonia won't hold out at all. And if they have 951 they might not even need her," he said, bluntly. "So you might as well assume that weapon will be up within the next twenty-four hours. That means we have to find them before they go underground again. It took us an hour to get back here. It would have taken them twice that long to get to the coast. And that's why we have to intercept them."

Over the phone Moore exhaled audibly. "Things don't work that fast, Hawker. Even if I could get the president to agree, he'd have to issue the orders, move units into place. No one's standing by to do what you suggest. Getting units on-site in three hours would be a miracle."

"Give me a helicopter. I'll start myself."

"Getting you killed by an Iranian missile isn't going to help us," Moore said. "Sit tight. I'll call back in half an hour."

"Sit tight?" Hawker said, raising his voice.

"What else can we do?" Danielle asked.

Hawker hesitated. "We have one of their guys," he said. "We can break him."

"You want to torture him?" Danielle said, making no effort to hide her disgust.

"This is an extreme circumstance," he said. "Besides, we're on foreign soil, he's not an American, the Constitution doesn't apply. Isn't that what we've been told?"

Hawker was addressing his words to Moore, but Danielle had taken over. "Forget about the Constitution. This is insane. You're not a torturer."

"I've been on the other end of it," he said. "I know what to do."

"And what do you think you're going to get out of him?" she asked. "He's Arab. Probably just a local like the guys they hired in France."

"He is one of the guys they had in France," Hawker said. "He has the brand, the same one Ranga had. He's part of the cult."

"He might not break," she said.

"Everybody breaks," Hawker insisted.

Danielle shook her head. "It's still unreliable. Look at Ranga. They tortured the hell out of him. Did they get what they wanted?"

That pissed him off. "All the more reason not to give a damn about this guy," he said. "For all we know, he's the one that did it."

Danielle glanced at the satellite phone, seeming to notice Arnold maintaining his silence.

"You're not actually considering this?"

"We have to consider all options at this point," Moore replied.

"We have enough here to make Gitmo look like Club Med," Hawker said, trying to seize the initiative. "And we don't have time to waste."

"No!" Danielle shouted. "Even if you forget the morality, torture has been shown unequivocally to be a weak intelligence-gathering tool. At best. You both know this. Put that guy through hell and he'll tell you anything to stop the pain. By the time we verify what he's said, it's too late anyway."

Hawker hated how he felt. A fissure had opened up between him and Danielle in Paris. The slightest of fractures. He'd felt it in Lavril's office and afterward. Now a wedge was driving deeper into that gap, forcing them to opposite sides.

He held his tongue, trying not to throw fuel on the fire. Danielle took a step back as well.

"The most productive intel we got out of Iraq came from Saddam himself," she said. "And not because we put him on the rack, but because an interrogator did a great job getting inside his head."

"We don't have that kind of time," he said. "Billions of people are going to suffer if we fail. If there's a chance, even one chance in a hundred that this guy knows where they're going, then we have to break him and we have to do it now."

"It's wrong," she said, fury in her eyes.

"Right and wrong don't matter anymore," Hawker said, realizing he agreed with her to some extent but that nothing mattered except stopping the misery.

"Do what you can for now," Moore said, ending the discussion. "But no torture. Keep him awake, coerce him, pump him full of anything that might loosen his tongue. But let's not cross that line, yet. If we have twenty-four hours, let's use it."

Hawker ground his teeth and looked away. He wasn't sure he could follow that order for long but he'd try. Across from him, he could see the relief on Danielle's face: nothing like victory, just thankfulness mixed with exhaustion.

"In the meantime," Moore added, "I'm tapping every available asset. Something will turn up."

Hawker hoped Moore was right, but he doubted it. Unlike other enemies they'd dealt with—foreign nations, terrorist groups, rogue billionaires—this group lived off the grid. They still had the same questions about this cult that they'd started with. Another twenty-four hours wouldn't change that. But he feared it might change the fate of the world.

CHAPTER 42

Arnold Moore was used to facing difficulties head-on. Troubles didn't go away on their own; if ignored they grew. If pain was to come, let it come and get it over with. If hard decisions were to be made he favored making them quickly rather than putting them off. Perhaps that's why no one had ever asked him to run for office. Those traits did not work for politicians.

And yet he found himself in a precarious position of having to balance his natural instincts and the actions that would follow if he acted on them.

Part of him wanted to call Danielle and Hawker and authorize the use of any force necessary to get information out of their prisoner. History would surely judge him harshly if this plague hit and he'd done less than all he could.

On the other hand, it would be an illegal order anyway, perhaps just enough to cover Danielle, assuming she would even follow it, and Hawker, who most undoubtedly would.

But he had chosen to put off the decision in hopes that some other avenue would appear. In a world of black and white he was hoping for a third way. Hoping the trouble would go away on its own.

It was an uncomfortable feeling and it didn't free him of any angst or even protect him really.

The fact was, Hawker and Danielle were holding a foreign prisoner as a hostage, torturing him in minor ways already, some of which would not pass the Geneva Convention. That they were doing it in a foreign country, violating not only American law but also the laws of Iraq, made it worse.

The NRI had no police power. They didn't even have the wink-and-nod status that had been granted to the CIA. If the truth came out it would be disastrous. Especially for an agency with as checkered a recent past as the NRI.

Two and a half years earlier the Brazilian mission that had included Danielle and Hawker had turned into an unmitigated disaster. Later investigations showed the NRI's then director, Stuart Gibbs, to be up to his neck in fraud, embezzling from the institute accounts, responsible for at least one murder and for attempting to kill Arnold Moore days later. Gibbs was proven to be in league with a radical billionaire who wanted to steal what the NRI was looking for and was suspected of planning to kill the entire team in some "accident" once they found it.

After the whole thing blew up, it was widely believed that the NRI would be shut down, but a last-minute reprieve put Moore in charge and kept the doors open.

Two years later Moore had been forced to break ranks with everyone in Langley and the West Wing in an attempt to avert a worldwide calamity. Disobeying direct orders, he'd gone all out to do what he believed was necessary, being proved right only at the very last moment—and after being shot and run over by the director of the CIA.

By inches, the NRI had avoided death a second time.

The current situation looked like a third fastball coming right down the pipe. They'd fouled the other two off, but miss this one and they were out. Miss this one and the whole world might be out.

Tired of running it over in his mind, Moore considered contacting the president, informing him, and letting the nation's elected leader make the call. But as weak as Moore felt about the inability to make any choice, he felt even weaker passing the buck.

He, Danielle, and Hawker were closest to the situation. If they couldn't decide, how could someone who saw the events only on paper make a good decision? He might as well just flip a coin, or close his eyes and swing away.

Thankfully his intercom buzzed. A time-out to interrupt his circular reasoning.

"This is Moore," he said.

"Mr. Moore, this is Walter Yang," the voice on the other side said. "I've found something odd in the virus code. I'm wondering if we have any further information from the field operatives."

Moore had promised Yang data from Sonia's corporation, but the hit on their lab had stopped it from coming in.

"I'm afraid not," Moore said. "What do you have?"

"Just some patterns in the inert section that seem very odd."

"Dangerous?"

"No," Yang said. "They're still inert. But they aren't random. At least I don't think they are."

"Any guesses?" Moore asked, still convinced there was something in that code that mattered.

"Not yet."

"We're running out of time, Walter."

As if to emphasize that fact the intercom buzzed again.

Moore's assistant spoke. "It's the president's chief of staff," she said. "Line two."

"Get me something, Walter. Anything."

"I'll do the best I can."

Moore hung up, took a deep breath, and hit the button for line two.

CHAPTER 43

Hawker's thoughts drifted back to Africa.

The quiet of a humid night was broken by the sound of thunder. It drowned out the constant buzz of crickets and cicadas.

Hawker stared out through a warped screen door made of rotting wood and mesh, held together by rusted nails and a coat of peeling and faded paint. The door never closed right, but pulled tight it kept most of the insects out.

The rain began to pour through the darkness of the night. It rattled the corrugated tin roof above, hitting so hard that it sounded more like hail than rain. A second wave of thunder rolled in from the southwest, crashing overhead and shaking the fragile house like an earthquake.

A second later a bedroom door opened behind him. A young woman of no more than twenty came running out, startled and wide-eyed. Not a touch of makeup or even a wrinkle marked her tan face. She seemed to relax when she saw Hawker.

"I dreamt that you left us," she said, pulling her black hair back in a ponytail and sounding relieved to be wrong.

"I'm not leaving without you," he said. "I told you that."

"I know but if Father doesn't . . ."

Before she could finish, the phone rang. The sound was peculiar, tinny and dull, as an old worn-out bell inside a rusted metal housing barely managed to function. Hawker picked up the faded plastic phone and held the receiver to his face.

"Right," he said. "I figured that."

Sonia looked up at the ceiling in frustration. She knew what was being said.

Hawker hung up the phone.

"He's not coming back tonight," she said. "Is he?"

"They're not giving him much space," Hawker said. "They'll keep him at the lab as long as they can."

"I swear he wants to stay here," she said angrily. "He doesn't see what's happening."

She looked outside at the pouring rain. Hawker followed her gaze. Somewhere out there, somewhere through all the rain and the jungle and the danger was freedom and a normal life.

Sonia wanted it. Whatever reasons she'd had for coming with her father to Africa, months as a virtual prisoner had been enough to override them. But freedom had been slipping further and further away.

If Hawker hadn't interfered months ago, she might already be in the generals' possession, either as a slave or a bargaining chip or both. If that wasn't enough to fear, the generals' men, white mercenaries and black soldiers all, looked at her as if she were some prize they might claim.

Why not? She was beautiful, young, healthy. And this was central Africa. You took what you wanted by force. No one asked questions.

Despite his efforts to protect her, Hawker knew a day would come when the general or some of his men gave up caring about repercussions. One day, in this land Sonia would face rape, imprisonment, and eventually death.

Hawker had finally beaten this truth into Ranga's skull.

And despite Ranga's faith in Hawker as Sonia's body-guard, Hawker knew that if someone important decided that day had come, all he could do was make it costly for them.

As he watched Sonia, her chest heaved and fell in a sort of controlled panic. She moved to the sink in the small kitchen.

"Everything is flooding," she said, turning on the fau-cet. "The water will be no good in the morning. We should run some and boil it, so that way we have good water to drink on the journey and—"

Hawker walked up beside her and gently turned off the tap. "We have enough," he said, putting his hand on hers and pulling it away from the spigot.

She looked up at him with tears in her eyes. "Then we should go," she said, her voice cracking. "We can't keep waiting. They're going to know."

He could hear the panic in her voice, months of living on the edge having chipped away at everyone's calm and resolve. The last two weeks had been the worst, plan-ning to go each night, postponing it because of the rain or the fact that Ranga was held at the lab or other rea-sons, including a gut feeling Hawker had that they were being watched.

Their biggest fear was that the generals would suspect their plans to leave. To avoid that suspicion Ranga kept working hard at the task they'd assigned him, and Sonia and Hawker did their best to act as if nothing was wrong. But fearing that someone was watching you had a way of making people act just differently enough to tip off those who were watching.

On previous nights, during a break in the weather, Hawker had spotted military vehicles parked on the dirt road or even patrolling where they'd never bothered to before. Like Sonia, he feared that something had been given away, but to act rashly would only tip their hand.

He'd seen no one this evening. Perhaps that was because they'd planned to keep Ranga at the lab. Or because they knew the rains were coming hard tonight.

He glanced outside. The downpour was turning the dirt road into a bed of oozing red clay. A drainage ditch Hawker had dug to funnel water away from the house was already filled and flowing like a small river.

"We can't go yet," he told her.

"When can we go?"

"I don't know, but not yet. Not tonight."

She looked away, fighting the internal struggle, shaking her head at thoughts only she knew. Her eyes were welling up, her chest heaving and falling as if panic was setting in. She looked as if she might burst into tears, but instead she grabbed the keys to their four-wheel-drive truck and ran for the door.

She bashed open the screen door, crossed the flat wood planks that served as a porch, and rushed out into the pouring rain. Hawker chased her, grabbing her as she reached the truck.

"Look at this!" he said, raising his voice to be heard over the rain. "Look at the roads. We can't drive in this."

"Neither can they!" she shouted back.

"We can't ford the river if it's flooded. So if we go now, the only way across is the bridge at Adjanta," he said. "They'll have a hundred men there; you know they will. The only thing we can do right now is keep it together and wait out the rain."

"There must be another way," she said.

He shook his head.

"There must be," she begged, as if he could make it so.

Tears streaked her face, mixing with the rain. She pulled from Hawker's grasp and slumped down in the mud, her back against the truck. Her face registered surrender, exhaustion, and despair.

"I don't care what happens anymore," she said. "I just need it to happen and be over with."

"Sonia, just hang on," he said, crouching beside her.

"I can't wait any longer," she said, sobbing. "Father will never leave. Even if we all die here. He'll never go."

Her hands fell heavy into her lap. The keys splashed into the mud. In some ways she was right: Twice they'd had chances to make a break for it during gaps in the weather, and twice Ranga had found some excuse why they couldn't go just yet.

Reaching forward, Hawker put an arm under her legs and one around her back, scooping her up. She was limp, a rag doll, exhausted by an obsession and a life no twenty-year-old should have to live.

"Look at me," he said, holding her against his chest.

She turned her eyes toward him.

"I promise you," he said. "I promise you, I'm not going to let anything happen to you. When the rains pass we'll go. If your father doesn't want to come then he can stay on his own. But I'll take you out of here, whether he comes or not."

Her head fell heavy onto his chest, her arms wrapped weakly around his neck, and her body shook with chills and sobs. He carried her across the porch, up the two steps, and back into the house.

He brought her to the kitchen, placed her down on the counter, and brushed the wet hair off her face. He smiled at her and stretched for a towel. It was just out of reach.

"You're going to have to let go," he said.

"I don't want to."

She stared into his eyes and he sensed that calmness had returned to her. The fear was gone; she felt safe in his arms. And Hawker had to admit it felt good to have her there.

She leaned forward and kissed him. When he didn't pull away, she pulled him closer, holding on tightly and

kissing him harder. He kissed her back, feeling the warmth of her body through their wet clothes and giving in to feelings he'd kept at bay for months. Feelings that Sonia had made clear to him but Hawker had chosen not to act on.

It wasn't that she was too young; she wasn't. She was twenty. He was only thirty. It wasn't that he worked for her father. Or that they spent their days as virtual prisoners who could not let their guard down. Those reasons had never really mattered, and to whatever extent they had, they evaporated as he kissed her and pulled her close.

In the heat and the passion of lust and love and breaking away from the fear, all thoughts left him except one: The moment he got Sonia and Ranga to freedom, to some civilized part of the world, he would have to let her go. There was nowhere for this to go, nothing ahead except pain for both of them.

That thought lingered, even as they pulled off each other's soaking wet shirts and their hands began exploring each other's bodies.

"Take me with you," she asked, giving voice to Hawker's lingering fear.

"I can't," he said. "It won't be good for you."

"It can't be worse than this," she said.

"It's always worse than this," he said. Until recently, guarding her and Ranga had been like heaven. Whatever was next would be closer to hell.

"I don't care," she said, her eyes closed, her words breathless as she pressed the side of her face against his. "I don't care."

Hawker wanted not to care, but he knew in his heart that he couldn't do that to her. Not if he loved her. Not even if he didn't.

The door banged open behind them. Hawker turned with a start.

Two men in fatigues, one white, one black, stood there. The white man held the keys to the truck.

"You lose these?" he said.

The men had been watching. From where, Hawker didn't know, but this was a bad sign. It may have tipped their hand.

Hawker turned and stood with his back toward Sonia. He put his hands against the countertop. His fingers found a knife.

"That's a nice piece of ass you got there," the white man said. He turned to the black soldier. "What do you say we get some of that?"

As the man spoke, Hawker gripped the knife and charged. The white soldier swung his head back around just as Hawker slammed into him, plunging the knife into his chest. Gunfire sprayed into the floor and off to the right as the soldier squeezed the trigger on his weapon reflexively.

Hawker pushed him back, slamming him into the black soldier. The three of them crashed to the ground. Hawker pulled the knife out and plunged it into the black soldier's neck. It erupted with blood. The man's head tilted back and his eyes rolled up.

Hawker held it there, held the two men down as they died. And then a shot rang out.

He snapped his head around in time to see a third soldier fall in the doorway.

He turned back to the kitchen. Sonia held his pistol, her hands shaking. She and Ranga had sworn they would never kill, but to save him Sonia had done just that.

Hawker stood, grabbed one of the rifles, and scanned the terrain outside the door. A military jeep with a hard-top sat there. It appeared to be empty.

He backed up to Sonia. She was still shaking, still aiming the pistol where she'd fired it.

"It's okay," he said, helping her to lower the gun.

Her eyes blinked and she refocused on him as the sound of thunder rumbled again.

"Put this on," he said, handing her shirt back to her.

She nodded slowly and slipped her arms into the shirt.

"We have to go," he said, pulling his own shirt on.

She seemed confused. "What?"

"We have no choice now," he said.

She turned to him and instead of fear or concern, all he saw was relief. They would finally be leaving this horrible place, and whatever happened they would never be coming back.

CHAPTER 44

Danielle came out of the interrogation room exhausted. She and Hawker had been taking four-hour shifts. Keegan had gone out. Like Moore he was trying to "tap any contact" he could find in hopes that there was information on the street about this group that the intelligence agencies did not have.

Trying to get information out of the prisoner, they'd kept the lights blazing, forced him to sit with his hands tied behind his back and questioned him repeatedly. When they weren't firing questions at him, they taped a pair of headphones to his skull, blasting Western rock and roll into his ears. Danielle had also injected him with various stimulants and barbiturates that were supposed to weaken his resolve and loosen his tongue. But so far they'd gotten nothing from him, except a name he claimed over and over: *Scindo*.

As she left the room, she propped the door open and sat where she could keep her eyes on him. Considering the nature of the cult they were dealing with, she feared he might try to kill himself. It wouldn't be easy with his hands and feet taped but she wasn't taking any chances.

Hawker was supposed to be sleeping during her shift, but she found him sitting at the kitchen table with one of the 9 mm Berettas lying in front of him. He had the clip out and was loading it methodically, carefully slot-

ting in one bullet after another, making sure they seated correctly, as if it mattered.

She'd seen the odd-looking type of shells before. It wasn't a good sign. Hawker was nearing the breaking point.

"We can't wait much longer," he said.

Over the past sixteen hours Hawker had grown quiet, aloof, as if he couldn't talk to her now. He hadn't slept much more than their prisoner. Certainly she'd found it hard to sleep during his shifts, fearing Hawker would take the situation into his own hands.

They'd discussed several options, none of which she liked. And since then, Hawker had been brooding in silence.

"I'm not the enemy," she said.

He looked up.

"I know that," he mumbled, then went back to the loading.

At least they were talking.

She thought how heavy his heart must be. Feeling betrayed from all sides.

"You sent a text to Lavril," she said.

"Tapping my phone now?"

"Keeping an eye on my partner."

He didn't seem to buy that answer. "I need to know what caliber gun was used at rue des Jardins," he explained. "Lavril said it was a small caliber, maybe twenty-five."

"Why?"

"Sonia mentioned being in Paris the day that all went down. She said she was looking for her father but now I'm not so sure."

Danielle sat back, surprised. "You think she's involved in this?"

He exhaled heavily, sounding worn-out. "What if she was at the house?" he said. "What if that .25-caliber pistol she gave you is the one that finished off those guys."

"Hawker . . ."

"She and Ranga had a falling-out," he added. "She told me she led that cult to Ranga. That she had contact with them before he did. What if all of them were involved, desperate to figure out how to save Nadia, and then Ranga bailed? His message said not to trust anybody."

"You're overthinking this," she said, understanding how he was drawing the conclusions but feeling he had to be wrong. "What about the attack in Dubai?"

He reached into his pocket and pulled out his phone, pressed the Internet button, and slid it across the desk toward her. She looked at the page displayed on his screen.

Drug company executive killed in ambush. Authorities have recordings linking him with the Dubai shootout.

The photo showed a burned-out car with an inset of the executive's smiling face. The photo came from the company's PR file.

"You don't necessarily believe this?"

"The guys in Dubai were different," he said. "They weren't locals, they were well equipped, they came in a five-million-dollar helicopter, for goodness' sakes."

"Aum Shinrikyo had a helicopter, too," she said. "A Russian gunship, minus the guns. No one says cults have to travel on foot."

"Remember the guys in France? One of them had a knife as a weapon. The guys in Dubai were professionals."

She put the phone down, not interested in looking at the burned-out hulk of a car anymore.

"We have two chunks of that stone," he continued. "Maybe seventy-five percent of the whole brick. Do you see any golden ball in our sections?"

Danielle had taken the two pieces apart and found nothing, except a curved interior wall that looked as if something round or spherical had been pressed up against it when the mud dried.

It reminded her of the Styrofoam that came with everything big enough to need a cardboard box. After you emptied the box you could tell what had been in it by the shape of the preformed Styrofoam packaging.

She remembered what Sonia had said. *The ancients sealed the seeds in a waxen ball and then covered them in gold, before hiding it within the secret vessel.*

If that golden ball existed it seemed likely that it had been contained entirely within the small section that Sonia had taken.

"She just grabbed what was in front of her," Danielle said.

"She grabbed it first," he said. "Before either of us reached in. Before I even said anything."

"That doesn't mean she knew what she was getting."

"I think she did," Hawker said. "She studied it, when it broke."

Danielle remembered Sonia looking at the broken pieces, staring at them like she was in shock. It had seemed like confusion and sadness to Danielle; now Hawker seemed to see it as cold, calculating study.

"For an instant, in the dark," she said, defending the young woman.

"She slowed us down on the way back to the ATVs and then she slipped and gave us away."

It all made some sense, but Danielle couldn't believe it was true. More likely lack of sleep and desperation were getting the better of Hawker. "Don't do this to yourself," she begged. "In the end it doesn't really matter, does it? She's not the important thing here."

He tilted his head slightly, pursing his lips as if another blow had just landed. Instantly she regretted the choice of her words. Tact was often the first casualty of exhaustion.

"I need to know," he said.

"Why?"

"Because I want to believe in her."

Danielle could understand that. "If Lavril says the wounds are from a .25-caliber that doesn't prove anything. Even if it did, it'll just leave you hating her for betraying you and hating yourself for believing in her."

He remained silent and she hoped her words were reaching him.

"And if it comes back that the kill shots were fired from a .32 or .380 or a .22, then you'll hate yourself for failing her somehow even though you did everything you could."

Hawker took a breath. He put the last bullet in the clip and slid the clip home in the handle of the gun.

She reached out and put her hand on his hand and the pistol at the same time. She wasn't good at this part, at healing or helping. It had never been her nature.

He looked up and this time he held her gaze. "What would you have me do?" he asked.

She did her best to answer honestly. "I'd try to forget about her and finish the mission. I'm not saying it's easy."

He looked at the wall, bitter and tense.

"Why else would she run to them?" he asked, getting to the point that obviously hurt him the most.

Everyone had their blind spots, things they just couldn't see because their temperament prevented it. She guessed that maybe Hawker had manufactured his own blind spot in regards to Sonia.

"Do you really not get it?" she asked. "She saw you on the hill. You think she didn't know what was going to happen? You think she didn't know you were going to die up there trying to save her?"

Hawker looked away, considering the thought.

"You think either of us wanted you to stay there?" she added. "If it had been her—or me—up on the hill, what would you have done?"

Hawker seemed to get what she was saying, but she couldn't tell if he believed it. Maybe didn't want to. Maybe it was easier not to.

"She loves you," Danielle said bluntly. "You were willing to die to save her and she was willing to return the favor."

"I wasn't planning on dying," he said.

"But it was a distinct possibility."

"She couldn't know they'd follow her," he said.

There was still anger in his voice, a ragged edge.

"She knew they weren't shooting at her. She made a choice. You have to decide if you think it was for her benefit or for yours."

Beside her, Hawker's phone lit up. She noticed a French country code. But it was a text, not a call.

"It's Lavril," she said.

He nodded. "And?"

She pressed the View Message icon, then hesitated for a moment as she read it. "The gun was a twenty-two. Not Sonia's."

A look of relief eased onto Hawker's face. And then a new kind of anger took its place.

"So she's at their mercy," he said, and then nodded toward the detention room. "And that son of a bitch in there knows where she is."

Before she could react, he snatched up the pistol, stormed toward the interrogation room, and kicked the door open.

CHAPTER 45

Sonia stood in an open doorway looking into an advanced genetics laboratory. It was spotless and clean and equipped with everything she and her father could have ever asked for. In fact they—or at least he—had asked for this equipment at one time. The sight of it made her sick.

"Move," a man said, jabbing her in the back with a rifle.

She stumbled forward into the gleaming room. Another man sat on a chair inside, grinning at her. He had a rectangular tattoo that curved around his neck and covered some kind of scar. In a strange way it almost looked like a bar code. A snake tattoo slithered down one arm from under the cuff of his black T-shirt. His eyes were points of black ice in a gleaming white room.

"Leave us," he said to the guard.

"Who are you?" she said.

"Don't you recognize your master?"

So this was the leader, the one she'd spoken to but never met.

"You're no 'master,' " she said. "You're just a murdering psychopath with a bunch of fools following you."

She expected venom from him, a slap across the face or hand to her throat to choke half the life out of her for what she'd said, but he seemed unmoved.

"See things so deeply, do you?"

She didn't respond.

"You're the fool," he said with disdain. "You and your pathetic allies. Hawker . . . Danielle . . . the ridiculous Arnold Moore."

She didn't recognize the last name, but a wave of trepidation swept through her as he spoke Hawker's and Danielle's names. She hadn't expected him to know or care who had been helping her. How could he know? she wondered. Why did he care?

She tried not to react.

"You think this is about you?" he said. "How vain."

She suddenly felt afraid even to speak. Was there something going on beyond what she understood?

The "Master" changed the subject.

"Your father bowed down before me," he said. "You will do the same. And then the whole world will follow."

It was the danger that had driven Ranga and her apart. In their own ways they'd attempted to mitigate that danger, Ranga going into hiding, Sonia trying to take Paradox public and raise enough money and publicity to the point where she'd be safe. But none of it had worked and this sick, twisted man in front of her was gloating over it.

Feeling a wave of strength flow from her anger, she looked around. For some reason a hammer lay on the bench beside her. She grabbed it and lunged forward, swinging it at him, but he caught her wrist as if he was waiting for it, twisted her arm around until it felt as if it might snap, and then swatted the hammer out of her grasp.

She expected him to let go now that she'd been disarmed but he continued to twist her hand, turning her wrist outward and down until it felt as if her elbow, her wrist, and her shoulder were going to come apart at the same time.

She let out a meek cry of pain but he didn't stop. Instead he pushed harder, stepping forward, pressing her

down until she was forced to her knees. With a shove he let her go. She fell backward and hit the floor.

In more fear than ever, Sonia scooted away from him until she hit the solid block of the workstation behind her.

The man with the tattoo stepped toward her, grabbed the hammer off the floor, and then yanked her up to her feet.

"Let me show you something more useful to do with this tool."

Grabbing the back of her arm he walked her over to another table. Resting in the middle lay the section of the tablet Sonia had placed in her pack. She knew what it held. She prayed she was wrong, but she doubted it.

The man grabbed a carbon steel chisel, placed it against the center of the tablet, and swung the hammer rather lightly.

One blow, one chime of metal on metal, and the tablet split in half. At the center, three small objects half the size of golf balls rocked back and forth. The baked clay clung to them but in places the gold leaf showed through.

The seeds of the Tree of Life lay inside.

"You think they're just going to stop?" she said, thinking of Hawker and his American government friend. "They want this as badly as you do."

"Maybe worse," the man said in a mocking tone.

"They'll come for me," she insisted. "And even if you kill me, they'll come for you."

"I believe you," he said sadistically. "In fact I'm counting on it."

Once again Sonia had been thrown off balance. The situation was terrifying. She was quite sure she was going to die before it ended, but each time her captor spoke or reacted differently than she expected, she grew even more afraid.

"You will bring me riches," he explained, looking down at her. "And you will bring me power over every-

one on this earth. But most important, you will bring *them* running to me."

Sonia felt weak and fearful and somehow culpable.

She'd expected Hawker would die trying to save her on the sand hill in Iran and she didn't want to think of it. She didn't want anyone else to suffer for what she and her father had begun and chased all these years. But the way this man talked . . . Something else *was* going on here. And suddenly she felt as if she were just a pawn.

"Go to hell," she said.

"There is no hell," he said. "Except the ones we make for ourselves."

"I don't care what you do," she said, trying to be strong. "I'm not giving you a damn thing. I'll kill myself before I let you make me the world's murderer."

The laughter came again. Derisive, mocking.

"I won't do anything to you," he said. "In fact, I'll let you live at the end. If you still want to."

He grabbed a radio. "Bring them in," he said calmly.

A second later the door opened and two more men came in, pushing other smaller figures in front of them, shoving them forward.

"Oh God," Sonia said, her knees buckling. Only by holding on to the table was she able to stand.

In front of her, at the hands of the men who had apparently killed her father, were Savi and Nadia. Savi was pushed to the floor; Nadia was shoved forward. Her glasses were gone and she smacked into the workstation as if she didn't see it.

Sonia ran to her. Tears were streaming down the little girl's weathered face. Sonia felt her heart breaking.

"It's okay," she said, corralling Nadia in her arms. "It's going to be okay."

She looked over at Savi. Her face was bruised, her nose badly broken.

"Please . . . ," Sonia begged, beginning to cry. "Please no."

Her tears flowed unabated. Her lips and her body quivered. Nadia was crying in her arms.

"They hurt Savi!" the little girl cried.

"I know, baby. I promise it's going to be okay."

She looked up at the man who'd called himself her master. He was now in every way. She would do anything to keep Savi and especially Nadia from harm. "Please don't hurt them," she pleaded. "I'll do whatever you want. Whatever you ask."

"I know you will," he said. "But to prove you should not doubt me, I give you proof of my resolve."

He snatched a gun from his belt and aimed it toward Savi.

"No!" Sonia shouted, covering Nadia's face, burying the child's face into her chest.

The gun sounded like a cannon when it fired. Sonia closed her eyes and heard the sickening thud of Savi's body hitting the floor and then nothing.

She held Nadia tight, cradling the young girl's head. "It's okay," she whispered over and over, not wanting the girl to look or to know or even guess. As it was, Nadia sobbed and held on to Sonia.

"Finish the serum," her master said. "Give me what your father promised and I'll let you all go when we're done."

In her heart Sonia knew it was a lie, but she couldn't speak it, couldn't force the truth out or stand or fight anymore. All her adult life she'd been fighting against the truth, and she couldn't do it anymore.

"And don't be too smart for your own good," the Master said. "You can still save her, but whatever you give us, she gets first."

She'd made a terrible mistake. She'd feared so badly for Hawker, been so certain he was going to die defending

her on the sand hill in Iran, that she'd let herself fall off the ATV. She knew the men wouldn't shoot her, she knew they would take her and scurry away for fear of losing their master's prize, and she'd been certain when she did it that she would probably end up dead. But she and her father were responsible for all this misery, so who better to sacrifice?

In dying she might right the wrong. End the trail that was leading the world to perdition. She even had a plan, a thought in her mind of how she could trick these men into thinking they had what they wanted and give them nothing. But now that they had her sister and they had 951, she was powerless.

"And if I don't give you anything?" she managed to ask.

"Then I'll torture you both to death and I'll release 951 instead."

At that moment Sonia wanted to die. She found herself wishing she'd died either the day before in the desert or back in Dubai or years ago in Africa. As irrational as it was, she cursed Hawker in her mind for saving her. He'd preserved her life just long enough to send her to hell. A hell of her own making.

CHAPTER 46

Caught flat-footed because something on Hawker's phone had distracted her, Danielle raced to catch him before he went too far.

As he slammed the door open, she saw Scindo stirring, a look of fright in his eyes. Hawker grabbed him, yanked him out of the chair, and threw him against the wall. Dropping down beside him, Hawker ripped the tape off the man's mouth.

"You're going to tell me where they are, you bastard!" Hawker yelled. He hoisted Scindo up, just far enough to knee him in the gut and then fire a right cross to his jaw. Scindo's lip burst open with blood.

"Hawker, stop!" Danielle shouted. "We don't have to do this!"

Hawker wasn't listening. When Scindo didn't reply, Hawker threw him to the ground again, kicked him again, and then stood on his chest.

"Listen to me," Danielle said. "There's something wrong here."

"Get out of here!" Hawker shouted. He grabbed a pair of pliers off the shelf, dropped onto Scindo with a knee, and jammed the pliers into the drywall beside him.

Scindo's eyes were as large as saucers as Hawker gouged out a huge hole right above the electrical socket. Slamming his fist into the wall, Hawker widened the hole, then

he reached in and, using the pliers, tore the copper wires loose from the socket.

"Hawker, there's a message on your phone. It came from my phone but I didn't send it."

Hawker wasn't listening. "You murdered her father!" he shouted.

For the first time the man replied, his eyes filled with fear. "I did not," he said in English.

Danielle took that as a positive and a negative. Scindo's determination not to talk might be breaking, but did that mean Hawker's insane plan needed to be tried?

"You lie!" Hawker Shouted, yanking more of the electrical cord through the wall.

"I don't," Scindo said. "It was not me. I never saw him."

Hawker stood, pulled the gun out of his belt, and put it down on the table behind him.

"Where are they taking her!" he yelled.

No answer.

"Where!"

When Scindo refused to speak, Hawker moved away from him an inch or two. Careful not to touch him, he jammed the two copper leads into Scindo's side. Sparks jumped, the lights dimmed and came back on, and Scindo screamed.

Watching this, Danielle's heart went into her throat. She knew what was coming. There was no way to turn back now.

"Tell me, you son of a bitch!" Hawker shouted.

"Stop it!" Danielle screamed at him.

"Tell me!"

Scindo held quiet and Hawker shocked him again.

The lights in the room dimmed and Scindo screamed. Hawker held the prongs on him, singeing the man's skin. The smell of hair and skin burning filled the room.

"For God's sake, Hawker!"

"Get out of here!" he yelled back.

"Please," she begged.

His response was to shock Scindo again. And Danielle could wait no longer.

She grabbed the gun off the table and cocked the hammer. The sound got Hawker's attention.

Hawker turned and Scindo's eyes followed. Both of them stared at her.

Tears were streaming down her face, welling up in her eyes, and rolling across her cheeks.

"Get away from him," she said firmly.

A look of utter shock appeared on Hawker's face. "Are you out of your mind?"

"Please," she begged. "I can't do this. I can't go where you're going."

"You're saving him?" Hawker whispered in disbelief.

"I'm trying to save you," she said.

Hawker's face hardened, as if this was another betrayal. "No," he said. "Go to hell. You're not stopping this."

He turned back to Scindo and shocked him again. The prisoner writhed and slammed his head into the wall.

"Hawker!"

"Tell me what you know!" Hawker shouted.

"Hawker, please!"

Hawker shocked Scindo again, only this time a gunshot echoed along with the prisoner's screams. Hawker fell forward, dropping the electric wires and slamming into the metal chair in the corner of the room.

It collapsed with a loud clang and Hawker rolled over on it. Lying prone, he turned back to face her. Staring back from the corner, he clutched a bleeding shoulder.

"Are you insane?" he grunted.

She ignored him. "Get up!" she shouted to Scindo.

If Hawker was in shock, Scindo was even more surprised.

"Get up!"

Scindo staggered to his feet, the shackles making it hard to walk, traces of smoke rising from his charred skin.

Hawker moved as if he were about to get up but winced in pain and fell back down. "What the hell is wrong with you?" he shouted.

She backed out the door, motioning for Scindo to follow. He shuffled through and she shut and locked the door behind her.

"Come with me," she said, heading toward the front door and wrapping a coat over Scindo's taped hands.

She opened the front door, her heart sick, her mind spinning. She hadn't wanted to do this, but Hawker had forced her.

"Down the stairs!" she shouted. Scindo hesitated as muffled sounds came from the interrogation room, where Hawker was shouting at the top of his lungs and slamming something against the locked door.

"Move!" Danielle shouted.

Scindo complied, hustling down the stairs as fast as his shackled feet would allow. Danielle followed, wondering where the hell she was going to go and not even wanting to think about what would happen now.

CHAPTER 47

Danielle found an abandoned building two miles from the safe house. It looked like it had once been a garage for large vehicles or a military depot, but heavy shelling or bombs from above had obliterated much of it. Half the roof was gone and the place was filling with sand and desert plants.

She pulled into the most sheltered part and hid her car. She ordered Scindo out and forced him into an abandoned office. File cabinets in one corner sat scorched and partially melted from the heat, either from the bombs that fell or the fires that must have followed.

She helped Scindo in, leading him to a place against the wall, where he sat knees up, hands in front of him, the bandaged hand Hawker had fired a round through bleeding heavily once again.

"Thank you," he said.

"Shut up!"

She pointed the gun at him.

She thought of Hawker's words, the devil always fights by dividing, dividing people against each other, Eve from Adam, mankind from God. She felt as if she'd been torn apart herself.

"The people you're protecting are murderers," she said, glaring at Scindo. "Even if you didn't kill Dr. Milan or the French policemen, you're part of it."

"Then why did you save me?" Scindo asked defiantly.

"I was trying to save him," she said.

He went quiet.

"Why are you protecting them?" she asked.

"They took me," he said. "I am part of them."

He spoke English well, but with something of a French accent.

"If you were part of them they would have come back for you," she said, trying to gain the upper hand.

"They did."

"Not here they didn't," she said. "And they're not going to, unless it's to put a bullet in your brain and keep you quiet. Like they did to your friends in France."

This seemed to hit near the mark. "You shot those men," he said sharply.

She shook her head. "Did we kill you when we had the chance? No, we captured you. We interrogated you. Murdering people is not what we do."

He glared back at her. He didn't believe her, she could see that. Or he didn't care. "What do we gain by killing off people who can tell us things? Huh? We didn't kill your friends. We would have interrogated them if we could have. So would the French. One of your people murdered them to keep them quiet."

Scindo stared. He seemed to be drifting toward anger. Whether it was at her or the feeling that she might be speaking the truth, she couldn't guess. She had to push.

"There's no rescue for you here," she said. "They left you out there once they had what they wanted. You're expendable, whatever your name is."

"I'm Scindo."

She shook her head.

"They must've thought I was dead," he stated.

"They could have checked," she said. "They could have killed all of us with ease and then checked on you.

But they didn't—they left. I'm telling you; you're alone now."

This seemed to bother him more than anything so far. "You shot your friend," he said. "Maybe you're alone, too."

She certainly felt alone, sick to her stomach at the turn of events, but she couldn't show it, not until there was no other hope.

"I did the right thing," she said proudly. "If you don't agree, I could take you back to him."

Scindo did not reply. He seemed to be studying her, trying to figure her out. Obviously he didn't want to be back in Hawker's clutches.

"So what will you do with me?"

"I'm not letting you go, if that's what you mean."

Other than that, she wasn't sure. There was no script for this. But at least he was talking. Maybe the madness could have some value, if she could coax even a little bit of intel out of him.

"Did you kill the policemen?" she asked.

"No," he said defiantly. "I'm not a killer, either."

He seemed proud of that, adamant, in fact. "Then why do you stand by while the people who left you plan to butcher half the world?"

Finally she seemed to be reaching him. He seemed moved by her statement, somewhat off balance. "I know your tricks," he said defensively.

She ignored him. There was a crack in his armor and she had to exploit it.

"They're going to release a virus that will cause misery everywhere. Do you understand that? Millions will end up starving, maybe billions. There'll be wars and hatred and violence. You can stop it."

"I live in it every day," he said.

"Where?" she asked.

He hesitated.

"And for that matter what's your real name?" she added. "I know my Latin. You weren't born with the name Scindo."

"What does it matter what name I was born with?" he said. "They don't call me by it. They call me *dirty Arab*. They spit at me. I'm French but the French hate me. If we fight they beat us; if we don't they ignore us. If we would just die and go away they would be happier."

"We?"

"All of us," he said, growing more agitated.

"Like the friends this cult of yours killed?"

"I didn't . . . they . . ."

He was agitated, straining at his cuffs, nostrils flaring. He was talking freely now. He was shouting.

"Where are you from?" she asked softly. "What can it hurt?"

It was a question she'd asked a hundred times before, only now she realized she already knew the answer. She needed him to say it first. A little crack, a trickle of truth, and then the flood. Or so she hoped.

"La Courneuve," he said finally.

"And your name," she said, speaking as kindly as possible. "Your *real* name."

His eyes darted around but he said nothing.

"You should really tell me," she said.

"Why?"

"Because if your friends find us before mine do, I'll probably be the last person to ever hear it."

"The Master named me Scindo," he said.

"What does your mother call you?"

He hesitated, a kind of sad pause.

"It's just a name," she said. "Mine is Danielle."

He looked around. He seemed to be thinking. His eyes fell for a moment and then he looked at her again. She could only guess at the war going on inside him.

"My mother named me Yousef," he said as his eyes found the floor. "Yousef Kazim. It was her father's name."

"Do you love her?" she asked.

"Of course. I love all my family." His voice rose. "That is why I fight."

This was the opening. This was her chance.

"Don't you understand what will happen if these people get what they want? Don't you realize that everyone you know will be harmed; everyone you care for will be worse off than before. They will suffer."

"It will be equal," he said defensively.

"No," she said. "It'll never be equal. Not on earth, not at the hands of men. The rich will still prosper but the poor will be worse off. They will see more misery and starvation, more destruction and pain."

"The rich will fear them," he said.

"Yes," she said. "And when they fear them they will pay armies to attack. Your family's lives will go from tough to miserable. It will happen everywhere. It will be a nightmare. And whatever chance they had once had, whatever hope you thought any of them had, will burn up like paper in the fire. And what will you have accomplished, but to seal their fate forever?"

"This is not true," he said, growing angry.

"It is," she said softly. "You know it is."

"And how will it be any different if I help you?" he said. The question was spat at her with venom, but she sensed there was at least a hint of honesty in it. *How would it be different?*

"Lives will be spared," she said. "Millions of lives. Maybe billions."

"And my family in La Courneuve?"

"I can't promise you it will be better," she said. "But it won't be worse. At least your mother will still have a son."

"I will not tell you," he insisted.

She sensed it slipping away.

"There's nothing to be gained from this," she said, feeling desperate now. "No riches, immortality, or fame. Only punishment."

"There is no God to punish me," he said.

"Maybe some believe that," she said, "but you don't. You have to believe in God to be angry with Him. You hate Him for what He's given you, but you believe He's out there."

"I don't," he insisted.

Now he looked away and Danielle knew this was the moment. She had to make him speak or he would retreat back into the shell of Scindo, the false persona that protected him, and they'd never break him in time, no matter what they did.

"Even if that's the case, you're still at the end," she said. "My friends will find us. They'll take me in chains and they'll take you somewhere that will seem like the darkest pit of hell. And I promise you, Yousef, they will not stop until they have made you speak every last secret you hold."

"I will not talk."

"You will," she said, pitifully. "If not to me, to them. They'll break you and you'll hate yourself for being broken. *And you will have nothing left.*"

He looked up at her.

"And what do you have left?" He finally sounded as sad as her.

"I have myself, Yousef. I did what was right in trying to save you."

She saw him quiver and look down. The drugs, the lack of sleep, the mental strain, she hoped it had weakened him enough.

"Please," she asked quietly.

He gazed at the floor.

"Please."

He did not look up, but staring at the ground, as if in a trance, he finally spoke.

"There's an island," he said.

"Where?"

"Out there," he said, still looking at the ground but nodding toward the south and the Persian Gulf. "There are buildings there, bombed and full of holes. A ship, a freighter I think, it sits on the rocks. That is where they took me."

He swayed back and forth but still did not look up. "They must have taken your friend there."

"Does the island have a name?"

"I don't know," he said.

"Yousef, please. I can stop them," she said. "But you have to tell me."

"I hope you stop them," he mumbled. "It is only an hour by boat. But I don't know if it even has a name. There are lots of birds there."

She took a breath. She hoped it was the truth, and she sensed it was the truth. If there was an island with a bombed-out ship beached on the rocks at its edge, one satellite pass would find it. And if they could find it, the terror could be stopped.

"They have missiles," Yousef said. "I saw them. They are for the virus."

A chill shot through her as she heard this news. The cult had everything they needed. But it had been only seventeen hours. There was a chance. "Thank you," she said.

Yousef did not respond. He just stared at the ground. She saw tears hit the floor.

"I've done things . . . ," he said, sounding broken inside.

"We all have," she told him.

He looked up.

"I am a traitor to everyone," he said, tears filling his

eyes and a panic of sorts growing over him. "I wish you would kill me."

Her heart felt for him, despite all he'd been a part of, despite everything he'd probably done. He couldn't have been much more than twenty. He seemed as much a victim as anyone else.

"You don't deserve to die," she said.

"They will mock me," he said, shaking.

She reached out and touched his face, wiping away some of the tears. He was sobbing, breaking down. He looked up, unending tears streaming over his face.

"They will say: *Here is the traitor. Here is Scindo. He rejected the Almighty and then betrayed those who took him in.*"

"No," she said firmly.

"They will," he insisted.

"No," she repeated. "They will say *Here is Yousef Kazim. Who in his darkest hour rejected the devil and gave the world a chance at life.*"

He gazed at her with wide eyes, as if some hope had come back within him. He continued to sob but he said no more.

Several minutes later, Yousef's cries had ceased, the numbness had returned, and she allowed him, still cuffed, to lie down and finally sleep.

She walked out of the small room, shutting what was left of the door behind her. She continued across the work bay to where she'd parked the car.

A figure stood beside it.

"Did he tell you?" Hawker asked quietly.

She nodded, thankful but exhausted. "Sorry about shooting you," she said.

He rubbed his shoulder. "It worked. But don't ever let those riot police tell you rubber bullets don't hurt."

"Blood pack was a nice touch."

"Almost dropped it," he said.

She nodded, but felt almost emotionless after all that had happened.

"I'll bring him back to the house," she said. "I don't want him to see you."

There were many reasons for that. Strategically, it made sense to keep the lie going. But mostly she didn't want Yousef to feel he'd been tricked. He had made an honorable choice, an almost impossible choice. She wanted him to feel whatever goodness might come from what he'd done.

Hawker nodded.

"He's not evil," she said. "He just fell."

"We all fall," Hawker said.

He seemed to understand. It was one of the things that Danielle found most refreshing in him. He was filled with arrogance at times and self-righteousness, but it was balanced by pity. He could look at the fallen and see himself.

CHAPTER 48

With dusk settling over the Middle East, Danielle sat in the left front seat of a maroon powerboat as it skimmed across the glassy surface of the Persian Gulf. To her right, Hawker's friend Keegan piloted the craft, while Hawker sat behind them, studying an image on the laptop computer that had been downloaded from the NRI mainframe. The body armor and the AR-15s they'd taken into the desert rested beside him on the bench seat.

A mile ahead she saw the outline of a crude carrier heading their way. The ship rode high in the water, its tanks empty.

"Stay clear of the channel," she said. "Don't want to be confused for suicide bombers."

"Right," Keegan said. "Any idea where we're going yet?"

"South," she said.

"I figured that," he said, "since we'd need wheels to go north from where we were."

She moved back to where Hawker was and sat down beside him.

"What do you think?"

He turned the laptop toward her. She'd studied the image briefly when it arrived, but since it would likely come down to planning an assault on the island, she figured Hawker was more qualified to look at it.

"This image came from an NSA satellite?" he asked.

"A pass this morning," she said. "Caught the island in the sweep, but it wasn't the target, so the information isn't as detailed as I'd like."

"The buildings are all on the south side," he said. "What isn't blackened and burned looks abandoned."

Danielle zoomed in on the island. It couldn't have been more than an eighth of a mile across. On one side there were bundles of mangled pipes and what looked like pumping equipment. A few control buildings and a helicopter landing platform built out over the water looked shot full of holes and falling apart. A four-hundred-foot vessel lay against the west edge of the island. It was difficult to tell if it was docked or had been run aground.

"Looks like what Yousef described," she said.

"It also looks abandoned."

"I believe he told me the truth as he knew it," she said. "Doesn't mean they didn't clear out once they got Sonia or the seeds."

Hawker nodded. "I believe he told you the truth, too. Do we have an infrared scan?"

"Not on this pass," she said, then glanced at her watch. "But the second pass should have gone over a few minutes ago. We'll know if there is activity there any minute now."

Thirty seconds later the satellite phone lit up. Danielle grabbed it.

For a second all she heard was the buffeting of the wind, caught in her own transceiver's microphone. She turned to the side, sheltering the phone. Moore's voice came through.

"Danielle?"

"Go ahead, Arnold."

"Where are you right now?"

"We're out in the Gulf, heading due south. Do you have the latest pass?"

"We do," Moore said. "NSA confirms heat sources from the stranded freighter and some of the other structures. That island should be dark but it's not."

About as she'd expected. It was good news. "So this is probably the right place."

"Seems to be," Moore said.

There was a shortness in his voice that she didn't like. As if he was waiting to drop some bad news.

"Where do we meet up with the assault team?" she asked.

"Danielle . . ."

"We could trail them in," she said. "Or we could go in with them. Either way they're going to need our help to confirm what we're looking for."

"There's not going to be an assault team," Moore said.

That was odd. They'd been preparing one an hour ago.

"What are you talking about?"

"We're not raiding the place."

"Why?" she asked.

"That rock is in Iranian waters," Moore reminded her. "It's been in dispute between Iran and Iraq for decades. The damage you see was done all the way back in '86. No one's touched it since."

"So?" she said. "What does that have to do with us? Surely we're not letting Iranians deal with it."

"Yes," he said sarcastically, "everyone here is eager to tell Mahmoud Ahmadinejad that the weapon of mass destruction he's always wanted is just waiting for him a few miles off his coast."

"Then what are we doing?" she asked. "If there's no assault team, and we're not going to involve the Iranians . . ."

"The navy's going to hit the island with a spread of Tomahawks," Moore said. "It's a presidential order."

"When?"

"Twenty minutes from now."

She took a breath. "What about the hostages?"

"I'm sorry," he said. "Obviously they'll be lost if they're on-site."

Silence rang on the line and Danielle glanced over at Hawker. He could hear every word. He hadn't reacted, almost as if he suspected it would go this way.

She felt for him. She understood why the president would make the decision Moore had attributed to him, and sentiment was not going to override that. But there were logical reasons not to blindly obliterate the island.

"What if the cult isn't there?" she said. "What if these are just some squatters? We're going to end up thinking we've saved the world only to get sucker-punched one day."

"We can establish that after the fact."

"After you blow the island to hell?" she said. "Do you think there will be enough left to establish anything? Do you think the Iranians are going to say, *'Hey, go ahead put some inspectors on our island, why not? Nice of you to blow it up for us in the first place'*?"

Moore responded with evidence. "The freighter wasn't there six months ago," he said. "We've tracked it to an undisclosed buyer in Singapore. It was dumped for scrap. It should be in pieces somewhere getting melted down, not jammed up on the beach of an Iranian island in the Gulf. This is the site, we're sure of it. And after what we've learned no one's taking any chances."

Danielle knew he was right, but she could only think of the heartbreak, and not just Hawker's.

"The virus Ranga created can be used for good," she said. "You know that. It could lead to all kinds of treatments, things that are just theoretical right now. You destroy that ship, you destroy the research."

"Better than a worldwide catastrophe," he said.

"And if they have another base?"

He hesitated.

"Come on, Arnold. There's a reason the CDC keeps anthrax and smallpox and other nasty germs on hand, because we need to research them and understand them in case something happens. This ship is our only chance to get ahold of 951 and the Eden virus. Our only chance to understand them. You blow it to ashes and the next time we see a virus like this, it'll be too late for everyone."

"Danielle, I know all this," Moore said, sounding exhausted. "I've spent the last hour making the same arguments to the president and his staff, but one concern overrides all the others. According to your prisoner they have missiles. Unless they're extremely short-range that puts Kuwait, southern Iraq, and most of the Gulf in the red zone. One missile, one dispersal, and it's all over."

The weight of the truth pressed her down like a heavy stone on grass. She felt spent, exhausted, defeated. She couldn't even think of another argument.

After days of fighting with Hawker, Moore, and Yousef, after traveling from Washington to Croatia to Paris to Beirut and then Iraq, she had nothing left, especially since she knew Moore was right.

Moore sensed it. "I appreciate everything you and Hawker have done," he said. "But direct from the president, you're both to stand down."

The buffeting sound returned. It took all she had to speak another word. "Anything else?"

"Please tell Hawker I'm sorry," Moore said.

"I will," she said, and then she clicked off and Moore was gone.

On the speeding boat in the Persian Gulf, she placed the phone down and turned to Hawker.

"You don't even have to say it," he said.

"I'm so sorry," she told him.

"They do what they have to," he said, sounding oddly at peace with the order.

She could guess why. "You're still going in," she said.

He nodded.

"Then I'm going with you."

"You don't have to do this," he said. "It's not your fight."

"Your fight is my fight," she said. "Besides, this is my job. They bomb that place to hell without any idea what's there and we'll never know if we've dodged a bullet or if it just hasn't been fired yet."

Hawker nodded, then looked past her. "Keegan, you want us to drop you over the side with a life jacket or two?"

Keegan looked back from the helm as if Hawker had lost his mind. "You know I can't bloody well swim," he said.

"You grew up on an island," Hawker replied. "You were a Royal Marine. Last I heard *marine* means something to do with the water."

"What can I tell you," Keegan said. "Standards were lower back then. Besides, the chance to violate Iranian sovereignty for a second time in two days absolutely intrigues me. I don't think it's ever been done. We could be legends. I could retire, put on fifty kilos and still get free pints at every pub in London if I had that feather in my cap."

Hawker chuckled and squinted into the distance. "So it's the three of us against whatever they have waiting." He turned back to her. "How many guys do you think they have?"

Danielle exhaled. "Knowing our luck, at least a hundred or so."

The absurdity of it brought a smile to Hawker's face. He began to laugh. Keegan did, too. And Danielle joined in, giggling at her own joke.

"Poor bastards," Keegan said. "They don't stand a chance."

CHAPTER 49

Having given the order, Arnold Moore waited. With his eyes closed, and his tie long gone, he tried to relax. News would come eventually. Whether good or bad, it would come. He didn't have to go looking for it now.

He opened his eyes and glanced at the clock. Fourteen minutes remained until the air strike. In the silence and the dark, each second seemed like an eternity.

The phone rang, startling him. He focused on the small glowing numerals above the keypad and recognized Danielle's coding.

He hit the speaker button.

"We're a mile from the island," she said, before he could utter a word. "We see no activity."

Moore leaned forward. "What the hell are you doing, Danielle?"

"I'm sorry, Arnold," she said. "But we're going in."

He could hardly believe what he was hearing. Then again he almost expected it.

"We'll be on the island in less than a minute," she said. "I just wanted you to know."

"Goddamn it!" he shouted. "Don't do this, Danielle! It's suicide. It's a violation of—"

She cut him off. "Once upon a time, you violated every rule, order, and directive you'd been given to come get

me. You turned to Hawker when no one else would help. I'm not letting him down now that it's our turn."

She spoke calmly, with certainty, and Moore felt his throat tighten. He had no response that could stand the light of scrutiny. He'd done exactly what she'd said. He also knew there was no way for this to end well.

"We have some weapons," she said. "We'll do what we can to take them by surprise. But . . ."

"But what?"

"We've been one step behind this whole time and if this goes sideways and we disappear . . . then by all means, please obliterate that island as planned."

Moore's heart churned inside him. He was proud of her resolve and filled with fear for the outcome. The simple fact was he couldn't stop her. The truth was, he didn't know if he wanted to.

"You have fourteen minutes," he said finally. "Don't waste time talking to me."

The call dropped and Moore sat alone listening only to the static over the speaker. Reluctantly he reached forward and pressed the button, cutting the line.

He took a breath. He had no choice but to contact the president and update him on the situation, but before he could do so a knock sounded at his door.

Too tired to stand or even call out, Moore flipped the switch that controlled the wall's opacity. For the first time in months they turned instantly clear. Walter Yang stood on the other side of the door.

"Now's not a good time, Walter."

"I have information," Yang said. "It's about the virus."

In the Persian Gulf, the small powerboat moved through the darkness half a mile from the northern tip of the island. A bit of luck in their favor had the wind out of the south, which would help mask the low rumbling of their

engine. In addition, the night was black as ink, though the moon would be up in ten minutes.

Until then the darkly colored boat with its low profile would be difficult to spot unless someone was looking directly for them. A fate that was a distinct possibility.

Crouched in the aft section of the boat, dressed in a black wetsuit, Danielle stared through a thermal scope looking for signs of trouble. She saw no sign of men or machinery operating on this side of the island. Only small dots here, there, and everywhere that she took to be cormorants in their nests. The species was known to claim the island at this time of year.

Beside her Hawker was busy securing their weapons and strapping their body armor to dive harnesses.

"How close you want me to get?" Keegan whispered.

They were cruising slowly now, making almost no wake at all. Danielle wasn't sure at what point the need to conserve time would be trumped by their desire to maintain the element of surprise.

She glanced at Hawker.

He'd grown tremendously quiet, his demeanor changing and darkening. She sensed a fire of grim determination in his heart. He had to expect the worst when he stepped on that island. In all likelihood, whatever they found there would bring him pain.

If Sonia had held out against the cult's demands, she was probably in a horrendous state by now, alive because they needed her, almost certainly beaten and tortured. Savi and Nadia would have fared worse.

And if Sonia had given the cult what they needed, she might be dead already.

"See any lookouts?" he asked.

She shook her head. Hawker turned to Keegan.

"Kill the engine," he said. "Take us in as far as we can coast," he said.

"You sure you want to get that close?"

"If they're watching we're dead anyway," he said. "I'd much rather have them start taking potshots at us while we're still in the boat."

"And if they don't?"

"Then we save five minutes swimming."

Keegan goosed the throttle a touch, picking up some more speed, and then feathered it back and cut it. The narrow boat knifed through the calm water toward the rugged, tawny-colored rocks.

Danielle swept the coast with the thermal scope as Hawker did the same with a night-vision scope mounted to the barrel of one of the rifles. No one shot at them, no one challenged them.

"Too good to be true," Hawker whispered.

A minute later she and Hawker slipped off the back of the boat a mere hundred yards from the beach. Keegan turned the boat away and coasted north, drifting with the wind and the current. He would drift for a while and then circle the island and come in near the freighter to pick them up. If they had any hope of surviving, they would need his help to get off the island before those missiles hit.

When Danielle emerged from the water, she was a few yards from the shore. Ten feet ahead, Hawker crouched by a VW-sized boulder on the beach. She moved up beside him.

"See anything?" she asked.

"Not yet," he said.

They pulled on their flak jackets and began to move, traveling up over a ridge before pausing again. Another round of scanning revealed nothing to trouble them.

In a crevice to the right a pair of bird nests sat empty, prodigious droppings marring the ground all around them.

"Let's not disturb the flock," Hawker said.

Danielle agreed. A hundred cormorants suddenly launching into the air would probably give them away.

She covered Hawker as he began to move, navigating across the weatherbeaten island before coming to a sudden stop. He dropped to the ground and then signaled her to stay put. She held her position.

He moved to the right, stepped around a large boulder with his weapon raised and ready, and then he stopped again. For several seconds he stood there, appearing from a distance to be confused. He poked at something on the ground with his rifle and began looking around.

What the hell was he doing?

Wearing black in the darkness he was nearly invisible, but even so, standing in the open was foolish.

Finally he crouched and waved her up.

She dashed forward, pressing against a boulder as she reached him.

"What the hell was that all about?"

"Something's wrong," he said.

"What are you talking about?"

He motioned to the other side of the boulder and she moved forward to see what he'd been inspecting.

There, lying across a bundle of pipes and hoses that seemed to spread across the island like vines, she saw two men. Armed men. Dead men.

"Look at this," Hawker said.

With the tip of his rifle, he opened one of their shirts. Danielle could see the branding on the man's chest. GEN 2:17, just like what they'd found on Ranga and Yousef.

"Members of the cult," she whispered.

"Shot in the head," he told her.

She bent closer, examining the wound and realizing it was from a small-caliber weapon, just like on the bodies of Lavril's men in Paris. She noticed something else.

"They're still warm," she said.

"Not dead long," Hawker replied, looking at her. "What the hell is going on here?"

She wasn't sure but a thought sprang to her mind. "Endgame," she said. "Jonestown, Waco, Aum Shinrikyo."

"But these bastards didn't kill themselves."

"Neither did all those people," she assured him. "Plenty who didn't want to go were *helped* along."

Hawker seemed to understand what she was saying, but he also seemed to have doubts. "Yeah, but those groups were about to lose. These people are in their moment of victory."

She agreed that was a difference, but they were still dealing with an apocalyptic cult.

"I'm telling you something's wrong here," he said. "I don't know what it is, but we're misreading something. I feel it in my bones."

She felt differently. "Endgame," she repeated, looking at her watch. "And we have eight minutes."

CHAPTER 50

Captain Laurence Petrie of the guided missile cruiser USS *Shiloh* stood watch on the bridge studying the orders that had come in from the commander in chief of Persian Gulf forces. His communications officer and the officer of the deck stood at attention, awaiting a response.

The orders directed him to launch a series of eight Tomahawk missiles against a single target. That alone was strange. The Tomahawk carried a hell of a kick, either a thousand-pound high-explosive warhead or what the navy called a combined effects bomb, which spread a hundred smaller warheads over a wide area, all designed to explode roughly simultaneously.

The combined effects bomb created a wide killing zone filled with flying shrapnel, explosive concussion waves, and, from the incendiary core of the charges, a storm of overlapping flame that burned well above a thousand degrees Celsius.

The fact that eight such weapons were being directed against the same target surprised him. In Iraq, Afghanistan, and most recently Libya, the weapons were used primarily in ones and twos, usually against air defense systems or hardened command and control bunkers. When the papers reported a hundred missiles fired they were usually fired at a hundred different targets. The idea

of launching eight missiles against a single target sounded like massive overkill.

The fact that the target was an abandoned rock in Iranian waters made the order seem even stranger.

"Did you confirm this order, Lieutenant?"

"Yes, sir," the communications officer said. "All proper communication protocols were followed and verified. The order is authentic."

"I'm not worried about its authenticity," the captain said. "I don't think anyone broke into the communications suite in Qatar and pranked us. But I'm concerned with its accuracy. I don't want to find out after the fact that we fired eight of those multimillion-dollar birds when we were supposed to fire one."

The officer of the deck spoke up. "Sir, the rest of the order indicates this is a joint operation. The *San Jacinto* and the *Bunker Hill* will be firing equivalent number of missiles as well. The *Normandy* has been placed on standby should either we or any of the other vessels have operational difficulties that prevent us from firing."

Captain Petrie glanced at the rest of the order. *Twenty-four missiles aimed at a single target.* He'd never heard of such a thing.

"Whatever's on that island," the officer of the deck added, "command wants it erased from existence."

Silently, Captain Petrie had to agree. He folded the order sheet and handed it back to the officer of the deck.

"Sound general quarters," he said. "Prepare to launch missiles."

Within seconds the whooping sound of the general quarters alarm was reverberating throughout the ship, accompanied by the words *This is not a drill.*

CHAPTER 51

Hawker and Danielle continued across the island, arriving in sight of the ruined buildings, pump houses, and battered helipad.

Hawker studied the layout. One building had a small amount of light inside. The others were dark. The grounded freighter lay just beyond, leaning toward the helipad. It loomed large in the darkness, tilted at such an odd angle and far too close to the buildings on the land.

There was a strange, apocalyptic aura to the scene, as if the world had already run down and all that remained was dark, lifeless rock, still waters, and the battered machines of man.

A muted hooting to the left reminded him that some life still existed.

Through the night-vision scope he could see one of the gangly long-winged cormorants moving around in its nest, plucking and pulling at what looked like a power cord or a drip line of some kind, like those used in landscaping.

"There's a heat source in that shack," Danielle told him. "No movement, though."

Hawker could guess what she was thinking. "Better hit it anyway."

He raised his rifle, screwed in the suppressor, and aimed. Pressing lightly with his finger, he activated the laser sight.

The red dot appeared on the building, clearly visible for both him and Danielle to see.

"Left four feet," she said, matching the thermal reading with the reflection of the tiny laser.

Hawker adjusted his aim.

"Down one foot."

He lowered the rifle.

"Fire."

Theut, theut. Two shots went out. Then two more.

"Anything?" he asked.

"Whatever it was, you hit it," she said, staring through the scope a little longer. "But it never moved."

Hawker got up and dashed to the small building. It was nothing more than a metal frame with blown-out windows. It looked like a tollbooth.

Inside lay pump controls, some corroded, others looking newer. One of the cult members lay dead on the floor, exactly where Hawker had hit him. The bullet holes from his rifle were obvious, but there was little blood oozing from the wounds.

Danielle came in behind him.

"Dead?"

"Already dead when I hit him," Hawker said. "These guys are killing off their own, just like you said."

"That's not a good sign," she replied.

"No," he agreed. Even though he couldn't understand it, even though it still felt slightly off to him, it certainly seemed like a final act. It only increased his fear for Sonia.

"Come on."

They climbed down a rickety flight of steps that clung to the edge of the rock wall and led to the helipad. From there they dropped onto the ship. Moments later they were crawling along the aft section of the beached freighter. And still no one challenged them.

A new thought sprang to mind. Maybe the final act was over. Maybe they were already too late.

The accommodations block at the rear of the freighter stuck up like a giant tombstone from the flat deck of the ship. They made their way inside, checking several compartments.

In one they found two more dead men. One of the bodies lay slumped forward in a chair, its head on a desk as if the man were asleep. The other lay sprawled on the deck.

Hawker pulled the sitting man's head back. The man was blue, his tongue bulging in his mouth as if he'd been poisoned.

Without someone to tell them if the lab or the prisoners were even on board, they'd have to go compartment to compartment.

"You need to go for the missiles," he said. "Whatever else happens we have to make sure they don't launch."

She nodded. "What are you going to do?"

"I'm going deeper," he said. "This isn't a cruise ship. If they're here, they'll be in the accommodations block. The rest are just cargo holds."

Danielle nodded. "Be careful," she said, and then she ducked out the door.

Hawker placed the dead man's head back down on the desk and began to move. He continued to be cautious for a moment and then began to move faster. From door to door, compartment to compartment. Most were empty, but a few held dead bodies.

Down the stairs he went. The next level was the same. A ship of the dead. He hoped Sonia, her sister, and aunt were not among them.

Sonia Milan stood in the gleaming white confines of a lab in the deep recesses of the grounded freighter. Draco

and a man he called Cruor, who seemed to be his first lieutenant, stood by.

She finished looking through the microscope in front of her. There would be no proof that what she'd done would work until it was tested and the test subject's altered DNA was examined, but she knew what she was doing and the samples in front of her all showed the desired effects.

"It's working," she said. "The cell cultures are dividing as they should. The new DNA is in place."

The Eden serum had been extracted from the seeds. The dormant virus revived and mated with the UN carrier virus. Under the electron microscope, the DNA fragment from the seed they'd recovered at the Garden had taken its place perfectly. The new cells showed lengthened telomeres.

Beside her a series of tubes marked with white stripes were filling slowly with the virus she'd created. The delivery system now had its payload.

"You're sure," Draco asked.

"We should test it on—"

"We have our lab rat," he said. He moved to the rear of the lab, where little Nadia lay strapped to a gurney like a patient in a psych ward. She wasn't moving.

"What have you done to her?" Sonia exclaimed.

"She wouldn't stop crying so I had her sedated," Draco said. "But if you've done what you said, she will soon be on the road to recovery."

"And the rest of the world?"

"Different road," he said. "Different destination."

"There's no need for this," Sonia pleaded. "We can test it on the animals. We can test it on rats, not people."

"I have no argument with the rats," he said. "It's humans I want to fear me."

"It wouldn't take long. I would—"

"You would stall and procrastinate!" he shouted. "You

would keep me waiting hoping that some rescue would come."

"No," she said, realizing she would have tried exactly that. "But this might not work as we—"

"You'd better hope it works," he said. "Or Nadia will die and then we'll start dragging people off the street and you can accidentally kill them one by one until you get it right. Do you understand me?"

Before she could answer, an alarm on some hastily rigged piece of equipment began chirping.

"Motion sensors," Cruor said. "We have visitors."

Draco looked surprised, and for the first time, uncomfortable. "They're early. They're more resourceful than I thought."

"They'll kill you," Sonia said, trying anything to put some fear and doubt into the man. "Even if you kill me, Hawker will find you and he'll kill you. I promise you that."

The backhand she'd expected the day before finally came, catching her across the face and sending her to the floor. Her eye began to swell.

"You think I didn't expect this?" he said. "It's just a timing problem. Fortunately our two viruses are ready."

"What do we do?" Cruor said.

"We get to see their end in person, and then leave," Draco said.

Cruor seemed nervous to her. Strange, since he was huge and menacing, but apparently he was the follower.

"They're eminently predictable," Draco insisted. "The woman will go for the missiles, because that's her job and she does what she's supposed to do. The man will come for this one, because that's what he does. Orders don't matter to him. But a damsel or two in distress . . ."

"I will wait with you," Cruor said.

"I have a place for you," Draco said. "Are the others dead?"

Cruor nodded.

"Good," Draco said. "They were not worthy. We will do better next time."

A second alarm began to chirp.

"They're splitting up," Cruor said. "One on the deck, one inside."

Draco began to laugh. "As I said: predictable."

Hawker had made it to the bottom deck. He broke into a larger bay and stopped. Crates lay on the floor. Long, rectangular crates. They were empty, but he knew what they were. He'd seen them before, in La Bruzca's warehouse.

"What the hell?" he whispered.

These were the very crates La Bruzca had insisted were for another buyer. In some ways it didn't surprise him that La Bruzca had sold the missiles to the cult, but like everything else it was just too convenient.

He thought back to the meeting with La Bruzca. He could hear La Bruzca's sinister tone as he intimated that he knew more about Hawker than the rest of the world did. Could it have some connection? He found it hard to believe events could really have come full circle.

There are no coincidences, he reminded himself, but what the hell did it all mean?

He glanced at his watch. In seven minutes it wouldn't matter.

As Hawker continued the search below, Danielle crossed the main deck. A hint of moonlight had appeared on the horizon, though the moon had yet to show its face.

Getting her bearings she moved toward the bow. She remembered Moore saying the missiles appeared to be located forward, placed on rather obviously built launch rails.

Getting away from the accommodations block, she darted forward in spurts, passing various cargo hatches and covers. Every step out into the open felt like she was inviting a sniper to put a round through her heart.

It was still coal black in the shadows but that didn't stop someone from having a night-vision scope. And in a minute the moon would be up and she would be painted with each step.

She hurried and quickly reached the forward section. There, between the two crane booms that might have once hoisted cargo out of the holds, she saw the launch ramps Moore had mentioned and a gray metallic structure the size of a small bus. It seemed nothing more than a crude covering, probably erected just to keep the missiles out of sight.

Even the launch rails seemed crude. She didn't know what missiles these people had, but she couldn't actually remember a missile old enough to need a launch ramp. She hoped they were so old that they wouldn't operate.

She moved toward the housing, staying under cover, looking around for any signs of danger. If anyone from the cult remained alive and present they would be here, protecting these weapons, waiting to fire them.

No one shot at her and Danielle stole a glance through an open doorway that had been cut in the metallic housing. Inside, two missiles the size of truncated telephone poles sat on the launch rails. She pressed her back against the outside wall of the shelter and checked her rifle.

She would dash through the cutout door, swinging her rifle to the right, firing blind, because she didn't have the chance to wait. And then once she'd cleared the area, she'd find a way to sabotage the missiles and prevent them from launching.

She took a deep breath, tensed her body, and looked toward the doorway.

The first sliver of the moon had risen over the water. It
pale light spilled across the deck. In that light Danielle
saw something she hadn't expected, hadn't even consid
ered: a tripwire, strung across the doorway, like the thin
nest strand of spider silk.

CHAPTER 52

As Arnold Moore sat listening to Walter Yang, he hoped the young man was about to tell him it was all hoax, that they could call off the dogs and let it all be, but the look on Yang's face suggested something else.

"Be quick," Moore said.

"I've been studying the virus like you suggested," Yang said, "not the data Ms. Laidlaw recovered but the original Magician virus from the UN."

"What did you find? Anything that will change our response."

"Not really, but something interesting."

"It's a little late for interesting, Walter."

Yang nodded. "I know what you mean but—"

"You don't know what I mean," Moore said curtly. "Two of our best are moving on the site right now. It's probably heavily defended. Even if they've survived the insertion and the recon, the island will probably be blown out from under them before they can find what they're looking for and get off of it alive. So trust me, you have no idea what I mean, when I tell you: *it's a little late.*"

Moore knew his pain had gotten the best of him. Yang's face said he regretted coming in, but he didn't flinch.

"You don't understand," Yang said. "That's why I'm here. I've been studying the inert section that you asked me to look at."

Moore exhaled and shook his head. "I thought you said it was just blank space reserved in the DNA, a space that would be replaced by the payload?"

"It is," Yang said. "But I think it's something else as well. I think it's a message."

Moore felt as if ice water had just been poured down his spine.

"A message?"

Yang nodded.

"What are you talking about?"

"You know what the DNA molecule looks like?" Yang said.

"Basically," Moore said.

"The parts that go up the side are called nucleotides, the molecules that go across the middle—the rungs in the ladder if you want to think about it like that—they're called bases or base pairs."

"Right," Moore said. "Go on."

"In standard DNA there are only four types of bases, adenine, cytosine, guanine, and thymine. We abbreviate them A, C, G, T."

"You're saying someone coded a message in these base pairs," Moore guessed, trying to jump ahead and hoping that it would be something they could use.

Yang nodded. "The primary parts of the virus are designed as we would expect, but the inert section is different. Successive rungs show a repeating pattern. You see this in certain sections of DNA. Often the telomere sections are the same over and over again: TTAGGG. But I found something different here. The repetition starts, stops, and then restarts."

"How is that a message?" Moore asked. He felt the clock ticking.

"Because the pattern is neither consecutively repeating nor sufficiently random. That means it has to be purposeful. In this case, I found fourteen consecutive rungs of one

ype of base pairing, eighteen consecutive rungs of a second type, nine consecutive rungs of a third type. Then the
pattern started over again. Fourteen, eighteen, nine. Fourteen, eighteen, nine. It seemed odd to me."

It seemed odd to Moore, mostly because it seemed
odd to his geneticist. "But what the hell does it mean?"

"Genetically it means nothing," Yang said. "But then I
remembered what you said about Ms. Gonzales working
for the NRI years ago and the connection hit me. *N* is the
fourteenth letter in the alphabet, *R* is the eighteenth, *I* is
the ninth. Fourteen, eighteen, nine, three times in a row.
NRI, NRI, NRI. In a virus sent to a former NRI employee."

Moore felt the hair on his neck stand up.

"Could there be any other reason?" he asked, feeling
the claws of panic pulling at him. "Any reason at all for
such a pattern?"

Yang shook his head. "I don't think so."

"How can you be sure?"

"Using the same logic, I 'read' the rest of the inert
strand," Yang said. "The next seventy-eight base pairs are
arranged as follows, repeating patterns, eighteen in a row,
then five in a row, then twenty-two, then five, fourteen,
seven, and then five again. If you take those as letters they
spell out one word: *REVENGE*."

Moore felt the room spinning. Someone was after them.
Whoever it was wanted them to know it at some point.
Perhaps they'd been meant to discover this earlier, or per-
haps well after the fact. But who and why?

Moore ran through the facts in his head. Ranga's in-
volvement brought Hawker in. The letter to Gonzales
tipped the NRI and brought Moore and Danielle into the
fray. All along whoever they were dealing with had been
one step ahead of them, to the point where they'd even
found or guessed the location of the safe house in Kuwait
where Hawker had stashed Savi and the little girl.

Ranga.

Hawker.

Danielle.

Information that no one outside the NRI should have known.

Revenge.

The answer hit Moore like an anvil.

Each of them had plenty of enemies, plenty of people who might want to see them suffer or die, but Moore could think of only one person with reason to hate them all.

He grabbed his phone and hit the button to autodial Danielle's satellite phone.

"Pick up!" he shouted to the air. "Pick up."

A British voice came on the line. "This is Keegan."

"Keegan, put Danielle on the line," Moore said.

The response brought added pain.

"It's too late," Keegan said. "They're already on the island."

It was too late. And if Moore was right, Hawker and Danielle were walking into a death trap.

CHAPTER 53

Aboard the USS *Shiloh*, Captain Petrie watched as his men ran through the prelaunch sequence for the Tomahawk missiles and reported back in. Guidance was confirmed, warheads were armed, safeties removed.

"Preparation sequence complete," an officer at the tactical station said. "Vertical launch system ready. TLAM four, seven, eight, and eleven ready to fire. TLAM units twelve, fourteen, fifteen, and nineteen on standby."

Captain Petrie looked at the ship's clock, watching as the second hand swung across the bottom of the hour and up the side. The ship was prepared, the board was green.

"Safeties off," Petrie ordered.

The fire control officer flipped up the plastic guard on the launch trigger, uncovering the Fire switch. The second hand continued to sweep higher, passing the 11 and closing quickly on the vertical position. Precisely as it hit 12, Petrie gave the order.

"Commence firing."

The weapons officer pressed the switch. A flaring sound was heard and the black night was lit up by blazing white flame as the first Tomahawk launched from its tube and lit its booster.

The missile fired off the ship at an angle, leaving a trail

of smoke that the next missile blasted through only seconds later.

Somewhere in the Persian Gulf, two other cruisers were doing the same thing. And sixty miles north of the *Shiloh*'s position, whatever existed on the small rocky island had approximately four minutes to live.

CHAPTER 54

Leaving the missile crates behind, Hawker continued his search. A chart room, a room filled with welding equipment, a room filled with moldy stores of flour and rice. Finally, at the heart of the lowest deck he found a door that looked different from the others. In fact, it looked like an airlock with rubber sealed edges and a handle that would have been at home on the inside of a commercial aircraft door.

He glanced in through a small window above the handle. It looked like a lab in terms of styling and modern equipment. He saw movement in the corner. Sonia sitting in a chair, sobbing, covering her face.

Left to die, he guessed.

He threw the handle open and rushed toward her.

"Hawker, no!" she shouted.

A shot echoed through the room. Hawker felt an explosion hit him in the back and he flew forward, slamming into the wall face-first. He fell and his rifled clattered out of his hand.

Rolling over, he looked back toward the doorway. A man with jaundiced-looking eyes, sunken into a narrow, hatchetlike face, stared at him. A snake tattoo coiled around his right arm, and a dark scar lay hidden beneath a block of ink that curled around his neck.

"Welcome to my parlor," the man said, raising Chinese-made SKS rifle to a resting position.

The SKS fired the same slug as the AK-47. A heavy 7.62 mm shell. The blast had thumped Hawker hard. Part of it had penetrated the vest.

Now on the ground, Hawker felt as if he couldn't breathe, as if the vest weighed a ton. He could feel blood flowing down his side. The only sound that came through the ringing in his ears was Sonia's muffled screams.

She dropped down beside him as another man came in the door. This second man was a hulking brute, with a different tattoo on his forearm, a knife dripping with blood. He stood a step behind the first. He guessed the snake man was the leader of the cult. Their prisoner, Yousef, had called him Draco.

Sonia reached Hawker's side. "I'm so sorry," she said.

"Get away from him," Draco ordered.

Tears streamed down Sonia's face. "I'm sorry," she whispered again. "I'm so sorry."

The hulking man stepped forward, grabbed her by the arm, and dragged her back.

Hawker tried to rise but the wind had been knocked out of him. Based on the sudden shortness of breath he felt and the immense pain on his right side, he guessed he might have a punctured lung.

"You don't look so dangerous now," Draco said. "Hardly enough to cause anyone pain. And yet you are the bane of my existence."

Hawker stared in utter confusion. "I don't know what you're talking about," he said. "I don't even know who you are."

The man snapped off a shot at Hawker. The bullet took a chunk out of the wall by Hawker's head. Hawker flinched and contorted his body away from the impact. The pain in his side tripled.

"You don't know me?" Draco shouted. "After what you did to me?"

Hawker's chest heaved and fell awkwardly as he fought for breath and understanding. Perhaps he could buy some time. His hearing had come back and some of his strength seemed to be returning. More important, Danielle was still out there.

He pressed himself against the wall and used it as leverage to force himself up. He stood facing Draco.

"You were only hired to take the fall," Draco said. "Don't you know your role? You were supposed to die or disappear and be blamed for what happened."

"I still don't know what you're talking about," Hawker said.

"They cast me out because of you!" Draco shouted. "Cast me out into the darkness, where there is wailing and gnashing of teeth and they took you in. You: a traitor."

The man knew something about him, wherever the information came from. But Hawker was no traitor.

"I never betrayed anyone," Hawker managed. "I just wouldn't . . . betray my conscience."

"Well, that's the problem with a conscience," the man replied. "It can really mess up your day."

As Hawker spoke he realized for the first time in a long time that he had nothing left to make up for. He'd done what was right. Not just what was right for him, but what was right in and of itself. And even then he'd spent years struggling with the choice that had banished him.

His only guess was that this man must have been involved somehow, though he didn't recognize him.

Just then a thunderous explosion rocked the boat. Hawker steadied himself with a hand on the wall, hoping it was the first of the Tomahawks, but it was followed by only a few rumbles and then slowly the odor of smoke began to seep into the room.

Draco glared at him. "Have you no respect?" he said.

"Bow your head. You've just heard the sound of M?
Laidlaw's death at the hands of a tripwire."

The smug arrogance and the words themselves lit
fire in Hawker. Not waiting, not thinking, he charged
He pushed himself off the wall and lunged forward. Th?
SKS fired. A shot hit Hawker on the side, a glancin?
blow. The vest took most of the energy and Hawker col
lided with Draco, wrapping his arm around the man'?
neck, trying to tackle him.

They stumbled together but didn't fall. They crashe?
through the door into the bay where Nadia was strappe?
to the gurney. Hawker drove the cult leader into the wal?

Still standing, Hawker slammed his knee into Draco'?
stomach and then butted his forehead into Draco's face
The man's nose shattered and he cried out. The back o?
his head hit hard against the wall as he tried to get th?
rifle loose and shoot Hawker.

Using the leverage he'd gained, Hawker wrapped on?
arm around Draco's neck and grabbed his weapon wit?
the other. Gripping it with all his might, he kept Drac?
from turning it at either him or Sonia.

Draco pulled the trigger anyway and gunfire spraye?
the room. The recoil hammered near Hawker's wound
The pain was incredible, but Hawker held on, and Drac?
fired again, unwittingly forcing his own man, Cruor, t?
take cover.

As the latest shots ended, Hawker could feel his han?
burning where he held the rifle. He let go, slammed ?
punch into Draco's face, and then turned him and ben?
him backward, pulling the man off his feet and body
slamming him to the ground.

Hawker landed on top of him and began to pumme?
the bastard, slamming his fist into Draco's face.

Before he could beat Draco to death, Cruor lunged fo?
him, grabbing him around the neck and choking him?

he brawl became all disjointed, a glimpse here, a punch
ere, another blow here.

Out of the corner of his eye he caught sight of Sonia
mashing something into Cruor's skull, and the man
ent off to the side. But as the thug landed, he rolled,
rought his own weapon to bear, and blasted Sonia in
he stomach. She fell backward against the wall, clutch-
ig her abdomen and doubling over.

At almost the same moment shots rang out from the
ther direction, blood splattered on the far wall, and
Cruor collapsed to his knees and then fell on his face.

Draco scrambled away, ducking through the door to
here Nadia lay. A pair of shots chased him, puncturing
he glass between them. Fissures spidered across the
lear plate and it crumbled in toward Hawker.

As the shattered glass fell away, it revealed Draco hiding
ehind Nadia. His right hand held an injector attached to
er IV line; his left hand held another one that hooked
ito the same line at a Y connection. They were large sy-
inges, the size of toothpaste tubes, with thumb-sized
lungers. One had been marked with a red stripe and one
vith white.

Hawker looked around wondering where the hell the
hots had come from. Danielle stood in the doorway
vith a rifle raised to her shoulder.

"Never one without the other," Draco managed. The
vords came raggedly from his busted mouth. "I trust *you*
ecognize me, Ms. Laidlaw."

"Gibbs," she said, sounding disgusted. "I have to say
ou've looked better."

Hawker finally understood. Gibbs had been director
f the NRI before Moore. He'd ordered Danielle to hire
Hawker for the ill-fated Brazilian expedition, planning
o eliminate the team once they'd discovered what they
vere looking for, to take the discovery private, and to

force the blame off on Hawker, a known fugitive an
criminal at the time.

But after it all went wrong, Hawker had pulled Daniel
and the other survivors out of the jungle. Gibbs's partne
had been killed and Gibbs had fled, disappearing into th
underworld before he could be arrested.

Hawker didn't recognize him because he'd never me
the man. But Danielle knew him well.

"Fire and my body tenses," Gibbs/Draco said. "Th
plunger will go down even if I die."

Gibbs crouched behind Nadia, using her as a shield i
her upright sitting position.

On the floor across from Hawker, Sonia was bleedin
out, her shirt soaked through with blood, the floor be
neath her turning red. He was torn between moving t
Sonia, whom he couldn't help, and holding his position
few feet from Gibbs, almost in striking range. He crawle
to Sonia. She had to be in terrible pain, her eyes barel
focusing.

Danielle eased closer, the rifle still trained on Gibb
"What is it you want, Gibbs? What the hell was all th
about?"

"I want to be king," he said, laughing. "But I'll settle fc
making the world beg for my mercy and pay me billions.

"So why do all this? You could have taken the viru
and left."

"You arrived a little early," he admitted. "But I wante
to be here anyway. To show you that you'd lost to me, t
find you writhing on my deck filled with shrapnel an
throw his"—he looked at Hawker—"dead body besid
you. I wanted pictures to send to Arnold so he'd know I'
taken you, his prize student, as payment."

"You're delusional," she said. "You blame us? For wha
you did?"

The anger returned. "They hunt for me with dogs an
they fawn over you," he said. "They give you the keys t

the kingdom, even as they try to destroy me. I've seen you. I've seen you both. I could have killed you many times. Just a shot here or there. But you would never have known it was me. And I would never have had the chance to do what I'm about to do. Punish the whole world for casting me out."

Hawker listened to the voice. He heard madness and instability. He sensed that Gibbs would destroy the world if he couldn't be part of it. Especially now.

"And killing your own people?"

Gibbs smiled through his busted face. "I didn't need them anymore," he said. "The definition of expendable, so I expended them. Besides, they were bad for the bottom line and I had to let you in somehow."

Hawker listened to the two of them. It felt as if Danielle was trying to keep Gibbs talking, trying to stall him from acting until the air strike hit. But strangely enough, it felt as if Gibbs was trying to stall as well. In his weakened state, Hawker tried to see through the fog. One last attempt to put the puzzle together.

It seemed as if everything Gibbs had done was a smoke screen. The cult, the threats, the cryptic language that never quite made sense, all these things now seemed no more than various means to an end. It some ways it had worked. It had kept the NRI guessing, kept them in a state of self-imposed blindness as they searched for some clue that would link it all together. But that clue was a ghost. It didn't exist because the whole thing was a con, a trap designed to get them here and get Gibbs's hands on 951 and the Eden virus.

The missiles, the old Soviet missiles La Bruzca had sold him, were probably the last piece of bait. But the information Danielle had coaxed out of Yousef had gotten them here early and Gibbs had struggled to finish, ending up on his own sinking ship.

All guesses, he realized, and probably only half-right, but they were all Hawker had to go on.

Gibbs seemed acutely deranged but still calculating. So why wasn't he running now? Why wasn't he backing down the hall with Nadia's wheeled gurney in front of him as a shield? He had to know some type of air strike would be on its way. Did he think it was going to be held off until Hawker and Danielle resurfaced? Probably he knew better. He'd been in command once.

The only answer Hawker could come up with was that he wanted the air strike to hit for some reason. If he was cornered, maybe he was playing for a tie. Or more likely he had some other way of winning even if they all died in flames.

"And all this," Danielle asked. "The cult, all this insanity?"

"New religion for the fools," Gibbs said. "If you want someone to reject God you have to put something in His place. I chose . . . me."

Moving his hands in such a way as to show the syringes better, Gibbs continued. "And now you get to choose. Red for death, white for life."

"We're all going to die here," Danielle said. "And your dream is going to die with us."

"My *dream* is to see you suffer," he said. "And this planet will suffer for what you've done to me."

"I destroyed your missiles," she said, moving sideways as if she were trying to get a better line to shoot her old boss. He turned, moving the gurney on its wheels; the child seemed to stir.

"You were lucky," he said. "But do you think I would have left them in plain sight if they were my weapon of choice? Missiles to spread disease are very hard to come by. Even with all I've accomplished, I couldn't manage that. But at least I thought they'd draw you in."

Hawker's thoughts raced. Gibbs did have something

else, one more trick. He glanced at the wall. A series of beakers filled with clear liquid were secured there. Each one was hooked up to an electrical pump and a length of thin tubing that left the room. Hawker recognized the thin, irrigation-like drip lines.

"The birds."

Gibbs turned to him, careful to stay in his crouch.

"You're smarter than you look," he sneered. "I've been feeding them sugar water and fish guts for weeks. At this point they're well trained. Airborne versions of Pavlov's dog. I hit that pump and they suck down whatever comes out of the tube. This time it'll be the virus. And when the inevitable shock and awe air strike obliterates this ship, it will scatter those birds to the wind. Some will live and some will die, but those that survive will land in other places. Qatar, Dubai, Kuwait. It'll give a whole new meaning to the words 'bird flu.' "

Hawker noticed the beakers were divided into those with a red mark and those with a white one. *Red for death, white for life.*

Gibbs inched toward the beakers.

"Don't," Danielle said, tightening her grip on the rifle.

"You won't shoot," Gibbs said. "Not till the very last second at least. Because in your weak little mind you still think there may be a way out for you and him and this girl. Shoot me and she's Typhoid Mary on a whole different scale. You'll have to leave her here to die."

As Gibbs spoke, Nadia opened her eyes. She looked out across the room. "Sonia?" she cried. "Savi?"

She was groggy, coming out of sedation. Hawker guessed she couldn't see without her glasses. Sonia tried to respond but couldn't. She reached out, her face contorted in pain.

"Sonia, don't," Hawker pleaded.

Grunting in agony, Sonia fell back into a pool of her own blood. Hawker put his hands on her shoulders, trying to calm her.

She looked up into his eyes. Her skin was pale, her lips turning blue, her pupils massively dilated. "I'm sorry . . . ," she said, barely audible.

Behind him Gibbs was inching closer to the pump. Across the room, Danielle was trying to get a bead on him. They were closing in on one minute. Maybe they would all die together after all.

Sonia reached out, touched Hawker's face, the blood of her hand covering his cheek. Her other hand was clenched and trembling. She looked at him and then right past him. Her eyes were blank, most likely blind. "I . . . changed . . . it," she whispered.

"Changed what?" he asked.

"White . . . for life. It will heal Nadia but it can't . . ." She gulped for air. "It can't live . . . outside . . . the body."

Her strength failed and she collapsed, but Hawker found a surge of energy.

"Shoot red," he shouted, turning and lunging for Gibbs.

He heard a shot fire and expected to see Gibbs's hand fly off the red plunger, a bullet hole through his forearm or wrist. But instead the IV line split. Danielle had shot it out, eight inches above where it hit Nadia's arm.

It was brilliant. No matter which plunger Gibbs pressed nothing would enter the child.

Gibbs seemed to realize this too, and he dove for the pump switch.

Hawker charged, hitting the gurney and driving it forward; he pinned Gibbs against the wall.

Gibbs stretched for the switch, which was just out of reach, and then convulsed suddenly as Danielle blasted three holes in his chest. Blood splattered the wall behind him. His arm fell and he slumped forward.

As Hawker took his weight off the gurney, Gibbs slid down the wall. He ended up facedown on the floor.

Hawker looked at the two syringes. Neither had been depressed. He glanced at his watch. Fifty seconds.

"Let's get out of here," Danielle said.

As fast as his weakened body would move, Hawker stood and pulled the straps off Nadia.

"I got her," Danielle said, picking the girl up and carrying her out the door.

Hawker had to go, but for a second he dropped down beside Sonia. She was dead. He touched her face. He was sick at the thought of leaving her there, but there was no time. He went to stand and noticed something clutched in Sonia's hand. It was a syringe, capped off and marked with a stripe.

White. White for life.

He grabbed it, stood, and lumbered down the hall.

By the time he reached the main deck he was choking and coughing up blood. He saw Danielle and Nadia go over the side. Saw Keegan come racing up in the boat.

He jumped after them, hitting the black water. His world went dark and silent.

Inside the laboratory, Stuart Gibbs twitched. He was not yet dead and somehow through the pain and the blood, he realized it. With great effort he managed to push the gurney away, get to his knees, and begin to crawl. He was beyond hope now, but hate drove him on. He would not let them survive. He would curse the world that had rejected him.

He reached the table beneath the beakers, pulled himself up, and stretched for the pump switch. The pain was incredible and the agony coursing through his body caused him to scream aloud as he stretched for it. He flicked the switch and fell back to the floor.

Lying in an awkward heap, Stuart Gibbs heard the pumps engage. He felt the vibration throughout the room as they drew the viral suspensions into the driplines.

Through his failing eyes, he saw the levels in each bea-

ker begin to drop. He would die but his last act would bring hell to the world one way or another.

Kicking hard, Hawker made it back to the surface. The body armor weighed him down; he slipped free of it. As he came up, powerful hands yanked him out of the water and into the speedboat.

He heard Keegan shout "Go!" as he sprawled out onto the deck.

At the driver's console, Danielle shoved the throttle to full. The boat leapt forward, accelerated away from the freighter, and raced south at top speed.

Hawker lay in the back, exhausted, barely able to breathe and facing the sky. Overhead he saw the cormorants circling like dragons in the dark. And then they suddenly veered off and dove toward the island en masse.

No, he thought. *It can't be.*

Seconds later the sound of whistling death shot over their heads, as the first of the Tomahawks raced past them on its way to the island. Two others followed, converging from different angles.

The cormorants swarmed over their feeding places, jostling and pushing against one another to get at the free buffet they'd grown used to finding. Liquid oozed from the thin black tubes. They squawked and flapped, stretching their beaks down, snatching the line from one another and then fighting to keep it.

And then they looked up and turned to the south in unison. A strange whistling sound came toward them. Thunder boomed a second later and a concussion wave blasted through them, ripping their feathers and wings apart. Some of the birds tumbled, others tried to fly, but

even as they flapped their wings, a wave of thousand-degree flames crashed over them, engulfing them from every direction and incinerating them on the ground and in midair.

Aboard the powerboat Hawker stared back at the conflagration. A half mile off, the explosions were still deafening. In the moments after each impact, chunks of rock and flaming debris rained down like small meteors.

At one point, three or four missiles hit simultaneously. A blinding explosion stretched across the island like a halo before rising skyward like a mushroom cloud.

Behind him, Keegan held the little girl, who was now fully conscious and confused. "Sonia?" she asked. "Where's Sonia?"

Hawker felt his heart break even more. He continued to stare at the island behind them as another round of Tomahawks hammered it, once again raising fire to the sky.

CHAPTER 55

Sunion, Greece

In the shade of some trees, fifty yards back from a white sand beach and the warm waters of the Aegean, Danielle Laidlaw sat on an old stone wall. The wall wasn't ancient enough to be from the classical Greek era or from Roman times, but she guessed a few generations had passed since its construction.

Enough time for the world to change and the height of technology to go from steam engines to spacecraft, from vacuum tubes to computers, from penicillin as *the* only miracle drug to the manipulation of DNA and the very building blocks of life.

All paths of growing knowledge that might lead to either paradise or perdition.

She wasn't sure they'd ever know the truth about the place they'd found, whether it was connected to the biblical Garden of Eden or not. She wasn't even sure if such a fact *could* be determined. But with the Iranians fuming over the incursion and the bombing of the cormorant island, and the American government trying to explain why they'd unleashed twenty-four missiles on a flyspeck in the middle the Gulf, she doubted anyone, particularly an American like McCarter, would get the chance to try.

In the end, it probably didn't matter. Those who wanted to believe it would, and those who wanted to believe

something else would believe that something else. Like all things connected to religion and spirituality, it wouldn't require faith if you could prove it one way or another.

She looked out to the beach where Hawker sat, shoes off, shirt open, watching the waves as his skin grew darker in the sun. For reasons known only to him, he'd insisted they come here and avoid hooking up with the authorities of any country or any representatives of the U.S. government, including the NRI.

After what he'd been through, what he'd lost and what he'd already done for her in his life, she didn't question it, even as the days passed.

They were staying in Keegan's place, a decent-sized chalet on the beach. But Keegan wasn't there. He'd gone out on some mission for Hawker.

Since then life had been a model of consistency.

Every day Hawker would check in with Keegan by phone and then he'd bring Nadia to the beach and let her play, watching over her as if she were his own. Every day Moore would call Danielle on the satellite line and ask when she and Hawker would be returning for debriefing. And every day Danielle would say "maybe tomorrow."

Truth was, she didn't know. Even as Hawker's physical wounds healed—helped on by a local surgeon—his mental anguish only seemed to deepen. Watching him, as he watched Nadia, Danielle felt a tremendous need to protect and shelter him. But he wouldn't let her in, and so she had to do it from afar.

Back in Washington, Moore was doing the same, deflecting and redirecting the thousand questions that were probably pounding down his door. In a way, it felt good to raise their shields around Hawker. After all, he was one of their tribe.

Sliding the satellite phone into her pocket, Danielle started across the beach, walking across the warm sand until she'd reached a spot beside him. She sat, brought

her knees up toward her chest, and rested her arms on them, leaning forward.

Ahead of them, a small wave swept in and over the sand castle Nadia was building. The young child, looking like a tiny old woman, shrieked with delight as the foamy water swirled around and then slid back into the ocean.

"She wants to know where Sonia is," Hawker said. "Where Savi is. And when her father is coming back."

He looked down at the sand and then over at Danielle. "How do you tell a little girl that everyone she loved is gone?"

"What about her mother?" Danielle asked.

"She died giving birth to Nadia."

"Cousins? Uncles?"

"No one yet," he said. "She's all alone."

Danielle turned toward him, brushing the hair out of her eyes. "Is that why we're still here?"

"I don't know where else to go," he said, sounding lost.

As long as she'd known him, Hawker had always been sure of himself. Even when he was wrong he made his mistakes at a thousand miles an hour. To be suddenly uncertain about things might feel worse than being wrong.

"You can't keep her here," she said. "You can't stay here forever, even if Keegan says you can."

For the first time he looked at her. "I know that. But where do we go?"

"We?" she said. "There are agencies. I'm sure with our influence—"

"A child with her problems?" he said. "You're going to put her in foster care?"

"I'm not saying that but . . ." She started and then stopped, finding that she didn't know what to say.

Hawker spoke again. "Sonia told me she'd only live

another year. God help us if we dump her on the system for the last year of her life."

Maybe he did plan to keep her here, maybe he planned to take care of her for the rest of her days and somehow honor Sonia's memory that way.

"Why are you putting yourself through this?" she asked. "You did everything you could."

"A long time ago I promised Sonia I'd never let anything happen to her."

"You kept that promise when you dragged them out of Africa," she said. "You put them on solid ground. They chose to go back into the land of snakes. Maybe they did it with good reason. But it was their choice. Not yours."

He looked over at her. Obviously he knew that.

"I know," she said, gently, thinking she might have overstepped her bounds. "Rational arguments aren't going to do much for you right now."

He nodded and gazed back toward the water.

"Did you love Sonia?" she asked.

He hesitated.

"It's a yes-or-no question."

"I loved the idea of her," he said, proving that it wasn't. "After five years looking over your shoulder and hoping the people you're working with or the woman you're sleeping with aren't planning on killing you, you end up wondering if the world would be better off without you. Then you run into someone good who needs help and suddenly you matter."

"And you're not alone," she said.

He nodded, then turned her way again. "I'm not big into psychoanalysis, but I wanted to feel alive. To feel normal. It almost felt normal."

"There's nothing wrong with that, Hawker," Danielle said. "There's nothing wrong with any of that."

"There is when you know it can't last," he said. "I

couldn't go back into the light where she was going and I sure as hell couldn't bring her with me or she'd have ended up dead somewhere."

He stopped. He didn't have to say it. She knew his next thoughts. She put a hand on his knee.

"Hawker, right now you're feeling guilt stacked on guilt, but even at twenty Sonia was a grown woman and nothing that happened since had anything to do with you. The only people to blame are Gibbs and the others he corrupted.

"We destroyed them," she added, thanking God that the president had chosen to obliterate the whole island instead of just the freighter.

"There's no indication that the virus escaped that island. There are teams looking for infected cormorants, but they haven't found anything, not even a bird with singed tail feathers. Nothing got away, not in that firestorm."

He nodded.

"You don't feel it now, but Sonia gave herself for something that mattered, even if she was misguided at times. Who isn't? Who wouldn't want to be? Talk about life not meaning anything."

She hoped her words were affecting him, but he remained silent.

Before anything else was said, a white Range Rover pulled up in the drive and parked next to the old wall that Danielle had been sitting on.

The horn sounded. Out on the beach Nadia perked up. She looked over her castle and toward the white SUV.

Keegan stepped out on the driver's side and an elderly woman with olive skin and white hair stepped out on the passenger's side. Almost immediately Nadia got up and began to hobble toward them. The woman came out past the wall and met Nadia halfway.

A look of relief swept over Hawker's face.

"Who's that?"

"Nadia's grandmother. Keegan's been looking for her all week. She's from Barcelona. We didn't know if she was still alive."

Danielle felt as if a great weight had been lifted off Hawker's shoulders and she couldn't help but smile.

"This is a good thing," she said.

He stood.

"It's a start."

"You gonna be okay?" she asked.

"Someday," he said,

"What about today?" she prompted.

"Today," he said, pulling something from his shirt pocket and studying it. "Today I'm going to get even."

He turned and began walking toward Nadia, her grandmother, and Keegan. Danielle quickly stood and followed. She caught up with Hawker as he reached them, picked little Nadia up, and sat her on the wall.

It was strange. The little girl looked exactly like a miniature version of the woman in the flowing dress, even though the woman was her grandmother and had to be in her seventies.

"Remember what Sonia told you?" Hawker said to Nadia, straightening her glasses, which had gotten crooked.

"That she'd fix me," Nadia said.

"That she'd fix you," Hawker repeated. "I have the medicine she gave me for you."

As Danielle watched, Hawker showed Nadia a large syringe marked in white. Danielle recognized it as coming from the lab on the freighter. *White for life.*

No wonder he'd been unwilling to meet with any government officials. The sample would certainly have been taken.

Realizing what he was about to do, she felt a pang of fear.

"Hawker."

"Sonia changed it," he said, without looking up. "She couldn't let Gibbs have what he wanted, but she wasn't willing to hurt Nadia or take away her chance for life. She changed it so the virus can't live outside the body. Once Nadia is healed and her body destroys the remnants of the carrier, the Eden virus will be gone."

Nadia stretched out her arm, no doubt having received so many injections in her short life that she knew what to expect. Hawker found her vein, rubbed a small amount of antibacterial gel on her arm, and pulled the cap off the syringe.

Danielle took a deep breath but held back as he pressed the needle through the young girl's skin and into her vein.

Nadia winced and made a little noise but that was it. Hawker slowly pressed the plunger down until 75 percent of the serum was gone. He stopped, pulled the syringe out, and capped it.

"I think the rest should go to the lab," he said, handing it to Danielle. "Maybe Walter Yang can find other uses for it."

Danielle took the syringe, thinking about the medical possibilities and worrying about the possible effects of what Hawker had just done.

"What if you're wrong?" she asked.

He turned toward her and she could tell he'd already considered the possibility. Maybe that's what he'd been pondering all these days on the beach.

"Then maybe we'll start caring about this planet if we have to live on it forever."

Danielle understood why he'd done what he'd done. She prayed he was right.

"Will she be well?" Nadia's grandmother asked.

"I hope so," Hawker said.

"Thank you," the woman said.

"It was your son and Sonia," he said.

The woman smiled.

"Come on, Nadia," Keegan said. "All the ice cream you can eat inside."

Excited, Nadia got down from the wall and headed for the beach house, not waiting for any of the adults.

"I'll see to it," her grandmother said, following after the little girl.

Keegan watched them go in, then turned to Danielle and Hawker. "So does this make me part of the team?" he asked.

"What team?" Hawker said.

"Your team, mate. The one with the big government pension and the expense accounts for all the Jags and the business jets. I could enjoy all of that."

Hawker turned to Danielle. "Tell him all about it," he said. "Break his heart."

Hawker began walking toward the bungalow, leaving them behind.

"He's your friend," Danielle said, catching up to Hawker and looping her arm through his.

For a second Keegan was left alone. He sounded stunned.

"Is this because I'm a Brit?" he asked, turning to follow. "What, a Brit can't earn a few dollars from America? I mean come on, you already took all our rock and rollers, and Beckham. Why can't I hop across the pond? I could be huge there."

"Keegan," Hawker said, "look at this place. The big government pension you're talking about wouldn't cover your cleaning bill."

"Sure," he said, pushing between them and putting one arm over Hawker's shoulder and the other over Danielle's. "But I could lose all this in one bad week at the tables. And then what would I have to fall back on? There's my good looks and charm, of course. I'll always 'ave those. But that only goes so far."

They reached the door and stopped.

"Where did you get him?" Danielle asked Hawker.

Hawker shrugged. "Apparently I pick up strays."

Somehow she felt like the one who picked up strays. Looking at Hawker and now Keegan, she suddenly felt the tribe growing.

"Who else is going to have your back?" Keegan said. "Did you see how I swooped in with that boat?"

"It was damn good to see you," Hawker admitted.

"Exactly," Keegan said. "And that's exactly how you're going to feel every time you see my smiling mug from here on out."

Hawker looked over at Danielle. She felt like she was being conned, but there was no resisting at this point. "I'll see what I can do," she said.

With that Keegan opened the door and the three of them went inside.

EPILOGUE

Mina, Saudi Arabia
Two months later

The crowd swirled around him in white and tan. Pilgrims numbering in the tens of thousands pressed forward, moving toward the three walls known collectively as the Jamarat. Most were eager, even emotionally overcome at the chance to complete this part of the hajj, the holy pilgrimage of Islam.

As soon as the noon prayers ended, they'd rushed toward a small bridge and toward the other entry points that would take them in front of the walls. In their ardor, few noticed or paid attention to a figure moving slowly, reluctantly. A man whose shoulders remained hunched, his head scarf pulled forward, hiding his neck and face.

Yousef Kazim had come on the pilgrimage not knowing what to expect. After the American woman let him go, he'd found his way back to France, to let his mother know he was alive, and then to Saudi Arabia.

Most poor Muslims had a hard time making the pilgrimage, but all were expected to do it at least once in their lives. Now, standing on this ground, Yousef felt a sense of nervousness, a heartsickness that he found hard to explain.

He had rejected Allah and then betrayed those who took him in.

He thought often about the conversation with the American woman, trying to hate her, trying to blame her for tricking him, but he realized she'd handed him a chance to redeem himself. In not giving in to him, she'd saved him somehow.

But now, standing only yards away from one of the holiest shrines in Islam, he did not feel any right to go inside. He tried to hold back, but the crowd flowed like a river, and despite his efforts Yousef was slowly swept along until he stood in front of largest of the walls, the most important of the three.

This was the tenth day of Dhu al-Hijjah, the last month of the Islamic calendar. On this day the pilgrims would throw stones at the large wall, the Jamrah al-Aqabah, which represented the devil. The ritual was meant to re create the time when Abraham had thrown stones at the devil to chase him away.

On the following days, the pilgrims would throw stones at all three walls, the others representing the devil's temptation of Abraham's son and of Abraham's wife. But today was only for the large wall.

As hundreds of others stood and threw their stones, Yousef hesitated. The noise, the heat, the sound of stones ricocheting off the wall were foreign to him. He felt out of place, not only among the people and the noise, but among Allah's holiest sites.

He braced against the crowd, trying at least to remain in the back, but inexorably he was pushed toward the front. Long before he was ready, Yousef found himself facing the wall.

The words coursed through his head.

He had no right. He was the worst kind of heretic. If the others knew the truth they would stone him instead, he was certain of it.

He wanted to run away and escape this place, as if he could hide from his shame. He twisted his body in hope

of sliding through the surging crowd. But then the American woman's voice came to him. He remembered its unexpected kindness and strength. He remembered her words.

He was Yousef Kazim. Who in his darkest moment had resisted the devil and given the world a chance at life.

He knew it to be true. He knew of the explosions on the Iranian island. He knew the Americans had destroyed the laboratory and the cult and the biological weapon they were building. He had played a part in that, as much as he'd had a part in all the evil that had been done before.

He was Yousef Kazim.

He held the first of seven stones in his hand as a sensation of fire built inside him. He felt a type of anger that was very familiar, a mix of bitterness and guilt, but he also felt a sense of peace that he had never known.

He thought of the woman who had saved him. He thought of his mother crying when she saw him again, and he thought of the people who had lured him away, Cruor, the man of blood, and Draco, the serpent, and what they had made him do. The anger grew as these images flashed through his mind.

Yousef Kazim raised his arm slowly, gripping the stone so tightly his knuckles turned ashen. And then, with all his might, he began to hurl his stones at the devil.

BY GRAHAM BROWN

The Eden Prophecy
Black Sun
Black Rain

BY GRAHAM BROWN AND CLIVE CUSSLER

Devil's Gate

BLACK SUN

"Will appeal to Clive Cussler fans . . . a good thriller that fans will not want to put down." —*RT Book Reviews*

"Armchair travel for the adrenaline set . . . Brown infuses non-stop action with spiritual, scientific and ideological elements, without ever pausing for breath."
—SOPHIE LITTLEFIELD, author of *A Bad Day for Pretty*

BLACK RAIN

"Action-packed . . . The fast pace . . . will keep readers forging ahead." —*Publishers Weekly*

"A unique and compelling thriller that will keep your interest start to finish. *Black Rain* is fast-paced, dangerous adventure at its very best. A sequel is in the works, and I can't wait to read it." —Fresh Fiction

"A successful thriller—exotic location, innocents in danger, overwhelming odds against the good guys and the inability to know who they can trust—this enjoyable read is very frightening. . . . A lively read." —*RT Book Reviews*

"*Black Rain* is an adventure that's not only a terrific read, but is smart, intelligent, and poised to shake up the whole thriller community. Every copy should come with a bucket of popcorn and a John Williams soundtrack to play in the background. Loved it."
—LINWOOD BARCLAY, #1 internationally bestselling author of *Fear the Worst*

"*Black Rain* sizzles with tension and twists that both entertain and magnetize. The plot envelops the reader into a brilliantly conceived world, full of strange and amazing things. Graham Brown is an exciting new talent, a writer we're going to be hearing a lot from in the years ahead. I can't wait."
—STEVE BERRY, *New York Times* bestselling author